Of All Faiths
& None

Of All Faiths & None

Andrew Tweeddale

To my wife, Keren

First published in the UK in 2022

Text copyright © 2022 Tweeddale Consultancy Ltd

Edited by Dominic Wakeford and Robin Seavill
Book design by Adam Hay Studio

ISBN: 978-1-7396122-0-7

Preface

Of All Faiths & None is a work of fiction. It includes references to real people and events, which are used to give the fiction an historical reality. While some of the facts relating to the Lutyens family, the Drewe family and Krishnamurti are accurate and have been taken from letters, books and biographies, the dialogue and the story are fictional and a creation of the author.

The novel has its origins in 2004 when I went with some university friends on a trip to Castle Drogo on Dartmoor, which had been built for the tea baron Sir Julius Drewe. The castle had been designed by Edwin Lutyens and the gardens by Gertrude Jekyll. It is England's last great castle and was commissioned in 1910. There is a room devoted to Adrian Drewe, Sir Julius' son, who died in the Great War. It is a cold, austere and sad place but also quite beautiful. As we walked around the castle and came to the wine cellars, a friend joked: "I'm afraid Master Robert has fallen down the stairs again." It occurred to me, as I discovered the castle and grounds, that this would be the perfect place to base a novel. The grey, rectangular castle was a wonderful symbol to illustrate a society out of step with its time.

I also had some knowledge about World War I and went regularly to the battlefields of the Somme, Ypres and Flanders with friends, who were keen World War I historians. Whilst there I came across many of the war memorials designed by Lutyens, including the Stone of Remembrance, which was used in war cemeteries containing 1,000 or more graves, or at memorial sites commemorating more than 1,000 war dead. It was this memorial that was intended to be for all fallen soldiers, irrespective of their religion or beliefs, and would be a symbol of all faiths and none. Lutyens initial thoughts about the design of the Stone of Remembrance were:

"On platforms made of not less than three steps... place one great stone of fine proportion 12 feet long... and inscribe thereon one thought in clear letters so that all men for all times may read and know the reason why these stones are placed throughout France – facing the West and facing the men who lie looking ever eastward towards the enemy."

The words chosen were "Their Name Liveth For Evermore".

I started drafting the novel in 2004 with a great deal of input from a writing group I had joined. The working title of the novel at the time was 'Castle Drogo' and was referred to as 'Drogo' around the dinner table. It was developed chapter by chapter between 2004 and 2010 with the first draft being completed on 30th April 2010. It was clear that the novel needed an extensive edit with some redrafting of the first sections of the book. However, life as a lawyer was taking up a lot of my time, as was a young family. In 2011 I found some time for redrafting and sent out extracts to publishing agents without success. The book was then put on the back burner until 2021, when I decided to employ a developmental editor from Reedsy. The book then passed through a copy-editing process and final proofing and preparation for publication. Although it has taken nearly eighteen years to publish, I hope that the novel is as relevant today as it was when I started drafting it.

I would like to thank the following people for their unreserved support and enthusiasm during the writing of the novel: Alexander Tweeddale, Eoin Tweeddale, Kim Brown, Lee White, Anthony Stern, Elizabeth Wardle, Rachel Wolcott, Adam Elston, Laura Fowler, Jean Nichols, Azalea Dalton, Steve Lugg and James Robinson. My prayers go out to Howard Phillips and Robert Sadd, both of whom have since passed away, for being there at the start of the journey.

Thanks also to Dominic Wakeford, Robin Seavill and Adam Hay for their editorial input on the novel and the cover design.

A special note of thanks to Patrick Dodds who took the beautiful photograph for the cover and Rosa Hatton who leant her hand for the picture.

Finally, this novel would not have been completed but for the never-ending support, good humour and love of my wife, Keren.

We can truly say that the whole circuit of the earth is girdled with the graves of our dead... and, in the course of my pilgrimage, I have many times asked myself whether there can be more potent advocates of peace upon earth through the years to come, than this massed multitude of silent witnesses to the desolation of war.

King George V, Flanders, 1922

PART I

Chapter 1

"Once upon a time," said Edwin Lutyens, "the devil and his friend were walking along the street when they saw ahead of them a man stoop down and pick up something from the ground. The man looked at what he had found and then put it away in his pocket. The devil's friend said to the devil: 'What did that man pick up?'

"'He picked up a piece of the Truth,' said the devil.

"'Oh,' said his friend, 'isn't that very bad for you?'

"'Not at all,' the devil replied, 'a piece of the Truth is like a piece of cotton. It can be spun into anything.'"

Edwin Lutyens' two youngest children were unsure what to make of the story. The kind of story that Mary and Elisabeth preferred were ones like 'The Ugly Duckling' or 'The Ant and the Grasshopper'. However, occasionally Lutyens would tell them a fable that they did not understand. There was no point in asking him to explain, as Lutyens had by now kissed them goodnight and was leaving the nursery. They knew they would have another story on another night.

"I am not sure they liked your fable," said Celia Lutyens, who had been listening at the door.

"I heard it recently, when I was in India," replied Lutyens to his eldest daughter, "at a talk, given by a young boy."

He turned towards the stairs.

"Why were you at a talk given by a young boy?" asked Celia.

"Your mother asked if I would go. She was told by a friend of ours that the boy was special."

"Is he?" asked Celia.

"We'll see," said Lutyens, "we'll see." He left Celia outside the nursery and walked down to the kitchen, hoping to find some bread and cheese in the larder. After being on a boat and then a train for the whole day, he felt famished.

"What did you think that story meant?" Mary asked her sister Elisabeth after their father had left. They both looked up as Celia wandered in.

"Well," Celia paused. She took a breath in and said with all the conviction that a fourteen-year-old could muster, "what it means is that sometimes a little bit of the truth is as bad as a lie."

"But mother says we must always tell the truth," replied Elisabeth.

"Of course, you must," said Celia.

"Even if it's like telling a lie?" asked Mary.

"If it's like telling a lie then it's best to say nothing at all." She decided now was the perfect time to go and find her brother Robert and she left her two younger sisters in the nursery after wishing them a good night.

*　　*　　*

Breakfast in the Lutyens household was a particularly noisy affair on the morning of the 5th of September 1910. Edwin Lutyens, having returned from India the evening before, was surrounded by all his children. Over breakfast the children asked him a score of questions about his travels, as he ate his cereal and then his eggs. Edwin Lutyens had attempted to answer each question and now wanted to read a copy of *The Times* in peace.

He sipped at a cup of Darjeeling tea as he read his paper. He would soon turn his attention to the morning post and then make his way to the converted office in the damp basement of the house. It had been a routine that he had followed for over a decade. He noticed that Celia was chewing a lock of hair, impatiently waiting for her parents to leave the breakfast table. He also noticed that she had changed in the four months he had been away. It was not a major change, but she appeared more confident and he thought, with a little trepidation, more headstrong.

Edwin Lutyens recognised that his eldest daughter had many of the traits that her mother possessed. She held opinions about almost everything and would express those opinions with only the slightest encouragement. He disapproved of this in a girl so young. She also had a possessive instinct that she had inherited from her mother; when she wanted something she would persevere until she got it. There were, however, other talents she possessed and

Lutyens had no idea where she had acquired these from. She loved dancing – something he and his wife detested. She was a romantic, whereas he and his wife were practical people. However, most of all she loved horse riding. Her new horse had been a present on her last birthday and she had managed to persuade him to buy it, despite his own view that he just couldn't afford it.

Lutyens put down his paper, reached into his Gladstone bag that was by his feet, and pulled out a small, red book. He passed it to his wife.

"Annie Besant asked me to give you this. It's Krishnamurti's book. The one they're all talking about."

"Did you read it?" Emily asked.

"Yes, on the way back home."

"And what did you think?"

Lutyens took his pipe out of his pocket, chewed at the stem and thought for a second before replying: "I haven't made up my mind whether there is any truth in it. It's certainly not the whole truth."

"Celia," Emily said as she watched her daughter across the breakfast table chewing at the ends of her hair. "You will ruin your hair if you carry on doing that."

Emily Lutyens continued to eat slowly from a bowl of sago. Once she had finished, she settled herself comfortably onto a green satin upholstered chair where she opened the small, red book and began reading.

Celia had already become accustomed to her mother's quiet breakfasts. It always surprised her how little her parents spoke to each other, despite the fact that they would write to each other every day when he was away. Perhaps, she thought, they had said everything they had to say in letters. Celia watched as both her parents became absorbed in their own worlds that seemed to revolve on different orbits.

Celia decided that now was the time to be excused, as both her parents had finished eating. She looked at her mother who was already engrossed in her new book, *At the Feet of the Master*. Celia assumed it was just another book on theosophy. She kept on meaning to ask her mother about it, as her understanding of theosophy was, at best, vague. Her mother had said it had something to do with spirituality, being a vegetarian and treating everyone as equal. However, precisely what it all meant and why it was still acceptable to have a house full of servants if everyone was equal, Celia did not quite understand.

"May I be excused?" she asked. Emily looked up from her book and nodded her head. Celia assumed that her father would also nod his head, which would be the customary thing. In her mind she was already riding through Hyde Park on her horse, Dido, a beautiful chestnut with dark brown eyes which had whinnied when Celia had given it an apple the last time they went out. It had made her best friend, Margaret Ellis, seethe with envy. She looked over to her father to see if she might leave the table.

Edwin Lutyens was, however, lost in thought. He had a letter in his hand, and he was reading it slowly. On the table was an envelope with a wax seal with a lion rampant on it.

"May I be excused, Father?" said Celia again.

Lutyens continued to read, unaware that anyone was speaking to him. Once he had finished the letter, he placed it on the table and looked over at his wife.

"I've got a letter from Sir Julius Drewe," he said. The name was enough for Emily to close her book.

"Sir Julius Drewe, did you say?"

Lutyens nodded.

Celia wanted to interrupt and ask why Sir Julius Drewe had written but decided she wanted to be excused as quickly as possible and so just listened.

"What does he want?" Emily asked.

"A possible new commission. Drewe wants me to design a castle for him."

"A castle?" said Celia, who could not help interrupting. "But you design country houses."

"Your father does a lot more than just design country houses," said Emily. "But I have to say no one has built a castle in possibly a hundred years; though with Sir Julius Drewe, nothing surprises me anymore."

"Aren't we related?" asked Celia.

"Distantly," said Emily. "His wife, Frances, is my second cousin. No one in the family approved when she married him."

"He's written," said Lutyens, rearranging his steel-rimmed spectacles in order to read from the letter, "that a relative of his has been researching his family genealogy and that the Drewe family can be traced all the way back to Norman times and the knight, Drogo de Teigne."

"Nonsense," said Emily, "he's new money. Everyone knows that his family has no pedigree."

"Well," repeated Lutyens, "he claims he has managed to trace his family lineage back to a knight of the twelfth century who had manorial title to Drewsteignton. Sir Julius has already bought a plot of land on Dartmoor and now wants to build this castle."

"A castle on Dartmoor in these times. What vanity!" said Emily.

"I think it's romantic," said Celia, to which both her parents gave her withering looks. "I do," repeated Celia.

"And he wants me to design it," said Lutyens. "Do you think I should try to change his mind?"

"You could try," said Emily, "but you know Julius; once he sets his mind to something he doesn't budge."

Chapter 2

There were three things that Celia remembered about her father as she was growing up. The first was that he was often not at home; the second was that when he was at home, he always had a new story; and the third was that he always smelt of warm, rich pipe tobacco. Celia could not remember, when she was a small child, whether her father had been overweight or had begun to go bald or whether his hair had gone grey. It was the smell of him and his absence that made an impression on her. However, more than anything else, it was his love of stories. When he returned from his trips abroad, he would have an abundance of new tales and she, her brother and her two young sisters would wait with anticipation for him to come up to the nursery so she could hear another adventure about a Persian princess or an evil mullah or a courageous pirate.

There were times when she could not remember her father being there from one month to the next. There were no hugs or kisses goodnight. When she was seven, she started to make up her own stories about what her father did and why he was often not there. She told her friends that he was an explorer, like David Livingstone. She made up tales about him meeting maharajas and queens. Then, one afternoon, when she was playing with Margaret Ellis, her father came home unexpectedly from a trip abroad. Margaret, a precocious child even at the age of seven, asked whether he had just been to meet the Emperor of Nepal.

"Oh yes," Lutyens had said. "He's a rather fat fellow with a wonderful crown." He smiled at Celia as he left the two girls to play, and at that moment Celia did not believe she could care for him more.

As Celia grew up, she noticed that her father was becoming a little more tired. He was not so energetic when he came home from his trips away and he did not tell his stories so frequently. He went out to dinner more and the notches of his belt grew fewer. Any pretence at vanity went. Edwin Lutyens knew what he liked and if this led him to be slightly overweight, then he saw this simply as a reward for success. He was not extravagant, and his wife was equally as frugal. In his club it was rumoured that he only had two suits, perhaps an unkind remark. He had three, but one suit he did not particularly care for.

After Emily became a vegetarian in line with her new-found beliefs, Lutyens ate at his club more and more. He took the view that it was not appropriate to invite either friends or clients to his home for dinner if he could not offer a meat or fish course. However, the more time he spent at his club, the more he relaxed into its comfy atmosphere. He could smoke his pipe without his wife complaining of the smell, and he was also able to do business there. He knew everyone at the club, and he made it a point to know if anyone was thinking about designing a new house or changing an estate.

Unusually, things were not too hectic a week after Edwin Lutyens received the letter from Sir Julius Drewe regarding the castle. Lutyens therefore thought he would leave his office early and wander down to his club just before five in the evening. He was surprised, therefore, when his secretary stopped him and told him that a Mr Hall was waiting to see him.

"Hall?" said Lutyens. "Do you know what he wants?"

"He said that you had written a reference for him about six months ago, that you knew his father and he wanted to thank you."

Lutyens remembered the letter. Peter Hall's father had studied architecture with him, and was quite a few years older than him. However, like many associations that do not develop into friendships, Lutyens lost touch with Duncan Hall and thought no more about him until twenty-one years had passed and a letter came out of the blue. The letter asked whether Lutyens knew of a firm of engineers who were looking to take on a newly qualified graduate and whether he could send a letter of introduction for his son. Lutyens made some enquiries, found out that Duncan Hall was down on his luck, and wrote a letter of introduction for Duncan's son, Peter, to a firm of engineers, Babtie, Shaw and Morton. He had worked with the firm in Scotland and understood that they had recently set up a new office in London. He was pleased to learn a few weeks later that Peter Hall had been employed.

Peter Hall was tall, far taller than Lutyens had expected. He had a thin face, unruly mousy hair and sharp blue eyes. When Hall entered Lutyens' office he looked around, taking keen note of what was there. Judging by the cut of his suit, the architect guessed that the salary of an apprentice engineer was not to be envied.

It did not take long for Lutyens to form a good impression of Peter Hall. He was not someone to take to the club but he was obviously diligent, hardworking and capable. He listened more than he spoke and asked the right questions. Inquisitiveness and prudence were the hallmarks of a good engineer, Lutyens thought, and smiled at his little play on words.

After fifteen minutes Lutyens started talking about the commission for a castle he was hoping to obtain and, on a whim, he asked Peter, "Which partner at your firm has the most experience with geology?"

"Alistair Morton," said Peter. "He has a huge amount of experience in soil mechanics."

Lutyens scribbled down a note and asked Peter to give it to Alistair Morton the next day. "Hopefully," said Lutyens, as Hall was about to leave, "this might be a project we can work together on. You might even meet Sir Julius Drewe."

"What's he like?" Hall asked.

"He is fastidious when it comes to money. He owns the Home and Colonial Stores and made his fortune from importing tea from India and the Orient. He also has a shipping company and a number of other import businesses. They say if Julius Drewe became bankrupt tomorrow, you and twenty million other people in England would go without a cup of tea."

Lutyens was surprised when a knock on the door interrupted his meeting. It was rare for his secretary ever to interrupt him, and he apologised to Peter for the disturbance. He opened the door to find Celia standing next to his secretary. He frowned. Celia ignored the frown.

"I wanted to speak to you before you went to your club," Celia said. "I've had some ideas for your castle."

Lutyens looked at his secretary who stammered in response that Celia had said it was a matter of urgency.

"I'm busy," said Lutyens. "Now run along, we can talk later."

"I can wait." Celia suddenly saw Peter Hall behind her father who had stood up. She smiled at him.

"Celia," said Lutyens sternly.

"Sorry," said Celia to Peter, "I really didn't think that anyone would be here at this time of the evening. I honestly didn't mean to disturb your meeting. I'm Miss Celia Lutyens."

"Peter, Peter Hall, miss."

"It's very nice to meet you, Mr Hall."

"We had just finished our meeting," said Peter, unsure of whether he should say anything more. It was clear to him that Lutyens did not want his daughter there but, on the other hand, he did not want to appear discourteous. "We were just discussing the castle."

Lutyens groaned.

"That's precisely the matter that I wanted to discuss with my father," Celia added. "Do you work for my father, Mr Hall?"

"Celia," said Lutyens with some warning in his voice, "Mr Hall is an engineer. His firm may be asked to assist with a survey and, if you would allow him, he no doubt has pressing things he needs to do."

"I do hope we shall meet again, Mr Hall," said Celia as she offered her hand to Peter. "I thought it might be interesting to help." Celia noticed that her father had gone red. Now, she decided, was a good time to leave. She shook Peter's hand and turned and left.

"Please excuse my daughter," said Lutyens as he showed Peter to the door. "She sometimes rushes in where angels fear to tread."

As Lutyens later walked to his club, he thought about what he should say to Celia. A short reprimand was in order, but what punishment would be suitable? The simple solution was to ban her from riding for a week, but he didn't feel that the punishment fitted the crime. The sentence should follow on from the offence; it fitted with his thinking of how the world worked. An action always has an equal and opposite reaction. Buildings stood up because of foundations – it was something that he had learnt in his first lessons as an architect when he sat next to Hall's father.

He pulled out his pipe and chewed on the end as he walked and then the answer came to him. If Celia wanted to help with the design of the castle, then he would encourage her. However, it would have to be done properly and Celia would have to understand some basic principles of architecture and engineering. A fitting punishment, he thought, and he knew a young engineer who might also be made to help administer the punishment.

"You're looking very well this evening, sir," said the porter. Lutyens took off his calf leather gloves and passed them to the porter with his coat and brolly.

"I'm feeling well," said Lutyens.

Chapter 3

Peter Hall lived in lodgings at Deptford Strand. His rooms were small, and the house was old and run-down. His landlady, Mrs Braithwaite, claimed that the house stood on the very spot where Christopher Marlowe had been murdered over a dinner bill and maintained that her family had owned the house for six generations. When telling the story, which was not an infrequent occurrence, she would let out a sigh and claim that death duties had ruined the Braithwaites.

Peter had two rooms in the attic – a small bedroom and a slightly larger living room, which contained an old chair, a threadbare sofa and a small table. The curtains and the rug on the floor were newer, as a result of constant complaints from a previous lodger. There were two reasons why Peter had chosen to take rooms at this house: it was close to the ferry that went to London, and it was cheap at ten shillings a month, including meals.

Peter Hall's salary as an apprentice engineer was barely enough to get by on, even with Peter being parsimonious. He would never take a cab if he could take an omnibus; and he would never take an omnibus if he could walk. He woke up early and prayed every morning. His faith was rooted deep in the Presbyterian traditions. He had been given a second-hand brown suit by an uncle when he got his job in London. The material was of a good quality and although the jacket fitted perfectly, the trousers were just a little short in the leg. Peter was nearly six feet tall; his uncle had been two inches shorter. The cut of the suit had dated; the lapels were slightly larger than was now fashionable, and the waistcoat buttoned up almost to the collar of his shirt. His mother had packed him three cotton shirts and six collars when he left home.

"Get your landlady to launder them daily," she had told him, "and make sure she starches the cuffs and collars; they'll come up nicer and last longer." From his father he received a silver watch and fob. The hour hand kept perfect time, although the minute hand no longer moved and remained forever pointing at the six. It was as if time had taken its toll and the hand could no longer make the struggle up the face of the clock. Peter had tried to fix it; however, nothing that he did could make the minute hand move. Peter soon learned, like his father before him, the art of telling the time solely from the position of the hour hand.

Peter had, since the day when he had been employed by Babtie, Shaw and Morton, felt indebted to Edwin Lutyens. He had thought about writing a letter of thanks but decided to see Lutyens personally. He had called at Lutyens' office on three previous occasions, but each time Lutyens had been abroad.

Lutyens and Gertrude Jekyll were, at that time, the talk of London. A Lutyens house and a Jekyll garden were said to go together like salt and pepper, a demonstration of good taste. Peter liked the style of a Lutyens house. He was impressed how effortlessly Lutyens seemed to make a house feel part of its environment. He could see the sense in building with locally quarried materials and this, he thought, was why a Lutyens building seemed immediately to become part of the landscape.

Peter's job was going well. He had been told that if the small practice in London developed, there could be a permanent place for him when he finished his apprenticeship. That he had been referred to Babtie, Shaw and Morton by Lutyens was certainly a feather in his cap, and now Mr Lutyens had written to Alistair Morton, after speaking to him.

Peter was not affected by the constant noise in the house or the shouting of the Braithwaite children as they played in the yard. He had grown up in a similar type of house in Glasgow. However, one thing did grate on his nerves. Mrs Braithwaite had a habit of trying to push him and her eldest daughter, Rose, together. This would not have been an issue, but Peter was prone to blushing even for the most innocent of reasons, and his landlady seemed to enjoy making him blush.

"Mr Hall would be a bit of catch," she would say to her daughter in earshot of Peter, "our Mr Hall is on the up. It's just a matter of time, mind you, before our Mr Hall has finished his apprenticeship and is earning well. A girl would be lucky if he was interested in her."

Rose was three years younger than Peter, having turned twenty on her last birthday. She worked as a nurse and lived most of the week at St Thomas' Hospital but came home on her days off. She pretended to take no notice of her mother's suggestions or when Peter blushed furiously. She knew that if she paid the slightest attention, her mother would take pains in making their embarrassment worse. She therefore let the comments wash over her and inwardly bit her lip.

Peter was not what she had in mind for a boyfriend, let alone a husband. He was too quiet, and she doubted whether he could even dance. He rarely seemed to go out except to church on a Sunday or talks on rocks or similar topics that she considered boring. He wasn't too bad-looking, she admitted to herself, and he was tall. She even hoped that his Scottish accent might wear away over time. He also had no money and, although she thought that one day he would earn a comfortable living, Rose wanted to enjoy her life now.

On the days when Rose travelled back to St Thomas' Hospital, she would take the seven a.m. ferry from Deptford with Peter. They would sit together saying very little. From the ferry terminus at Blackfriars, she would walk along the embankment to the hospital, and he would take an omnibus to Fitzroy Street, in order not to be late. Rose eventually became used to his ways, and they developed a sense of familiarity, like a warm bath or daffodils in spring.

On Monday morning on the 26th of September 1910, like a dozen times before, Peter and Rose walked along Deptford Strand to catch the seven a.m. ferry to Blackfriars. However, Peter was wearing a new suit and tie and carried a small briefcase.

"Are you going to tell me why you're all dressed up?" she asked.

"I have a meeting with Sir Julius Drewe."

"Mixing with the toffs are you now?" responded Rose. Peter started blushing. "Sorry, I didn't mean anything..."

They carried on walking and bought their tickets for the ferry. Peter gripped his briefcase that contained a file of papers that Lutyens had given him. He had spent the weekend at the desk in his room with some drawings that Lutyens had prepared. They were mainly sketches, some preliminary ideas that Lutyens had had regarding the castle. Lutyens' idea was a rectangular building chiselled out of granite. Block after rectangular block seemed to be placed next to each other. The sketches were austere with little decoration. He did not know what to make of them. The granite walls rose vertically from the edge of the escarpment on the Teign gorge. It had straight lines with almost no curves. It was so different to the work that Lutyens had done before. Nothing in the design undulated as he imagined the moor would. It was so different to what he had expected, that Peter wondered whether Lutyens had even designed it himself.

Peter would be meeting with Lutyens, Sir Julius and Alistair Morton later that morning. At the request of Sir Julius, the meeting was to take place at the Bristol Hotel. Peter recognised that this was an opportunity for him. He had briefed Alistair Morton during the previous week, and they had a further meeting with Lutyens. Alistair Morton had given Peter clear instructions that at the meeting he was not to say anything unless he was asked a direct question. From his point of view the major engineering concern would be the shear strength of the cliff. The escarpment would need to hold the weight of the massive granite walls. From the Teign valley the castle would redefine the skyline.

"So, what are you designing?" asked Rose, as the ferry moved slowly through the water to Blackfriars.

"It's a castle," said Peter. "Would you like to see a sketch of it?" Before she could answer Peter had one of Lutyens' sketches out of his briefcase. She stared at it for a minute and considered the rectangular shapes of the walls and buildings, the small windows and the austerity of the whole design. She did not say a word and then her brow furrowed.

"Is he pulling your leg?" she asked.

*   *   *

Sir Julius Drewe had panache; one could tell that from the cut of his Savile Row suit. His tie was made of the finest silk and the collar of his shirt was starched but unglossed. His shoes were made by Church's and polished to the point of reflection. There was a faint scent of an eau de cologne that was now the fashion. His black hair was oiled and combed to the side and his moustache was clipped. There were a few grey hairs, but the oil seemed to gloss over them. Sir Julius was tall. His manicured hands indicated a man of leisure and, like many men of leisure, his waistline had started to grow with each passing decade. Peter guessed he might be fifty, although he could still pass for a man in his mid-forties.

Sir Julius obviously knew where to eat in the City. Not those places that still served mutton chops and where one sat on red velvet chairs, but the restaurants where one could get the freshest sole *bonne femme* and a bottle of Pouilly-Fuissé and where the waiters were French. Although Sir Julius had made his money in trade, he was not a shopkeeper. He was a man of substance, and he knew it.

The drawing room of the Bristol Hotel was brilliantly alight. The polish on the parquet flooring shone. A table had been placed in the middle of the room and there were cushions of ivory silk on the chairs. An impressive fireplace on one side of the room had an impressionist painting hanging above it. In one corner, in tall pots of Chinese-style porcelain, palms were growing. In the opposite corner was a piano.

After the introductions Sir Julius sat quietly but attentively as Lutyens gave his presentation. The drawings came out one by one. First there was the presentation of the barbican – something that Sir Julius had insisted on. The great gate tower straddled the driveway, and the rampart wall then circled the castle. The driveway led to a courtyard. There was a portcullis and above it, carved into the granite, was a lion rampant, the Drewe heraldic symbol.

Lutyens ended by saying, "What I am trying to achieve is a balance between a traditional Norman castle – something which would have been built in the time of Drogo de Teigne – and something modern. The castle is intended to be a representation of both modernity and tradition."

Lutyens leant back in his chair and lit his pipe. Sir Julius took a cigarette from a silver cigarette case and lit it. He watched the match burn down, blowing it out when the flame got down to his fingers.

"Modernity and tradition," said Sir Julius and then paused.

"Yes," responded Lutyens, "that's what we discussed on the telephone."

"But, perhaps, it is a little too traditional," said Sir Julius.

"Norman castles were designed as fortifications and the design I am proposing is for a modern family to live in, with windows and heating."

"I see," said Sir Julius. He picked up a glass of water and took a sip. "I suppose some of the details can be worked out later."

"Of course," said Lutyens.

"And the budget for all of this is sixty thousand pounds? Fifty thousand for the castle and ten thousand for the gardens?"

"More or less," said Lutyens. "The next step is to take a more detailed geotechnical survey of the area. Mr Morton and Mr Hall can tell you about what will be needed."

Alistair Morton commenced his short presentation, based on the scant information he had been given. After a few minutes Sir Julius stopped listening. He was not interested in this level of detail.

Lutyens then interrupted. "Given the location of the chapel," he said, indicating one of his drawings, "we shall need to ascertain whether we can build this close to the cliff edge or whether the building will need to be moved further back."

"I don't want a chapel there," said Sir Julius, "it's a waste of good money. I want a ballroom with a courtyard to the side and views out across the moor."

Lutyens made a scribble on one of the sketches. "Changed already," he noted.

"There are also some preliminary surveys that I had done," said Sir Julius. "Perhaps they could be sent over, if they would be of any use."

"Mr Hall can pick those up, Sir Julius," said Alistair Morton.

"When could you do that, Mr Hall?" asked Sir Julius.

"Tomorrow?" suggested Peter.

"Agreed," answered Sir Julius. "He will need to come down to Wadhurst Hall. I have a meeting in the morning," said Sir Julius, looking at his diary, "but if Mr Hall could arrive at around eleven-thirty, that would be convenient." And with that, Sir Julius Drewe brought an end to the meeting. He shook hands with everyone and excused himself, saying that if they needed to discuss any matters, the room was available to them for the rest of the day.

When Sir Julius had left and tea was brought in, Lutyens settled himself to talk with the two engineers.

"As indicated on the sketches," said Lutyens, "everything is to be built with local granite, which will cause you problems at every turn because of the weight of it." Lutyens drew out from his Gladstone bag some further sketches. "I am proposing," he said, "to put a cantilevered staircase in the north tower. What we will need to do is have the load spread along the length without need for supports inside." Another sketch was brought out and they discussed the scullery, with its five small rooms huddled around an octagonal lightwell. Lutyens also had sketches for the kitchen, where he had designed curved edges to the walls and floor, the boudoir, the drawing room and the dining room.

Peter saw that, even though the building was austere from the outside, it was beautifully crafted on the inside. It had nothing to do with furniture, paintings or decoration, but rather the positioning of light wells and windows meant that light would flood into many of the rooms.

The conversation finished at one o'clock and Alistair Morton excused himself as he had another meeting to attend at three.

When alone, Lutyens looked at Peter and asked, "Didn't you like the design?"

"It's nae what I expected," said Peter, as if by way of explanation.

"At the end of the day, life is all about legacy. No one is ever remembered for merely being rich. Sir Julius wants to leave a legacy, and this is it. Remember, Peter, this castle is not for him, it's for his children and grandchildren. He is building it so that he is not forgotten. That's what Sir Julius fears; fading into obscurity."

"Aye, and who was Drogo de Teigne?" asked Peter. "Ye mentioned him as part of your presentation to Sir Julius."

"Drogo de Teigne," said Lutyens, "and the heraldic lion are the most important things about the castle. For Sir Julius, these are the things which stop the endeavour being frivolous."

Lutyens' pipe had gone out and he relit it.

"But the design of the castle is everything for me," he continued. "You may not like it now, but you will grow to love it, absolutely and completely, and Sir Julius will too. He is buying something original, something permanent. It's not a pastiche, nor is it cheap or garish. It's something that others will envy, and for Sir Julius that will make it a possession worth having. It's not the size of the castle but what others think of it."

Peter nodded his head, as if he agreed.

"Just one last thing," said Lutyens, as he got up to leave. "You remember my daughter, Celia? She expressed some interest in this project and I hope you won't mind if I ask her to attend one of our meetings."

"Not at all," said Peter.

"That's very decent of you," said Lutyens, taking his hand and shaking it vigorously. "Perhaps we can see you tomorrow after your visit to Wadhurst Hall. Say five-thirty at my office?"

As Peter Hall walked away from the Bristol Hotel towards his office in Fitzroy Street, he wondered why a fourteen-year-old girl would be interested in a castle.

Chapter 4

Peter Hall had lost track of time as he turned the pages of a copy of Craig's *Soil Mechanics*. The sketches that Lutyens had given him were on the table. He needed to have his dinner, get his suit pressed and bathe. On Wednesday nights Mrs Braithwaite boiled up water for bathing in the outhouse; unfortunately, it was a Monday. Peter looked at his pocket watch, it was nearly seven o'clock and dinner would soon be served. He went downstairs and knocked on the parlour door.

"Yes, dearie?" said Mrs Braithwaite.

"I was wondering whether ye could boil a copper for a bath this evening? I have a meeting tomorrow and..." Peter finished his sentence with a shrug.

Mrs Braithwaite looked at him coldly. "It's not Wednesday," she said, "and I have dinner to serve soon."

"I was also hoping," added Peter, slightly hesitantly, "that ye might also press my suit. It's very important and I don't mind paying a little extra this week."

"If Rose is around, she won't mind helpin' out, Mr Hall. Ask her to put the coppers on the boil." Mrs Braithwaite thought for a moment. "I'll put the iron on the stove – but it'll cost you thruppence, mind you."

Peter left the parlour and went looking for Rose. He heard her arguing with one of her younger siblings outside. She spoke in a measured, authoritative tone that would not accept any nonsense.

"Rose," he said, when a natural break in the argument came about. Rose's younger brother was sniffling and when he saw that Rose had turned her attention to Peter, he made a dash for it.

"I need a favour," said Peter. "I was hopin' ye might help me with a bath?"

"Why? Do you want your back scrubbed?"

Peter blushed to the roots. Rose bit her lip and apologised.

"I just wanted to get a copper boiling. Your ma said it was fine, but she was too busy to help."

Rose agreed, saying that it would take twenty minutes or so to get the coppers boiling.

After Peter had quickly eaten his supper of mutton stew, he went back to his room. He took his towel, a comb and clean underwear and made his way to the outhouse where Rose was pouring a pot of boiling water into the bath.

"Just about ready," she said. Peter looked at the water – there did not seem to be a great deal, but it would be sufficient. He waited for Rose to leave with the copper and started to undress. He placed his foot in the water; it nearly scalded him, and he added some cold water until the temperature was bearable. He climbed in and gingerly sat down.

There was not even a knock on the door when Rose entered, another copper of boiling water in her hand. Peter frantically leant over the side of the bath in a vain attempt to grab his towel and shouted at Rose to put down the water and get out. He thought she took an inordinately long time to do so.

*　　*　　*

The following morning, Peter sat next to Rose on the early ferry to Blackfriars. He had little to say and looked out over the side of the boat at the muddy water and the riverbank as it passed by. The river reeked and the stench was only broken by the occasional smell of malt as the boat sailed by a brewery. Behind him was Deptford, where he felt comfortable. Ahead of him was Wadhurst Hall, and a world where the people and the customs were different. Familiarity was fading in the wake of the boat. The ferry sailed under Tower Bridge, and he could see Blackfriars Bridge in the distance and the white stone walls of the Carmelite houses and red brick of the Temple, with its gardens of red and white roses. Further ahead, just out of sight, was Westminster. Law, politics and religion were the professions of the wealthy that had their own languages which he did not fully understand. He felt comfortable with things that he could see and hold. Engineering was logical. He knew why a boat sat on water, what made an engine work and why a crankshaft turned a propeller. He continued to stare, devoid of any sense of humour, at the brown, dirty water as it swept along the side of the boat.

"What's wrong with you?" asked Rose.

Peter found himself going red again.

"You've hardly said two words."

"Just thinkin'," he muttered. He had not forgiven her for the night before, although he knew he was being petulant. He did not really believe that she had come into the outhouse deliberately; and it was perhaps because he knew in his heart that it was nothing more than a mistake that it annoyed him. He also did not wish to be once again the butt of a joke and if Rose had not already told her friends and her mother, he worried that she might. However, nothing had been said that morning by Mrs Braithwaite as he ate his breakfast in the dining room and once again, he felt that he might be being unjust to Rose.

"It's nothin'."

In the face of Peter's sullenness, Rose moved to the gangway, an unspoken but intended snub. The act didn't go unnoticed by Peter, but he continued to stare at the water. It was not until he got bored that he saw a young man standing next to Rose and he felt a pang of jealousy, which he attempted to quell immediately. Behind her dark eyes and pursed lips, he wondered what was going on in her head. He watched her for a few minutes as she nodded her head when the man spoke to her and then she started to bite at the corner of one of her nails. Peter smiled. Rose always bit at the sides of her nails when she was bored. He stood up. Rose looked in his direction and her eyes seemed to say: 'Please rescue me'.

Peter and Rose were laughing when they disembarked at Blackfriars. Peter had towered above the young man standing next to Rose and scowled. Rose said on cue, "Hello, darling," and for a horrible moment Peter wondered if the young man was going to try and jump onto the gangplank before it had been fully placed.

"My mistake," the young man stammered.

As they walked towards Waterloo, they were still laughing.

"Aren't you going to your office?" asked Rose.

"Nae," said Peter, "I have to take the train to Ticehurst and then go to Wadhurst Hall. I'm collecting a survey from Sir Julius Drewe."

"You've been invited to his home?" said Rose, impressed that someone she knew would be invited to such a place. "Will you be meeting him again?"

"I would have thought so," said Peter.

"Will you tell me what Wadhurst Hall is like when you see me next?"

"Of course," said Peter. "I could tell you this evening if you wanted. We could get some supper. After I see Mr Lutyens this evening, I could be here at about seven?"

"Can I ask you something?" said Rose. Peter nodded. "Do you dance?"

"Of course," said Peter. "In Scotland we all have to learn to do ceilidh dancing at school, but I can also do a passable waltz."

Peter in return wanted to find out something about Rose, some tiny, unimportant secret that only he would know. Something that she would not have told her friends or mother, not because she was embarrassed about it, but because it was so small and insignificant.

"Rose," he said, "would ye tell me a secret about ye'self?"

Rose looked at him, confused.

"I was just wondering whether ye had a secret wish like sailing to America or seeing the Great Wall of China or something like that."

She didn't know what to say. She loved to dance, but that was hardly a secret. Anyone who knew her for five minutes knew that she loved to dance. She couldn't think of an answer and then it came into her head.

"A pineapple," she said. "I would love to try pineapple."

Chapter 5

The main drive to Wadhurst Hall was flanked by cedars planted by the previous owners, the Murrietas. They obscured the view of the Hall until the final turn when the house came into sight. From the front, it appeared as if it were little more than an ordinary country residence made of red brick, built for a well-to-do magistrate or the squire of the parish of Ticehurst. The only distinguishing feature of Wadhurst Hall was a tower on one side with a pointed red slate roof.

Over the row of cedars, Lady Edith Facey could just make out the tower and the two chimney stacks, which twisted up from the roofs and puffed out smoke. The Cadillac Model 30, in which she and her husband sat, thudded and misfired as it slowly went up the driveway. Edith knew, however, that the heart of the house was the old wooden panelled drawing room with its minstrel gallery, which opened onto the gardens. There were small formal gardens which cascaded down to a long lawn that went back some fifty yards with a croquet pitch on one side and stables on the other. Behind the stables were workmen's cottages, and behind these and a dry-stone wall was a farm. Surrounding all of this was woodland, which contained a dozen paths that led down to a large lake. A summer house had been constructed to afford those who wished to walk through the grounds some shade.

"Sorry to drag you out here, old girl," said her husband, Lord Facey, who was in the process of lighting a cigar.

"I wish you wouldn't," replied Edith tartly, "at least not before lunch." She pulled down the window of the Cadillac. Lord Facey ignored her and exhaled a cloud of blue smoke.

"I needed to see Drewe about business and you expressed an interest in visiting."

It had been fifteen years since Edith Facey had last been to Wadhurst Hall. Her father was a friend of the previous owner, Raphael de Murrieta, before he lost his money. Despite the austerity of the physical appearance of the house, Raphael de Murrieta would throw the most decadent parties. On a weekend the music and the dancing and the champagne seemed never to stop, and, in the morning, there were plates of eggs benedict, smoked salmon and more champagne. Sir Julius Drewe bought Wadhurst Hall for a song when Raphael de Murrieta went into bankruptcy in the Panic of 1896. While Sir Julius and Lady Francis Drewe continued to throw parties, especially the New Year's Eve ball, it was rumoured that they were simply a shadow of those held by the Murrietas.

"Drewe's eldest boy would be quite a catch," said Edith.

"Humph," grunted Lord Facey and puffed once more on his cigar.

"They're rich," said Edith pointedly.

Lord Facey grunted again and flicked the ash from the end of the cigar out of the car window.

"And we must think about Jane," she continued.

"There's no hurry for that," said Lord Facey, "she's only eighteen."

"She's nineteen," Edith responded. "Unfortunately, everyone I've spoken to says Drewe's wife is dreadfully dull."

"One more thing," said Lord Facey. "When you speak to Frances Drewe, ask her about the castle they're building. I heard from someone at my club that they commissioned Lutyens to design it. Awful man! He's always trying to cadge work off anyone at the club. He treats the place like an office."

Edith Facey said nothing but raised an eyebrow in curiosity.

Fifteen minutes later, she was alone with Mrs Frances Drewe in the summer house at Wadhurst Hall. It was a warm morning and the sweet smell of wild grasses hung in the air. The church bells from Ticehurst could be heard as they struck the quarter hour, as could the animals from the farm. The summer house had been painted a light pale blue and there were small painted scenes on wood panels on each of the walls. Edith Facey remembered that, years earlier, the summer house had been whitewashed with sunflowers in thin, tall copper vases. It all now looked too ornate. The simplicity of what the Murrietas had designed had gone. New money, she thought, can buy you anything, except taste. The maid brought out a tray of tea and Frances Drewe busied herself pouring two cups.

Edith smiled as Frances sat next to her. She noticed how Frances straightened a loose curl at the side of her face and rearranged her crimson velvet dress. The dress, thought Edith, would have cost a pretty penny, probably designed by Worth. However, no one she knew would have worn it for morning tea.

"How long have you lived here, my dear?" said Edith.

"Just over thirteen years, though I lose track of time. There's always so much to do here."

Edith Facey kept the smile painted to her face. So much to do here, she thought. She could think of nothing worse than attending local summer fetes at the church on weekends or judging the local farmstock.

"I used to come down here when the Murrietas owned it," replied Edith. "It was about fifteen years ago. I remember the balls that Raphael de Murietta used to throw, and I believe that you keep up the tradition."

"We still have a ball each summer and winter," said Frances. "You really must come to the next one."

Edith again sipped at the tea and smiled.

"I'm told," continued Frances, "although I don't want to sound my own horn, that our little soirées are even grander that those thrown by poor Mr Murrieta before us."

"I've heard that," said Edith with a wry smile. "And both Cecil and I and our daughter Jane would be delighted to come."

"Of course," said Frances, "though Julius didn't tell me you had a daughter; he never tells me anything important. He really is the limit."

"She's just come back from Paris," replied Edith, "having finished her schooling. I doubt that your husband even knew we had a daughter. She'll be presented this year. You have three sons, don't you?"

"Yes," replied Frances, "Adrian, Christian and Basil. Christian is down by the water meadows painting and more likely than not Adrian and Basil will be out on some horses – halfway to Brighton if I know them."

"Well, perhaps if they are back later, I shall get to meet them," said Edith.

"Oh, they will be," said Frances. "We have an engineer coming down from London later this morning and Adrian wants to discuss the new property. He'll be back in a few hours."

"This would be the castle everyone is talking about," said Edith. "You must be very excited."

At this, Frances' eyes unexpectedly welled up with tears.

"I am so sorry, my dear," continued Edith, "I didn't mean to say anything to upset you."

"No, it's nothing," said Frances Drewe taking out a small handkerchief from her clasp bag. "It's just that... well... I have always thought of here as my home."

Edith put down her empty cup and picked up the teapot and refilled her cup and Frances'. It was going to be a long, dull morning of tea and inane chatter, thought Edith, as she picked up her cup once more.

Lord Facey had grown fleshy in his old age. He may have once been described as handsome, but a penchant for brandy and cigars had made his complexion pallid and with unruly iron-grey hair, he gave the impression of an aging army colonel. He sat in a Chesterfield chair of soft burgundy leather. Sir Julius had poured him a glass of Oloroso that he sipped at as he smoked his cigar. Lord Facey was not known for his small talk. As the permanent secretary to the First Lord of the Admiralty, he considered such trifling details as the weather and the price of property beneath him. Lord Facey's interest was in politics.

When Lord Facey had requested the meeting, Sir Julius had set in motion an investigation. He was provided with a list of Lord Facey's friends, his habits, his political affiliations, his clubs, his mistresses, his assets and, most importantly, his debts. As Lord Facey sat before him, Sir Julius Drewe knew more about the worth of Lord Facey than Lord Facey knew himself.

The meeting between them started cautiously. Lord Facey expressed his views on the economy, the return to Ireland of the republican James Connolly, and the expansionism of Germany. Sir Julius was non-committal on everything except the return of James Connolly, where he clearly set out his opposition to Home Rule in Ireland. Lord Facey then steered the conversation back to Germany and referred to "its increasing arrogance as it challenged British naval power with the building of more battleships." Sir Julius listened, tapping his fingers on the desk, as he tried to understand where Facey was taking the conversation.

"Wilhelm II said that he wants Germany to have its 'place in the sun'," said Lord Facey.

"That's no different to what the French or the Italians have said," replied Sir Julius.

"The difference is that Germany is actively trying to make sure it happens," said Facey.

Sir Julius took a sip of coffee and Lord Facey finished his sherry.

"Togo, Cameroon and New Guinea," said Sir Julius. "They are the only countries that Germany has. They were too late to the game."

"And they are now producing steel at an inordinate rate and have a navy which is nearly the size of Britain's," said Facey.

Sir Julius countered, "But we have alliances with France, Russia and Japan."

"And they have alliances with Turkey and the Austro-Hungarian Empire..." Lord Facey paused. "The point is that Germany is more than a nuisance in our view, and the First Lord of the Admiralty wants to ensure that if things deteriorate, we have contracts in place with all our merchant shipping companies to bring in supplies."

So that's the nub of it, thought Sir Julius.

"Our shipping companies work out of many countries," said Sir Julius.

"Well, there could be a way for this to benefit both the government and you."

Sir Julius leant back in his chair. Here it comes, he thought to himself. Someone like Facey did not simply invite himself down to Wadhurst Hall on a whim. The permanent secretary to the First Sea Lord of the Admiralty did nothing on a whim, except, according to Sir Julius' investigators, bet on the horses. Sir Julius' information was that Facey was in debt to the sum of ten thousand guineas and a mistress in a small flat at Kensington did nothing to help his finances.

"I am always happy to come to an arrangement with those I trust," said Sir Julius, "and if I can support my country, all the better."

"I'm pleased you see things that way," said Facey. He seemed to visibly relax, as if he had passed a landmark in the conversation. He looked down at his empty glass. Sir Julius got up and refilled it.

Sir Julius and Cecil Facey spoke for another hour. Facey wanted to have stock in at least two of Sir Julius' shipping companies and for that Sir Julius would be given a fixed-price, fixed-term contract with the Admiralty for the importation of uniforms and weapons. Sir Julius could not see a downside, except that he would have to work with Facey and, contrary to what he said, he did not trust him one iota.

"One of the attractions of a joint stock company," said Facey, "is that no one can find out who actually owns the stock." He grinned, took out another cigar and lit it.

The conversation between the two men was interrupted by a knock at the door. Sir Julius opened it and Adrian, his eldest son, was there. Father and son were similar in appearance. Both had dark hair and green eyes, both were tall, although Adrian was slightly taller. When they spoke, they both had a measured tone, although Adrian's accent was pure Oxbridge.

"I just thought you ought to know," said Adrian, "that the engineer you invited arrived about half an hour ago. He's been sitting in the library. Would you like me to speak with him?"

Sir Julius thought for a moment. His conversation with Facey had gone about as far as it was going to go today. He decided to ask Adrian to join them for a few minutes.

"Adrian is studying Classics at Cambridge and then I hope he will take an interest in one of the businesses," said Sir Julius by way of introduction. He turned to Adrian. "Lord Facey and I have been discussing the possibility of war."

"It's really no longer a question of if," added Facey. "Nothing will happen for a year or two, even longer perhaps, but I believe that war is quite inevitable."

Adrian looked perplexed. "Who with?" he asked. As far as he could see, Britain had secured alliances with France and Russia and war seemed, if anything, something unlikely to occur in his lifetime.

"Germany," said Lord Facey in a matter-of-fact tone.

"But I'm sure the government will be able to manage the situation," said Sir Julius.

"I doubt that there is anything anyone can do," said Facey, shaking his head. "The only question is what must we do to meet the inevitable?"

"Inevitable?" said Adrian. "No one is going to be foolish enough to start a war against a country with the most powerful navy in the world."

"That's true for now," said Facey, "but at the rate the German navy is expanding, they are likely to have more ships than us within a few more years. They are also trying to extend their empire and it is the government's view that, sooner or later, we will have to put a stop to their expansionism."

"But will it come to war?" asked Adrian.

Lord Facey shook his head again as if he carried the burdens of every Englishman. "If it's thrust upon us," he said, "then what can one do? But you're right, no one wants war and as Asquith has so often said: 'if you are going to go to war, then it's better to have the public behind you.'"

Sir Julius brought the conversation to an end. He walked Cecil Facey out to the summer house where Edith Facey, exhausted by two hours of conversation with Frances Drewe and five cups of tea, was waiting. He watched them leave and then went back to Adrian in his study.

Ten minutes later, Sir Julius and Adrian walked towards the library with a copy of the survey that Peter Hall had come to collect.

"He seemed very affable," said Adrian.

"The widest smile hides the sharpest knife," said Sir Julius in response.

When they opened the door to the library, where Peter Hall had been waiting, Adrian was surprised to find him standing by the dresser with all the fruit from the fruit bowl turned out, and a smile on his face.

Chapter 6

The library, with its old Spanish furniture, smelt of beeswax polish and woodworm oil. It had a slightly acrid smell that left a bitter taste in Peter's mouth after a while. Peter sat in a wing chair until boredom got the better of him. He started first by looking at the paintings on the walls. Old gentlemen or ladies, not in their first bloom, who could afford to be painted and each wore the same look of boredom, indifference or disdain. Each had sat before an artist for no other reason than they did not want to be forgotten by the next generation. In many ways, thought Peter, they were no different to Sir Julius and his desire to build a castle.

The room had few decorations; its attraction was the beautiful carved wooden panels around the bookcases and crystal chandeliers. Some silver ash trays, a bowl of fruit and a Chinese porcelain figurine were placed on an ornate dark, wooden dresser. There was an oriental rug on one wall. When Peter got to the French doors, he stopped and looked out across the lawn to a little summer house at the far end of the garden. He could just make out two women sitting there, drinking tea. He watched them for about ten minutes but soon became bored with them and continued his investigation of the room. He moved on to the dark wooden bookshelves and inspected the books. Complete sets of journals, some in Spanish and some in English, were on the shelves. He took one down to look at it, but found the paper riddled with bookworm.

On a small table was a photograph in a silver frame. The picture was already fading and there were black spots starting to eat away at the paper. The photograph was of a woman, the same woman as in one of the paintings. She was now older and less attractive, and next to her stood a man, the spitting image of Sir Julius, except for the fact he was much older. Peter stared at the picture. The features were so similar but there was also a difference. Peter couldn't put his finger on it immediately and moved away from the table back to the dresser where the bowl of fruit had been placed. He was just about to sit back down in his chair when he turned back. He removed an apple, a pear and two oranges from the bowl until he found what he had caught just a glimpse of.

He was smiling to himself when Sir Julius and Adrian came in, and quickly he attempted to put the fruit back in the bowl. He blushed as if he had been caught with the family silver.

"Were you looking for something in particular?" asked Sir Julius.

"No," replied Peter, he began to stammer, "well... nae exactly..."

Adrian, however, stepped in to relieve Peter from his embarrassment and offered his hand. Peter shook it firmly and managed an introduction.

"Scottish?" Adrian asked.

"From Glasgow," replied Peter.

"Not a city I have visited," Adrian remarked.

Sir Julius handed the survey to Peter.

"There is something I would like you to see," said Sir Julius. They walked out into the garden through the French doors and along a path beside the house. Peter looked towards the summer house and noticed that the two women had gone. The front and back of the house was traditionally English, nineteenth century, Peter guessed. However, from the front of the house, one would never have guessed at the size of the estate. He could see stables and next to them were the garages. As they walked through an archway in one of the stable buildings, he saw dozens of workmen's cottages.

They stopped at one of the outbuildings and Sir Julius unlocked the door. The room was empty except for a large table in the middle of the room, covered by a large board, a filing cabinet in one corner and photographs on the wall. When Peter moved closer to the table, he saw that on the board was a model of a castle and its terrain.

"An exact replica of the landscape where the castle is to be built," explained Sir Julius.

"Except for the Teign gorge," added Adrian. "If we had done that to scale, we would have had to dig up the floor."

The photographs on the walls showed the landscape around where the castle was to be built, and the nearest village of Drewsteignton. There were photographs of the Teign gorge and copies of Lutyens' sketches. A small model had already been made of the castle and placed on the mock-up.

"Up to last week we used to have a fort," added Adrian, "instead of the castle. My brother Kit spent the whole of last night making the model based on Lutyens' sketches."

"He certainly has a talent," said Peter.

"He wants to be an artist," Adrian replied. Peter thought he heard Sir Julius make a derisive sound but carried on paying attention to Adrian. Adrian explained about the topography of the site and the extent of the boundaries. Adrian pointed to where the roads were being built and where the utilities would be laid.

"It's all in the survey that you've been given," said Adrian.

Peter opened the copy he held and ran his eyes across it. It was too basic to be of any use to an engineer. It gave general descriptions of the surrounding area and a brief description of the ground. However, it had almost no detailed information.

Adrian kept on talking. Peter tried to pay attention but the warm room and the smell of hay from the farm was affecting him. He sneezed and sneezed again. He looked at Adrian and Sir Julius standing beside each other. Two peas from the same pod, he thought. Adrian, however, had an openness. He showed none of the disdain which his ancestors had displayed in the paintings. It was, however, there in Sir Julius.

"I'm afraid that this may have been a wasted trip for you," said Adrian when he had finished telling Peter about what was at the site.

"Nae," said Peter, "but we'll probably need t' do a full survey of the escarpment. I'll confirm that with Mr Morton when I get back to the office."

"Really, will that be necessary?" asked Sir Julius. "As you can see from the survey, the walls of the gorge are granite."

"It's really not for me to say, sir," said Peter, "but you'll be putting hundreds of tons of weight on the edge of the escarpment and ye need t' be sure that it'll not fail."

"I suppose I won't convince an engineer to throw caution to the wind," said Sir Julius. "You'll test anything and everything and then you'll test it again just to be sure you haven't made a mistake and then you'll charge me for both sets of tests which will prove I was right."

Peter feigned a smile and said nothing. Sir Julius continued.

"We've been dynamiting up on the top of the escarpment in order to level the ground for the road to come in and our surveyor has said that not even a pebble has slipped from the escarpment. However, Mr Hall no doubt believes he knows best."

Adrian took out a cigarette case from his jacket and offered one to Peter. Peter shook his head and sneezed again.

"I'll have the survey copied and sent back," said Peter.

"No need," said Adrian. "We have another copy. I'll arrange for our driver Poley to take you back to the station."

Peter thanked him.

"There is one other thing," Peter said, before he left. Adrian and Sir Julius looked at him. "Ye had a pineapple in yer fruit bowl. I was wondering whether I could take it. I'd be happy to pay for it."

As Peter sat in the car on his way to Ticehurst station with a survey in the inside of his jacket and a pineapple beside him, he remembered the look that Adrian had given him when he had asked for the pineapple. He had smiled broadly, and his green eyes had shone. He remembered then the photograph in the reception room. That was it, he thought. Adrian and the man in the photograph at that moment had the same look, as if they were laughing at the world. Peter looked at his pocket watch, with its minute hand fixed on the six. The hour hand stood between the one and the two and with a little luck, and no mishaps, he could be on the five-past-two train back to Waterloo.

Chapter 7

The smile faded off Edith Facey's lips as Wadhurst Hall receded into the distance. Her husband had lit another cigar in the confined area of the car and even with the windows pulled down, she felt she was being suffocated by the smoke. She had smelt alcohol on her husband's breath when Julius Drewe had brought him back into the garden and although he was not drunk, there was still an hour before lunchtime. No doubt he would be off to his club when they got back, she thought. It seemed to her that no one in the civil service did anything after lunch and precious little beforehand. Even though her husband was the permanent secretary to the First Lord of the Admiralty, he seemed more interested in drinking and gambling than with politics. She doubted that he would even bother to leave his club if he was given news that there were German battleships coming up the Thames.

"How did you find Frances Drewe?" he asked her.

"Simply dreadful," replied Edith. "Living out in this wilderness seems to have robbed her of any sense of wit that she might once have had."

"So how did you pass the time?"

"She told me all her little secrets about managing staff. And you?"

"Drewe was amenable to my suggestion. When we renew the supply contracts for the Admiralty, they will go to one of Drewe's companies if I have stock in it. He can smell a deal. And I met that boy of his, Adrian. We talked for ten minutes or so. He looks like his father, but the resemblance stops there. I quite liked him, although he's still wet behind the ears."

"It was clear to me that they both dote on him," said Edith.

"Yes," said Lord Cecil. "Drewe dragged him into the room just to show him off to me."

"We were also invited to their next ball," said Edith. "They have one every New Year's Eve and I said that we would bring down Jane. Do you think that they would make a good match?"

Cecil Facey scoffed and the unanswered question hung in the air like the smoke from his cohiba. The Cadillac continued its fitful journey back to London. Edith Facey stared out the window as the motor went through the undulating Sussex countryside. Cecil Facey finished his cigar and threw the butt out of the window.

As they were passing near Croydon, and the beauty of the Surrey hills was fading, Edith Facey once again started the conversation. "We also had a long chat about their castle that Lutyens is designing for them."

"I suppose they chose Lutyens because Frances and Emily Lutyens are second cousins?" said Cecil.

"Not at all," said Edith, shaking her head slightly. "It was Julius' choice that they have Lutyens. I must admit to being somewhat surprised. I had heard that Lutyens' recent trip was not a success and he had made the worst sort of impression. He made some awful *faux pas* but of course it's the kind of thing for which Lutyens is known. He stopped off at Cape Town on his way back from India and at dinner with the Bishop of Cape Town and his wife, a Mr and Mrs Pim, he asked them whether there were any little Pimples. Unfortunately, the South Africans don't have our sense of humour and there was a terrible silence and Mrs Pim went bright red with embarrassment. My friends told me it caused something of an incident. There is a certain age that people reach when it looks rather desperate if one clowns around in public, and Lutyens has certainly reached that age." Edith moved her head slightly closer to her husband's before whispering, "I also heard that Lutyens' wife has locked the bedroom door. It's all to do with this theosophy sect that has sprung up in town. They are all talking nonsense about reincarnation and the need for celibacy. There's a delicious story about Emily Lutyens telling everyone that she knew the secretary of the theosophical society in a previous incarnation, possibly as a mouse. And now there are rumours that a boy is going to be sent over from India. He's got some unpronounceable name, and they're all convinced that he's going to become the World Teacher or something or other. You must have heard about that little red book that is doing the rounds? He is supposed to have written it. The whole group is nothing more than a laughing stock."

"It's too rich," said Cecil. "But then she was always a bit strange. It's the Lytton blood. All the Lyttons are that way. Her sister Constance is always in and out of jail, demonstrating about this and that. The only sensible one is Betty, and the rest of the family hardly recognise her since she married a Tory." Cecil paused for a second. He thought about lighting up another cigar but decided to give his wife some breathing space. "It's a wonder that Lutyens has any work at all. Drewe probably thought he could get Lutyens to do the design of his castle on the cheap." He laughed, took out a cigar from the inside pocket of his jacket and lit it.

When the Cadillac pulled up in front of their house in Chelsea, Lady Edith Facey got out. Cecil Facey said that he would carry on and go to his club. Edith watched as the motor turned at the end of their road and wondered whether he would actually go to his club or whether he would go off gambling or see his mistress in that flat in Kensington or, on the off chance, go to his office.

Frankly, she didn't care.

Chapter 8

Lady Emily Lutyens was in an exuberant mood. She had just received a letter from her dear friend, Annie Besant, the head of the Theosophical Society in Adyar, India, confirming that they were bringing Krishnamurti and his brother Nitya to England to be prepared for school. Through Annie Besant's spidery handwriting, Emily Lutyens ascertained that Krishnamurti was arriving in London on the 1st of March 1911 and then, after a week or two, he would go down to Bude in Cornwall. Emily was asked whether she would introduce herself to the two boys and then escort them to Cornwall and, if possible, stay with them until they had settled into life in England.

Krishnamurti was fifteen, a year older than Celia, and his brother Nitya was thirteen, a year older than her son Robert. She decided that it would be the most fabulous vacation and wondered whether Edwin would be able to take time away from his work to join them. She would be able to introduce her four children to the World Teacher and his younger brother. Krishnamurti and Celia could be the closest of friends, she decided. However, when she thought about it a little more, she realised that her daughter knew almost nothing about theosophy or Krishnamurti. She decided she would need to introduce Celia slowly to the teachings of theosophy and picked up her copy of Krishnamurti's book and went to find her.

Celia was on the landing, in her riding clothes and boots.

"Are you on your way out?" her mother asked.

"I'm going riding," said Celia looking down at her clothes, "with Margaret Ellis," she added by way of further explanation.

"I have something important for you," said Emily. "It is probably the most important present I shall ever give you."

"Jewellery?" said Celia, her face brightening up.

"No, no! Nothing like that," said Emily tersely. "It's a book, *At the Feet of the Master*."

"Oh, that thing," said Celia, who had seen her mother reading it continuously for the last few weeks. "What's so important about a book on mumbo jumbo?" Celia regretted the words as soon as they passed her lips.

"What did you say?" said Emily, emphasising each word.

"That..." said Celia.

"That, what?" asked Emily.

Celia could see her morning of horse riding evaporating with every word that passed her lips.

"That I'd love to read it when I get back from my ride."

*　　*　　*

Emily Lutyens was not a naturally tactile person and never had been. Even with her children she was not what one would call overly affectionate. She would kiss them goodnight and sometimes hold their hands when they were out together. However, when her children were out of sight, they would be easily forgotten and Emily could then focus on one of her more pressing causes.

She believed that her children should be independent, and each was enrolled in a multitude of different activities. She was especially keen on them exercising outside and thought that a healthy mind would be found in a healthy body. She encouraged Celia to take up horse riding, Robert to play rugby and cricket, and the two younger children to attend ballet classes.

Her relationship with her husband was, unusually, one of equals. Edwin Lutyens encouraged his wife to take up causes thinking that she would become bored and restless otherwise, while he travelled the country and often the world. In public Edwin Lutyens was the supportive husband and Emily the dutiful wife. However, they rarely held hands and the thought of being kissed in public made Emily shudder. Perhaps, surprisingly, no one seemed to notice. In another country they would have been the talk of high society, but in England it was accepted as the most natural thing in the world that a married couple would treat each other with a certain indifference.

Emily was waiting for her daughter to return from her riding lesson. After Celia had bathed and changed, they ate a light lunch of a cheese soufflé followed by a pineapple fritter drenched in sugar. The other children were out for the day and Edwin Lutyens had travelled down to Sandwich in Kent in the hope of obtaining a new commission.

"What do you know about Krishnamurti?" asked Emily.

"Almost nothing," said Celia, who was cutting her pineapple fritter into little pieces, "sorry."

"Well, where to start?" said Emily. "He was born in Madanapalle in South India. His father got a job with the Theosophy Society in Adyar and moved his family there." Celia dipped one the pieces of her fritter into a small mound of sugar. "There are a number of very spiritual people who are able to see a person's aura," continued Emily. "This aura is called a chakra and Krishnamurti has the most perfect chakra anyone has ever seen."

"Would I be able to see his chakra?" asked Celia. Emily's mouth pinched a little as she considered whether her daughter was making fun of her. She gave Celia the benefit of the doubt and continued.

"No, chakras can only be seen by the most spiritual of people. Only the very wisest and most perfect of people can have a perfect chakra and we believe that Krishnamurti will therefore become the World Teacher." Emily paused to let this sink in and looked at her daughter. Celia put the piece of fritter into her mouth and slowly chewed on it.

"What exactly is a World Teacher?"

"The World Teacher," said Emily, "is also known as the Lord Maitreya. He is a spiritual entity..."

Celia cut her short in her explanation. "You said Krishnamurti would be the World Teacher, so how can this Lord Maitreya also be the World Teacher?"

"Oh, do stop interrupting," said Emily. "When Krishnamurti is ready the spirit of Lord Maitreya will enter him and he will be given the knowledge about the existence of all humankind, just like Jesus had this knowledge."

Celia was not, however, dissuaded from interrupting and asked, "Are you saying that Krishnamurti is going to be like Jesus, all because of Lord Maitreya? That's not what the bible says."

All the teachings at Godolphin and Latymer school had not prepared Celia for news of a return of the messiah; a flaw in the British education system, she thought.

Emily decided that they had gone as far as they could. One more interruption and she would lose patience. "Well, the important news," she said, "is that Krishnamurti is coming to England, and you will be meeting him and his brother over the Easter vacation."

Celia did not say anything.

"He'll be like an older brother to you." Emily thought about putting her arms around her daughter but decided against it.

Later in the afternoon, as Celia sat in her room, she tried to piece together the conversation with her mother. She looked at the cover of the red book she had been given and opened it.

*"From the unreal lead me to the Real.
From the darkness lead me to Light.
From death lead me to Immortality."*

She turned the pages of the book, trying to understand one paragraph after another, but the meaning eluded her. After a while she went to the window and looked out. A woman sat on a bench in Bedford Square, a perambulator next to her. She was making cooing sounds to the baby. At her feet, a small Pekinese with a piggish face sniffed the ground. She wondered who they were, as she had not seen the lady in the square before and she knew most people who lived there. The woman looked incredibly serene as she looked down at her child.

A few minutes later, Celia went back to the little red book. She knew her mother would quiz her on it later and so she lay on her bed, read a few pages, and effortlessly managed to fall asleep.

Chapter 9

Celia stared at the choice of eggs for breakfast. None of them looked appetising, but she decided that the scrambled eggs appeared to be the lesser of all evils. The new cook would have to go, she thought. How could anyone cook eggs so badly? Both her parents were sitting at the table. Her father was reading the post. She noticed that he had left one of his poached eggs that appeared to resemble a deflated tennis ball. Her mother was sitting with a bowl of sago and hot milk. Celia decided she would have to break the monotony and, as she sat down, said:

"I thought I should have my hair cut."

"That's nice, dear," said Emily.

"I thought I might have it short – Margaret Ellis' elder sister is thinking of having her hair cut short. It's becoming fashionable in Paris right now." Celia put her hands through a mass of auburn-coloured curls and held them up to try and show the effect she was after.

Her father looked up.

"Do you think it would suit you?" he remarked.

"The problem with short hair, dear," said Emily interrupting, "is – well – well, it will probably make you look like a boy; however, ringlets would look lovely."

Celia bit her bottom lip. Being compared to a boy was, she thought, hardly tactful. In fact, she considered it just plain rude.

"But what can I do with this?" Again, Celia raised the mass of hair. "It just won't do anything. I brush it fifty times in the morning and at night, but it just has a mind of its own. Anyway," said Celia, already thinking about changing tack, "I could keep it cleaner if it was shorter. Isn't that what Krishnamurti said? 'You must keep your body strictly clean, even from the minutest speck of dirt.'"

The next few seconds surprised Celia. Her father stood up, threw his post on the breakfast table and said, quite firmly: "Don't get mixed up with that damned nonsense." He took in a deep breath. "Your mother's old enough to make up her mind but don't you start up with that foolishness."

Emily looked at her husband; her mouth was already pinched before she spoke.

"Don't," she said firmly, but Lutyens was already leaving the room. "Don't you dare try and stop her. You have to let her set her feet on the Path. If she believes like I do, nothing in the world should stop her."

Celia found there were tears welling up in her eyes. The door to the breakfast room slammed behind him and Edwin Lutyens left dead silence in his wake. Celia sat down and ate her breakfast quickly. Better get out, she thought, and let the air clear. She would take her horse out for a ride in the park and then see her friend Margaret Ellis. However, she would have to be back at four as her father had organised another meeting with Mr Hall, who she thought was as dull as dishwater.

Celia stood outside her front door, waiting for their chauffeur to bring the motor round. There had been a downpour during the night and the detritus on the streets around 31 Bedford Square had been washed away. However, the air was still humid, and it would take another storm to clear the air. More thunder is coming, thought Celia, but not just yet. It's still a good day for a horse ride.

Six hours later, Celia again stood in front of her house. She had hoped that riding would blow away the cobwebs, and lunch and a long chat with Margaret Ellis would put the world to rights. Unfortunately, she returned to 31 Bedford Square as despondent as when she left. Margaret had done her best to cheer her up and had views on nearly everything: on fashion, nice boys, music, not-so-nice boys, politics and, to Celia's surprise, even theosophy.

"Theosophy is a fad," Margaret said, "like pompadour hair styles or Home Rule in Ireland." Celia listened, wanting to be reassured, but in her heart not holding out much hope that her mother would drop this particular fad. Her mother had been fervent about it for months. She had not, however, realised that her father had become so set against theosophy. The only objection he had previously raised was to the imposed vegetarian diet, which he said was the hardest bit to swallow.

Celia went down into the basement of the house where her father had his office.

"You're expected, Miss Celia," said her father's secretary as she walked in. "He's in his office with Mr Hall." Celia knocked on the door, chewing the ends of a lock of hair until the door opened.

"Celia," said her father, "Mr Hall has been down to Drewsteignton to look at the site and kindly said he would update me on his return." Lutyens took out his pipe, filled and lit it. He let out a satisfied puff. "We can't keep Mr Hall for long as he is extremely busy." Celia nodded her head and Lutyens then looked at Peter. "Mr Hall, would you be kind enough to give me a summary of your most recent survey."

Celia listened to the presentation, which she considered unduly long and technical. Half an hour later, she could not hide a smile as Peter folded up his sketches and put the survey back into his bag.

"That's it," said Peter, "not much to report; however, we'll need to monitor the escarpment when the works start."

"Thank you," said Lutyens. "Any questions, Celia?"

"Nothing about your recent trip to Drewsteignton, but Father says that you met Sir Julius a few weeks ago. What was Wadhurst Hall like?"

"Aye, it's impressive, full of tapestries and grand furniture. On the estate there are stables, courtyards and lots of cottages and, aye, even a farm. They have their own loch where they go fishin' and swimmin'."

"You saw all of it?" asked Celia.

"No," said Peter, "Master Adrian Drewe told me about the estate as I was leaving."

"And what do you think of my father's design for the castle?" asked Celia. Peter hesitated before answering.

"Aye, it'll be grand," he said. "A castle fit for a princess. It will have stables and a grand banqueting hall."

"And will there be a chapel?" Celia asked her father.

Lutyens hesitated for a moment. "Sir Julius doesn't want a chapel," he replied.

"He has to have a chapel," said Celia, "otherwise there will be nowhere to pray for their souls."

Lutyens made a note on one of his drawings.

Chapter 10

"You know how much I hate change," said Celia. Edwin Lutyens looked up from his eggs. "However, we have to get rid of cook."

"Getting rid of staff," said Lutyens, "is easy. It's getting others that's the headache."

"But can't we get a French chef? Margaret Ellis' parents have a French chef, and everyone says that he cooks like a god."

"I'll discuss it with your mother," said Lutyens, and as he finished his sentence Emily Lutyens walked in.

"What will you discuss?" asked Emily.

"Nothing," said Lutyens. Celia stared at her father.

"We were discussing whether Cook is really up to the job."

Emily placed her bowl of sago onto the breakfast table. She stared for a moment at her daughter.

"Cook's position in this household, Celia, is not a subject for breakfast table tittle-tattle. If you don't have anything nice to say about her, then the best thing you can do is hold your tongue." Celia looked down at the white linen tablecloth. "And you should stop encouraging her," she said acerbically to her husband.

The last four months had been a trying time for Celia. She had read Krishnamurti's book and a dozen other pamphlets and articles on theosophy that her mother had chosen for her. However, when push came to shove, she just thought it all nonsense and said so quite bluntly one evening over dinner. Her mother appeared unaffected by the outburst and her father said nothing, but she felt afterwards that her allegiances in the household had somehow shifted. In fact, thereafter her father had not appeared to object to her spending evenings in the library with him when her mother went out or while she meditated.

"Changing the subject," said Lutyens quickly, "I spoke to Julius Drewe on the telephone yesterday evening and he's planning to have a stone laying ceremony at Drewsteignton later in the year."

Celia stopped herself biting into a piece of toast she was holding. She had met with Peter Hall three times since his first visit and Celia now considered the castle as much hers as her father's or anyone else's. She knew the general topography of the land and where the castle would sit on the lip of the escarpment of the Teign gorge. She knew what type of stone the gorge was made of. She had seen the calculations regarding shear strength and for a day or two she almost understood how they had been calculated. She had even made some suggestions regarding the design to her father, who had not dismissed them out of hand.

"Who's going, Father," she said excitedly, "and what does one wear to a stone laying ceremony?" She thought about asking what exactly a stone laying ceremony was but decided against it.

Lutyens took off his glasses and rubbed his eyes.

"Everyone who has been involved with the castle is invited, Celia. It will be Sir Julius' fifty-second birthday and he wants to lay the foundation stone, now that the design has been developed. There will be his family, me and Mr Hall and Gertrude Jekyll, if she wants to come."

"Can't we all go?" said Celia.

"Actually, he did invite us all, but I assumed your mother would not be interested in coming."

Emily looked up from the pamphlet she was reading.

"You assumed wrongly then," said Emily. "I haven't seen Frances Drewe for years and I wouldn't miss the chance of seeing where they are building this castle."

"Thank you, Mother," said Celia, "and I get to see Aunt Gertrude again."

In truth, Aunt Gertrude had always scared her a little. She was a true Victorian in spirit. She had views on young people that were very uncharitable and views on politicians which were even less so. Celia could guarantee that she would get at least one scolding for either having unruly hair or wearing improper and indecent clothing; that is to say, a lady's dress that went above the ankle.

"I have to tell everyone that I'm off to Castle Drogo," said Celia and she left her untouched breakfast and ran towards the stairs.

"I am pleased you're coming," said Lutyens. "We don't seem to do anything together anymore."

"You're always away," replied Emily. "By the way," she added, "when will this stone laying take place?"

"In September," answered Lutyens.

Emily again looked up from her pamphlet. "That's seven months away," she said.

"I suppose it is," said Lutyens.

"You might have mentioned that to Celia before she ran off."

"Well, she never gives you time to finish what you're saying."

Lutyens finished his breakfast and went up to the nursery. Celia was still there and after Lutyens had said good morning to his three youngest children, Robert, Mary and Elisabeth, he turned to Celia.

"What did you call the castle?"

"Castle Drogo," replied Celia.

"You know, I like that name," he said. "It'll do, it'll do very nicely."

PART II

Chapter 11

The seasons come and go, and years fade one into another. Winter turns to spring, and spring into summer and in no time, autumn is upon us. The fogs fall and suffocate the world and the coldness of winter creeps in. As one gets older, caution replaces exuberance when looking at the first snowfall. An ache is felt deep in the bones and the promise of spring is something to look forward to. Within no time whatsoever, in Edwin Lutyens' opinion, most of 1911 had flown by and the stone laying ceremony at Castle Drogo was upon him.

The design for Castle Drogo was in a state of flux. Sir Julius was again arguing about every penny and, as a result, the west wing of the building had been postponed. Postponed was a euphemism for omitted, thought Lutyens indignantly, knowing the castle had lost its balance. However, even with that part of the design removed, Lutyens knew that his first estimate would still be exceeded. Sir Julius also knew it and in the last month he had begun to question whether the great hall was just an indulgence. Lutyens knew he would have to put his foot down about that. However, already he was spending the potential omission and perfecting the sculptural virtuosity of the elevations, bringing a sense of classicism into the austere design.

Lutyens had spent far too long on the design of the castle and, as he would only get a percentage of the building cost, he doubted he would make a penny from it. However, something kept on drawing him back to the design. He was not precisely sure why, but it marked a change in what he had done before. Perhaps it was the struggle with his client. Sir Julius wanted a castle at a certain cost and cost seemed to be driving the design. For Lutyens it was the design that was important and when he thought more about it, he concluded that perhaps it was not the castle that was in a state of flux but himself. It was also the first of his designs that Celia had taken an interest in and, on occasion, she still attended his meetings with Peter Hall.

Time to get packed, thought Lutyens. The stone laying ceremony at Castle Drogo would take place tomorrow and they needed to get going if they were to arrive in Drewsteignton by the afternoon. Lutyens looked around his office. He placed his sketchbooks and some detailed drawings in his portfolio. He had a score of pen and crayon drawings, his small attempts to charm Sir Julius. He was pleased with them, and Celia had adored them. He looked at his desk; there was still one sketch on it, a drawing of Sir Julius' bathroom. Celia had only last night asked him about it because not only did it contain the layout of the room with sinks, baths and lavatory but also a column standing next to the bath, which seemed to be there for no reason.

"It's a Tuscan pillar," was his reply to Celia's question. He spoke in such a matter-of-fact tone of voice that Celia had for a moment thought that every bathroom in England might have a Tuscan pillar. "I added it to the design when Sir Julius decided to omit the west wing. I thought that Sir Julius could contemplate it when in the bath. A lesson in taste you might say."

Lutyens smiled when he remembered the look of shock on Celia's face and then he had winked at her.

"You won't actually include it in the design!" Celia said.

"Of course not," he assured her. However, he decided to slip it into the portfolio. One could never really tell what Sir Julius would or would not like. He looked at his pocket watch; time to go.

*   *   *

Lutyens had hired an Oldsmobile to take them to Gertrude Jekyll's house. He rightly considered that his little Austin 10 was not man enough for the long drive. The motor pulled away from Bedford Square. The sun was still in the east on the early September morning. Edwin Lutyens could see his three youngest children waving from the nursery on the third floor of his house. He and Celia put their arms out of the Oldsmobile and waved back. The motor slowly picked up speed and then turned into Bloomsbury Street and they were gone from sight.

In the bright morning light, the car swept by the British Museum, and turned south towards Trafalgar Square. In no time they had passed the Houses of Parliament, crossed the river at Putney and were out on the main road to Guildford. Edwin Lutyens settled himself down and opened a book. Celia wrapped a blanket around her and was happy to watch the world go by. She had also brought a Latin book with her, however, reading Virgil's story of the Trojan wars two thousand years ago seemed a little too dusty. Nothing exciting ever seemed to happen now, she thought to herself. There were no Trojan heroes or warriors like Achilles. She dreamed about falling in love and marrying such a man. It seemed to Celia that there had been no one since Byron who could be described as a romantic hero. They had all been replaced by politicians with starched collars and walrus moustaches.

Celia looked over at her mother. She was immersed in a book by her friend Annie Besant, a short, well-built woman with a suntanned face, white hair and a dominating voice. Celia remembered her because her mother seemed exuberant before she visited them and a little in awe after she left. Celia recalled that her mother had said that Annie Besant was the woman looking after Krishnamurti in India.

All in all, thought Celia, the past year had been a strange one. Her mother's fascination with theosophy continued unabated. Her family had taken Krishnamurti down to Cornwall and stayed there for a month. Her father had been abroad all that time in India. If the truth be told, she found Krishnamurti quite shy and a little stupid but then, as her mother had said, he had only received the most rudimentary education in India. Celia felt that neither parent had been there for her that year and, now she was sitting with them both, she had nothing to say. She did not want to talk about Krishnamurti. That seemed to be the easiest way to cause an argument between her parents. She even admitted to herself that she felt jealousy for this boy who, without doing anything, had stolen her mother's affection. She continued to stare at the countryside and without noticing that she was doing so, began to chew the end of a piece of hair. However, many stars cannot be concealed behind a small cloud and soon Celia's mood improved.

"When will we get to Aunt Gertrude's house?" said Celia, to no one in particular.

"We're nearly there," said Lutyens looking out of the vehicle. It was still morning, if only just, when the car arrived at Munstead Wood, Gertrude Jekyll's house. Gertrude was standing outside waiting. She was not tall, in her stockinged feet just over five feet, and she seemed just as wide. She wore a three-piece green tweed suit and what she liked to call a 'going out hat'. It was made of the same green tweed with an ostrich feather stitched to one side. Even in millinery circles, the style of the hat had no name and perhaps only one was ever made before it was crucified by fashionable society. However, Gertrude Jekyll thought it a practical hat, which to her was far more important than the foolishness of fashion.

They greeted each other as only the English can. They knew each other far too well to shake hands; however, the intimacy of kissing cheeks was just a little too foreign. First, Edwin and then Emily approached Gertrude, and each pretended to kiss the other. Only Celia was favoured by a proper kiss and she had now reached an age where she hoped that this would soon stop.

"You've been chewing the ends of your hair again," Gertrude observed after having kissed Celia. "My mother would have known how to stop that."

Celia had little doubt of that. If half the stories about Gertrude's mother were to be believed, then the woman had been one of the original Harpies.

Gertrude watched as her case was stowed in the back of the motor, making sure that it was not thrown in unceremoniously but placed properly. She then got into the car and settled herself beside Emily and opposite Celia. Having got herself comfortable, she proceeded to talk to Lutyens about when they would arrive, so that she could see where the castle was to be built, and thus where the gardens would be. Lutyens explained that they would be going to Guildford next and then take the train to Southampton where they would change for Exeter. Sir Julius had arranged for a car to pick them up and take them to the site where the castle was to be built. Their luggage would be taken to the hotel in Drewsteignton.

"We have lots to discuss," said Lutyens. "After our walk around the grounds this afternoon, we will be having dinner with a distant relative of the Drewes in the evening. He's the rector of Drewsteignton, who first wrote to Sir Julius about his infamous ancestor. The stone laying ceremony is the next day."

After listening to half an hour of dry conversation between her father and Gertrude, Celia reached for her Latin book. Perhaps Virgil will grow on me, she thought to herself as she opened it. However, after fifteen minutes she began to appreciate what it was to be between Charybdis and Scylla.

It was not until they were on the train from Southampton to Exeter that the conversation changed from the castle to politics. It was only then that Emily put down her book. Celia also began to listen, as the conversation moved to the suffragettes.

"I see your sister's been making news again," said Gertrude to Emily. "I read that she was arrested for breaking windows in Downing Street."

This was a story of which nothing was said in the Lutyens household, although it had been a subject for both the broadsheets and the gutter press. Celia was not supposed to know about it, but both she and Margaret Ellis had read almost everything written regarding her Aunt Constance, who had been arrested.

"The right of women to vote is something which is worth going to prison for," said Emily. "We've protested peacefully and marched a thousand times, and Constance felt she was left with no choice but to do something to make the politicians listen. Asquith could have seen us and heard what we had to say but instead he turned a blind eye. If you ask me, there's not been one good argument yet as to why women should not have the vote."

"I don't disagree with you, Emily," said Gertrude. "But it's not just a question of right or wrong, it's a question of politics. The mistake your sister has made, as has every other suffragette in my opinion, is that they have not managed to get the support of either the Liberals or the Tories. Until the battle lines are drawn down party lines, the government will do nothing. Asquith just doesn't see the issue as one of importance."

"But it's not a matter of opposition," said Emily. "Balfour said that he was not averse to putting forward a suffragette bill to the House, but he thought that the problem would arise if ever there came a time when women made up the majority. That's why he is a fool. He said it would be a perverse thing if women could decide on a position of policy, which they did not have the physical strength to enforce. I wanted to throw a brick at him myself."

"But you can hardly be surprised," Gertrude said. "A government in power hates change and it will never enfranchise the disenfranchised or change the basis on which it obtained its mandate. Politics is only ever about keeping power and those who have power are always the most conservative."

"So much for living in an age of enlightenment," added Lutyens.

"An age of enlightenment!" said Emily. "Whatever made you think that, Edwin? We live in a patriarchal society."

Gertrude looked at Celia who had sat quietly listening to the conversation.

"Well, let's have your tuppence-worth," she said. Celia took a deep breath. She tried to think of what her form tutor would say if asked the question. However, Mrs Deare was fifty, bitter and unmarried, and was likely to stay that way. In Celia's opinion, she probably didn't even care about voting. How would Margaret Ellis answer? Margaret was far too flippant. She found herself chewing at the end of one of her locks of hair and stopped immediately when she caught Gertrude's eye.

"It shouldn't be wrong to steal a loaf of bread to stop a man from starving," Celia said slowly, "and it shouldn't be wrong to stop a person who is beating a child." Gertrude was smiling and Celia began to warm to her theme. "It therefore shouldn't be wrong," she continued, "to throw a stone at a window if it will result in the lives of ten million women being better. Aunt Constance was probably right and when she went up in front of the magistrate, she had nothing to be contrite about, even if you've always got to be contrite in front of the beak because that's the law."

"Celia!" said Lutyens and Emily together.

"Well, she wasn't contrite," replied Celia. "In *The Times* it said that when the magistrate asked Aunt Constance why she had thrown the brick she replied that she thought she was at a coconut shy. Even I know that wasn't true."

"Celia!" said Lutyens and Emily again together, and Gertrude Jekyll roared with laughter.

Chapter 12

Archibald Drew was the rector of Drewsteignton. He was in his late fifties, overweight with a round red face and mutton chop whiskers. His curly grey hair had for some years been progressively getting thinner. Life in a quiet village suited Archibald. He had an opinion on nearly everything and an informed view on very little. The church had been his perfect vocation. He had shuffled through life without ever having to question anything, because his answers were determined solely by his faith. He believed that everything was pre-ordained and therefore there was little point in worrying. His sermons were not of the hell and damnation variety. He preached about the meek and forgiveness and his parishioners looked forward to going to church on a Sunday accordingly, even the ne'er-do-wells.

Archibald Drew stood at the rectory door greeting Lutyens and his family as they came in one by one followed by Gertrude Jekyll.

"Miss Jekyll," he said, clasping her by the hand, "now there's no need to hide."

"It's pronounced 'Jee-kill'," she corrected him. She pulled her hand away from his slightly clammy grasp. "The mispronunciation of *that* novel will be the death of me."

"Yes, yes of course. Well, everyone's here now. Sir Julius came earlier. He's in the sitting room."

Sir Julius Drewe was very much as Celia had expected from her conversations with Peter Hall. She had once overheard her mother describe Sir Julius as an arrogant little shopkeeper but to Celia, he looked nothing like any shopkeeper she knew. When he stood up, he looked down at her own father. His suit was hardly creased, and his hair was in place as if he had just stepped out of his bathroom. Celia thought him dashing, although a little overweight, realising how shabby her father looked in comparison as the two men shook hands. Sir

59

Julius then inclined his head slightly to Emily and Gertrude.

"Good evening," he said. "Emily, it's been far too long and Miss Jekyll, it's a pleasure." Emily answered, apparently indifferent to Sir Julius, but Gertrude was quite taken with him. Suddenly Celia was standing before him with a dry mouth and butterflies in the pit of her stomach.

"I hear from Mr Hall that you've taken quite an interest in the design of my castle."

Celia curtsied. "Pleased to make your acquaintance," she said quietly.

"And this is my wife, Lady Drewe," said Sir Julius, indicating a woman who was sitting in the corner. Frances Drewe had been sitting quietly, unnoticed, on a large wingback chair which was covered by a number of mismatched tapestries. Celia turned in her direction and curtsied again. Frances got up. She was thin with long golden hair that had been pinned up. Unruly curls hung down on each side of Frances' face and Celia felt that here was a kindred spirit. Frances smiled warmly and Celia returned the smile.

The sitting room had several chairs randomly placed around the room and a battered sofa. Celia guessed that the furniture had probably been donated from parishioners over the years. Books and dusty papers were piled up in cluttered corners. On the mantelpiece were Toby jugs and small China ornaments. The French doors of the sitting room were open and dust mites danced in the air as the early evening sunlight streamed in. Archibald Drew waited for everyone to get comfortable before offering them a drink.

"A glass of lemonade, or maybe a sherry?" He pulled on a cord for his housekeeper. Archibald looked at Celia.

"All the young gentlemen are outside, Miss Lutyens," Archibald said. "Would you mind asking them if they want a libation as my housekeeper's legs aren't what they used to be? You might also want to have your drink with them; you might find it all a bit too stuffy in here." Archibald tapped the side of his nose as if he were letting Celia into a secret. Celia took no longer than a second to decide that outside with the young gentlemen was the better option and looked towards her father, who nodded. She got up.

"I have planned to eat *al fresco* this evening," Archibald continued, waving at the garden outside. "*Al fresco*; that is the correct phrase, isn't it? I've heard that everyone does it abroad and it would be so very pleasant in this humid weather. We've had hardly a drop of rain in nearly a month and the moorlands have gone to scrub and now my gardener tells me there is a storm coming." Archibald looked at Sir Julius. "But what does a gardener know?" he said with a shrug. Gertrude Jekyll, who was sitting behind him, made a derisory sound. "However, you must want to hear all about my research, and I can honestly say that there is the most marvellous story of your ancestor Drogo de Teigne."

Celia stepped quickly out of the French doors. Archibald Drew sounded too much like her Latin teacher and if she was any judge, Archibald would be starting a long, involved, rambling story ending with a terrible joke or anecdote. As she walked down the path to the end of the garden, she could visualise Archibald fully apprising everyone in minute detail of his excavations through the church archives. She could also imagine the glare that her Aunt Gertrude would be giving him.

Celia was surprised by the beauty of the garden. It seemed out of place in comparison to the ramshackle rectory. Beside the path of slate stepping stones, the garden had been allowed to grow and interspersed in various types of grasses were white daisies and purple heather. Japanese maples flanked the garden, although the red leaves looked shrivelled from the heat and were waiting to fall with the next rain. At the far end of the garden was a wooden fence that separated the ordered world from the untamed moors. Celia could see, sitting on the fence, looking out at the darkening sky, three young men.

'Arrogant, argumentative and stand-offish,' were the adjectives that came immediately to Celia's mind when she spoke to Christian Drewe, who everyone called Kit. There was a slight condescension in the way he looked at her, being four years her senior. It was not anything he said, of course, but she felt that he considered her interruption a nuisance rather than a pleasant interlude. She decided that she did not care for him one iota and would not grow to like him. Sitting on the left of Kit was his twelve-year-old brother, Basil Drewe. He sat listening and piped up quickly that he would have a glass of sherry rather than lemonade. It resulted in Kit clipping him around the ear. On Kit's other side was his older brother, Adrian. Celia's first thought was that he was dashing, more so than Sir Julius would ever have been. He smiled at her, and she stammered when she asked him whether he would like lemonade or a sherry. She went a little red.

"There's a storm coming," Adrian told her. "You can see the clouds building up over there on the east of the moors."

"It's not coming this way, is it?" said Celia. "It's such a beautiful evening."

Kit stared at the clouds.

"The weather here can change at the drop of a hat," he said. "You don't want to be on the moors when the weather is like this; one minute it's bright and the next you can't see your hand in front of you."

"Kit was at school near here," said Adrian in explanation. "He once got caught out on the moor in a storm and was out there for two days."

"It was worse at night," Kit added. "You can't see anything in the blackness, and you wander around blind. It suddenly goes desperately black and there is nothing to help you get your bearings."

"Now Kit's afraid of the dark," added Basil.

Celia could not help but notice the look Basil got from Kit. There was something malicious in the stare, which said that this would not be forgotten quickly.

"What's going on up in the house?" asked Adrian, changing the subject quickly.

"When I left, the rector was talking about your family genealogy."

"God," said Adrian, "we had that all afternoon. It seems that finding out about Drogo de Teigne has now become his life's work."

"He's just looking for a handout from Father," added Basil. "We're always getting them knocking at the door – poor relations."

Now it was Adrian's turn to look sternly at Basil.

"Sorry," said Basil, noticing Adrian's expression, "I didn't mean anything by it; it's just what everyone says."

In the distance the dinner gong sounded.

"Race you up the garden," said Basil and suddenly Celia found that she was standing all alone.

Chapter 13

Dinner, thought Celia, was taking forever. The food was overcooked and bland. Celia looked at her mother's meal. Emily had caused an incident when she had told Archibald Drew that she was a vegetarian. The cook finally agreed to throw together an omelette and lightly fried some mushrooms with a handful of parsley as a starter. Celia looked down at the overcooked leg of chicken and bread sauce on her plate and wished that she had also asked for the vegetarian option. The request for a vegetarian meal had resulted in a discussion between Emily and Archibald. Emily was emphatic that the suggestion that man needed meat was mere superstition.

"No different to sacrificing animals to appease the angry gods," she said. Archibald attempted an acquiescing sound but as eating meat was not prohibited by the bible, he saw no reason why he ought to give up one of the main pleasures of his life.

As the meal entered its third course, the subject of conversation once again turned back to the Drewe genealogy. "The Drewe name," Archibald declared, "has a wealth of history behind it whether you have an 'e' at the end or not. The family name goes back to Richard, Duke of Normandy who was the grandfather to William the Conqueror. Our ancestors sailed with William when he invaded England and for this assistance William provided our family with seventy-three manors." Archibald took a sip of his wine.

"Back to William the Conqueror," said Emily, with just the merest hint of sarcasm. "I suppose that if you trace your name back far enough, sooner or later you will stumble across a relation of a king."

"It's all recorded in the Domesday Book," Archibald said, mistaking Emily's remark for genuine interest. "The most well-known manor was here, of course, Drewsteignton. The town of Drew standing on the river Teign. However, our family only came to prominence during the reign of Henry II."

Celia looked around the table. She had been placed between Basil Drewe, which she considered inappropriate as his interests seemed to be limited to cricket, and her father. Gertrude appeared to be flagging. The only person who she could not see properly at the table was Kit and she could imagine the look of tedium on his face. She found herself looking at Adrian and began to daydream until Basil tapped her on the shoulder and asked her:

"Do you like the castle your father has designed?"

"Of course," said Celia, "don't you?"

"I don't know what to make of it," said Basil. "Adrian likes it, but Kit says that it looks like a mental asylum."

Celia heard her father laugh.

"The castle will symbolise the essence of Englishness," said Lutyens across to Basil, "so if you think all Englishmen mad then perhaps your brother might agree that it is the perfect design. It brings together a sense of modernism and our past; an island standing in a wilderness." Lutyens took out his pipe and began playing with it.

Gertrude Jekyll suddenly perked up as Lutyens was speaking.

"Two themes, Edwin, traditional and modern. We could have formal terraces, balustrades, trellis work and small flower gardens around the castle and then long lawns which finally blend into the moorland."

Archibald Drew saw the conversation suddenly taking a different and unwelcome course and so he tapped his glass with his spoon.

"And now," he said, "I will tell the story of Drogo de Teigne and the fair Rosamond. It's a tragic story for after Drogo de Teigne's first wife died in childbirth he grieved for a year and could think only of himself. Over time he noticed that the child's nurse cared for the baby as if it were her own, so that the child never cried or wanted for anything. Little by little Drogo found that the child's nurse, Rosamond, brought laughter back into his dark heart and one day decided that he should marry her not only for the child's sake but for his own. However, Drogo was a Norman knight of King Henry's court and to marry a Saxon lady, he needed the King's permission. Drogo therefore brought Rosamond to the court of King Henry II. Drogo could not have guessed that on seeing Rosamond the King's heart would be filled with a relentless passion.

"Now Henry was married to Elinor of Aquitaine who was cruel and heartless; however, carried away by his passion he abducted Rosamond and, so the legends say, he took her to an enchanted castle hidden in a magical garden. The castle was known as Labyrinthus because, in order to arrive at it, you needed to travel through a maze, which, to anyone who did not know the way, was impossible. The Queen went mad with jealousy and plotted to have Rosamond killed and so would wait outside the maze hoping to find its secret. One day, the King snagged his tunic as he was going through the maze and left a trail of silk thread.

Elinor saw this and returned later with her knights and was able to follow the silk thread back through the maze and kill Rosamond."

Celia listened intently. It reminded her of one of the stories that her father used to tell her when she was a small child and which, if she were honest with herself, she would admit she missed.

"When Henry discovered that Rosamond had been killed, he believed that it had been Drogo de Teigne, who had sworn to avenge the insult that the King had done him. Henry summoned his troops and his hunting dogs and rode to Drewsteignton to settle matters with Drogo, but Drogo fled onto the moors. Folklore in these parts," continued Archibald, who had noticed his guests' interest had stirred finally, "says that Henry's pack of hounds were unnatural beasts who would not give up the scent. They were giant dogs with blood-red eyes. After tracking Drogo across the moors for three days and nights they found him on Watchet Hill. They surrounded him and though he managed to kill three of the Whist Hounds they finally got the better of him."

"Whist Hounds?" asked Celia.

"It's the name the locals gave to these dogs of hell. Nonsense of course! Anyway, so passed away Drogo de Teigne, although his child survived, and our lands were not taken by Henry II. It is not precisely clear how and when the family name changed but over time Drogo became Drugo and then Dru and finally Drewe."

"And that's exactly what I shall get," said Sir Julius, "a magnificent castle surrounded by a magical garden."

The sky suddenly became darker, and the rain began to pour.

"I told you that the weather here changed on a whim," said Adrian to Celia as they busied themselves helping to get everything indoors. Celia noticed that there was a disconsolate look on Archibald's face and a satisfied one on her aunt's, as they started to carry in the tableware.

"You're getting soaked," said Adrian, as the rain started to pelt down. He took off his jacket and covered Celia's head. She could smell a hint of sandalwood as he got close to her. They made a final dash through the French doors and back into the living room. Adrian put down his jacket. Celia stared as his wet shirt stuck to his chest. He shook his head and then with his fingers combed backed his hair. Everyone should have black hair, Celia decided to herself.

"What did you think of Archibald's story?" asked Adrian.

"It was tragic," said Celia in reply. "But then all great love stories are tragedies."

"Don't you believe in happy endings, then?"

Celia didn't answer, as Kit came wandering over to them. To Celia's surprise he was perfectly dry. She could not remember him helping when the rain started pouring and she doubted that he had managed to skip between the raindrops. Irritation flared up for a moment that he had remained dry, and she had nearly got drenched.

"I bet that you're wishing you hadn't agreed to stay at the farm," said Kit to Adrian.

"It will still be fun," said Adrian.

"In this weather?" said Kit.

"Where is the farm and why are you staying there?" asked Celia.

It was Kit who answered. "Father has arranged accommodation for some people on the farm near where the castle is being built and that engineer fellow, Peter Hall, is staying there. I had a wager that Adrian would not last a night staying there."

"It will be the easiest guinea I've ever earned," said Adrian.

Kit turned to Celia.

"Would you stay on a farm?" he asked.

Celia could see the rain hammering down outside. In the distance there was the sound of thunder rolling in. She liked animals but not enough to live with the smell of them, and she could imagine that the beds would be hard as a slab.

Now would be as good a time as any to tell a white lie, she thought to herself.

Chapter 14

A phosphorescent glow lit up the sky and the rumble of thunder was heard soon afterwards. The approaching storm moved closer. Something other than the thunder had woken Adrian, like the howl of an animal. The second sheet of lightning brought the world into luminescence and the sound that followed shook the barn. Adrian lit a candle and looked out of the window. More lightning followed and was accompanied by a clap of thunder. In that moment of illumination, Adrian could see people in the farmyard. Their forms were marked out like rubbings from a church stone. The rain continued to drum down on the roof of the barn so that even between thunder claps it was impossible to hear what was going on outside. Adrian grabbed his clothes, found a waterproof by the door, and went out.

The ferocity of the storm surprised him. The wind whipped his face, and the driving rain stung his eyes. He could just make out figures moving towards the outbuildings at the far end of the farm. He followed them until he came to the stable block where smoke was billowing out of the doors. In the midst of the darkness, he felt a hand on his shoulder and turned to see someone carrying a bucket of water.

"Hall," shouted Adrian, "is that you?"

"Aye," said Peter. "They've got a horse trapped in there. Everyone's getting water to put out the fire."

Adrian followed Peter into the stable block. He saw Henry Bowden, the farmer, hurling water at a stack of hay at the far end of the stable. It hissed for a moment and then fire leapt up again from the top of the stack. Even from where Adrian was standing, he could feel the heat. Opposite the haystack a horse was trapped in its stall, it whinnied wildly and kicked its feet against the stone walls. The kicking stopped and the horse suddenly reared up and Adrian could see its taut neck as it tried desperately to find an exit from the advancing flames. Adrian stared at its watery, brown eyes filling up with panic. For what seemed minutes he could not move his eyes away from the horse and then its head disappeared, and Adrian once again heard the horse kicking at the wall. The fire was crackling viciously and spitting as it licked its way along the timber roof. Peter ran forward and threw his bucket of water at the top of the fire. The farmer attempted to placate the horse, but it proved a vain effort as the fire, the sound of thunder and the smoke had now maddened the animal.

"Get more water," shouted the farmer. Peter turned and ran. The farmer's wife came in carrying another bucket and was followed by two farmhands.

It's a wasted effort, thought Adrian; they might as well shout for the fire to withdraw. He could see that it was now only minutes before the fire would run along the timbers of the stable and be over the head of the animal. Adrian moved forward. He looked at the walls dividing each stall. Each was made of stone, and he guessed it would take an hour to knock one down even if they could get close enough. Peter returned and threw another bucket of water on the haystack. Adrian stopped Peter running back out.

"The fire's spreading," he shouted, "and there aren't enough hands to get it under control. The kindest thing we can do is put the animal out of its misery."

"Nae," shouted Peter. "We can save it! If I had something we could drag the fire outside!"

Once again, a thunderclap deafened them. Peter started looking around the barn. Suddenly he ran past Adrian to the other side of the stable where a pitchfork was hanging and brought it back.

"Get more water!" he shouted. The fire continued to spit and hiss, and clouds of dark smoke belched out.

"I'll see if I can drag it outside!" He jumped forward and stuck the fork into one of the bales of straw at the top of the stack. However, to obtain enough leverage to move the bale he had to lodge his left foot into the base of the haystack. The bale came down and Peter jumped back, cursing as the fire scorched his leg. Adrian watched as the bale fell and broke apart. Fire washed in front of them, stopping anyone getting near the stack. The horse began to throw its whole body against the stone wall.

"Get a bloody shotgun!" Adrian shouted at the farmer, who turned and ran back to the farmhouse. Peter started to move closer to the haystack again, but this time Adrian stood in his way. Thick black smoke now engulfed most of the barn.

"Get out!" Adrian shouted. Peter hesitated. He looked at the fire as it crept along the roof of the stable. The smoke suddenly overwhelmed him, and he started coughing.

"Come on!" Adrian screamed, leading him out. As they left the stable Adrian could see the farmer running back with his shotgun.

"It's too late," Adrian shouted at him, "you can't breathe in there."

"I'll not let it suffer," cried the farmer. "No animal deserves that kind of death." Adrian watched as he ran into the stable; a minute later Adrian heard the gunshot. He waited for the farmer to come out. He waited for what seemed an eternity.

"Shit!" spat Adrian. Peter was still choking. Adrian pulled out his handkerchief and wrapped it around his face. The barn was full of smoke, and he could see nothing. He got on his hands and knees and crawled forward, hoping that he might be able to breathe more easily lower down. His hand went forward trying to feel for the body of the farmer. He could hold his breath no longer and gulped for air. The smoke choked him. Above him, he heard the timber roof splitting and prayed that it wouldn't all come crashing down on him. He began to cough and then his hand touched the still form of the farmer. He wasn't sure what limb he had grabbed, but he got hold of it as tight as he could and pulled backwards with all his strength. As he got outside, he slipped on the mud. He tore off the handkerchief and breathed in the clean air. Peter and the farmhands pulled the farmer clear from the stable. Adrian sat in the mud, exhausted, breathing quickly in between bouts of coughing. The rain continued to fall, smearing the black soot down his face. When he stood up his legs felt weak, but he needed to know how the farmer was.

Henry Bowden was also coughing and was equally as black. Adrian came over and Henry's wife was making him drink from a pitcher of water.

"I'm sorry about your horse," said Adrian.

The farmer looked up at Adrian. He didn't answer. His wife, Bess, handed Adrian the pitcher of water.

"Thank you," she said, as Adrian took the pitcher. "It's bad enough losin' a horse but..." She looked at her husband. "He's an old fool." She then looked at Peter. "And you as well, Mr Hall. Both of you risked your lives in there."

Wet and weary, Adrian and Peter sat in the farmhouse with the Bowdens and their farmhands an hour later that night. Henry Bowden had broached a cask of ale and was pouring tankards for everyone. The fire had been extinguished mainly due to the heavy rain. Henry Bowden, after his first two pints of beer, was reflective.

"Well, Mister Hall, Mister Drewe," said Henry, "you should know that you'll always be welcome here." They drank up.

"It's the strangest thing," said Adrian. "It wasn't the storm that woke me up. I heard something else."

"It was probably all of us shoutin' in the courtyard," said Bess Bowden.

"No," said Adrian, "it wasn't that either. It was the weirdest sound."

"You hear some strange sounds coming from the moor," said Henry. "It's just the wind but there's many a story round these parts; stories to frighten the young 'uns. They'll tell you in town it was the huntsman with his pack of wild hounds. They call them the Whist Hounds – the Hounds from Hell – and they say that anyone who meets up with the pack and the huntsman will die within a year and a day."

"Shut yer nonsense," said Bess and she once again filled up everyone's tankards. They carried on talking for another hour until tiredness started to take its toll.

Adrian could not, however, go back to sleep. At five o'clock that morning he had washed in cold water and had walked to where the castle was to be built. He wanted to see the sun come up and send its first rays to where his father planned to set down the family's roots. He looked out to the east. The world still appeared in hues of grey and ash. He noticed how cold it was in those seconds just before dawn, before the air moves and the temperature rises, just as the corona of the sun appears on the horizon. He felt the cold breeze race over the moor. Adrian put his hands in his pockets as the north wind suddenly whipped past him, having travelled from the icy clouds at the boundaries of civilisation.

The sun rose and Adrian thought that, away in the distance, the world would be waking. Soon the sounds of church bells would be heard calling the superstitious to prayer and would meld with the shrieks of morning birds, with the water from the stream below him, with the night animals as they scurried back to their lairs and the creak of the trees. Adrian listened to the sounds, unusual and strange and often unnoticed. He stood on a half naked, half tree-covered escarpment that blended itself into the fathomless greys of the morning. Away across the moor, a pallid mist hung just above the ground like a soft grey cloud. In those tired hours his mind jumped from one thought to another but always it came back to the sight of the horse's watery, brown eyes that seemed mad with panic.

He promised himself that if he was ever again in that situation, he would do something different.

Chapter 15

Edwin Lutyens woke from a fitful sleep. He could not remember his dream, nor did he want to. His eyes gradually opened with several blinks, and he saw his wife still curled up under the blankets, hiding from the world. She had slept through the storm and the crowing of cockerels. Lutyens heaved his legs over the side of the bed, put on his steel-rimmed glasses and looked around the room of the old coaching inn. The worn rug rubbed at the soles of his feet as he made his way over to the wash basin. He washed with cold water. It wasn't the type of place where he would usually stay but because Sir Julius had arranged the rooms, he could not complain. Sir Julius had said it would be convenient, being a five-minute walk from Archibald Drew's rectory in Drewsteignton and close to where the castle was being built. Gertrude Jekyll's estimation of Sir Julius had lowered considerably when she first saw the old coach house.

Lutyens took from the wardrobe a tweed jacket and a pair of corduroy trousers and found a clean shirt in the chest of drawers. He dressed quickly and made his way downstairs. Emily turned in her sleep, unaware that her husband had left the bedroom. The breakfast room was small; it didn't need to be big as there were rarely more than half a dozen guests staying at the inn. Celia, who was having breakfast with Gertrude, waved across to him.

"They haven't even got a copy of *The Times*," he complained as he sat down to join them. However, his face lit up when he saw the plate of sausages, bacon, kidneys and scrambled eggs that were in front of Gertrude. A waiter arrived immediately with a rack of hot toast and conserves.

"Coffee or tea?" the waiter asked.

"Darjeeling and the full breakfast with two lamb chops," said Lutyens.

"I'm afraid we don't have Darjeeling," said the waiter.

"Lap-san-sue-shong?" said Lutyens, as if the waiter might be a bit slow. He waited for the inevitable response.

"Lap – san what, sir?"

"Breakfast tea will be fine, if you have nothing else."

"There's something I wanted to talk to you about," said Gertrude, who then turned to Celia and asked her whether she wouldn't mind running up to her room and fetching a powder case. Celia stood up, a piece of toast still in hand. Gertrude gave her the room key, smiled and said, "Don't hurry, dear."

When Celia was out of earshot Gertrude began. "Edwin, we couldn't talk yesterday but I am afraid that there is some nasty gossip about that theosophy group of which Emily is so fond."

Lutyens looked at her over his steel-rimmed spectacles.

"We've been friends a long time Edwin," she continued, "You ought to know that I wouldn't say anything against either you or Emily and that I'm having this conversation because I feel it is necessary."

Lutyens still said nothing.

"I don't pretend to understand anything about theosophy but it's all the talk of society." Gertrude lowered her voice slightly. "Actually, there are two things," she said. "First, there's gossip about a man in India called Leadbeater. He and Annie Besant seem to be the people running the theosophist group. It hasn't been published yet but there is an allegation of impropriety with some of the Indian boys by Leadbeater. I was told by a most reliable person that some of the parents are now demanding their children back and have started a court case. The fact of the matter is that he's rumoured to be a nasty little pederast, and neither you nor Emily really can be seen to have anything to do with that group."

"I don't have anything to do with them," said Lutyens emphatically, "and as far as I know Emily has only met this Leadbeater person once, when she went to Cornwall at Easter."

"There's sure to be an almighty stink when this gets out in the press, so I thought I would just put you on notice. The other thing is this Krishnamurti boy who came from India. Emily and her theosophist friends are apparently running around saying that he will soon become the new messiah. People are laughing at her, Edwin. And while of course she's not the only one, you don't want your name to be associated with such talk."

"Gertrude," Lutyens said slowly, "I will speak to Emily again; however, you must understand she's unlikely to listen to me. For her, it's a matter of faith."

"Faith," said Gertrude. "So, there is no hope of making her see sense?"

"None," said Lutyens. "She believes in theosophy as much as a saint believes in Christ. Emily and Celia are very much the same in that regard. Once they get their minds set on something then there is no stopping them. They are both possessive people."

"Celia?" said Gertrude. "I always thought she was quite flighty."

"About some things she is," replied Lutyens. "But once she gets her mind set on a subject, neither hell nor high water will stop her."

Celia re-entered the breakfast room and walked towards the table.

"This may amuse you," said Gertrude. "I recently heard this *bon mot* which made me smile: 'a casual stroll through the lunatic asylums shows that faith does not prove anything'."

Lutyens smiled and turned to Celia.

"If we are to get to Bowden's Farm by nine, then we'll have to get going fairly soon." He looked around the breakfast room. "Where is my breakfast? I can't be expected to walk up the Teign gorge on an empty stomach."

Celia was relieved when she saw the waiter carrying in her father's breakfast but wondered how he could walk anywhere if he ate the whole plate. Celia was astonished how he made short work of the food, and they got up from the table where Gertrude was still sitting. She saw another couple in the corner, who must have come in while she was getting Gertrude's powder case. She wondered why they were in Drewsteignton on this September morning. Had they come down to meet friends or relatives or had they eloped?

She hoped it was the latter, because they looked like they were in love.

*   *   *

Few people made a living on Dartmoor. The Romany earned just enough from turf cutting or trading in gorse, bracken, or heather. The feudal rights of 'common in the soil' were hardly ever taken up by the locals because of the peatiness of the land. The farmers survived by turning out their oxen and draught horses to graze in springtime after the ploughing was done. In summer, the moor gave some pasture for cattle and sheep and then the livestock were returned to cover when the weather became inclement. In the areas where heather, bracken and blackberries grow in abundance, a living could be made from beekeeping. The honey, often a rich reddish-brown colour and slightly bitter, fetched a good price in the local market towns.

Celia Lutyens fell in love with the moor the first time she saw it. It reminded her of where her grandparents lived in Frensham. She adored the vivid colours of the heather and gorse and the smell of peat and bracken.

"Most people can't make enough to rub two ha'pennies together," Lutyens was saying as he walked with Celia, "but I suppose that if I had Sir Julius' money there isn't a better place in the world to set down roots."

"It's so perfectly quiet," said Celia as she looked down into the Chagford vale.

"Do you think so?" said Lutyens. Celia listened as they walked away from the town. She could just hear the lowing of cows in a nearby field and the sound of a shrike, screeching in the sky. When the breeze blew, it caught the leaves of the trees and made them rustle and then she heard water tumbling over pebbles and stones, slowly wearing them away on its way to join the river Teign.

"I didn't sleep well at all last night," said Lutyens. "There were too many strange noises."

"I slept like a log," replied Celia. "Adrian Drewe told me that the moors were the most dangerous place on earth. How can somewhere so beautiful be so dangerous?"

They turned off the main path as soon as they arrived at the river and walked beside it. The earth was wet from the night before and Celia was grateful that her father had made her pack a pair of walking boots, however unladylike they looked. It seemed to Celia that all around her was a lost world, fascinating because of its look and colour, and she felt the enchantment of the moor, like the magical Labyrinthus in Archibald Drew's story. Her father was now talking about the plant life, how the ling can survive for up to forty years and how the heather hides areas of mire, which can ensnare the unwary walker. Celia made the occasional sounds acknowledging her father's explanation, but she was only half listening, lost in her own imaginary world.

"You're not listening," Lutyens suddenly said, turning to Celia.

"I was," she replied and hoped that he would not ask her about anything that he had said in the last fifteen minutes. She looked along the riverbank and saw that there was a stone bridge ahead. "Do we cross?"

"Yes," answered Lutyens, slightly exasperated. "As I told you five minutes ago, if we carry on, we come to Watchet Hill. We have to cross the river and take the path up the escarpment and then walk down to Bowden's Farm where Adrian Drewe and Hall are staying."

Her father continued talking but already Celia was back in her daydream. At fifteen it was a barrier against the mundane, the dreary and the dirty. As they reached the bridge, she looked up at the escarpment. It looked steep and she hoped that the path would not be too arduous. No wonder both her mother and Aunt Gertrude had said they did not want to walk to Bowden's Farm. Her mother had never liked walking and now she had no time for anything but her precious theosophy. Celia made up her mind at that instant never to like Krishnamurti, even if she lived to be a hundred.

"I'm told," said Lutyens, "that there are salmon in the river. Next time I come down I must remember to bring my rod."

"I didn't know you liked fishing," said Celia.

"I used to fish a lot as a child. However, in London there's nowhere really to go. Can you imagine me sitting on a towpath? But here, if I owned a castle,

I would go fishing every day."

"And I would go riding," added Celia. "And then we could go fishing and riding every day and be a fine family and there would be no corners in the nursery so that none of the children would ever be made to stand in a corner, and we would all be perfectly happy. Even Mother."

Celia did not know what had made her say that and Lutyens did not answer. They walked on silently. Celia felt that she had said something inappropriate but did not know what it was. She wanted to lighten the conversation and so asked her father to tell her a story. "It must begin with 'once upon a time'," she added.

"Once upon a time," Lutyens began, "Mary Magdalene dreamt that she was walking along the seashore of Galilee with Jesus. She knew it was a dream because Jesus had been crucified many years beforehand. Jesus held her hand and they looked back along the shoreline. At that moment she saw all the things she had done in her life and also saw Jesus' footprints and her own. She then noticed something which disturbed her. When she saw the darkest moments of her life, she saw only one set of footprints. 'Jesus,' she said, 'before you died you promised that if I had faith then you would stay with me forever. Why then at the darkest moments of my life do I only see one set of footprints? When I needed you most, why did you leave me?' Jesus answered: 'I have never left you. On those most painful moments when you suffered, I carried you.'"

"Is it true?" asked Celia. "I mean, is it true that if you have faith then that helps when things are bad?"

"Faith or a belief," said Lutyens. "A belief can be as strong as any faith."

Celia wanted to ask whether this was why Mother believed in theosophy, but she instinctively felt it was the wrong thing to say at that moment. She therefore said nothing. They walked on until they reached Bowden's Farm and entered the courtyard. The farmyard was still in disarray, there was a smell of burnt wood, and Celia asked her father what he thought had happened. Lutyens shrugged. They knocked on the farm door and a young girl opened it. Lutyens asked to see Hall and the maid led them into the farmhouse, pulling her skirts straight and tidying her hair.

"I'm not sure if Mr Hall is up yet after the troubles we had last night," she said.

"Troubles?" said Celia.

"The fire, miss," said the maid. "In the early hours. Got us all out of bed."

"Was anyone hurt?" asked Celia. What she wanted to ask was whether Adrian or Peter had been hurt.

"None too serious."

Celia had a dozen more questions on the tip of her tongue but before she had a chance to ask any of them, the maid had gone. Lutyens sat down and

Celia stood at the window looking out. She could see the stable block with only black charred remnants for a roof.

Peter entered the sitting room and she looked at him. Lutyens didn't get up as he entered. It was clear that Peter had been dragged from his bed. She noticed that he was limping slightly.

"Do you mind if I sit down, sir?" he asked.

"Of course," said Celia. "But you're hurt! What happened?"

Peter walked over to an armchair and sat down, telling them the story. At the end of it, Celia asked whether he was badly hurt. He shook his head.

"It's not too bad; a small burn on my leg."

"Will you be able to come to the stone laying ceremony?" asked Celia.

"Aye," said Peter, "you couldn't stop me. Anyway, I said I'd pick up Sir Julius' two youngest boys who are going fishing this morning."

"Well, in the meantime," said Celia, "we'll arrange for a doctor to come and see you and dress the burns."

"I'm fine really, Miss Celia..." Peter began, but Celia interrupted him.

"Father will arrange for the doctor to come..." she hesitated for a second, "and of course he will take care of everything. Isn't that right, Father?"

Chapter 16

Celia did not mean for her mouth to open, but it did so involuntarily. She had been told that Sir Julius had arranged a tent for them to have their lunch in. However, she would not have described this as a tent; it was perhaps the largest marquee she had ever seen, except at the circus. It was palatial in size and made of a green and white striped material with the corners rising into small minarets. Each tower had a flag with a lion rampant blowing in the breeze. A host of staff stood waiting to serve at the entrance to the tent, all in olive green livery with the heraldic Drewe lion embossed in white on the front of each tunic.

Adrian wandered over to Celia and began telling her about the stone laying ceremony that his father had insisted upon. They were going to be setting the first foundation stone that marked the start of construction works, and even though the stone would be covered and never be seen, the words written on it would still be there even after it had become a ruin. Celia stopped staring at the marquee and turned her attention back to Adrian.

"What words?" she asked.

"I don't know," replied Adrian. "It's supposed to be a secret, and Father knows how to keep a secret."

Adrian turned to Edwin Lutyens. "You don't happen to know what it says, sir?" he asked.

"Actually, I do," said Lutyens.

"You couldn't tell me, could you, sir?"

"I couldn't possibly say." Lutyens lit his pipe and smiled to himself.

"It's just that Kit, Basil and I have a small wager; a few pennies, nothing serious. I thought that Father would have his name and 'laid on this 5th day of September 1911'. There would be nothing ostentatious. Kit thought the opposite and thought that Father wouldn't be able to resist the chance to put something down for posterity. He thinks that Father won't resist a bit of irony and guessed at, 'In my house there are many mansions.' Basil guessed at the family motto: *Drogo Nomen et Virtus Arma Dedit* – Drewe is the name and valour gave it arms, and the date. It's fair to say that, on reflection, the sensible money is on Basil."

In between puffing at his pipe, Lutyens repeated that he really couldn't possibly say.

Celia stared once again in disbelief as they entered the marquee. White roses and green ferns were presented in glass vases on pedestals. An oval table covered with cream linen stood on a dais in the middle of the marquee with eleven wicker chairs surrounding it. Sheets of matted rush lay on the ground. Everywhere was pristine and clean as if the previous night's storm had never happened. Celia felt she ought to take her boots off, which were covered in mud, but resisted the temptation.

Sitting on the wicker chairs were Sir Julius and Frances Drewe, as well as Gertrude Jekyll and Celia's mother. They joined them.

"Our first tenet is that all people are equal, irrespective of their race, colour or creed," Emily was saying to Gertrude. "How can anyone object to that? Our second tenet is to encourage the comparative study of all religions, philosophy and science. Again, what can possibly be objectionable?"

"None of that is objectionable," said Gertrude, "if you just stopped there."

"But there is existence beyond what we can see and touch," said Emily, "you must see that, Gertrude. The third tenet of theosophy is just to investigate the supernatural and the latent powers of man."

"To investigate the supernatural is fine," said Gertrude, the feather on her going-out hat visibly shaking as she leant towards Emily. "No one would say anything if all you did was investigate but it's all the other comments. 'I was reincarnated from this animal' and 'in another life I was the King of Siam'. It's these kinds of comments that makes your group into a laughing stock."

Emily let out a heavy sigh. "Having faith in theosophy has made me a richer person."

"It certainly made Blavatsky a richer person," added Lutyens, smiling at his own little joke. However, he only got a withering look from his wife.

"Who is Blavatsky?" asked Celia.

"The woman who started the theosophy movement," said Lutyens. "She was given a lot of money by the people who joined."

The conversation ended in that uncomfortable way and Emily, Frances and Gertrude sat for a few moments in silence staring out across the moor. It was Celia who broke the silence.

"How will the garden look when you have completed it, Aunt Gertrude?"

"Ultimately it will have to blend in with the moor..."

"You will bring in the heathers and lavender, won't you?" Celia interjected. Gertrude raised a finger to her lips. Celia stopped speaking.

"I thought you wanted me to tell you how the garden will look. It will have a formal and an informal part. The informal part will lead down into the moor itself with no fence to delineate where the moor begins, and the informal garden ends. As the castle will be both modern and traditional, the garden will have a similar theme. And yes, the heathers, the ling and lavender will all become part of the garden so that it will feel the most natural place in the world."

Frances Drewe motioned her hand to a crystal jug on the table and one of the staff came over and refilled the long crystal glasses with homemade lemonade. The sun was now getting above them. Celia guessed it must be nearly eleven o'clock.

"Where is Hall?" asked Sir Julius.

"Ah!" said Lutyens. "Now there's a story to tell, and your son plays a somewhat heroic part in it." Everyone looked at Adrian and Celia noticed that he was blushing slightly. She thought it appealing. She hated people who were so full of themselves.

"There was a fire last night at Bowden's Farm. Both Adrian and Hall ran without a moment's hesitation into the burning barn and tried to save the animals. They got out all the animals except for one poor beast. Hall even tried to drag burning bales of hay out of the barn with a pitchfork. When nothing more could be done, the farmer got his shotgun and went back into the barn to put the horse out of its misery. Unfortunately, the farmer was overcome with smoke and when he didn't come out of the barn, Adrian dashed back into the inferno and saved him."

Frances Drewe stood up and hugged her son. Sir Julius then came over and shook Adrian's hand and patted him on the shoulder. Celia had been looking at Sir Julius as the story was being told by her father, and she could have sworn that his first reaction was one of displeasure.

"So where is the other hero?" asked Gertrude.

"His leg was burned slightly. It's nothing too serious but we called the local doctor this morning and are having it treated and bandaged. He said he would be here by twelve-thirty and that he would round up Basil and Kit who have gone fishing at the bottom of the gorge, and bring them safely up the path."

"He had no care for his own safety," said Adrian. "When I had given up trying to save the horse, he still wanted to do something even if it meant getting hurt himself. Actually, he was the only hero."

Celia didn't agree but stayed silent; it hadn't been Peter that had gone back into the fire to save the farmer. She watched as Adrian's mother effused about his bravery and then the conversation changed, and the men started talking about the castle.

Suddenly, Celia had a feeling of self-doubt that Adrian only saw a young girl nearing adulthood, or a younger second cousin of no importance. Life seemed so unfair. Why couldn't she be four years older – but even then, would he even notice her? Even her mother described her shape as boyish, and her father referred to her as a young lady. 'A young lady' – it was such a pejorative phrase. She was either a lady or she wasn't. She felt everything, probably more intensely than her parents or even Adrian.

However, Celia said nothing and smiled contentedly.

Chapter 17

For young boys, time evaporates when lost in a world of running and hollering, playing soldiers or hide and seek. Mothers, with a vague sense of disbelief, watch their sons as they create make-believe worlds with made-up rules. The more cynical believe that their boys never really grow up but simply change the games they play. The army, politics, the church, and the law were manifestations of boyish imagination, from which women were excluded. Emily Lutyens was one of these cynical types and felt a deep resentment at the fact that she was supposed to sit quietly listening to her husband and Sir Julius talk about their castle. Except for gossip and the tittle-tattle of the gutter press, she was not expected by society to express her views on anything.

Emily watched her daughter as she sat listening to the men's conversation. She was at an age when she would be taking her first steps on a path of false hopes and disappointment. Society was an unforgiving place and only the very brightest women could get away with *ad libbing*. Emily knew her daughter was clever, but she was not the very brightest of women. She was intuitive and she would not make too many mistakes. However, if she were too headstrong, the frowns would sooner or later start and she would be told what was expected of her, how a lady ought to behave. Celia would then have to make a choice. If she played her part impeccably, she could expect to attend the best balls, have a well-arranged marriage and a life of tedium. For many women, like Frances Drewe, they were not even aware of the dreariness of their lives. They were genuinely pleased by any trinket or bauble thrown to them at Christmas or on their birthdays. If Celia did not play the game, then she risked having no place in society.

And then there was love. Emily hoped that no one would recognise the way that her daughter looked moon-eyed at Adrian Drewe. Even when he was not speaking, she continued to stare at him and when she thought he had noticed her gawping, she turned and started chewing at a lock of hair. When Frances Drewe suggested that Celia and Adrian go and find Kit and Basil, who had not returned with Peter Hall, Emily felt relief. At least she would not have to suffer the embarrassment of Celia making a fool of herself in public. Emily decided that a firm and unequivocal word was needed when they got back home. Nip it in the bud and put a stop to any such foolishness. When Celia was older, there would be time for the idiocy of love and all its pitfalls. Love, thought Emily, is the one thing that can be the ruin of a young lady, as she knew herself.

The weather, staff and the education of the children were the subjects of conversation that Frances Drewe excelled upon. As the women spoke it was discovered that Gertrude, Emily and Frances had all been reading about the theft of the Mona Lisa from the Louvre and Emily's mood improved as the conversation went to a subject that was of some interest to her. It then moved on to the government bringing in universal education, where even the men took some interest. While she was in favour of universal education, Sir Julius took a different view.

"The problem," said Sir Julius, "with giving everyone a bit of an education is that people then get above themselves. They have had a few art lessons and think they're artists. They are taught how to read and write and then we find we have created nothing but a world of civil servants. They aspire but none of them want to learn anything properly." Frances, of course, immediately agreed with her husband. Emily had wanted to cut him short but when her husband laughed and made an approving sound, she felt that she had no option but to bite her tongue.

The clouds from the night before blew effortlessly away and a hot September sun came out. Gertrude Jekyll listened quietly to the conversations, adding only the occasional comment. Champagne had been served and she sipped contentedly from her glass. As soon as the glass was half empty it was replenished, and just as the sun was directly overhead Gertrude closed her eyes. Emily heard her breathing get slower and fuller and, left with no one else to talk to, she asked Frances about the castle and why they wanted it. However, Frances was vague about the reasons, and every time Emily tried to turn the conversation back to the subject of the castle, Frances seemed reticent. For all her faults, and Emily thought Frances had many, this monumental piece of vanity was not hers and Emily realised that Frances would have loved nothing more than to have remained at Wadhurst Hall. Emily thought it ironic that a seemingly intelligent man like Sir Julius, with more money than he knew what to do with, would squander it on something just to give himself false airs.

Sir Julius Drewe, in Emily's opinion, epitomised everything she hated about modern England. Sir Julius only had a desire to make money without any discrimination. He represented the wealth and the greed of the new bourgeoisie. Honesty and integrity were not virtues that Sir Julius was said to have in abundance. In Emily's circle there was rarely a good word when Sir Julius' name was mentioned.

Emily recognised that he had qualities, such as determination of the mind and confidence. Focussed the right way, these were assets, but, in her opinion, that was something Sir Julius did not do. He represented everything Emily loathed and those who envied Sir Julius' wealth, and aspired to become like him, adopted those self-same attitudes.

As she listened to Sir Julius indicating where his castle would stand and how big and impressive it would be, she feared that the country was going to the dogs.

Chapter 18

"You're not like your brothers," Celia said to Adrian as they walked along the line of the escarpment.

"I wish I was," said Adrian. "Kit can see something beautiful in the most mundane things, and Basil is enthusiastic about everything."

A tumbling wind swirled up from the Teign gorge and blew back Celia's hair. She had a feeling like putting her head out of the window of a motor vehicle.

"Kit is barely nineteen years old and he's studying art at the Slade. They offered him a scholarship and the last person to be offered that was Augustus John. He even had a picture submitted for the annual Summer Prize. As a first year there, that's almost unheard of. It was a painting of Sir Lancelot sleeping under the Tree of Life surrounded by the Four Queens. It was judged by Augustus John and even though Kit did not win, he was told that he had no small amount of talent."

"And what about Basil?" Celia asked.

"Well Basil is always outdoors somewhere. If you look for him, he'll be with the chauffeur's son, George Poley, on the estate. They'll be out riding or playing cricket or swimming in the lake. Basil can fill every hour of every day. He doesn't care so long as he's busy. The other day, for example, he and Poley helped cauterise a calf."

"Why on earth would they do that?"

"It had been injured. It had run into some razor wire and couldn't free itself. Finally in its struggle to get away, it must have cut an artery because when Basil found it, it was near enough dead. Basil sent Poley to run and get his father and they brought the calf back to the estate where they cauterised the wound. Both Basil and Poley held the animal down as they sealed the gash."

"Nothing interesting ever happens to me," Celia pointed out. "So where are they?"

"At the river, fishing. If I know Basil, he will have fallen in by now or Kit will have pushed him in. Hopefully Mr Hall will be able to keep those two from fighting again."

"Do they always fight?"

"Just about every day, and it's got worse since I went up to Cambridge. Kit wants to be top dog and Basil – well, let's just say that Basil doesn't know when it's time to keep his mouth shut."

"What are you reading at Cambridge?"

"Classics," answered Adrian.

Celia looked down over the lip of the escarpment. Neither Kit nor Basil could be seen.

"They're not there. We'll have to walk down," she said. "I know the way. I came up the path this morning."

The pathway down was slippery. It was more slippery going down than it had been coming up, and on at least one occasion Adrian had to reach out and take hold of Celia's arm. Next to the path were harsh furze and gorse and bramble and only the wild creatures for companions. The gorse was a vivid yellow, now in full bloom, and its sharp green needles were hidden behind the beautiful flowers. A Dartford warbler screeched as Adrian and Celia walked by, warning the other birds of unwelcome visitors.

Celia could see the river Teign below and could hear the fast-flowing stream. The sun was now fully overhead and a radiant yellow. She could see its brilliance reflected in the water below her. As her eyes tried to find the course of the path that led down to the river, she noticed that there was a reddishness to the soil. The locals called this blood earth, Adrian told her, where the iron in the earth had rusted. The rocks of the coast near Teignmouth were of a similar colour. She was about to suggest that they go back when she caught sight of Basil and Kit coming up the path; however, she couldn't see Peter Hall and guessed he was somewhere behind them.

As Kit and Basil got closer, Celia heard them arguing. At first, she did not hear what they said but the swirling wind blew the words towards them.

"If you ever go telling tales out of school," Kit was shouting, "I will give you such a beating that you will be bruised for a month of Sundays."

"What did I say?" Basil said, with an attempt at innocence that was not believable.

"You know damned well what this is about. You don't ever tell anyone that I'm afraid of the dark."

"But you are. You're afraid of the dark. You're afraid of the dark."

"Come here, you little bugger."

Celia could just make out that Basil had turned and was starting to run back down the path. Kit didn't follow and carried on walking slowly. Basil ran back, jeering that Kit couldn't catch him. Kit ignored him. Basil continued to jeer and got closer and then Kit turned and lunged for Basil with his fishing rod still in his hand. Basil tried to avoid the rod as it whipped towards his head and fell. Celia lost sight of him but could hear a scream.

"For God's sake, be careful!" Adrian shouted down the pathway.

Celia could suddenly hear Kit shouting. His voice was higher than it had been, full of panic. "Adrian! Adrian!" Kit shouted. Adrian started moving quickly down the trail towards him. His calves knotted underneath his wool trousers as he tried to stop himself from slipping and falling.

"What's happened?" Adrian screamed.

"He slipped!" Kit shouted. "I didn't mean to, he just slipped. I didn't mean it! Honest!"

When Celia got to where Adrian and Kit stood, she could see Basil lying flat on his stomach about thirty feet below her. Kit was as white as chalk and was shaking uncontrollably. Adrian suddenly started running down the path as if his life depended on it. Now's not the time for daydreaming, Celia thought to herself. Standing under the sunshine, she told Kit to go and get help. Of course, he was upset but she could not afford for him to dither. She had to make him notice her, otherwise he would stand there like some simpleton. She shouted at him, but he seemed not to hear her. She slapped him across the face.

"I need you," she said each word slowly, making sure he understood what she wanted, "to get help. We must get Basil to hospital. Have your parents bring their motor down to the river." She looked at Kit. "Do you understand?" He mumbled a reply. It was the first sense of recognition that counted. She realised that as soon as Kit appreciated what had happened, the need to do something would outweigh the fear that was making him freeze. Without further word, Kit ran up the path towards the top of the escarpment.

Celia thought about what she needed to do. She had to talk to Adrian and tell him that Kit had gone to get help and that his parents would be coming. She felt it crucial for him to realise that she would not go to pieces. That, although she was younger than him, at that moment she had a clear head and knew what she was doing. Up above her, hovering on eddies, she could hear a shrike screeching as it spotted its prey. She started to move quickly down the path, unconcerned about her own safety. When she got to the bottom of the ravine, she saw Adrian next to Basil. She stammered something about it being all right; spots of burning colour rose in her cheeks because she did not know whether it was true.

Adrian had turned Basil on his back, and Celia could see that a shard of bone had torn through the skin of his leg. She felt nausea well up in her stomach. There was blood seeping out where the bone had split the skin and she wondered whether there were other breaks. Time dragged its heels more slowly than she could ever recall as she watched Adrian examining Basil.

"He's still unconscious," said Adrian, more to himself than to her.

"Your parents will be coming. You need to carry Basil."

Adrian looked at the leg. Celia could see from his expression that he did not want to move him.

"We must," she insisted. "We need to make a splint for the leg. I know how to do that, and then you have to carry him." Suddenly, she felt his equal.

She was not unhappy to go and search for two staves of wood to make the splint. She would need something to tie the splints together – she could afford to lose a petticoat. Horribly clear, she could see Basil's ashen face, and the bone moving as they tied the splints. Then Basil screamed and opened his eyes but only the whites could be seen. Adrian carried Basil in both arms, and she walked beside them. Basil cried. She remembered the crying and the tears in dreams to come for the next week. When she saw her father and the Drewes and the motor on the roadside, she kissed Basil on his forehead in relief. She talked to him and told him how brave he was. She said a thousand splendid things that she could not later remember.

When Basil had been taken to the hospital with Frances and Emily, Sir Julius Drewe set out upon the task of examining the facts with forensic exactitude. He approached the case in the same way that his great grandfather, Reginald Drewe, would have done; that is to say, like a magistrate. He said nothing until he got back to the marquee. Sir Julius first took Celia to one side with her father and spoke to her quietly. Celia explained what she had seen. He then spoke to Adrian and finally to Kit.

"And where was Mr Hall?" asked Sir Julius to Kit.

Kit shuffled uncomfortably where he stood. "I told him to go back to the farm."

"You told him what?" said Sir Julius.

"I told him that he didn't need to come with us. He was limping and I thought it was better if he went back to the farm and took a wagon from there to here."

"So where is he?"

"I would guess," said Kit, "that he's on his way."

"I'm here, sir," said Peter, who had arrived at the marquee as Sir Julius was speaking. Sir Julius took him and Kit to one side.

"I thought you were going to look after my sons?"

Peter went red. "Sorry," he mumbled.

"You just left a twelve-year-old to make his way up the pathway after the rain we had last night?"

Peter looked at Kit.

"It wasn't his fault," said Kit.

"No?" said Sir Julius. "Then whose fault was it, if Mr Hall is not to blame?"

Sir Julius looked back at Peter. "I am not a vindictive man," he said. "However, when someone says they will do something I expect them to do it. You didn't. I will not make this an issue with your employers, but I don't want you working on this project any longer. I don't want people I can't trust."

"Father!" said Kit.

"I've made my decision and it's final."

Peter turned without a word and began walking towards Bowden's Farm. He took out his pocket watch. The hour hand pointed to the ten, and he realised that finally it had given up working. He threw it out over the Teign gorge as he started to go down the path.

Sir Julius turned to Kit after Peter had left. He looked at his son with more than a hint of annoyance. "What am I going to do with you? You are nineteen years old, and you sometimes act as if you were younger than Basil."

"It was an accident, sir," said Kit.

"It may have been," said Julius, "but it was an accident that you made happen." His green eyes looked accusingly at his son. "If Basil doesn't make a full recovery, I won't forgive you."

PART III

Chapter 19

Sir Arthur Conan Doyle, perhaps the greatest Edwardian, was said by his friend Mr E.W. Oaten to possess all the characteristics of an English gentleman. These characteristics were defined as courage, optimism, loyalty, sympathy, magnanimity, love of truth and devotion to God. Being a friend, he omitted from the list 'arrogance' and 'folly'. God, however, does not overlook such details and, therefore, while to be healthy and an English gentleman in 1914 was perhaps the greatest privilege bestowed by God, it should not be forgotten that God has a black sense of humour – why otherwise would he have created Death?

Kit Drewe was very much an English gentleman. He sat in an uncomfortable and overcrowded train carriage and put down his paper with a sense of resignation and listened to the conversation. He had been sitting for the best part of five hours as the train made its way from Vienna to Rotterdam and his mood was deteriorating quickly. Having finished his novel – *The Man of Property* – and now his paper, he found himself unable to do much but listen to the conversation which had been ongoing since they had passed over the German border.

Like the enlightened thousands of his class who did not care about money and had been privileged to travel abroad, Kit Drewe held liberal views. He tried never to see the world in black and white and thought it a duty to help those less fortunate than himself. He hated pre-judging things, but then every rule has an exception. He found, for example, that he despised bankers, whom he considered money-grubbing, and lawyers who always discussed fees before giving a word of advice that was rarely of any value. As a result, he took an immediate dislike to a banker who had been speaking for the last twenty minutes on a pet theory that the killing of Archduke Franz Ferdinand was a plot by the secret service of Austria. Kit had heard similar rumours spread about by the foreign press in Vienna. He had spoken to his Viennese friends about the killing and believed that there was not a word of truth in that particular rumour. His friends thought it scurrilous to suggest that their country's secret service could order the execution of its future Emperor and believing them without reservation, Kit therefore thought such views ungentlemanly.

Kit let the banker drone on for a few more minutes. He made a show of pretending to be interested and then interrupted suddenly saying: "Do you really think so? That's the kind of speculation I would expect to hear from a Bolshevik." The banker demanded an apology. Kit suggested that if he did not like his remark, he find another carriage to sit in; however, both knew that there was not another seat on the whole train and so the banker made a few indignant sounds and stopped talking.

The rest of the carriage remained silent for a further ten minutes until an old lady in a raffia hat said that she no longer felt that Vienna was safe. Although Kit had lived in Vienna for the last two years, and although he would not admit to feeling frightened on its streets, there was a growing sense wherever he went, that foreigners were no longer welcome. He had seen demonstrations outside the French embassy; stones had been thrown and the cavalry had charged in. He had heard about the arrest and torture of suspected Serbian terrorists. It had been time to come home but he left with a certain amount of regret as he was not unsympathetic to Austria's position.

There had been a score of stories about the assassination of the Archduke Franz Ferdinand. Kit had heard each one repeated in the cafés of Vienna, but there seemed to be one that was repeated more than any other. It was said that the assassination attempt had gone horribly wrong and that only by chance had the Archduke been killed. A young terrorist, Čabrinović, had thrown a grenade at Franz Ferdinand's vehicle as the Archduke was visiting Sarajevo. The grenade bounced off the Archduke's shoulder and exploded near the following motor vehicle. The Archduke had escaped the attempt, and everyone thought that was the end of the matter. However, there were two other assassins. One of these, Gavrilo Princip, panicked and ran. He realised that it was only a matter of time before he would be named. He entered unthinking into Moritz Schiller's food store on Franz Joseph Street and ordered something to eat.

Franz Ferdinand lunched in the Town Hall and then decided to go to the hospital to visit the soldiers injured in the attack. No one told the chauffeur of the change of plan and by mistake he was driven into Franz Joseph Street. The Archduke, who realised he was going the wrong way, ordered the chauffeur to stop the car and turn it around. Gavrilo Princip came out of the food store and stood no further than six feet away from Franz Ferdinand who sat in the open vehicle. He pulled out his revolver took a step towards the open car and fired twice. The first shot hit Franz Ferdinand's wife in the stomach. They said that Franz Ferdinand turned and looked at his assassin. The second shot hit the Archduke in the neck. Čabrinović and Princip were both boys, no older than nineteen. Both were Yugoslav nationals and both wanted Serbia to be free of Austria and the cruel conditions Austria imposed on Serbia; but the assassination attempt had nothing to do with the Serbian government.

Kit had not anticipated that the Austrian press would be so ferocious in its condemnation of the Serbian government. Things deteriorated when the Serbian press called it a legitimate act to overturn oppression. The Serbs then refused to hand over members of the Black Hand, the terrorist group to which the assassins belonged. The old Emperor returned to Vienna from his hunting lodge in Bad Ischl and mobilised the army. Once that happened war was inevitable, but, thought Kit, it was so easily avoidable.

And like so many times in history, when the fear of war grabbed hold of everyone, the anti-Semitism started. Kit got himself into one fight when he saw some Viennese men throwing stones at a Jewish woman. He had not been frightened to step in even though he came off worst in the scuffle. On his last night in Vienna, he bolted the door to his apartment. He had never done that in two years – it was time to leave. His friends had told him things were likely to get worse. The army was everywhere. He did not pack much – a few essentials in a grip bag and a portfolio of paintings. His friends promised to send his belongings on when they could. He got to the train station and all the trains leaving Vienna were full. He bribed a porter in order to get a seat. He had never bribed anyone before and suspected that he had paid at least twice as much as was necessary. He despised himself for giving a backhander; it wouldn't have happened in England.

As the porter led Kit down the platform, he was horrified by the chaos. People were moving about attempting to find any empty compartment. Families tried to keep together. Kit noticed a woman pushing through the crowd, a child in her arms, shouting for someone. For a moment he thought about stopping and seeing if he could help but the porter would not wait and so he moved on, only briefly glancing back. There seemed to be every nationality from every corner of Europe trying to board the train. The most orderly country in Europe had suddenly gone mad.

Bags and cases were stuffed full of personal possessions. As Kit entered his compartment, he saw that the luggage racks above the seats were jammed full. The most valuable belongings did not leave one's sight and no one expected to get the rest of their property. Nobody thought that they would ever see their furniture again. Kit didn't have much of value; just his watch, a silver cigarette case that he had received from his brother on his eighteenth birthday and his portfolio of paintings that had been stowed in the baggage compartment.

Knowing that things were likely to get worse, Kit did not say much on the journey. He felt like an outlaw who had been given thirty days to leave the realm.

He read his book, read his paper, and when he did speak it was just the few objectionable words he said to the banker. He had no interest in taking part in the conversation. When would Russia attack, people were asking? When would France join in and was war inevitable? Some said yes and others shook their heads but said that something had to be done about Germany and Austria. Kit closed his eyes and pretended to be asleep. He heard the banker once again join the conversation. He wondered what he would do when he got back to England or if England would join the madness.

Chapter 20

arrive london saturday 18 july [stop] no money [stop] arrange hotel for me [stop] not expensive [stop] send case champagne [stop] kit

*   *   *

Kit felt a sense of relief, but it did not feel like he was coming home. As he got closer to London, the names that the station master called out became more familiar. As a child Kit had not been intimidated by the size of London, or its noise, or the crowds pushing in a hundred different directions. Two years in Vienna had if anything made him more nonchalant. It was shown in the way he carried himself, a belief in his own superiority. Even if the whole of Europe was to fall apart in a frenzy of madness, an English gentleman would retain his composure and London was the heart of England. It was why half of the world woke up each morning under the shadow of the Union Flag and knew that without the empire, life would be harder still.

The fog that had followed Kit in from Harwich lay like a monstrous blanket upon the world. He had breakfasted by gaslight on the train as it came through Essex towards London, thankful to be alone in first class. The people who had travelled with him initially from Vienna and then on the overnight ferry from Rotterdam had been relegated back into second or third class; the banker had found another first-class carriage. England closed its eyes to what was happening abroad, and everything remained in its right and proper place. Even copies of *The Times* and *The Telegraph* had been neatly folded and left in the paper rack for him to read. He decided to read *The Telegraph* and take *The Times* for later. However, as he arrived in London he could not say that he was happy to be there. For all his arrogance, there was still a feeling of regret for what had happened to his brother three years ago.

As Kit left the train the darkness of the fog encircled him and muffled him from the world. It was as black as a night on Dartmoor. He shivered. Walking down the platform, he could see only ten paces ahead of him. Whistles and voices seemed to taunt him from every direction. 'Kit's afraid of the dark,' he seemed to hear in the undercurrent. He turned to see if someone was talking to him, but no one was there. 'Kit's afraid of the dark,' 'Kit's afraid of the dark.' For a moment he thought that if he left the station he would be lost. The sounds continued to mock him and then he saw a light coming from the tea room on the concourse of the station and pushed open the door.

"Morning, sir. Are you all right?"

"Yes, fine," he said to the woman pouring tea from a copper urn. More quietly to himself he said, "Why wouldn't I be fine?" All the tables were occupied. For a few seconds Kit wondered whether he should go back out into the fog but decided against it. He hadn't felt like this in nearly a year. It was like a skeleton he thought he had locked away in a forgotten cupboard and he now despised himself for being so weak. He could not stand there forever and made up his mind to ask a young lady, who was sitting alone reading a book, whether he might share her table.

"Do you mind if I join you?" he asked. The young woman smiled and said not at all.

Kit sat down and opened *The Times* that he had taken from the train. His eyes swept across the main headlines. Everything was again about Germany, Austria and Serbia. The troops were on the move, and it was all speculation about a needless war. He turned the pages until he caught sight of a headline that grabbed his attention: 'Lutyens to build like Wren.' There was a name he had not heard for a few years. He remembered quite liking the old man when they had met.

He read through the article. England was building a new capital for India even though India was shouting for its independence; it did not surprise him at all. Those who ran the empire were blinkered and tradition-bound and therefore, he concluded, the empire was in decline. Most people in England could never imagine losing India; but his friends in Austria thought that England's grip on the world was becoming weaker. There was a quote from Lutyens: 'Anyone who wanted to know what New Delhi would look like could do worse than spend a day examining the dome of St Paul's Cathedral.'

Kit smiled to himself as he thought about his father's castle. The design for Castle Drogo was nothing like St Paul's Cathedral, more like an asylum. The one memory triggered another, and he thought about his brother, Basil, and the smile fell from his face. He remembered Basil screaming as he was placed in the motor and driven to the hospital. His father had then decided to apportion the blame. He wondered whatever happened to that young Scottish engineer. He frowned.

"Are you unwell?"

Kit looked up from his paper. The young lady at his table was looking at him with an expression of concern. Kit glanced at her, not wanting to stare. He had failed to take much notice of her when he had sat down. She was about his age or maybe a year or so older, in her mid-twenties. She had an open face with large eyes, and black hair that was pinned up. Her nose was small and straight and her mouth was slightly too wide but all the features fitted perfectly together. In fact, thought Kit, she was more than a little attractive and her brown eyes were set off by her pale complexion.

"I'm very well," said Kit. He wondered whether he should initiate a conversation and decided, because she was too pretty to ignore, he would and added, "Thank you for asking."

She carried on looking at him. Kit noticed a slight show of teeth and perhaps the merest hint of a smile.

"It was rude of me not to introduce myself – Christian Drewe."

"Rose Braithwaite."

"I'm sorry if I appeared somewhat distant but I'm a little tired. I've just come back from Vienna and I've hardly slept for two days."

"Were you on holiday?"

"No, I lived there for two years. Have you ever been there?"

"No." The girl leant forward. Kit took this as an indication that she was interested in hearing what it was like and continued.

"You must see Vienna if you ever get the chance, it's a magnificent city. The buildings are made of white stone and marble and look very imperial. In the evenings the cafés fill up with all sorts, especially after the theatres close. There's always a band playing, and the dancing goes on until the early hours. In the bars near the *Volkstheater*, if you're lucky, the opera singers, after they've finished of an evening, will sing an aria or two. The Austrians like to drink and sing. Once you get to know them, they are a very friendly people. Sorry, I'm going on. What about you?"

Rose thought for a second.

"There's nothing special about me," she said. "I'm a nurse in a hospital and when I'm not working I go home to see my mother. If it wasn't for this fog, I would have been at Dartford an hour and a half ago."

"I wanted to wait until the fog cleared as well," added Kit. "I didn't want to try and find a cab."

They continued to talk. Rose asked more and more questions about Vienna and about what Kit did. Kit became oblivious to the whistles, the shouting and the hisses of steam from the trains outside the café. He ordered a mug of tea for himself and one more for Rose and they had two rounds of hot buttered toast. Two hours later when the fog had risen, they were still talking and when Kit finally left the café and found a taxi, Rose Braithwaite probably knew more about him than anyone in London.

In the cab to the Bristol Hotel, Kit closed his eyes. It wasn't far from Fenchurch Street Station to Bloomsbury and he could picture the buildings as they went along, so different from Vienna. London was more diverse, less ordered and shabbier. He could imagine the brick-built container houses by the wharfs and stench rising from the river Thames. The journey would take him along Fleet Street, into Chancery Lane and then the Regency Squares of Bloomsbury. There were so many different types of building. It was a city that had grown and matured. London would still be there – a sundry assortment of styles and peoples – long after the Austrian Empire had fallen and been forgotten. He was in a good mood when he got out of the cab and gave the driver an extra shilling.

"Your 'ealth, sir," shouted the driver, who thought the tip more than generous and drove off quickly before Kit could change his mind and ask for change.

At the reception of the hotel was a telegram:

'please come to exeter monday [stop] meet you at station 7 pm *[stop] champagne sent [stop] not best quality [stop] sorry [stop] adrian.'*

Chapter 21

Summer had taken hold after an indifferent June. The leaves on the trees were a vibrant green and the fields of yellow corn shimmered as the train passed by. Kit seemed to have spent the last week in one train or another. He had first crossed Europe and was now crossing England. The English countryside was so different to that of Austria. It was less regimented. In Austria and Germany the forests were larger, the manufacturing areas more built up and industrial and the farmland more cultivated. In England a train could pass from town to countryside in a matter of minutes. In England, if you closed your eyes for fifteen minutes and then opened them again, you might find the view was of green hills or a field of wheat, maize, corn, mustard, or just untouched pastures with dry-stone walls. So much is in such a small place that one is always surprised by the variety.

Exeter station was in contrast grey and unclean. There was a smell of stale tea and cabbage. Soot had blackened the stone walls and the glass ceiling of the station. Kit did not dare even touch the dirty, black wrought-iron railings, a hidden trap for unsuspecting children who would leave black smears in their wake for the rest of the day. In Austria the stationmasters lived at their stations and took pride in them. There would be an outcry from the *Bürgermeister* if a station was not spotless or covered with flowers.

Kit handed over his ticket to a guard at the gate who examined it.

"Why doesn't someone clean up this mess?" he asked as the ticket was handed back.

"Not my job, sir," was the sullen reply.

Kit left the station and saw Adrian standing by his car. He had changed little in two years. He looked a little older perhaps, and maybe a pound or two had been put on, and then Kit looked again. Adrian had grown a small moustache. It was a short, neat, thin moustache in the style of those American actors in silent films that were all the rage. He was tall, lean and suave, and Kit would have recognised him anywhere.

"Is that all you brought?" asked Adrian, as he took hold of Kit's small overnight bag.

"Nearly everything I have is somewhere between Vienna and Rotterdam, I hope," said Kit. "A friend of mine, Tomas Skeres, promised to send my things on to me."

"A grey suit in the country; you'll stand out like a sore thumb!" said Adrian.

"I was hoping to borrow some of your things, but it looks like you've put on weight."

Adrian looked down at his stomach. He had hardly put on more than a few ounces over the last few years. He still rowed, still kept himself in shape. He was just about to protest when he saw the grin on Kit's face.

"At least I can afford to eat," Adrian remarked, getting into the Ford. He handed Kit the starting handle. "If you have the strength, can you turn her over?"

"I have a small house in Drewsteignton," said Adrian, when Kit had got in the car. "I spend as much time as I can there, but to be honest I don't get down here nearly as much as I would like. I thought we might have a walk up to the castle later."

Kit lit himself a cigarette and passed one to Adrian. They said nothing as they smoked. Kit's thoughts went back to the last time he had been at Castle Drogo. He remembered the story that Archibald Drew had told about Drogo de Teigne and how Henry II had hunted him down because the King suspected that he had murdered Rosamond and therefore had killed the wrong man. He had not guessed that the true culprit was his own wife.

There was still a tension between Kit and his father, as a result of Basil's accident. He knew that Adrian had tried to play the peacemaker, but his father could hold a grudge longer than anyone he knew. Kit was sorry for what had happened to Basil, of course he was. He had apologised and apologised again, but the incident was neither forgotten nor forgiven by Sir Julius.

Kit stared at the world as it flew by, and his thoughts flew back to Vienna. He had exhibited some of his artwork some months previously. He had even sold a number of paintings to some foreign buyers through a gallery on the Ringstrasse in Vienna. His two years in Vienna had been a success; all his friends there had said so. However, he was able to pack his bags and move at a moment's notice.

"When did you learn how to drive?" asked Kit.

"About two years ago," said Adrian. "I can get down here from London in less than eight hours with a good wind. Had her up to thirty-five the other week – Mother nearly had a heart attack."

"Have you told her I'm back?" asked Kit.

"I thought it would come better from you."

"And how's Basil?" asked Kit.

"That's the reason I asked you to come down. Basil has to go into hospital next week to have the plate in his leg changed. This should be the last operation and then that's it. It's been nearly three years, Kit, and I was hoping that the past could now be forgotten."

"That's a matter for Father."

The motorcar turned off the main road. Kit threw his cigarette out of the window. The embers sparked, tumbled and rolled as they hit the asphalt.

"And if he were able to forget and forgive?" said Adrian, taking his eyes off the road for a second.

"That's the whole point," said Kit. "He can't. How many more times can I say that it was an accident and that I'm sorry?"

Adrian again looked at Kit and they remained silent for the rest of journey until they arrived at Drewsteignton.

*   *   *

Drewsteignton was a prosperous little village and Adrian's house was on a quiet lane that marked the southern part of it. There were several houses that bordered the lane with substantial gardens and cars parked in the front. Money had moved to Drewsteignton. Adrian turned into a short driveway lined with yew trees on one side. The house was what Kit had thought it would be. It was made of a yellow stone with a red brick extension added unsympathetically to it. It was unpretentious and solid with a foot in the modern world. It was what the home of an English gentleman should look like. Behind the house was a garden with a wild, overgrown look that folded down to a wood and beyond that was the river Teign. A hedge filled with yellow flowers like dew drops bordered the property and separated the garden from the neighbours.

They walked up the gravel path to the front door. It had a sense of sturdiness, even down to the mullions in the windows. Adrian took out his keys and opened the door. The first thing Kit noticed was the assortment of hats, coats and wellington boots, as if a party of fishermen had decided to drop in for tea. Kit wondered whether there were others staying; for a moment he thought that his father might be there and what they would say to each other. He had not come all the way down here just to be made to apologise again. The second thing Kit noticed was that there were three of his paintings on the walls. He felt annoyed, as if he had been cheated out of a genuine sale.

"I would have given them to you if you had wanted them," said Kit.

"I know," said Adrian.

"I didn't even know that you liked my paintings."

"I've always liked them. My favourite one is the crying clown."

"Pagliacci." Kit walked up to the painting and looked at it as if it were a long-lost friend. "I didn't think I would ever see it again."

"You're not upset with me, are you? I wanted to buy them." Kit put his finger up to the tear drop of the clown's face.

"No, I'm not upset; just surprised. Are these the only ones you bought, or will I find another half dozen scattered around the house?"

"You've sold more?"

"Don't sound so surprised," said Kit. This time he could not keep a hint of irritation out of his voice.

"I only meant – well, they weren't exactly cheap…" Adrian started to blush slightly.

"Forget it," said Kit. "Anyway, are we going to stand in your hallway or are you going to invite me in and pour me a drink?"

The house was smaller than it had looked from the outside. It had no rooms of intimidating grandeur, like Wadhurst Hall. It did, however, have a myriad of different rooms and corridors and spaces for one to look out across the garden. Adrian poured two glasses of sherry, an old, sweet Oloroso that smelt of dates and figs, which he had borrowed from his father's cellar. They talked about very little and nothing about their family. When Kit had finished his drink, which he found a little too cloying in the hot July afternoon, Adrian suggested that he unpack and then they take a walk up to the castle.

Kit was given a room that had a high window at which he had to stand on tiptoe if he wanted to look out over the back garden. He had little to unpack and so examined the room to see what Adrian had left him. The carved oak wardrobe was empty. An enamel wash bowl of Dresden china and a matching pitcher of water sat on an oak chest of drawers. Towels had been left on a wooden towel rail. He sat on the bed, bounced to test its firmness and then suddenly felt tired. He guessed that he had travelled nearly two thousand miles that week. He wondered whether Adrian would mind if he passed on the suggestion of a walk up to the castle and lay back, looked up at the ceiling and then closed his eyes. When he awoke, he found that he had slept around the clock.

* * *

"It's difficult to march an army on an empty stomach and it's more difficult to run an empire when people are starving." Kit continued to express his view that the greatest export of the British Empire was pragmatism. Between mouthfuls of sausage, he repeated a monologue he had often expressed when in Austria that the empire had grown on trade.

"Remember," he continued, looking for the brown sauce, "we were invited into India in order to trade. There was no army marching through Afghanistan and down into the Punjab states. The army came only to protect the trading routes that had been established and it was the maharajas who invited the East India Company to bring soldiers. Mark my words, when Britain leaves India, and it will, India will find itself in civil war. It's not really a single country but made up of a hundred and one different principalities."

Adrian ate a piece of hot buttered toast. If he closed his eyes, he would think that he was breakfasting with his father. It was the exact same attitude his father had and that was the reason Kit and Sir Julius clashed. It had nothing to do with Basil and his accident. The fact of the matter was that Kit may look more like his mother, but he had the same opinions as his father. Even when Kit was a child, he and Sir Julius were at each other's throats. It was not that they were different; it was because they were so much alike. Adrian had realised this for as long as he could remember. He realised that you could not tell either of them what to do. Both Sir Julius and Kit thought the other self-opinionated, arrogant and controlling. They both had to be right, thought Adrian, and added a good spoonful of marmalade onto his last mouthful of toast.

He watched as Kit leant over the table and picked off another sausage. Kit handled the fork delicately, as if it were a paintbrush casting a stroke upon a precious canvas. His fingers were long and elegant, with the nails cut short, possibly even manicured. There would be no calluses on his hands, thought Adrian. He doubted whether Kit had ever done anything close to manual labour in his life. As a child Kit had hated sport. Adrian still went rowing twice a week to keep himself in shape. A brisk walk up to the castle; that would make Kit sweat a bit, thought Adrian.

Adrian suggested that they get going. Kit pushed the last bit of sausage into his mouth and got up.

"You don't mind if I borrow your Panama hat?" he said. "I saw one in your room."

"Not at all," replied Adrian and Kit went off in search of the hat. Adrian noticed as Kit went by that he was wearing eau de cologne; *his* eau de cologne. He suddenly felt that he would be distinctly poorer when Kit left. He picked up the paper as he waited for Kit to come down.

The state of England had been getting more and more on Adrian's nerves. It was a rum thing that the liberal press could even suggest that England might not honour the *entente* with France, but then everything was a little rum nowadays. Everyone wanted to talk the country down, and he felt in a glum mood as he read through the headlines and in a glummer mood when he put the paper down again. Of course, the government would support the French, but the French would never thank them for it. The French press was even now having a jab at English foreign policy, complaining that by sitting on the fence England was allowing the conflict in the Balkans to escalate and then they would try and make some money out of it.

"Do you think we will be going to war then?" asked Adrian as Kit returned with the Panama fitted firmly on head. "Will this Liberal government honour the *entente* or let France bleed to death in a war with Germany? It's not a very liberal thing going to war, is it?"

"Actually," said Kit, "it is because we have a Liberal government that we will go to war. As soon as the opposition taunt the Liberals that they can't govern in a crisis, they will be bound to overreact. If they didn't then the Tories would have a field day."

"You've grown cynical in the last few years," said Adrian.

It was the first time that Kit had walked along the road from Drewsteignton to the castle. It was a cloudless morning in late July. The road was slightly dusty, and the hedgerows were bursting with flowers and Brimstone butterflies. There was almost no sound but the chatter of the two intruders, whose words seemed dulled by the hot summer haze that could be seen coming off the moor. Adrian knew the route and as he passed a sandstone pillar at the side of the road, he lengthened his stride.

"So, what have you done since you got back?" Adrian asked.

"Not much. I slept most of Sunday."

"I suppose that even you would have difficulty getting into too much trouble in forty-eight hours."

"Actually, I met a nurse the other day," said Kit.

"And what was she like?" asked Adrian.

"Rather attractive," he said by way of understatement.

"And where does she work?"

"In a hospital," said Kit, and realised he had not even asked which hospital she worked in. He decided to change the subject and asked how far they had to walk.

"No more than a mile to go," Adrian said. Kit began to struggle to keep pace as the road began to wind upwards. After fifteen minutes of walking, Adrian turned off the road along what appeared to be a cart track. There was nothing to mark that it was private property or that there would be anything beyond the path but the moors. A small copse of trees parted to allow the track to pass through it and then the trees were gone. They came to a building site where large granite stones, seven feet thick, rose out of the ground in rectangular shapes. Kit thought of the druid stone circles. In two thousand years, if these stones were found, would civilisation guess that this was a place of worship, or a stone clock, or where an arrogant Englishman decided to build a castle?

"Well?" said Adrian.

"Well?" said Kit.

"Is it what you imagined?" Adrian asked.

"How can anyone imagine madness?" answered Kit.

However, even Kit's cynicism could not dull Adrian's enthusiasm for the castle. Adrian seemed to know each workman by name and when he got to the walls he stopped to speak with the two stonemasons, Cleeve and Dewdney. Kit wandered down to the escarpment.

"Be careful there," shouted Adrian, as Kit got to the edge of the promontory.

Chapter 22

To say that Sir Julius Drewe thought the whole shooting match absurd would be too crude a way to express his feelings at the declaration of war. At the heart of it was the fact that he had yet to see how he could profit from it. Taxes would be raised, and all the patriotic tin-shakers would be knocking at his door for a handout. He sat in his club, low in spirits, having read in *The Times* an account of the preceding day's events. Asquith had said to a packed House of Commons, 'We have made a request to the German government that we shall have a satisfactory assurance as to Belgian neutrality before midnight tonight.' The Germans hadn't waited and the British ambassador in Berlin was given his passport and from seven p.m. on the 4th of August 1914, the two countries were in a state of war.

There was talk everywhere and as Sir Julius Drewe sat in the library, a place where the butler usually insisted upon a rule of silence, he heard the chattering of at least a dozen voices each expressing their own views on the situation. They said that Asquith had seen the King as soon as he heard the news, and later that evening the King had sent a telegram to the Admiral of the Fleet telling him to renew the old glories of the Royal Navy which would once again be the sure shield of Britain and her empire in the hour of trial.

Sir Julius hoped that the hour of trial would not turn into a year of endurance. The costs of importing food to his stores would go spiralling upwards and he doubted that he could pass on the increases without an accusation of profiteering. Everything was happening quickly, and he worried that normally sensible heads would be turned. There were meetings with his board just after lunch and he was now waiting for Lord Cecil Facey, who had telephoned him the previous night out of the blue, asking him to be at the Carlton Club at nine the next morning. Sir Julius realised it must be important if Cecil Facey was up and out by nine.

The absence of any politician breakfasting at the Carlton Club was unusual. Usually, a handful of Conservatives stayed at the club from their constituencies in Scotland, ostensibly there to deal with an important bill on rural affairs but who would in fact spend most of their time with their secretaries. That morning there was the stench of excitement and not a politician to be seen. Club members were freely expressing the view that Germany would soon get what had been long overdue. Retired colonels were opining on strategies and others demanded that Kitchener be returned to lead the army. People kept looking around, hoping that a politician might turn up for them to glean some piece of news, and when Cecil Facey arrived, he was surrounded immediately.

"It will take some time to get the army mobilised," said Lord Facey to the group around him, "but from the reports this morning there are tens of thousands of people who are trying to enlist."

A question was asked whether the army could deal with tens of thousands of new recruits. A retired general coughed in derision at the question and Lord Facey continued: "An Englishman is not like the European. Last night there was a mob outside the German Embassy in Carlton House Terrace, chanting for the Germans to get out. In Europe they would have sent in the army and there would have been blood on the streets. In London it only took one policeman to ask the crowd to move on, and they went quietly." The retired general made an approving sound. "An Englishman understands authority. They may not always like it, but they realise that it is what makes society function." Cecil Facey extracted himself from the small crowd and went looking for Julius Drewe. He sat down next to Sir Julius, waved over the butler, and asked for a small glass of Madeira.

"It was decent of you to come on such short notice, Drewe," Cecil Facey said, his voice low and gravelly.

"Not at all," said Sir Julius, leaning toward Lord Facey in order for their conversation not to be overheard. He could smell on Facey's breath that this would not be the first drink that he had had that morning. There was something about Facey that he didn't like or trust.

"Things will play out this way," said Lord Facey taking a cigar from his jacket pocket. "Tomorrow we shall say that Germany has tried to bribe us with peace to betray our friends and our duty. We shall say that Britain has preferred the path of honour. That's what you will read in *The Times* tomorrow."

Sir Julius folded his arms. This was not the news that he wanted to hear. He had thought that there would be a good deal of sabre-rattling but did not think the government so mad as to charge headlong into a battle with Germany.

"Now more than at any other time we need our entrepreneurs to support their country. I told you this was coming years ago." Sir Julius continued to listen without interruption. Already Facey was playing the patriot card and he realised that he would soon find out why he had been asked to come to this meeting.

"This war is going to be quite different to anything this country has ever faced. We're not fighting Boers or Chinamen. Germany has been equipping itself for ten years and has scores of divisions of well-trained soldiers ready to go to war." Lord Facey lit his cigar. "The best we can hope for is that Germany doesn't overrun France in a matter of weeks. We can get an expeditionary force together quite quickly but if this drags on then God help us."

"And you think this will drag on?" Sir Julius asked. Lord Facey looked intently at Sir Julius. His hand went to his iron-grey hair and he swept it back.

"Actually, I don't think that we have the men or the weapons to stop Germany taking France. However, Asquith's view is that unless we attempt this now there will be hell to pay later. This is not going to be a quick war and we're not ready to fight it. It will be a war that's being run by a committee and if twenty years in politics has taught me anything it's that all the worst decisions are made by committee. Good decisions are made by individuals, but Asquith hasn't the backbone. Until he's gone, this war is just going to stumble along."

"And so how can I help?" asked Sir Julius.

"I was hoping that I could help you," replied Facey. Ash fell from his cigar onto his dark grey-striped trousers. He ignored it and continued speaking. "We shall need equipment, food, and uniforms brought in from the Dominion countries. You are one of a few people who have the shipping connections, and the government will pay above market rates for what it gets. However, we cannot insure your ships." Facey did not smile. There was something else, thought Julius; Facey did not go to a meeting and not want something in return.

The butler brought over the glass of Madeira and a pot of tea for Sir Julius. The interruption gave time for Sir Julius to think. He wondered who Facey had seen that morning. He had said 'one of the few people'. Max Aitken was the only other person Sir Julius knew who had enough ships to compete with him. He decided he needed to press for more information.

"How is Max?" Sir Julius asked.

"He's fine," said Lord Facey, "sends his regards."

"I didn't know he was in London?"

"He came back last night."

Sir Julius took a sip of tea. Facey had been to see Max Aitken first and now he was here. He wondered what Aitken had offered and he surmised that it was probably not enough. Was Facey's first choice Aitken or had he gone to get a feel for what this contract might be worth? How would the negotiations have played out? If Max Aitken was true to form, then Facey would have got one of Aitken's notorious 'take-it or leave-it offers' and if that had happened, then because Facey was here, he had not accepted it.

"One always wants to help one's country and one's friends."

"Yes, I know," said Facey.

"And I've been meaning to speak to you about a place on the board of Home and Colonial." Sir Julius smiled and this time the smile was returned. "And of course, we would provide you with a greater interest in the company as you are bringing with you a vast amount of expertise."

"That's good of you to say so," said Facey, "and although I can't pre-judge matters, I think it likely that Home and Colonial will get an exclusive government contract. Aitken is Canadian and while a decent enough sort of chap, he isn't one of us."

Julius smiled at the words 'one of us'. He recalled that when he was making his fortune people like Cecil Facey had said the same thing about him. He so hated people like Facey – so full of their own sense of self-importance and who had never had to work.

"I'm pleased that we've managed to resolve things," said Sir Julius and leant over and offered Facey his hand. "I'll speak to the board this morning and draw up the agreement later today."

"And the percentage I'll get?" asked Lord Facey.

Sir Julius stood up, smiled one last time. "I assume 0.5% will be satisfactory."

Facey could not keep the look of disappointment off his face.

Sir Julius left the club, walked down through St James' and onto the Mall. He guessed that Max Aitken might have offered Facey twice as much from the look on his face. As he walked down the Mall, rather content with himself, he heard the noise of brass instruments and drumming coming up from Trafalgar Square. The banging reverberated off the cold stone buildings of Whitehall and across Horse Guards. He saw coming through Admiralty Arch a large group, moving in his direction towards Buckingham Palace. He took out his pocket watch. It was a quarter past ten. He had to be in the City for eleven and there would be a cab at Charing Cross. He decided to wade through the crowd.

A sense of fatalism swept over Sir Julius. He had felt that way when he had first heard news of war, and now had the same feeling as he approached the crowd. It had something to do with his age, he was certain of that, as he had never felt this way when he was younger. The young were too impetuous. Drum-beating and banging, it would lead to no good. It seemed to him that the only things young men were talking about were honour, glory and adventure. They had no real idea of what it involved. When it was all over, and the flags were furled, what would they say about the war? Would they say that it was an honourable war or that it was good sport? He doubted it. Would they count the dead and regret what they had done?

Sir Julius' pace slowed as he approached the crowd. A few people at the front moved apart so that he could get through but there were more people than he anticipated and soon the surge of the crowd was pushing him back up the Mall and towards the palace.

"Come on, mate," somebody shouted, "you're going the wrong way." Once again there was that surge of fatalism; Sir Julius tried to hold his position, but the push of the crowd sent him backwards. He could hardly hear himself think. Everyone seemed to be banging something and suddenly Julius felt his feet going beneath him.

"Oh God!" he shouted as he started falling. He heard shouting near him and saw a couple of soldiers in uniform trying to hold back the rest of the crowd. For just a few moments the line held, and an officer leant down and helped Sir Julius up.

"Thank you," said Julius, but the young officer was already lost in the parade.

Sir Julius stood for a moment shaking and then the crowd had passed. He looked back up the Mall to see if he could see the officer. His breathing became more regular as he became calmer. How old had the officer been – twenty-five, perhaps? He had hardly time to look at him. Even now, a few moments later, he could not even recall the man's face, except he did remember that the officer's hands were soft and his grip was firm. He had long fingers, like a pianist or an artist. Kit had similar hands. He always thought there was something feminine about Kit's hands with his long, delicate fingers. Perhaps it had been Kit. He hesitated a moment and then turned back down towards Trafalgar Square and carried on walking.

A cab took him to a large office on the corner of Bishopsgate and Houndsditch. The cabbie seemed unimpressed with the tip that Sir Julius gave him, although it was a fraction more than what he customarily gave. Julius pushed open the heavy wooden double doors of the offices of Home and Colonial Imports and walked into the marble reception area. The doormen lifted their top hats as he entered, and he walked up the staircase at the far end to his office and the boardroom.

He had a list of things to do before the board meeting that afternoon. He needed to contact his lawyers about Facey and see a few of the other directors to make sure the appointment went unopposed. He also needed to review all the charter agreements the company had in place. If what Facey had promised was half as large as Sir Julius suspected, it would stretch his resources to the limit. As he entered his office, he was told by his secretary that his son, Adrian, was there to see him.

"Some good news," said Sir Julius to Adrian. He noted that Adrian had poured himself a glass of water. "Cecil Facey has given the company a large contract. I never thought that he would ever come up trumps. You can never tell when you're dealing with a drunk." Julius sat down behind his office desk.

"I remember the first time I met Facey," said Adrian. "I would never have guessed that he was a drunk. Anyway, I'm pleased things are going well."

"Well as can be expected but our biggest problem will be keeping staff. I heard that a dozen office boys had enlisted this morning. The government is buying an army. A motorcyclist is being paid 35 shillings a week all found and a bounty of £10 paid to each man approved and £5 on discharge."

"It's the same everywhere," said Adrian. "You may not have anyone working on the castle until the war is over."

"That's the least of my problems," said Julius.

"I was there a week or so ago with Kit," said Adrian.

"You said he was coming back," said Julius. "I thought about him this morning. How is he?"

"Well," said Adrian. "It's one of the reasons I wanted to see you. It's been over two years since you last spoke to him; isn't it long enough?"

Adrian lit a cigarette. The blue-grey smoke whirled around the room, rolling around on a light breeze that came through the half-open leaden windows.

Sir Julius paused before answering: "He knows that he's always welcome at Wadhust Hall to see his mother. I won't object."

"So I won't tell him that you'll be killing the fatted calf," added Adrian.

"Tell him what you like. We both know why we haven't spoken for so long. He ran off to Vienna and hasn't been back. Despite the operations that Basil has had to endure. He hasn't once visited his brother." Julius looked at his watch – he had fifteen minutes before his next meeting .

"He did write to Basil," said Adrian.

"Did he?" said Sir Julius. "Anyway, how is the castle coming along?" Sir Julius picked up the telephone on his desk, placed the receiver to his ear and tapped the switch-hook a number of times until his secretary answered. "Tea for two," he said. "You will have tea," he said to Adrian, "or do you only drink coffee now? So many young people have taken up with the fancy of only drinking coffee."

"Tea will be fine." Adrian thought for a moment about the morning he had walked around the castle with Kit. "The walls are starting to go up but with only two stonemasons it's taking forever."

"I should tell you," said Sir Julius, "that the cost is crippling. The estimates for the castle are already three times as much as the original budget. I just can't seem to make Lutyens understand that when I said the budget was sixty thousand, I meant sixty thousand and not a penny more. We keep having the same argument. He says what I want will cost a little more than the original estimate. I reply that trebling the cost is not just a little more. He then goes away with the intent of making some savings, which inevitably ends up costing me more."

"Have you seen Lutyens recently?" asked Adrian.

"No," said Sir Julius, "but your mother's taken quite a shine to him. He comes down with his funny little sketches of the castle and keeps her amused. He sometimes even brings his daughter, Celia, the one who was at the stone laying ceremony. She turned eighteen this year and they're planning to present her."

"Eighteen?" said Adrian. "I still think of her as that skinny girl."

Sir Julius once again looked at his watch.

"Anyway, you haven't told me why you're here?"

"There were two things," said Adrian. "First, I spoke to the surgeon who said that this would probably be the last operation Basil would need. He'll be in St Thomas' Hospital for a while. Mother's there now and I'm sure she'll make a fuss of him for a few days. Drop round to see him if you get a moment. I left the name of the ward with your secretary."

"And the second thing?" said Sir Julius.

"The second thing is..." Adrian hesitated before continuing. "You don't think this will be a long war, do you?"

Sir Julius looked at his son. He had a horrible feeling in the pit of his stomach as he guessed what was coming next.

"Do you believe it will be over in six months, nine months, or a year?" Adrian was now speaking quickly. "I only ask because a group of us, who I know from my days in Cambridge, thought we could probably do more good helping to end the war quickly rather than anything else and– well – we all enlisted."

Julius groaned. "You idiot, you damned idiot!"

Chapter 23

Kit finished reading the note from his brother in his rooms at the Bristol Hotel and stared into the empty grate, wondering what he should do. He had been back in England for nearly two aimless weeks. Except for drinking with a few old friends from his student days at the Slade, he had done very little during that time. It had not taken long to realise that his popularity was due to a misconception by his old acquaintances that he was a success and had deep pockets. His triumph in Vienna, he now thought, was not nearly as great as he had believed. Vienna had only been a success because his family could afford to bankroll him. He hadn't even unpacked his canvases and paints and now he was wondering what he should do with his time.

The letter from Adrian was the usual brief note that he had come to expect from his brother. Adrian always had a hundred and one things to do. It was so different to the tedium that Kit was experiencing; so different to the late breakfasts and the occasional stroll in the parks. The prospect of work was also unpalatable. A gentleman shouldn't need to work. He read Adrian's note once again.

6th August 1914

Basil's operation went well, and I believe he would like you to visit. He's at St Thomas' in the Victoria Ward – visiting hours are between 11 and 5. I have spoken to Father, who said you should come down to Wadhurst Hall as Mother wants to see you.

I have enlisted. Father called me 'a damned idiot' which proves that you are no longer the black sheep. Will you be joining up? Two Drewes in the Royal Garrison Artillery – it would be good to know that you were beside me.

Adrian

Kit looked at his watch. It was a little after two and the desire to see his younger brother seized him. He thought about walking the mile to the hospital but decided it might be more comfortable to take a cab in the summer heat and so telephoned reception. As he walked past the mirror, he looked at himself. His mother might be at the hospital and he decided to comb his hair, shave and dab on some eau de cologne that he had borrowed from Adrian, although he did not care too much for the scent of sandalwood.

"St Thomas' Hospital," he shouted up to a cab driver as he slammed the door of the hansom closed. He could hear Big Ben chime the half hour as he arrived at the hospital. He climbed the twelve cold, stone steps and entered into a room full of the smell of carbolic soap and disinfectant. An elderly man in a bowler hat with grey lamb chop sideburns sat behind the reception desk and Kit asked where he could find the Victoria Ward.

Armed with this knowledge, he wandered down a corridor of scrubbed floors with whitewashed walls. There were no paintings or anything to break up the sterility of the whitewash except several small windows, which were too high up to see through. He turned left at the bottom of the corridor and expected to see the sign Victoria Ward but was faced instead with a large sign that informed him that he was about to enter the George Ward. Kit turned around. It was a five-minute walk back to the reception and he decided to enter the ward and see if he could ask a nurse for help.

"Excuse me," he said to a nurse who was carrying a stack of metal, kidney-shaped trays. "Could you tell me where the Victoria Ward is?"

The nurse peered over the top of the stack that she was holding.

"If you follow me, I'll show you, sir. I'm heading in that direction." However, she didn't move and Kit for a moment wondered whether she was expecting him to offer to carry the trays. "Sorry, sir," she continued, "but I didn't recognise you for a moment."

Kit thought she had mistaken him for someone else, was about to correct her then he looked at her face peeking over the trays.

"Daisy?" he said enquiringly.

"Rose," she corrected him.

"Sorry," said Kit. "Do you remember my name?"

"Christian," she answered, "Christian Drewe." He walked behind her back up the white-washed corridor until she turned down another corridor on her right. Kit realised that he must have walked straight past the turning without thinking. He wondered whether she was smiling to herself as she walked in front of him.

The main room in the Victoria Ward had a dozen or so noisy children who seemed to be everywhere. From the look of them Kit doubted whether they were ill. All of them were out of their beds. His eyes scanned across the various faces, but he could not see Basil and then he realised that eldest was no more than twelve and Basil was – he thought for a second – Basil would now be fifteen. They walked through the room and into a smaller corridor where rooms came off on each side. Rose stopped at a door and indicated to Kit that Basil was inside. Kit took a deep breath. Three years, it now seemed a lifetime.

He was partially relieved to find Basil asleep. He was also relieved that his mother wasn't there. However, he had decided to come and see Basil and for some reason he felt let down. He thought about waking him. A discreet cough or scraping a chair; but he recollected his father's favourite saying: 'let sleeping dogs lie.' He sat down at the farthest edge of the room and immediately found himself fidgeting. He should have brought a paper, he should have brought grapes, he should have brought something. He waited for what seemed an hour but according to his watch was only fifteen minutes. He had just about made up his mind to go and find a paper when the door opened, and he was once again looking at Rose.

"I can wake him," said Rose.

"No, please don't. I'll come again tomorrow."

Kit got up. Basil coughed in his sleep and Kit turned to look.

"How is he?"

"If you would like to wait, I can call the surgeon. He'll be able to tell you how the operation went."

"There's no need, I just wanted the gist."

"If you can wait ten minutes," said Rose, "I'll have finished for the day and there's a coffee house just across from the hospital where we can talk."

Kit sat in the coffee house waiting. He did not know why he was sitting with a cup of something that pretended to be coffee, but which would have been spat out in Austria. He missed the noisy cafés of Vienna, and lost in his own thoughts about them, had not appreciated that Rose had come in. He failed to stand up and then felt annoyance with himself for his lack of manners, quickly getting to his feet.

Her news about Basil was given concisely and professionally. She explained how the operation had proceeded and that she had even assisted. He gathered from what she said that he would always have a limp, but that they hoped in time it would not be too pronounced. He looked at her more closely as she spoke and noticed how her dark eyes flicked up when she thought he wasn't looking at her. He saw how she occasionally smiled and how that smile seemed to break across her whole face, like a small fan waved in an opera. He noticed how she tried to hide any emotion by hiding her face in her hands.

"And what do you do," said Kit, "when all the patients go to sleep and the world is yours to do with as you wish?"

"Sometimes," Rose said, "I go out with a few of the other nurses to the nickelodeon or a dance. Last week we went to see an American film called *Kid Auto Races at Venice* starring Charlie Chaplin. He's English, you know?"

"Who?" asked Kit.

"Charlie Chaplin. He used to live close to us down in Deptford and Mam and Dad have seen him in the music hall more than once. Mam says that he was the funniest music hall drunk she had ever seen. Do you think now the war has started he will come back to England to fight?"

"I doubt it," said Kit, "why should he? He's probably living in the lap of luxury somewhere in Hollywood. I wouldn't."

"So, you won't be enlisting?"

Kit noticed that Rose was looking directly at him, and he wondered what she was thinking. He decided the question was impertinent. He thought about telling her to mind her own business, that she was just a nurse, but of course he didn't. However, he had no answer to the question which had first been raised by his brother Adrian. Would he enlist in the Royal Garrison Artillery and go off and fight?

Kit felt embarrassed by his lack of decision. He had, for the last two years, been certain of his position and now he questioned the war and his role in it. He felt no compunction to put on a uniform and attack the Austrians who a few months ago were his friends, with whom he drank in bars and cafés. He looked at his watch. "I've kept you far too long and you'll want to get home. Perhaps next time I'll have an answer." He smiled but it was only half-hearted, and she did not smile back.

"What makes you think that there will be a next time?"

Chapter 24

Although Kit came regularly to St Thomas' Hospital during the next week, he did not see Rose. At first, he wondered whether she was avoiding him and so he asked Basil, who told him that she was working in another part of the hospital. By the end of the week, he had almost forgotten about her.

In that time, Rose had been busy. The hospital needed to put in place the resources to deal with the wounded from the war. They needed to recruit more nurses, find more beds and buy in more medicines. She slept and worked almost solidly at the hospital until her day off when she went home to Deptford. On her twenty-fourth birthday, she awoke in her own bed at her parents' house in good spirits. The morning started with hot sweet tea, toast and sticky jam, birthday cards and small presents. She received a St Christopher on a silver chain from her fiancé, Peter Hall, with a letter. On the reverse of the St Christopher, he had her name engraved. She had only seen Peter four times in the last ten months since he had become a full lieutenant in the Royal Engineers, and she put the letter in her bag and wondered how he was.

In appearance, Peter Hall had changed little over the years. He remained quiet and could bury his head in a book for hours on end. Rose smiled when she thought of Peter in his uniform.

Peter had been down after the accident at Drewsteignton. He finished his year-long apprenticeship; however, Babtie, Shaw and Morton decided to let him go after taking on the nephew of Mr Babtie. Alistair Morton came to his aid and helped him with an introduction to an acquaintance, Rory Campbell, a colonel in the Royal Engineers. Peter was given a commission and went to Sandhurst for training. He wrote to Rose regularly as he went through training and would come back to see her when possible. They even went out dancing, and although Rose thought he had the clumsiest feet in England, or Scotland, he was always willing to dance with her. Eighteen months later, when he had been made a full lieutenant, he had come back to see her and told her that he was earning well, his prospects were good and that he could now afford to look after her. Like his dancing, she thought it the clumsiest proposal she could imagine but eventually said yes. As her mother reminded her, his prospects were better than anyone else she knew.

Rose Braithwaite, soon to be Rose Hall, left her parents house on Deptford Strand and hurried towards the ferry. The letter from Peter was stuffed into her raffia bag. She closed the kitchen door at five to seven and ran down the road towards the dock. As she got onto the seven-fifteen ferry to Blackfriars, her fingers played with the St Christopher around her neck. Although the hospital did not permit the wearing of jewellery, even her engagement ring, no one would ever see the St Christopher and she decided that she would wear it every day.

As soon as she sat down on the ferry, she opened the envelope. The letter was written in Peter's neat handwriting and was dated the 4th of August 1914. It had taken a week to get to her. Rose's eyes ran down the first few paragraphs of the letter. He asked about her family and said that he was coming back to England now that the war had started. He said he missed her and that he hated being apart from her. He hoped to land in England in a week or ten days and would contact her when he returned. She continued to read as he described his last three months in India. The letter concluded:

'I know that we are now at war and once again everything is uncertain. However, if we are to wait until the war is over then perhaps there will never be a right time for us to marry. I am going to apply for some leave when I land. If you feel the same as I do then should we wait a day longer? Please think about it.

Affectionately yours – Peter

p.s. If I can make it to your party which you told me about in your last letter then I shall.'

Rose reread the letter and put it into her bag. She had been looking forward to her party at the Lyons' Corner House for weeks. The ferry arrived and full of high spirits, she headed along the embankment towards Waterloo Bridge. Eight o'clock rang out the bells of St Bride's.

"Rose!" someone shouted. She turned her head to see who had called her name but there were only tramps down by the river. She continued forward but, without looking, hit a gentleman coming in the opposite direction. She fell backwards onto the pavement, looking up to see a young man in a grey lounge suit. She recognised him instantly. Christian Drewe apologised profusely, even though it was all her fault, and leant down to help her up. "Nothing more than a clash of colours," he added with a smile. "Are you all right?"

"Fine, Mr Drewe," she said, as she started to shake the dust off her uniform.

He then bent down and picked up her St Christopher that had fallen from its chain.

"Is this yours?" he asked.

"Yes."

He handed it back to her and said, "It doesn't seem to be working too well today."

She blushed.

"Do you know the story of St Christopher?" continued Kit, as she put the chain around her neck and retied the clasp. "The tale goes that he was weighed down by the baby Jesus because when he picked him up, he found he was also carrying the burdens of the world. However, despite the load he managed to carry him safely across a raging river onto the safety of land."

She said nothing. Thinking that he may have embarrassed her, Kit turned to go but stopped after a step and asked her whether she would be working in the hospital later that afternoon. She said yes. "Then perhaps we can have that coffee after you finish work? I shall be seeing Basil later today."

Rose thought for a moment.

"Sorry," she said, "but I have another commitment." She mentioned that it was her birthday and explained that she was going out with some of the nurses and doctors.

"Perhaps you would like to come?" she added.

"This evening?" asked Kit. "I'm not sure I can make this evening."

"We'll be at the Lyons' Corner House on Coventry Street from eight if you change your mind."

*   *   *

The news that Rose had invited Christian Drewe to her birthday celebration at the Lyons' Corner House caused more than the occasional comment throughout the day. In fact, when Kit came to the hospital that afternoon for his daily visit to see Basil, he noticed more than one nurse looking at him. Rose went briskly about her routine until her closest friend caught up with her.

"Why didn't you tell me that you knew Christian Drewe?" said Dora. "He's a dish."

"I don't know him that well," said Rose.

"Well enough to invite him to your birthday party."

"He didn't say he would come."

"But he didn't say he wouldn't," answered Dora. "I'll have to get something new to wear."

"Don't be ridiculous," said Rose, "he wouldn't look twice at either of us."

"Speak for yourself – why wouldn't he look at me!"

"That's not what I meant," she insisted. "I just meant that he's a gentleman – and, well, he'll keep to his own. When we had coffee, I asked him what he was going to do in the war and he almost told me to mind my own business. He didn't say anything, but it was quite clear what he was thinking."

Rose looked at Dora whose mouth had dropped open.

"What's wrong with you now?" said Rose.

"You didn't tell me that you had gone for coffee with him. What else haven't you told me?"

"Nothing!" said Rose.

"You're not gettin' fancy ideas for yourself are you, Rose Braithwaite? You do remember that you're walking out with someone else?" Rose became annoyed and told Dora that she was talking nonsense, that there was nothing in it, that she had only spoken to him once before and that was about his brother and that she didn't know why she had invited him to her birthday party, but she had only done so because he had helped her up when they had bumped into each other that morning.

Morning flowed into the afternoon and afternoon into early evening and Rose rolled from one job to the next without purpose or direction. She felt a whole series of contradictions. She was annoyed but flattered. She felt restless and guilty. She made a point of going nowhere near the ward where Basil Drewe was recuperating. The operation had been a success and the patient was recovering quickly. Basil was now walking with crutches, and he would be discharged soon and then there would be no reason whatsoever for Kit Drewe to come to the hospital. She shook her head. Her fiancé would be home on leave soon and then she could plan the rest of her life with Peter. Dependable and honest; she knew where she stood with Peter, who cared only about his books and her. She decided that she would not wait to get married; why wait when tomorrow was such an uncertain day? However, a minute or two later she changed her mind. There was no hurry; she felt she was just being silly.

At seven o'clock Rose had finished work and was soon ready to go out. Rose, Dora, four other nurses and two junior doctors had booked a table at the Lyons' Corner House on Coventry Street. The Corner House had only been opened for a few years and each of its five floors was different. Rose's favourite was the third floor where there was a big band that usually played the latest dance tunes from America; their table was by the dais where the band played.

When they entered Rose caught her breath. Her table had been decorated in creams and pinks, with flowers at each end in small Delft vases. In the centre of the table was a cake, covered in pink icing and with twenty-four candles. The Marty Bridgewater Band was playing a foxtrot and Rose had no sooner sat down than she wanted to start dancing. However, six female nurses and two male doctors did not result in a perfect division for dancing and her friends were already surveying the ballroom floor for dance partners. As they waited for the band to stop playing, a waiter came over to the table holding two ice buckets with champagne in both.

"You've made a mistake," said Rose to the waiter, "we didn't order this."

In his black jacket and white apron, he looked at her coldly. "A gentleman telephoned this afternoon and requested that it be brought to your table when you arrived, madam."

"Did he leave any name or message?" asked Rose.

"Just that he apologised, would try to come later on and that he wished you a happy birthday."

Rose noticed that Dora was looking at her.

"Well?" said Rose.

"Well what?" asked Dora.

"Nothing," said Rose. "Let's dance." She looked at the two doctors who seemed to be paying more interest to the champagne that was being poured into their glasses than to the nurses. "I suppose it's you and me again, Dora."

Rose danced for what seemed an age and when she came back to the table, there were people there that she did not know. When the champagne ran out, bottles of wine followed. Dora was still on the dance floor; Rose had lost her in an 'excuse me' and had not been able to get her back. Three of the nurses had gone back to the dormitories, fearing that they would be locked out because it was now after hours. The doctors were talking to two ladies who wore, in Rose's opinion, too much make-up and of whom Rose immediately disapproved. There were two couples sitting and drinking at her table who she didn't recognise and so she sat next to the last remaining person she knew, a nurse who had recently joined the hospital, called Julie Coombes. Julie was a stout woman with a ruddy complexion and short curly hair. She never danced for any period of time, complaining of sore feet. Rose suspected that it was more to do with the fact that she was rarely asked to dance.

"Are you enjoyin' your birthday?" Julie asked, as she took another bite of a smoked salmon sandwich.

"Yes," said Rose, "although where all of this came from, I have no idea."

"It was from that gentleman you're engaged to," said Julie.

"He's not here," said Rose. She leant over and picked up a half empty bottle of wine and poured herself a drink.

"Of course he is," said Julie, helping herself to another smoked salmon sandwich. "He's been standing over there watchin' you for the last half hour." Rose turned round and looked for Peter. He had written saying that he would try to come and see her as soon as he arrived back in the country, and it was so like him to be the wallflower standing in the corner – not coming over or breaking up the party. However, she could not see him. There was no one she could see who was over six foot in height or in an army uniform. She asked Julie again where Peter was. Julie pointed to a man in a black dinner suit and bow tie. It was Kit.

"He's not my fiancé," whispered Rose to Julie. "He shouldn't be here. It was a mistake; I should never have invited him."

"I wish my mistakes turned out like that," said Julie.

Kit had the same purpose in his walk as he had on that day he had wandered into St Thomas' Hospital and asked to be taken to the Victoria Ward. He carried a glass of champagne in one hand and had a cigarette in the other.

"Happy birthday," he said.

"Thank you," said Rose, "but you shouldn't have done all of this."

"It's a tradition," said Kit. "One must always drink champagne on one's birthday."

"It's not a tradition I have," said Rose.

"It's a tradition everyone should have," said Kit.

"It's frivolous," answered Rose.

"It's my money to waste." The merest hint of a smile crossed Kit's lips. "I suppose a dance is out of the question?"

Julie Coombes looked at Rose. "If you don't dance with him I will," she said. However, Rose was already on her feet.

The darkness was spread out over London when they left the Lyons' Corner House. Rose had not realised how late it was. Dora and Julie had both returned to the hospital an hour earlier in order to get back into the nurses' rooms before the doors were locked. Time had got lost for Rose. The moon was high in the night sky and looked down on the West End of London. She would have to get a cab home and come in early in the morning, even then she was likely to get a warning from the staff nurse. Kit suggested that they walk back to his hotel, and he would arrange for a cab from there. As they went through Soho the moon cast shadows around the alleyways and squares. Rose had drunk more than she was used to, and she was laughing at a story he was telling about very fat Viennese men dancing.

Kit demonstrated by pretending to waltz along the side of the road. "*You maaade me looove you,*" he sang. "*I didn't wanna do it, I didn't wanna do it...*" When he came to a lamp post he took hold of it and danced elegantly around it.

"Stop," shouted Rose, who was trying to control her laughter.

Kit stopped dancing and came over to where she was standing. He still had a bottle of champagne in his hand and took out a glass from his pocket.

"One more for the road," he suggested.

"I have to get home," she said.

"I haven't got you into trouble, have I?" he asked.

Rose took the glass from his outstretched hand. "No, you've been a perfect gentleman." She leant forward and kissed him on the cheek.

Kit put his arms around her and pulled her close to him. He kissed her on the lips. One hand moved down her back; Rose pulled it away.

"Almost a perfect gentleman," she said reprovingly. Once again there was the faintest hint of a smile. She turned, laughed, and then began running towards Bloomsbury. Kit ran also, caught up with her at Russell Square and in the ghostly moonlight he again kissed her. The iron railings around the square looked like sentries at their posts.

"You never did tell me what you plan to do now the war's started," Rose said.

"No, I didn't," he answered.

"You don't intend enlisting then?"

"No," he said, "it's not my war and I really would make the most terrible officer."

Everyone else Rose knew seemed so eager to go to war, and she wondered whether Kit was the only sane man in England. Without thinking, she placed her hands around his neck and kissed him. The kiss lingered and once again Kit moved a hand down past her waist. This time Rose made no movement to stop him. He began kissing her more passionately and then moved his lips to her neck. Rose stood still with her eyes closed, unaware of the world and its sounds around her. She ran her hands through his dark hair. As he began kissing her again on the lips, Rose suddenly felt that she was being watched. She opened her eyes and saw a soldier standing on the path in front of them. He stood motionless. She started backwards. Kit turned.

"Get lost," Kit shouted.

The soldier took a step towards them, brought back his fist and swung it into the side of Kit's face.

"Peter, no!" Rose screamed.

Kit took a step backwards and then his legs gave way.

Chapter 25

"That hurts!" groaned Kit. He continued to stare upwards at the ceiling light as the doctor held his eye open.

"It will hurt less if you don't move, Mr Drewe," insisted Dr Harold Gillies.

Kit bit his lip and determined not to move again. All he could see were sunspots in a haze of white light. The doctor let Kit's eye close and moved back. Kit's vision started to come back into focus. He was in his room at the Bristol Hotel and then he looked at the person standing over him. It was one of the two doctors who had brought Rose to the Lyons' Corner House earlier that evening. Kit had taken almost no notice of him but now saw that he was no older than thirty, tall with a long aquiline nose and grey-blue eyes.

"I don't usually come out for street fights," said Gillies, "but in the circumstances I could hardly refuse. Fortunately, it doesn't look like there's any serious harm done." Gillies turned to Rose who stood holding a basin of warm water with some bloodstained cotton wool in it and told her to pour it away.

Kit sat up slowly.

"Christ!" he murmured. "I feel like I've been hit by an omnibus. What happened?"

"Just a right hook," said Gillies. "Now try not to move. Your eye will be sore for the next few days but fortunately your nose wasn't broken." The doctor once again turned and said to Rose, "I can take you back to the hospital if you like? I'll say that you were helping me with a patient."

Rose thanked him and said that it would help her out of a tight spot as she needed to be back on duty in six hours.

Gillies leant over and whispered to Rose, "I can wait for a little while if you like. I saw your fiancé standing out in the corridor when I came up. I suspect that he'll still be there, and you'll want to sort out this mess before you go back."

Peter was walking up and down the corridor. He was beating the side of his leg with his swagger stick. The brass buckle of the Sam Browne belt glinted in the gaslight as did his brown boots that had been polished with parade gloss and spit. On the sleeves of his tunic were two pips, denoting his rank of lieutenant. He had grown a small moustache since being given his commission and his hair had been cut even shorter. His attitude and anger were things that she had not seen before, things which she did not know he possessed and since it is the unknown that frightens, Rose felt scared.

When he saw her, he walked deliberately up to her until he was standing close, looking down at her.

"It looks to me," began Peter, "that you have something of mine which you no longer have a right to keep."

Rose tilted her head downwards slightly. He grabbed at her left hand and held it up to her face.

"You're not even wearing your ring," he said accusingly. "Don't pretend that I'm an idiot."

"I made a mistake," said Rose.

"A mistake?" said Peter. "A mistake is when you leave your shopping on the omnibus or lose your house keys. Being felt up like some common whore is not a mistake!"

"Don't be coarse," she said.

"Don't accuse me of being coarse. I'm not the one..." He didn't finish the sentence. "Just tell me how long it's been going on."

"There's nothing going on." Rose found that her eyes had filled with tears.

"Don't lie to me." He grabbed her shoulders and shook her. "I told you I'm not an idiot."

"Then don't act like one," said Kit. Peter looked down the corridor at Kit Drewe, who was standing by the door of his room. Kit's white cotton shirt was speckled with blood.

"You," shouted Peter, "you really are stupid. Didn't you have enough outside in the square?"

"Obviously not," said Kit, with a little more bravado than he actually felt.

"Go back inside, Kit," said Rose. "You'll just make things worse."

"Don't think I don't remember you, Christian Drewe! I don't forget a face," shouted Peter.

Kit reluctantly went back into his room. For the life of him he didn't have the faintest idea who the soldier was. Kit could still hear the argument continuing outside in corridor. "You really are something else, Rose," he heard the soldier shout. Things suddenly went quiet and then he could hear the march of boots down the wooden corridor. He imagined Rose running after him. He imagined her grabbing him by the arm and him swinging round. Would he slap her?

126

Would he strike her with his swagger stick? He wanted to go out and protect her and then he wondered whether there would be a reconciliation.

He looked at Gillies.

"I told you not to get involved," said Gillies. He lit a cigarette and offered one to Kit. "She's the only one who can sort things out with her fiancé."

"I didn't know she was engaged," said Kit. "He seemed to know me."

"He's an engineer in the army," said Gillies, "name of Peter Hall."

The name rang a bell in the depths of Kit's memory but for the life of him he still could not recall when, or even if, they had met before. He could not recall meeting any Scottish soldiers while he was in Vienna and was certain that he had not met a soldier called Peter Hall before.

It took another ten minutes before Rose returned. She knocked on the door of the room, asked Dr Harold Gillies to take her back to the hospital and said nothing to Kit. She had been crying and her mascara had streaked down the side of her face. She seemed paler than normal. The door closed behind them, leaving Kit alone in the room, staring at nothing.

PART IV

Chapter 26

In his bedroom Kit Drewe, still wearing the trousers of his dinner suit and white shirt, contemplated his life. He had not been able to sleep. He remembered the look Rose had given him just before she closed the door behind her. She had not said anything when she had come back; what could she say with her fiancé somewhere outside? He tried in his head to decipher what she was thinking.

By morning, when the light eased its way through the curtained windows of his hotel, he was still thinking about the night before. He had made inroads into the best part of a bottle of Scotch and had finished a packet of cigarettes. Similar to his father, he hated unsolved riddles, but what went through a woman's mind was perhaps a question that was unanswerable. As with some problems, the more he picked at it, the more opaque it became.

He deliberately tried to think about something different. He remembered the recent letter from Adrian and wondered whether he ought to join up, but just as quickly dismissed the idea. It wasn't his war and when he thought about it, he realised that most of his friends were Austrian.

He decided, however, that he had to do something. He thought about packing his bags and sailing to America like Charlie Chaplin. He could live inconspicuously over there; a quiet Englishman in a land of loud Americans, daubing at canvases until the war was over. However, would he ever be able to return and pretend that nothing had happened? It was not him and the cut of the cloth did not fit. Whatever he was, he was not a coward.

However, his mind kept coming back to Rose. Should he write to her or let sleeping dogs lie? There was the rub! He had not acted like a gentleman. A gentleman would let her go, he thought, she was after all engaged and to write to her now was beyond the pale. However, he felt alive with her. As he closed his eyes and started to drift into sleep, he had one word in his head – 'perhaps'.

When he finally fell asleep with his legs tucked up on the small bedroom settee, he was no closer to resolving anything.

He slept through a knock on the door, a letter being left for him, and even the maid coming in. He almost slept through lunchtime and when he awoke his legs ached. He smelt of stale sweat and alcohol. His nose was sore, but he was relieved to see there was not much bruising. He could not remember the questions that had kept him awake the night before or whether he had reached any answers, and decided that it would do no good to brood on matters. The quickest way to clear his head was to go out for a walk. He opened the windows of his room and let the August breeze blow through.

After he had bathed and dressed, he noticed the letter lying by the door. He tore open the envelope. The handwriting was large and shaky, almost childish. He was surprised when he looked at the signature: Gertrude Jekyll. He remembered her as a well-built, solid person who did not suffer fools lightly. The writing was anything but solid. However, it was the content of the letter that intrigued him. She asked whether he could contact her regarding some pictures that she wanted painted of her home, Munstead Wood. He immediately saw the potential. It could have taken years to rebuild his reputation as an artist and here was a chance of a commission from the *grande dame* of the Arts and Crafts movement.

In an instant his mind turned from the night before and he started looking ahead. He would go down to the Charing Cross Road and see if there were any books on Munstead Wood. He didn't want to appear completely ignorant when he met her. He would also telephone his mother and see if Poley could chauffeur him down and whether he could borrow her camera. He would also suggest that Basil join him. Basil was making a speedy recovery following his operation and could walk short distances with the aid of a walking stick. Suddenly everything seemed possible. He grabbed his hat from the coat stand and headed downstairs to reception. He felt it was time to grasp the nettle. He had been back in England for three weeks and had not yet spoken to either of his parents. He would also send a telegram to Gertrude Jekyll and suggest that he come down on the following day. *Carpe diem*, he thought.

As he waited for his mother to come to the telephone, he wondered what he would say. He hated telephones, a common device that in his view had only limited benefits and could never replace the written word. People either shouted or spoke in an inaudible whisper so that you found yourself asking them to repeat everything. The experience was not edifying, as one ended the telephone conversation either having sounded like a town crier or a deaf imbecile.

"Is that you, Christian?" his mother shouted.

"Yes."

"Where are you?"

"In London."

"What?"

"In London," he said loudly. He noticed the girl behind the reception desk looking over and lowered his voice.

"So why haven't you come down to see me?"

Kit took a deep breath. "I thought I would have bumped into you at the hospital. I went to see Basil nearly every day."

"He told us you had visited him." Kit noticed that her voice had softened.

"Anyway, I wanted to take Basil out tomorrow. I am going over to Munstead Wood and thought he might like to come as well." Kit took another deep breath.

"I am not sure he is up to taking the train," his mother said.

"I was hoping that you could send Poley up with the motor. It will be less strenuous for Basil." There was a silence. Kit wondered whether his mother would agree.

"Poley will be with you at ten-thirty but you will stay over and have dinner with us when you drop Basil back."

Kit knew that this was not a suggestion but a condition if he wanted the car, and so he agreed without hesitation. While he was riding high, he also asked whether he could borrow a camera and explained that he still had not received any of his things from Vienna. They chatted for a few minutes and when he hung up the receiver he felt that they had not really spoken; all they had done was exchange pleasantries and catch up on some family small talk. He realised that he missed having people to converse with. When he had first come back, he hoped that he and Adrian would have spent more time together, but Adrian had enlisted. The only other person with whom he had sat down and talked properly was Rose. In Vienna there had always been Tomas Skeres, the person with whom he had shared rooms.

He walked out of the hotel in the August afternoon. The roads around Russell Square were quiet but as soon as he got down towards Bloomsbury the noise seemed to increase exponentially. Cabs and buses pushed their way through the arteries of the city. It was so different to the broad boulevards of Vienna. Even the people were different; everyone walked around with their heads down, too busy to give you the time of day. In Vienna the café owners would be outside cajoling the passers-by to stop and have a coffee. People would be sitting drinking outside at tables on the wide streets. In nearly every European city he knew there was a café culture where people took time to watch the world go by. In London, with its narrow pavements and damp weather, no one ever sat outside – except, of course, for the tramps.

Tomas Skeres! He had not thought about his friend for weeks. Skeres had never liked London and had once said he would prefer to die rather than reside in London. Skeres had said that London had everything a man could want, but no one knew how to enjoy it properly. Skeres sucked pleasure from life. He enjoyed bars and restaurants and sitting outside in the cafés talking about politics and love. He would have laughed at Kit and his flirting with Rose. Skeres would have pronounced in a flamboyant manner that Englishmen are so funny; that they run their empires and trade with the four corners of the world but that when it comes to sex, they seem to lose their heads.

Tall, thin and slightly effeminate, Tomas Skeres would often speak on the differences between 'love' and 'sex'. If an Englishman was in love, Skeres would have said, and it was unrequited, then his countrymen would forgive everything, especially if it was a love that was doomed. However, the English were so backward when it came to sex. A Viennese man would take your girlfriend to bed and not think twice about it. An affair with a married woman was as natural as night passing into day. In fact, a man of means in Vienna would be expected to have a string of mistresses.

Kit stopped walking for a moment and the dialogue in his head also ceased. Why shouldn't he contact Rose; after all, it was for her to decide whether to see him again. Why should he be constrained by what others thought decent? She was attractive – perhaps not conventionally so but pretty nonetheless. He remembered her large brown eyes set off by a pale complexion, and her long black hair that hung down her back when they had danced. However, what he remembered most was her wide smile which made her whole face come alive. He could not remember when she had not been smiling as they danced together.

He continued walking along until he turned into the Charing Cross Road. Would it be so easy to be like Skeres – full of charm and frivolity, but in a way which was absolutely decadent? Kit did not feel he could live that way without any sense of responsibility. So many generations of tradition were bred into him that to give it all up on a whim went against the grain.

Of course, there was something in being English. He had felt it when everyone was trying to get out of Vienna. He had seen the madness in the eyes of the Viennese throwing stones at Jewish shops simply because they were different. Nothing like that had happened in England in six hundred years, and he hoped that that bit of barbarism had been bred out of the English character.

He started to play out in his head what he would say if he went to the hospital to see Rose. *I wanted to come and see you*, he might say, or *I wanted to thank you for helping me the other night. I realise it must have been difficult.*

He wondered whether she would walk away, or would she want to see him again and if so what she would expect from him? Would he be implicitly asking her to give up her fiancé? He had not thought of committing himself, but she might think otherwise. Skeres would want nothing more than a bit of fun, but

Rose would have expectations. She was engaged and if he went to see her, she would expect him to be serious.

"What do you really want?" he heard Rose ask.

"Nothing," he answered. It was such an inadequate response – not even true – but he had not yet worked out what was the whole truth.

The late afternoon was humid and by the time he had got to the bookshops on Charing Cross Road, his clothes were sticking to him. It was not until he appreciated that he was only a five-minute walk from the Lyons' Corner House that he realised he had retraced his steps from the night before. He had walked past the places where he had stopped and kissed Rose and where he had been hit. He had failed to recognise the lamp post that he had danced round. He suddenly recalled singing a song and smiled to himself, although he could not for the life of him remember the words, the tune was momentarily lost somewhere in his memory.

Across in Leicester Square, there seemed to be hundreds of soldiers milling about with young boys waving their enlistment papers. Many of them seemed to Kit to be no more than seventeen – so young that they were barely able to shave. He wondered how furious Basil would be when he realised that he would never be able to enlist or play any part in this war. Every cloud, thought Kit, even if it brings with it a storm.

Kit went into the bookshop and milled around for twenty minutes or so, looking at anything to do with the Arts and Crafts movement. He found nothing directly on Munstead Wood and was directed by the bookshop owner to another shop in Covent Garden.

"*You maaade me looove you,*" he whistled as he walked, "*I didn't wanna do it, I didn't wanna do it.*" That was it, he thought to himself; what a fantastic tune. He had heard it the previous year at a show in Vienna. He hadn't been to a show in an age and wondered what was currently on in the West End. He made a mental note to check the papers when he got back to the hotel.

Covent Garden was far busier, and he almost had to push himself through masses of soldiers. He stopped whistling and continued walking through the crowd while it cheered on the war. Everywhere there was khaki, and he felt out of place in his suit and Panama.

"Y're lookin' to join up, laddie?" a half-drunk sergeant shouted at him. Other soldiers from the sergeant's regiment cheered.

"If I join up it will certainly be in the infantry," shouted Kit. "What regiment are you from?"

"The 1st Edinburgh Division," replied the sergeant.

"Well, they're on my list now," said Kit lifting his hat.

The soldiers cheered once more, and Kit walked on until he came to the bookshop. He was in luck and found a book with a small article on Munstead Wood. When he left the bookshop, the bells of St Martin's could be faintly heard striking six. There seemed to be more soldiers everywhere and he decided to walk down to the Strand and hail a cab.

As he turned into Drury Lane, he saw a large group of soldiers coming up from the Strand. As he got closer, he heard them cheering, shouting for anyone to join them in the Royal Engineers. In the pit of his stomach, he suddenly feared that he might run into Peter Hall and that this time he would not get away with just a bloodied nose. He started looking around him. He thought about turning around and walking back the way he came but they would just be a few steps behind him.

To his left the foyer of the Theatre Royal opened up. The doors were open and a few people were queuing. He had no idea what was on, and he didn't care. He quickly skipped up the stairs and paid his shilling. Hopefully there might be a few good tunes, he thought.

Chapter 27

Kit Drewe nearly walked out of the theatre when he realised that, instead of a musical, he was there for a talk on theosophy. He could think of nothing less likely to have a few good tunes. However, when he read the penny programme, he saw that there would be an introduction by Emily Lutyens, a short address by Jiddu Krishnamurti, and then a talk about theosophy and the war by Annie Besant. He remembered hearing stories about Krishnamurti. He looked around the stalls, wondering who came to a talk on theosophy. There were less than two hundred people and almost everyone could fit into the first ten rows.

As he looked around the theatre he saw Edwin Lutyens, who appeared much the same as Kit remembered: a pipe in his mouth, a grey moustache, and inquisitive eyes hidden behind steel-rimmed glasses. He was standing with a young boy of about fifteen and a young woman. The young woman was thin and rather tall, taller than the boy by an inch or so. She had long, curly auburn hair that was tied at the bottom in order to prevent its unruliness, a Botticellian mouth and a straight nose. Kit knew immediately who she was, even though it had been nearly three years – Celia Lutyens.

He moved into the row behind the Lutyens family. He was in two minds whether to reintroduce himself. However, before he had made up his mind one way or the other, the lights dimmed, and a spotlight was shone onto the front of the stage. Emily Lutyens walked out from the wings.

"Mother doesn't look well at all," said Celia to her father.

Kit also thought that Emily Lutyens looked much older than he remembered. She was gaunt and her skin had become pallid. Her eyes, that were once a light pale blue, now appeared tired. Her reddish hair also showed signs of age and fatigue. At forty-one, Emily Lutyens looked ten years older and, if asked, she would have admitted to feeling more drained than she had ever done in her life.

"She wrote in her last letter," said Lutyens to Celia, "that she's not enjoying the travelling and gets nervous when she has to speak. She said that she often gets almost nothing to eat and that some of the guesthouses she has stayed at don't even know what being a vegetarian is."

"Can't you make her come home?" asked Celia.

"She'll be home this evening, but you know your mother," said Lutyens, "she believes in what she's doing and even if she is half-starved and exhausted, she's not someone just to give up. I can't make her stay at home and even if I could, I wouldn't."

It was not, however, just Emily Lutyens' appearance that had changed. The exhaustion had begun to make her waspish and quick to annoy. If Lutyens had suggested that she take a break or come home, she would have told him to mind his own business. Like an apostle, she felt it was her calling to introduce the young Krishnamurti to the world and, at the end of the day, being with Krishnamurti seemed to make everything worthwhile.

The introduction by Emily Lutyens lasted twenty minutes. Unlike the other people in the theatre, Kit Drewe had no preconceptions of what theosophy was and no understanding why these people would pay good money to listen to a young man talk about reincarnation and immortality. Kit grouped theosophists with the Mormons and the Jehovah's Witnesses – he knew they existed but did not really know what they believed in. He recalled his father once speaking of Emily Lutyens as being 'one of *them*!'

"He will offer you a glimpse of the end and the beginning," concluded Emily Lutyens, "and if you can find the God within you, and listen to His voice, you may perhaps grasp the message that he brings. Therefore, please stand and welcome Jiddu Krishnamurti."

Kit Drewe watched her as she sat down on a small, plain wooden chair at the side of the stage and then turned his attention to a young boy in long Indian robes who walked to the lone lectern. The audience at the Theatre Royal stood up and applauded.

Even in a theatre, sitting twenty feet from the front of the stage, Kit Drewe could sense that Krishnamurti was exceptional. Though he talked naturally and without any affectation, Kit could feel the warmth and passion in his voice.

There was a marked difference between what Krishnamurti said and the talk given by Emily Lutyens. Emily Lutyens was not a confident speaker; she looked uncomfortable on the stage, she fidgeted and did not know what to do with her hands. Krishnamurti spoke with a self-belief, as if he knew something important and was there to tell them that secret. Emily Lutyens spoke about other people's wisdom, about Euclid and Democritus. Krishnamurti spoke about the audience he was addressing; about the path that he had travelled and the path they could travel. However, most of all,

Krishnamurti spoke about faith and blind faith. He said that there was a need for doubt and that without doubt no one would question anything. Kit remembered, years later, that Krishnamurti had said that clarity of thought is achieved through doubt.

When Krishnamurti had finished speaking, the audience stood up and applauded. Kit sat watching, wondering whether he should stand up and applaud or stay seated. He had understood, from Krishnamurti's sermon, why all faiths were misconceived. However, Krishnamurti proposed nothing to replace them, except to follow on a path to wisdom. Kit felt unsatisfied with what he had been given.

As the audience quietened, a small woman with white hair and a powerful voice took the stage. Annie Besant was a dominating figure; the type who was not often contradicted. Emily Lutyens in her introduction had described her role in fighting for Indian Home Rule and her current post as president of the theosophical society. Emily spent some time describing how Annie Besant had found Krishnamurti in India and had seen his potential almost immediately.

Robert Lutyens, now sixteen, was two years younger than Celia. He was tall and thin like his mother and looked like a Lytton; that is, he had a thin face and a sharp nose, a pallid complexion, light blue eyes and reddish-brown hair. He had no academic flair but he did possess a love of cricket and a talent for painting, and an overwhelming desire to prove himself. He applauded the loudest as Annie Besant was introduced.

"Have you heard Mrs Besant speak before?" he asked Celia.

"No."

"She's wonderful," said Robert. "You can't help believing in theosophy after you hear her."

"Can't you?" said Celia. She frowned slightly. While she didn't want to publicly contradict the views of her mother and her younger brother, her cynicism regarding theosophy remained.

"I don't believe in any faith," said Celia.

"You will," said Robert.

Sitting behind them, Kit Drewe could hear Lutyens give a derisory cough to that last statement from his son.

"So, you don't even know what Mrs Besant's talk is about?" Robert said to Celia.

"No," was the whispered response. Robert put his hand into his jacket pocket and pulled out a cutting from the paper. "Read this," he said, shaking his head disapprovingly.

Celia looked at her brother, thinking that he had mastered some of their mother's mannerisms quite admirably. "Patriotism and theosophy," read

Celia out loud. "A talk by Mrs Annie Besant on theosophy and the obligation to fight a moral war."

"At school," said Robert, "we're all in favour of giving the Hun a bloody nose."

A moral war, thought Kit. What a contradiction in terms. Europe had drawn up the battle lines because the Austrians claimed that their Prince Regent had been assassinated and Serbia had done everything to hide the terrorists that had shot him. The Austrians claimed that Serbia had planned and then hidden the crime, and when asked to be open and honest with Austria, they had declined. The Serbians had said the opposite, and once the war escalated, everyone seemed to try and take the moral high ground.

"I just don't see that a war was necessary," said Celia.

Lutyens nodded in agreement and then looked at his son before saying, "Everyone just seemed a little bit too keen to get started and, well..." Lutyens kept chewing on his pipe. "I thought that diplomacy could still find a solution."

Robert looked disapprovingly at his father. He was about to say something, but Lutyens continued.

"I'll support our men and our country with every breath that I have; it's just that I don't believe we have to accept unquestioningly everything that our government does."

The audience went quiet as Annie Besant walked to the front of the stage.

"Theosophists," she began, "brothers and sisters. Each one of you here is my brother and my sister." Her voice was loud and clear, and Annie Besant commanded the stage. "There are great uncertainties in life, but I am certain of this," she paused for effect, "that the British spirit of honesty and fair play will prevail. It means that, despite the adversities that we must face in the coming months against the German brutality visited on our friends in Belgium, we shall ultimately prevail." Once again there was a slight pause. "We shall stand beside our friends and despite the lies that the Germans will tell about us, you can rest assured that we will unflinchingly follow a path of fairness and honesty." There was another pause. A number of the audience applauded vigorously. "The theosophists are part of a plan. We must each take a step upon a path, and we must endeavour to make the right choices when the great questions are placed in front of us. Krishnamurti talked about faith, but we must have faith that our leaders will take us along the right path."

"I have a question," said Kit, who had stood up. Annie Besant had not expected to be interrupted and it was a moment before she registered what was happening. The applause stopped.

"What you have so far said is just a piece of the truth," said Kit, "spun around a lie. I was there in Austria when Franz Ferdinand was shot. All that the

Austrian people wanted was to know the truth; all they wanted was for all the criminals who shot the Prince Regent to be brought to trial, not just that boy who pulled the trigger." Kit felt everyone looking at him. He didn't care. "They demanded justice and when Serbia would not hand over the criminals, they felt that they had no option but to go to war. Why is this brutality? Would we not have done the same thing? And now that Germany stands next to Austria, why do you criticise them?"

Annie Besant didn't answer the question but stared at Kit. Kit Drewe picked up his Panama hat, and in the silence, he turned and walked out of the Theatre Royal.

Chapter 28

Celia heard the front door thud shut soon after six. She had known that her mother and Krishnamurti would be going early, but it still brought about a deep ache in her stomach. She turned over the white cotton-covered pillow and placed her head onto the cold material. However, thoughts were spinning around her head; too many and too potent to allow her to sleep again. She considered getting up and going downstairs but decided that to stay in bed under the crisp white sheets was the lesser of all evils.

As a child she would have written all her disordered thoughts down in her diary, ordered each anxiety into a table of importance, and addressed her concerns one by one. However, now she simply let them flood over her. Some thoughts were so disjointed and strange that she did not even think twice about them. Her main concerns centred on her mother and how she never seemed to be at home. Celia had grown up accepting that her father would often be abroad; he had his jobs in India, Spain and Italy, but her mother had always been the bedrock of the family life. Now she was on the road giving her talks about theosophy and when she wasn't talking, she went to Cornwall to look after Krishnamurti. Celia was now the matriarch of the house with Nanny Gardiner, cook and the maid playing their parts.

That concern led on to Krishnamurti. However much she tried – and she had at times tried awfully hard – she found she could not genuinely dislike Krishnamurti. It was becoming a source of irritation, as she had made a promise to herself that she would never like him because he had taken her mother away. In order to overcome what she referred to as the 'Krishnamurti paradox' she had decided that the best way to treat him, when they were in each other's company, was to tease him – and to her great delight she found that she was rather proficient at this.

The second anxiety that kept her awake concerned the war, for though she supported her country, she felt that everyone seemed to have lost their heads. For the last week her friend, Margaret Ellis, had done nothing but wave the flag. Every time they had met, she had insisted that they go to some rally or event in support of the war. First, it was a meeting of the suffragettes in which it was agreed that they would give their full support to the war effort. Second, it was a parade along the Mall. In the last week Celia had only managed to get out once on her horse and then she couldn't get to a decent gallop as there seemed to be hundreds of soldiers walking in the parks. It did seem to Celia an obvious question that, in a time of war, why was half the British army hand in hand with their fiancées in Hyde Park? It appeared to her that, if the country really was in dire straits, they really ought to be doing something much more constructive.

An hour passed and the sunlight continued to creep through the curtains. Celia made one last effort to get back to sleep – put her head under the pillow to block out the light and closed her eyes. However, try as she might, sleep was not forthcoming. She had enjoyed herself yesterday – an afternoon with her brother and her father and then back home and dinner as a family and, of course, Krishnamurti. Her brother Robert had been surprised by how few people had come to hear Krishnamurti speak and even more surprised when someone stood up and criticised Annie Besant. Celia almost wanted to applaud the man behind her, but it would have embarrassed her mother if she had.

"I had expected it to be at least half full," Robert had said to her. Celia had looked around the near-empty theatre. The audience had been mostly made up of middle-aged, middle-class theosophists. She knew most of the people there by sight.

The final thing that was gnawing at her was her brother Robert. Like a lost puppy he had been following her around since the beginning of the holidays, and she felt she could hardly walk out of the house without him in tow. Like a shadow he had followed her on nearly every occasion when she, Margaret Ellis and Jenny Stanton had gone out; although, to Celia's relief, the suffragette meeting proved one rally too far. When Margaret had said she thought that if the war went on there ought to be conscription, he had agreed. When Jenny had said that any man who did not volunteer was nothing more than a coward, he also agreed. Celia was worried for a while that Robert would try and sign up and told Margaret and Jenny that because of his age they should not encourage such thoughts. She also noticed that he now seemed to spend more time in the bathroom than she did and, although she did not mention it, he seemed to be trying to grow the most ridiculous moustache.

Her father was now home for two weeks before his next trip to India, and she thought it might be a good idea if Robert spent some time with him. At the moment, they were like chalk and cheese; Robert was so like his mother in so many ways. Celia hoped that in the following two weeks Robert and her father could find some common ground as they appeared to be disagreeing on nearly everything, except the cricket. On the war, Robert had expressed his opinion that he was jolly well pleased that the Hun was now about to get their comeuppance. Her father had replied that he thought it sad that everyone was just a little bit too keen to start the killing.

Celia got out of bed. A few days away might be just what she needed, and Aunt Gertrude would be the perfect person to see. She had bags of common sense and would be able to give her some good advice. She realised too that it would also involve the usual lectures – Aunt Gertrude was probably the most Victorian person she had ever met. Celia washed and picked out from her wardrobe a long white cotton skirt and blouse. She packed a few other things into a small overnight case which she kept under her bed. She looked at herself in the mirror – she wondered whether she should wear her hair up or down, deciding on the former, and swept up her long auburn hair, fixing it in place with two sticks of black ash. A light layer of powder was added and a dash of lipstick. She was more than pleased with the result.

When she went down for breakfast, neither her father nor Robert was there. Just as well, thought Celia – one might object to me going and the other might want to come along. She scribbled a note to her father saying that she had forgotten to tell him that she had arranged a visit to Aunt Gertrude for a day or two – a small white lie, but one that wouldn't hurt anyone. She also thought that she had better send a telegram down to Munstead Wood to tell her aunt she was on her way. She asked the maid to telephone for a cab, looked at her watch and realised that if she put her skates on, she could still make the eight thirty-seven train to Thursley.

*   *   *

The train pulled out of Waterloo station on time, steam billowing out of the engine as it hauled the carriages towards the small Surrey village. Celia settled herself in a window seat and rested her face on the cold glass. She habitually did the same whenever travelling by train. She would look out of the window in a daydream until the pane became warm and then she would take her face away and find something else to do. In her bag, on the seat beside her, was a book by Jane Austen and her knitting. She knew from experience that her aunt would be asleep by ten and there would be little to do in the evening. Perhaps she could finish the jumper that she had started the last time she had been there.

There was smog over London so that, as the train pulled into Clapham Junction, she could not clearly see the new Arding & Hobbs building. She liked the building because it seemed to fit in with the surrounding architecture. So much of London now seemed to be changing. The new buildings that were going up were rectangular, large and utilitarian, as if cocking a snook at the grandeur of the Victorians. Everything seemed quick and loud, as if all the people had woken up and decided to live. While she liked the sentiment, she did not appreciate its look.

Thousands of people milled around – all waiting for trains to take them to the City, trying to continue with their lives despite the war. They were like a swarm of ants marching to the metropolis in bowler hats and dark grey suits. Celia noticed that most of them were middle-aged men and wondered how many young men had now enlisted.

The train stopped at a dozen or so small towns on its way out to Thursley. Her carriage remained empty as if, except for her, the world was going in another direction. Celia picked at the nail on her little finger on her right hand and then, when she noticed that she was doing it, stopped. She had not thought of a suitable explanation for going down and Gertrude would be sure to ask. The problem was that she did not want to pour out her feelings about her mother and Krishnamurti. While Gertrude would give practical advice, she was not the best person to go to for emotional support. Outside the sun was rising high in a brilliant sky and she looked out across the fields and began to regret the fact that if she had stayed at home, she might now be in the park riding.

She put down her book and placed her head against the glass of the window. It was once again pleasantly cool. What were her concerns that morning? She again arranged her thoughts into some kind of order. First, was her mother's absence and Krishnamurti; second, the war; and third her brother, Robert. She decided to tell Gertrude that she had come down because of her concerns that her brother might try to enlist, and that her mother was rarely there.

When the train arrived at Thursley Station, it was still a few minutes to ten and Celia thought about walking the two miles from the station to Munstead Wood. However, her choice of shoes that morning, the weight of her overnight case and the sight of an unoccupied taxicab outside the station hall changed her mind. She ran over to it before it had a chance to drive away.

"Munstead Wood," she said, getting into the cab.

"Miss Jekyll's house?" said the driver. "Are you expected, miss?"

"She's my godmother," replied Celia with a sense of self-importance.

The cab pulled away from the station. It was a journey with which Celia was familiar. She had been christened at the church near Munstead Wood seventeen years ago and then Gertrude Jekyll had held a party in the gardens. Of course, she could not remember the party, but she was told by everyone that it was a fabulous affair and there had been mention of the event in *The Times*.

The leaves of the trees along the road from Thursley station were still a bright green. Yellow asphodel could be seen flashing out from hedgerows, and in the fields white and golden daisies and buttercups bent in the slight breeze. It was a season which seemed unaware of the approaching autumn or the nakedness of winter. The asphalt road was grey as if the blackness had been scorched out of it by the sun. Ten minutes later, the taxicab turned off the road onto a cinder path. It came to a halt before a broad set of iron gates.

"Here is fine," said Celia handing the driver a sixpence from her purse. She opened the gate but instead of following the driveway around, took a short cut to the house along a stepping-stone path. The housekeeper, Mrs Hurley, was in the kitchen when Celia popped her head around the door.

"Hello, Hurley, is Aunt Gertrude up and about?"

"Not yet, Miss Celia."

The breakfast tray was almost ready to go up – Mrs Hurley was still waiting for one side of the toast to brown on the range.

"I'll take it up," said Celia.

"She'll be glad to see you, Miss Celia. She's been down in the dumps for the last few days."

Celia picked up the tray as Mrs Hurley continued.

"She feels that there ain't nowt for her to do since they started this war and even though she can't walk much now, Miss Jekyll just can't abide sittin' around doin' nothing."

Celia carried the tray out to the hall and up the stairs. She placed it on a small table on the landing and knocked on her aunt's bedroom door.

"Come in, Hurley," shouted Gertrude. Celia opened the door and whisked in the breakfast tray.

"Oh, it's you," said Gertrude, picking up her pince-nez from the bedside table and placing them on her nose. "I only got your telegram half an hour ago. You're not in any trouble, are you?"

"No," said Celia, keeping her head lowered.

"So, are you going to tell me why I have the pleasure of your company?"

"No reason," said Celia. "I just wanted to get out of the house and, well, I wanted to speak to you about Robert. I'm concerned that he might try and enlist."

"Is that it?" said Gertrude, keeping her eye on Celia. "Why didn't you just telephone?"

"I thought it would be nicer to come and see you, and as I was at a loose end I just hopped on a train."

"Well, I won't say it's not a pleasure; however, I do have company coming down later on this afternoon and I really can't put them off."

"Sorry," said Celia.

"Don't be," said Gertrude. "The men who are coming over are quite young and I had no idea how I would spend the afternoon with them. One of them has agreed to do some pictures of the garden."

Celia sat on the side of the bed.

"Toast?" said Gertrude, offering Celia the toast rack. "Hurley always makes me far too much." Celia picked up a piece and bit into it. "So, tell me," continued Gertrude, "what news do you have?"

"It's all very dramatic," started Celia. "They say the fighting is going to start soon now the first regiments have got to Belgium and everyone wants to do their bit. Robert wants to enlist, and I want it all to be over quickly."

"I meant," said Gertrude, breaking a poached egg with the side of her fork, "what's going on with you?"

Celia took another bite of toast and through a full mouth said, "Nothing much, I suppose. There's a boy, the brother of my friend Jenny Stanton, who's quite keen on me. I'm not sure Father likes him."

Gertrude asked why.

"Well, it's just that we went out last week and we got back home quite late. We sat down in the sitting room chatting for quite a bit and then Edward tried to kiss me. I think Father must have been listening because a minute or so later he was down, wearing his paisley dressing gown with his hair all over the place."

"Where was Emily?" asked Gertrude.

"She was out doing one of her talks somewhere in the north. Anyway, Father walked straight into the sitting room and poured himself a large whisky. He then sat in his old wingback chair, the one which Mother so hates, sipping at his drink without saying a word. Finally, after about five minutes, he turned to Edward, who, bless him, had no idea what to do, and said, 'I'm not keeping you up, am I?' Edward looked at Father and said, 'No, sir,' after which Father stood up and said, 'Well then, it was a pleasure meeting you.' He shook Edward firmly by the hand and led him to the front door. Poor Edward stood by the door without his coat and had to walk all the way home to Bayswater."

Celia and Gertrude continued to talk for the next two hours until Gertrude realised that guests were on the way and she would have to get up.

"Did I tell you who's coming?" said Gertrude as she got out of bed.

"No," answered Celia.

"Christian Drewe."

"I haven't seen him for years," Celia said, but just then the most intense feeling of *déjà vu* came upon her.

Chapter 29

"Where are we going?" asked Basil.

"To Munstead Wood," shouted Kit over the sound of the wind as it streamed off the aluminium-painted body of the Rolls-Royce Silver Ghost. The six-cylinder engine thudded as the vehicle made its way towards Surrey. Kit sat back on the tan leather seat and let the breeze fly into his face.

"Say what you like about Father," continued Kit, "but he has impeccable taste when it comes to motors." Kit breathed in deeply and then shouted to the chauffeur, "Put your foot down, Poley."

"We're already doing thirty-five, sir," replied Arthur Poley.

"Then take her up to forty!" hollered Kit in response.

After an indifferent, hazy morning in London, the air seemed fresh and clear in the Surrey countryside, weighed down only with the scent of summer. Lazy fields gave up clouds of soft dandelion balls as the car went by. Kit was enjoying being out and pleased that his mother had allowed Basil to come. A day in the country, thought Kit, was the perfect antidote to two weeks in hospital. It also meant that he had the car. However, after an afternoon at Munstead Wood they would have to go back to Wadhurst Hall and, for the first time in nearly three years, he would see his parents again.

"Don't expect Father to kill the fatted calf," Adrian had said.

Kit knew little about Munstead Wood except what he had read in *Home and Garden* the night before. It had been one of Lutyens' first designs and was immediately applauded as being a great example of the Arts and Crafts movement with a garden to match. It was built with traditional craftsmanship and Gertrude Jekyll had decreed that no bad work should be hidden behind dishonest plaster. It was to be her home, and so when the young Lutyens had suggested an expensive decorative addition to the external façade of the house, she had responded that, "My house is to be lived in and to be loved; it is not to be built as an exposition of architectonic inutility." Lutyens had no response and Gertrude had dined out on the fact that sometimes arcane words had their uses.

As they travelled, Kit thought about the commission to paint Munstead Wood. He concluded that Gertrude Jekyll must have seen some of his work before and liked it. He now felt that he must go ahead with his painting – it seemed to him to be the right path, his vocation, and he knew he must pursue it.

*   *   *

Gertrude Jekyll looked older than Kit remembered. She had put on weight to the point of being obese, and her hair was far greyer than before. There was a walking stick beside her, which she evidently needed. However, it was none of these things that made an initial impact on Kit when he first saw Gertrude Jekyll; instead, it was the young woman that sat next to her, drinking a cup of lemon tea. In a country of thirty-five million, he had now seen her in two places on two consecutive days.

"Good afternoon, Miss Jekyll," said Kit, as he walked towards Gertrude. "Thank you for inviting me down." He looked around and saw that Basil was a few steps behind him and struggling with his walking stick to keep up. "You remember Basil?"

"How could we forget the youngest Drewe?" replied Gertrude.

"Or the bravest," added Celia.

Basil looked down, trying to hide the fact that he was blushing.

"Now you've embarrassed the boy," scolded Gertrude. If Gertrude had intended to make Basil feel less self-conscious, her comment had the opposite effect. "The last time we met, of course, you managed to scare three old women out of their wits. Do you know that I blame you for at least a quarter of my grey hair, and I dare say that the same goes for your mother?"

"My mother doesn't have grey hair," stammered Basil.

"If she did," continued Gertrude, "then you would have been the cause." She took a sip of tea. "Perhaps you can get our guests something, Celia, and then perhaps, if he feels up to it, show Basil around the garden while I talk to Christian?"

"Of course," said Celia. "Can I get either of you some tea or a glass of lemonade?"

Two glasses of lemonade were requested and Celia stood up, straightened her long white cotton skirt and walked back towards the house. Kit again noticed how tall she had grown in the last three years, and also how she had changed

148

from a girl to a young woman. She had something of a Gaelic look to her, with her white skin, green eyes and reddish hair. Her voice had also dropped so that, at eighteen, she sounded as if she were some years older.

While Celia was away getting the drinks, Gertrude Jekyll talked about what she had in mind for the commission. It was to be a mixed media work – she had an idea of colour added to a sepia photograph. As she spoke, Kit looked around the garden trying to get a feeling for the media he would use. He struggled with watercolours, finding that often the diffusion of colours worked in a way different to what he intended, and he suspected that the problem might be worse on photographic paper. His preferred medium was oil paint, but oil paint would overwhelm the photograph. Pastel crayons were the obvious choice, but then everyone was doing that now.

A silence in the conversation followed until Basil suggested that he find Celia and that they start their walk around the gardens.

"An excellent idea," said Gertrude, "and have Hurley bring down Christian's lemonade. If Celia remembers anything that I have taught her, she will be able to take you to the parts of the garden that are in bloom."

Basil picked up his cane and began slowly walking towards the house.

"Oh yes!" shouted Gertrude after him. "Tea will be at three. You should be able to hear the church bells of Thursley. They ring on the hour."

Gertrude watched Basil as he went slowly up the pathway.

"You can tell a lot about the character of a person when they are faced with a problem. Some people make a meal of it. Your young brother just seems to get on with it with quiet modesty."

"The doctors hope that the operation he has just had will be his last. It all depends on how much more he grows. Something to do with the plates they had to put in."

Gertrude took another sip of tea.

"I hope you don't mind me asking," Kit said, "but what made you decide to commission these paintings of the house and gardens?"

"As you will have noticed, I also have trouble walking and getting around the gardens. If work needs to be done, then I'm reliant on others. I wanted to have a reminder of what my gardens look like now they're maturing and," she paused, "then there's the war. A week ago, when war was declared, I thought I would like to have the gardens painted. I wanted to preserve a little bit of England right now – before everything changes."

"And if I may also ask," said Kit, "why me? Landscapes aren't exactly what I'm known for."

"Perhaps not, but you paint with freshness and vibrancy and it's that feeling I want. I saw a catalogue with some of your work when you were in Vienna last year, and I don't like to see talent go to waste."

Gertrude then began to describe the three pictures that she wanted. The first would be of the house, with its extended roof of red tiles, the tall chimneys and the oak mullions at the windows. The second would be of the rose garden viewed from the house, with the yew hedges behind it. The third would be a view along a row of elm trees with Munstead Wood in the distance. Gertrude described each panorama in detail. She made suggestions where Kit should set up his easel, when the gardens would be lit correctly. Kit listened as she described the garden she had designed, planted and nurtured for the last eighteen years.

*   *   *

Celia was pouring the iced lemonade into a cut crystal jug when Basil arrived at the kitchen door. He watched her. Half a dozen squeezed lemons lay on a chopping board beside a bag of sugar. Celia placed the crystal jug on a tray and moved to a dresser, where she took out three glasses. Her white cotton skirt with its small pastel-coloured flowers embroidered on it appeared to dance around her ankles as she moved. Basil stood watching, noticing how the impression of her legs appeared as shadows whenever the light shone through the skirt.

Celia smiled at Basil and then she continued working, aware that he was still staring at her. She found it amusing for a few moments and then wished he would stop. His expression was the same as her own brother's whenever Jenny Stanton was around. It was a mixture of stupidity and serenity. She looked up from what she was doing and matched his gaze until Basil began to find her stare in that regardless manner exceedingly embarrassing.

"Miss Jekyll suggested Hurley bring out the lemonade for Kit and... if it won't put you out too much... whether you could show me around the gardens." Basil's eyes dropped and found their focus on a crack in one of the floor tiles.

"If you want," said Celia. "Shall we take our glasses with us?"

Celia poured two glasses and handed one across to Basil who took it in his left hand.

"Can you manage?" she asked, noticing that Basil was holding his cane in his right hand.

"I'm fine," said Basil, as he limped towards the garden. "It's nothing."

After some time, their conversation seemed to run out of steam. Basil liked cricket, motor cars and shooting. She had decided to read English literature at university the following year, and thus enjoyed reading, and also liked to dance. Even the subjects of horse riding and Castle Drogo could not ignite a conversation of any length. Basil could no longer ride, and she had not been back to the castle since the day of the accident. A pattern started to form as they walked around the garden. Every time Celia saw some unusual or beautiful flower, she would run off towards it and he would follow as best he could. They were therefore both quietly pleased when they heard the peal of the church bells from Thursley telling them it was teatime.

Gertrude, or rather Hurley, had set a table in the garden for tea. Steam wafted from the spout of a brown ceramic tea pot. Bread, honey, jam and a baker's dozen of plovers' eggs had been placed in the centre of the table. Beside this was a cake stand abundantly piled up with meringues and cream. Gertrude commanded the table as a field marshal commands his troops. She issued orders to Celia and reserved to herself those tasks that should not be delegated. She decided how many plovers' eggs each guest should have and gave to herself the additional one.

"Cook brings them up from Thursley especially for me – knowing they are my favourite," she said, peeling the first one. "I feel it might insult her if I ate less than my guests." With that, the first egg disappeared.

"And how are you progressing?" Gertrude asked Kit.

"I took a few photographs of each of the locations we discussed," he said, "and I made a few sketches. I think I have got a feel for the colours and perspectives. However, what I would like to do is come back again when I have more time and spend a few days just painting."

Gertrude agreed and the next ten minutes were spent looking at the pastel sketches that Kit had already done. Celia was impressed by how he had managed to catch the feeling of the garden in just a few simple sketches highlighted by some streaks or blocks of colour. As Kit put away his sketches, he remarked that he had seen Celia yesterday afternoon at the talk by Krishnamurti.

"I thought I recognised you," said Celia, as she poured more tea, "but I wasn't sure."

Basil, who had only eyes for the cake tray, leant over and took a small meringue boat filled with the rich pastry cream and strawberries.

"What did you think of Krishnamurti's talk?" asked Gertrude.

"There's certainly something extraordinary about him."

"You do know he's Celia's sworn enemy?" added Gertrude.

"Aunt Gertrude," said Celia, "you're exaggerating!"

"Perhaps," she replied, "but not much."

"So, you don't believe he is the reincarnation of Christ?" asked Kit.

"Actually," said Celia, "theosophists don't claim that he is the reincarnation of Jesus. What they say is that when his mind is ready the spirit of Lord Maitreya will inhabit him. It's difficult to explain." Celia paused for a second to gather her thoughts. "It's like a person who wins gold in the Olympics. Unless he exercises and trains every day, he will never win. It's the same with Krishnamurti. He has to meditate and study so that his mind is capable of accepting the spirit of the World Teacher."

Kit looked at his watch. It was three-thirty and he considered making his excuses. He was also aware that Basil was making inroads into his second meringue chantilly and feared that he might become car sick on the way back to Wadhurst Hall. And then there was an evening with his parents. Both he and Basil would need to get cleaned up and ready for dinner as his father still insisted on black tie. He suddenly realised that Gertrude Jekyll was asking him a question. He apologised. She repeated the question on how the castle was coming along.

"Slowly," said Kit. "I was there about three weeks ago. They've laid the foundations of the main building, but I understand my father is having second thoughts about the barbican and the west wing. Adrian told me that there were problems with building the west wing on the escarpment."

"And does anyone know whatever happened to that young engineer – the one who fought the fire with Adrian?" asked Gertrude.

"Hall," remarked Kit.

"I'm surprised you remembered his name," said Celia.

"We bumped into each other the other day," replied Kit. His hand instinctively went to the bridge of his nose. It was still sore when he touched it.

"What is he doing now?" asked Gertrude.

"He's in the army," answered Kit. "He's engaged to a nurse at St Thomas' Hospital."

"You must have had a good chat," said Celia.

"More of a short exchange," remarked Kit. The sun continued its journey westward. A cooler wind blew in from the east and Gertrude lifted her shawl that had rested on her lap and placed it around her shoulders. Basil persisted with his demolition of the cake tray.

"I'm afraid it's time that we made a move," said Kit, "before Basil finishes every pastry that you possess." Gertrude smiled. Kit got up. "I'll find our chauffeur and get him to bring the motor to the front of the house for Basil."

Celia also got up. "He parked at the back of the house," she said. "I'll show you the quickest way."

They left Basil and Gertrude together and walked back towards the house. As they spoke, Kit's view of her began to soften. On the surface she appeared very serious, but when she was talking, she had an enthusiasm which was almost childish. Three years ago he had found that irritating but now she was eighteen it was charming. He smiled to himself when he thought that her sworn enemy was the person whom her mother was following around.

"A penny for them?" Celia asked.

"Nothing," Kit replied. She looked as if she did not quite believe him. He embellished his previous remark. "I was thinking about these paintings that Miss Jekyll wants."

"Just do something similar to those sketches in your book."

"They're not very good," Kit answered. "They're just sketches."

Celia again looked over towards him. "Liar," she said.

"Sorry?"

"You said, 'They're not very good' and you were lying. They're beautiful."

"Have them," he said.

"Thank you," she replied, but when he handed her the sketchbook she felt uncomfortable taking it. They continued to walk along the path. "I didn't know you were a theosophist," she said.

"I'm not."

"Then why were you at the meeting yesterday?"

"It was a mistake," said Kit. "It's not much of a story. I was out and just wanted to get away from the crowds. Actually, I was hoping for a jolly good musical with some new tunes and I saw people going into the theatre."

"You wanted a musical and you got my mother, Krishnamurti and Annie Besant instead." Celia stifled a laugh. "I'm surprised that you didn't leave long before your argument with Annie Besant."

"Actually, I found Krishnamurti's talk interesting. I would love to believe that one day, despite religion or race, everyone will treat their neighbour with equal respect. Only then will there be an end to war."

"I didn't know you were a dreamer, Christian Drewe." Celia smiled and Kit could not help himself but smile back. It was only the third time since his return to England that he had spoken to someone about his feelings, and again it was to a young woman he hardly knew.

*   *   *

On the journey back to Wadhurst Hall, Basil shuffled uncomfortably in his seat. Out of the corner of his eye he watched Kit smoking a cigarette. He had wanted to enjoy his day out, but he hadn't. He had become embarrassed each time he had spoken to Celia and found himself staring at the shadow of her legs through the white cotton material. He thought he had acted pathetically and, in his embarrassment, had managed to talk only about cricket and shooting. She had taken him over every inch of the gardens, and he had tried his best to keep up with her but it just made his leg ache. After two weeks in hospital, it was more walking than he was used to. The only consolation was the tray

153

of cream cakes at the end of the journey. He then left the conversation to Kit, Celia and Miss Jekyll and had hardly said a dozen words. He hadn't spoken to Kit who had had to run around taking pictures and sketching and then impressed Celia with an effortlessness he could not imagine ever possessing.

"Do you ever doubt yourself?" asked Basil.

"Doubt myself?" repeated Kit. "That's a strange question to ask."

"Well, what I mean is, are there times when you're uncertain, when you just don't know what you should do or say?"

"All the time," said Kit.

"But you're always so confident."

"Some people call it arrogance."

"Well, you are sometimes a bit full of yourself – or at least you used to be."

Kit took the cigarette from his mouth and looked at his younger brother.

"I was joking you know." He waited a moment and then added, "Are you going to get to your point?"

"Well," said Basil, "what I wanted to know was why you don't support the war. Don't you mind what people think of you?"

"I do mind," said Kit, who stubbed out his cigarette as he spoke. "But as I keep on saying, I don't know if this war is right or wrong and therefore want no part in it. Everyone is warmongering – the government and the church. I read in the paper last week that an archbishop said that the passion of Christ is not love, it is suffering. Getting people to join up now seems to be the church's mission so that they can suffer and enjoy the passion of Christ."

"And what if you're conscripted?" asked Basil.

"Then I'd have to go," said Kit.

"And would you go for any other reason?"

"As long as you and Adrian understand the reason why I won't enlist, then I can't think of any reason why I should." Kit paused for a moment to collect his thoughts and to arrange them so he could explain things to his brother. "Let me explain," he began. "It matters to me what you and Adrian think of me. You, more than anyone else, have gone through a great deal because of me and I would hate you to think poorly of me. If I thought that you considered me a coward, I would join up in a minute."

"Really," said Basil, "you would join up if Adrian and I thought badly of you?"

"Really," said Kit. "That's why I need you to understand why I won't join up. I'm not afraid. I just don't believe that going into this war for the reasons the government have told us is right."

Basil turned towards his brother. "Of course I don't believe you're a coward."

154

Chapter 30

Kit Drewe, still in his dinner suit, straightened his black tie in the mirror. He had not set foot in his father's study for three years and in an already haunted house, he hoped he would now lay to rest the final ghost. There were memories in that room which trooped out in a disorderly pageant; it was a place often of silence, sometimes of lectures and, on rare occasions, laughter. It was here that Sir Julius had told him and Adrian that he intended to build Castle Drogo.

As Kit approached Sir Julius he was offered a cigar, something which his father had never done before. He took it, rolled it by the tips of his fingers and finally lit it, producing the smell he most associated with this room. He puffed at it and sent a cloud of blue smoke billowing into the air. His father had suggested that they retire to his study after dinner and, as had always been the custom in this house, he waited for his father to dictate the conversation. He had not come home wanting confrontation; nor would he have chosen to start a quarrel in his father's lair. He had little doubt that if there was an argument, he would come off the worse. What could he threaten his father with? He had been away from home for nearly three years and the suggestion that he could go off again seemed hardly a threat at all. However, he was also not prepared to be ridden roughshod over. If his father wanted honesty he would give him honesty, however unpalatable the aftertaste.

Sir Julius stood with his back to the open window. There was a hint of camomile caught on the warm breathless night. Kit moved over to a bookcase, where a large glass ashtray had been placed. He wondered whether his father felt equally as uncomfortable; how the conversation would start and where it would lead. It was bad enough to walk round someone on eggshells but to have to do it in your own house was intolerable. From the moment Kit stepped over the threshold, both men had realised that this conversation was inevitable.

"I heard you had some success in Vienna," began Sir Julius.

"Thank you."

"That you were accepted at Klimt's studio and then exhibited at one of the better salons."

"Yes."

"I don't see why there's all that fuss with Klimt but there's money to be made, I suppose, from those who are easily parted from it."

"So, you approve of me continuing?"

"I didn't say that," said Sir Julius, "and I don't think you would care anyway whether I approved or not. You never gave a damn about my approval." Sir Julius walked over to his drinks cabinet.

"Actually, I cared more than you probably thought," replied Kit.

"But you didn't need it," said Sir Julius. He passed Kit a glass of Armagnac. "Basil needs reassurance, even Adrian – but you – you have a mind of your own. You just need to take responsibility for the things you do. All your actions will have their consequences, and the trick is to see far enough ahead in order to work out what the consequences will be."

Kit couldn't keep the irritation out of his voice. Even now they couldn't talk as equals. His father had to talk down to him as if he were a child, receiving either a lecture or reprimand.

"I've taken responsibility for everything that I've done for the last three years and I don't need a lecture from anyone."

"Sit down," said Sir Julius, "and don't be so precious. I had the same conversation with my own father when he thought I might go off the rails."

"I hardly think that I've gone off the rails."

"Seducing a young nurse and brawling with her fiancé in public? In my day that was called 'going off the rails'."

Kit felt the irritation again welling up inside. It made him wonder what else his father knew about what he had done, even when he was in Vienna.

"I didn't realise I was being followed."

"Don't be so melodramatic," said Sir Julius, taking a sip of his drink. "I wouldn't waste my money having you followed and, to answer your next question, the hotel manager told me."

"Why would he do that?" said Kit, with more than a hint of annoyance. He simply hated the fact that his father had known what his next question would be.

"Because I own the hotel."

"And you're charging me to stay there," said Kit.

"Not the rack rate," said Sir Julius, grinning underneath his moustache. "Adrian made me promise to give you a fifty percent reduction."

"That was decent of him," said Kit.

"Not really," said Sir Julius. "I wouldn't have charged a penny, but Adrian pleaded your case so admirably that I thought I ought to concede."

Kit put down his cigar.

"Let me get this right; you would have let me stay for free at the Bristol Hotel but I'm paying because Adrian argued my case."

"You have to remember," said Sir Julius, "that Adrian has many qualities that you and I do not possess. However, I sometimes think that commerce was not a natural choice for him. You on the other hand... but you were dead set on becoming a painter."

Sir Julius filled up the glasses.

"I saw Celia Lutyens today," said Kit.

"Basil said so."

"She's grown up."

"They're a strange bag, that family," said Sir Julius. "I instruct Lutyens to design a castle for me and he gives me something which is likely to cost three times as much as the budget. His wife looks down on us because she thinks of us as new money. She runs around like some infatuated schoolgirl after that Indian boy with only thruppence to rub together and leaves her family to be brought up by their daughter."

"She's not like either of them."

"I remember her as being quite determined. Proud people never see their own faults," said Sir Julius.

"Well, she wasn't like that at all," said Kit. He puffed at his cigar. "Actually, she has a lot of humility. She showed Basil round the grounds and was quite happy to make lemonade for everyone."

"Did she?" said Sir Julius. "I understand you went to the hospital every day when Basil was there."

Sir Julius looked at Kit. Kit realised they might soon be stepping out on thin ice. He had not lived at home for the last three years with the operations on Basil's legs, with the limp and the cane, the tears at night and his young brother's frustration at not being able to ride or play cricket.

"I thought I should," replied Kit.

"But you were not there for the first two operations. You decided to run away to Vienna."

"I thought I was not wanted here," said Kit. "You made it clear to me that I was not welcome."

"I may have been wrong to have done that," said Sir Julius. "Anyway, Basil asked me to settle things with you."

"Basil?" said Kit.

"Yes, Basil," replied Sir Julius. "While you two may have fought like cat and dog when you were growing up, he actually looks up to you. And although he may walk with a limp for the rest of his life, he has channelled all that energy he used to have into studying."

Kit was worried that if he said "Basil?" one more time, he would sound like a broken gramophone.

"So, he's doing well at school?"

"Top of his class," said Sir Julius. "Everyone is saying that he is a shoo-in for Oxford or Cambridge. He's a perceptive young man."

The conversation finished and Kit was excused. Sir Julius said that he had some work to do. He mentioned that he had got a new contract for transporting supplies for the government but already the costs of freight had escalated and that he would need to raise some money – in fact a lot of money.

As he was leaving the room Kit stopped and looked back at his father, who was already getting out his papers. He had always admired how his father addressed a problem until it was resolved. However, he could not see the point of it all. It seemed to Kit such a ridiculous game; counting success or failure by the money accumulated. He could not understand why his father kept on at it, there just seemed to him to be no point when at the end of the game the king and the pawn would be laid back in the same box.

Chapter 31

Arthur Poley lifted a pewter tankard and drank a mouthful of beer. He could hear the footsteps of his wife and two sons in the kitchen as they washed the plates. On the surface his world had appeared to change very little with the commencement of the war, but he knew that a ripple on a pond is caused by a great commotion beneath. He had been a young man when the First Boer War had started; however, this time the feeling in the country was different. People seemed to be losing any sense that they had. There was a palpable taste of anger in the air and the government was whipping everyone up into a state where they wanted to destroy the Hun – where the fight was personal. He worried about this – after all, it was not very English.

Arthur Poley looked at his hands as he held the tankard. They were rough from thirty-five years working on the land, first in charge of the stables and now in charge of Sir Julius' prized motors. He thought that the change from horses to cars was a retrograde step. There was something solid about horses – they had souls. Anyone who worked with horses knew how intelligent they were and how each had its own character. There was nothing in a motor car except the cold metal. It was the same with the land. People were forgetting the old customs that he had been taught and that he had grown up with. There was now a feeling that nature was subservient to man and that people could do whatever they liked without consequence. You can't push nature around, thought Arthur Poley.

There was something about wars which made young men act strangely and he worried about his own two sons and those of Sir Julius. His two were young and headstrong and could be relied upon to get themselves into trouble. Fortunately, his youngest, George, was just sixteen and a few months older than Basil Drewe. Arthur therefore hoped that the war would be over long before George was old enough to join up. Luke, his eldest son, was however a different kettle of fish. He had little doubt that since Adrian Drewe had enlisted Luke would follow suit.

He was not surprised when Adrian Drewe joined up. He had known Adrian from the time when he could waddle. He had taught Adrian how to ride, in fact he had taught all of Sir Julius' children. Adrian was always the leader, always the one to get himself into scrapes, there was no subterfuge with Adrian. He had been captain of his cricket team at Winchester and then rowed for his college at Cambridge. Arthur had driven the whole of the Drewe family up to Mortlake when Adrian had rowed in the Boat Race and only lost by a hair's breadth. It was never said but everyone knew that Adrian would one day take over from Sir Julius.

Kit Drewe was different to his two brothers. Arthur Poley liked him; he stood up against his father just because no one else did. It had taken a while to teach Kit how to ride. Kit had found it difficult and therefore he had practised and practised until he was as good as Adrian. He set his own benchmarks and tried harder than anyone else to achieve them. He remembered that when Kit got his place at the Slade School of Art his mother had been so proud of him. Despite his apparent indifference to everyone and everything, Arthur Poley could tell that it was important to Kit that he had made his parents proud of him. Arthur Poley liked him because of this, because he did not wear his heart upon his sleeve.

Arthur finished his beer and placed the tankard on the table next to a corn doll that he and George had made two weeks earlier, after the first harvest of corn had been brought in. It was the custom to make a corn doll every year on the 1st of August. He had done so since a boy and his father and his grandfather had done so before him. Arthur made a mental note to put it safely away before he went to bed. The clock on the wall struck nine. His youngest son, George, would be going to bed soon and like nearly every other night, for as long as he could remember, his family came into the sitting room where Arthur had finished his pint of beer to hear a story before going to bed. Arthur Poley once again looked at the corn doll on the table.

"Generations long past have celebrated Lammas Day – the first day of August – and the day when the first corn of the season is turned into Eucharist bread. However, time has forgotten the festival except for a few men of the land who can still weave a corn doll from the last sheaf of grain. We then keep the corn doll safe until the next year. The reason we do this is because the doll is supposed to protect our family against the corn gods – whom my father called wanton and cruel. He told me that we needed to give an offering to these corn gods because if we didn't, they would refuse to cry and it was their tears that fell on the earth and fertilised the ground."

Arthur looked at George and said to him:

160

"Your great-grandfather told me that long, long ago the corn gods were thought to be amongst the most powerful gods for not only did they bring forth the new harvests, but they were also the divine mourners that brought back life after death. He used to tell a story that in his village, when he had been a boy, on Lammas Day a young girl would dance the whole of the day in order to feed new life into the weary corn gods and when she was exhausted and could dance no more, the villagers would make a sacrifice of a lamb. He used to frighten me by sayin' that in a time before Christ it was the girl herself who was taken to the sacrificial stones, and she would have her heart torn out of her and have it offered to the gods. He always said that unless somethin' were offered to the corn gods they would take their own retribution, which is why at the end of Lammas Day we make a corn doll as our own small offering."

"Now don't you go scaring George," said Arthur Poley's wife.

"I'm not scared at all," said George. "I'm sixteen and I've heard this story a dozen times and I can tell a tall story when I hear one."

"Don't go thinkin' that I was makin' that up," said Arthur Poley. "Your great-grandfather knew more about the land and its workin's than anybody I've known."

"I said I weren't scared and I ain't," and to prove his point George Poley reached across to the table where the corn doll lay and threw it in the open hearth.

PART V

Chapter 32

It rained almost every day in December of 1914, and as it came closer to Christmas the weather became darker. Slowly, and in dribs and drabs, news started coming back about life at the front. The war had changed, and the soldiers had dug trenches and now faced each other. The British generals decided that in the face of overwhelming firepower, a war carried out in trenches was the only option. They gave up their mobility to gain protection. It took an extraordinary feat by one army to overrun the trenches of the opposing force. It became a war where opposing armies attacked, counter-attacked, and defended from relatively permanent systems of trenches dug into the ground.

There were also rumours that these trenches were overrun with both brown and black rats. They would gorge themselves on human remains, eating at the dead soldiers' eyes and eating through into the stomach. They often grew to the size of a small cat. During nighttime the soldiers became more and more afraid of them as they would, with impunity, scamper across their faces in the dark. During their sleep the soldiers would sometimes convulse, as if trying to sweep rats from their faces. In the winter of 1914, they started causing increasing infection and contamination and then there was the never-ending problem of lice.

*　　*　　*

Rose woke just after six. She looked across the bed at Peter who seemed fast asleep and decided she had to get to work. His salary as a lieutenant in the Royal Engineers paid the rent on the two rooms that they had taken but there was little left for anything else. Rose slipped her legs from under the sheet and onto the worn carpet. She stood up, shivered in the chilly December morning, and made her way to the bathroom that they shared with two other families. Fortunately, it was vacant. Peter heard her leave and opened his eyes after she had gone. He was resting with his shaved head on one hand as she came back into the bedroom.

"Good morning, Mrs Hall," he said.

"Good morning, Peter."

He took her left hand and looked at the thin gold band on her fourth finger. "Happy?"

"Of course," she said.

"Nae regrets?"

"None."

"Do you really have to go to work?" Peter asked. "Can ye nae take a day off for your honeymoon?" He pulled her closer and lifted his head to kiss her. She moved her face away slightly and his lips pressed upon her cheek.

"No," she said and started to get dressed.

"I'll miss you," Peter said. "Anyway, we shall go out tonight. I've booked a table at the Corner House."

"There?" said Rose. "Why on earth did you choose that place?"

"I thought you liked it," said Peter. "It always used to be one of your favourites."

"It's fine," said Rose, but she did not feel fine. The last time she had been there was with Kit Drewe on that night when he and Peter had ended up fighting. Now Peter was suggesting that they go back. She wondered whether Peter was somehow testing her, playing a game that she did not understand. She decided it was unlikely. Peter wasn't like that and anyway, he couldn't lie to save his life. Perhaps, she thought, he was trying in his own clumsy way to say that the past was forgotten and forgiven. However, even if he had the best of intentions, she did not feel happy; how could she? How close had she come to throwing him over that night? But instead of following her heart, she had agreed to marry him and while she wanted the marriage to work, she did not feel she was in love with him.

Peter scratched under his armpit and then picked up an old copy of *The London Magazine* which was lying beside the bed and started flicking through it.

"Have ye read this?" said Peter.

"Read what?" asked Rose.

"This article about the trial of that Serb, Gavrilo Princip, who murdered Franz Ferdinand and started this war. It says here that he told the court he wasn't a criminal because it was Austria who had invaded his country. He did say he was sorry for killing Franz Ferdinand's wife. It also says that because he was only nineteen when he fired the shots, he couldn't be sentenced to death.

The lucky bastard's going to sit out the whole war somewhere safe."

"Don't swear, Peter, I don't like it."

"Well, he is a lucky so and so. Anyway, be a dear and put the kettle on before you go?"

He scratched himself again.

*   *   *

At the Corner House, Peter and Rose had been given a table next to the dance floor and ate their supper quietly with a bottle of sparkling wine. After he had finished his pheasant, Peter excused himself for a moment. As soon as he had left the table the waiter came over to clear away the plates and fill Rose's glass.

"It's always a pleasure to see Madam again," said the waiter. Rose looked up and recalled him from the last time she was there; she remembered that cold sneer.

"Thank you."

"Will Mr Drewe be joining you later this evening?"

"No," said Rose, looking around to see if Peter was coming back. "Unfortunately, Mr Drewe won't be joining us."

"Such a shame," said the waiter, wringing his hands. "A proper gentleman."

Was it a shame, thought Rose. The waiter drew back, leaving her alone with her thoughts. She smiled to herself. She could remember how Kit had skipped lightly around the dance floor. How he pulled her towards him as he danced and how his cologne smelt of cypress and lemon; like waking up in a cedar forest. She saw Peter coming back and hoped that they could go soon. While Peter could now dance, it was all so regimented. She decided that she would not dance again even if he suggested it. However, Peter stopped at the table next to them and started talking to a middle-aged lady.

"What did she want?" asked Rose when Peter came back to their table.

"She said that she had overheard us talking about our wedding and told me that she thought you were very pretty."

"Oh!" said Rose, smiling.

"And that I would have to keep you safe when I went back to the front."

"What do you think she meant by that?" asked Rose.

"She said that when I was not at the table and the waiter had come over, all you did was look around for me, smiling happily to yourself. She said, 'She's so in love – you can see it in her eyes.'"

The music stopped and Rose looked over to the woman who smiled back at her.

*　　*　　*

Rose continued to stare into the darkness of her small bedroom as Peter breathed heavily. He had fallen asleep soon after they had finished making love, and three hours later his heavy rhythmic breathing had not changed. Rose felt tired. She wanted to shake him by the shoulders and wake him up; scream at him that she felt trapped and lonely. It had been less than three days since she said, "I do" and she had already felt the first degree of separation.

Her eyes were full of tears. Tomorrow Peter would ask her if she was happy, and she would lie and then lie and lie again. She wondered how many lies she would have to tell before their lives drifted irretrievably apart. Would they wake up each morning a little further away from each other and by degrees find that they had nothing in common? That old woman in the Corner House could see that she was in love, but had wrongly assumed that it was with Peter. She had known Peter for over four years; however, he still had no idea what she was thinking. She wondered whether she ought to pack her bags and leave him, but that was not fair. He had done nothing wrong. He simply told her to choose on that night when he had hit Kit Drewe. He had given her an ultimatum – marriage on his next leave or that they would end their engagement. She had thought with her head rather than her heart – always a mistake.

She wondered how she would get through the next two weeks. She would talk about her day in the hospital, but he would not talk about the last three months in Belgium. And how she resented his silence! When he had worked as an engineer, he would talk about shear strengths and though she had understood almost nothing of what he said, she had enjoyed the fact that he thought she did. Now when she asked him about what it was like at the front, he would talk but say nothing: it was noisy, it was very muddy. She understood what a war involved. She had seen its effects as soldiers were brought back home and into her wards at St Thomas'. But now, she saw a different, more personal consequence.

She had asked Peter the night before about stories she had heard of young boys, some no older than fourteen, helping to build the trenches. She said that in the hospital wards there were rumours that the engineers had put young Belgian boys to work at the front because they could work bent over all day. He had shrugged. She had asked him how he would feel if they had a son and they made him go to fight at the age of thirteen.

"They're all sixteen now," he had answered and continued watching her undress.

"So there's no truth in those rumours then?" she had asked.

"I didn't say that," he had replied, "it's just that all those boys are dead."

He seemed so unaffected by it all – so disembodied from the horror of it. She had not wanted to make love but he had, and he had got his way.

His leave would be over in ten days and then he would go straight back to the front. She could have taken a week off work. The matron had said they could muddle on without her clumsiness for a week, but Rose knew they were desperately understaffed. There had been a surge of young middle-class girls joining up as nurses and many of them could not cope. She spent at least half an hour a day with her arms wrapped round someone's shoulders, wiping away tears, and an equal amount of time explaining that bedpans did not clean themselves. She could not afford the time off work, even if she wanted to take it, and had no idea what she would talk to Peter about for a week anyway. The thought of a lifetime with him made her want to cry.

"Are you still awake?" he said, through sleep-stained eyes.

"Yes," she said quietly, "go back to sleep." He did.

Too many thoughts were going on in her head. She could not believe that she would ever now find love or want to dance again. She got up and made her way out of the bedroom into the living room and tucked her legs up under her on the small living room settee. She felt no closer to knowing how to find happiness. She had always wanted to be in love, but getting married had not given her the key to that door. When she fell asleep, she was thinking of Kit Drewe. She remembered how he had looked that last time she had seen him. Although she had said nothing to him, he had looked at her with concern. She recalled him standing with his shirt half undone with blood on it, and such ferocious emotion in his eyes.

Chapter 33

The journey from Exeter to Drewsteignton took less than forty-five minutes. By the narrowest of margins, the car avoided a ditch at Cheriton Bishop and on Fingle Bridge a horse bolted. Kit Drewe felt rather pleased with himself and when he pulled into Adrian's driveway, Adrian leapt out of the vehicle and opened the garage doors.

"Not bad for a first attempt?" shouted Kit above the thumping of the engine. He managed to crash the gears again and the wince on Adrian's face said all that was needed.

"Come on, we're late," said Adrian, as Kit got out of the motor.

"If you had told me we were going to have to lunch with Archibald Drew, I don't think I would have come," said Kit.

"Sorry," said Adrian. "I promised to see him when I was back, and this was the only available day. He did say he would arrange a meal and anyway, except for the housekeeper and the cook, who only comes when needed, I couldn't keep staff on – not on my pay."

"Look, don't get me wrong, I have no problem cadging a free lunch, but couldn't you have done a little bit better than Archibald Drew?" Kit pulled his coat around him tightly as he left the garage. A cold December wind blew off the moor and nipped at any exposed skin. Adrian lit a cigarette and offered one to Kit who took it eagerly. They started walking the two hundred yards along the road to the old rectory.

"So, what's the story with Father?" said Kit.

"What do you mean?" asked Adrian.

"My allowance," said Kit, flicking cigarette ash onto the pavement. "It's been cut by half."

"Mine's been stopped," said Adrian. "He has money problems."

"Father?" said Kit.

"His money is tied up with importing supplies for the government and food for the Home and Colonial Stores. He has assets, lots of assets, but he is having huge problems finding money. He is also losing a lot of ships to the German U-boats."

"He's always been rolling in it," said Kit, with a hint of surprise.

"And he will be when the war's over," answered Adrian, "but as I said he's lost a number of ships and now the government contract is up for renewal. Cecil Facey is squeezing him for more stock in father's company."

"Cecil Facey?"

"He used to be something in the Admiralty but has now been made Minister of Trade in Asquith's government; don't you read the papers?"

"So will Father pay?"

"As far as I can gather, he'll have to," said Adrian. "Father needs that government contract and he'll give anything for it." He threw his cigarette on the ground and crushed it out with the ball of his foot. It hissed slightly on the frosted tarmac. "Let's get inside," he continued, "it's freezing out here."

Archibald Drew opened the front door of the rectory. He was very much as Kit remembered him. The top of his head was bald, and tufts of grey, wispy curls grew out vigorously from the side of his head. Once again Kit's initial thought was of a lapsed monk from an obscure monastic order.

Adrian and Kit were led into the living room. Nothing had changed much; piles of books were everywhere and even the dust still danced in the light at the window.

Sweet sherry and questions about the war would be how Kit later described that lunch at Archibald Drew's, but such a description gave no indication that he quite enjoyed himself. He learnt more about Adrian's training in Aldershot than if he had spent a dozen days with Adrian, and in addition to two helpings of rare rib of beef, he also got some family gossip.

"I understand that your name is being linked to a young lady," said Archibald to Adrian.

"It's one of my mother's little ideas," answered Adrian, "it's something and nothing."

"You didn't mention this to me," said Kit.

"As I said, it's something and nothing," answered Adrian a little more emphatically.

"But wouldn't she be quite a catch?" said Archibald. "I also hear that Miss Facey is rather attractive." Kit whistled when he heard the name.

"Miss Facey," he asked, "wouldn't happen to be related to Cecil Facey?"

"His daughter," said Archibald. "Do you know her?" However, Kit wasn't listening. He looked towards his brother.

"I don't even know her," said Adrian. "I've seen her at one or two of

Mother's balls but that's it. Anyway, even if I wanted to get married there's a war on and in three weeks' time, I will be going to the front. I'm in no position to marry."

"Nonsense, my boy," said Archibald, refilling his sherry glass. "You're single and there's no other impediment in God's eyes. When I was in the Transvaal in the Boer War, I married at least twenty soldiers. The happiest soldier is a married soldier." Archibald took another large sip of sherry and Kit noticed that his face was looking a little flushed.

"I could come back wounded," said Adrian. Kit could sense that Adrian wanted to change the subject, but Archibald carried on.

"All the more reason, my boy, to get married quickly. You'll have someone at home to look after you. It's in a woman's nature to want to care." Adrian stared at Archibald and Kit knew exactly what he was thinking. He had seen that stare a hundred times before as they were growing up and usually just before he got punched. Kit decided to intervene.

"Did you know, reverend, that our mother is having one of her New Year's Eve balls?"

"Actually, I did," answered Archibald, "and I also know that Miss Facey will be there as well." Kit inwardly groaned. "And I have also been invited," Archibald added.

"I can hardly wait," said Kit sarcastically.

He did not catch precisely what Adrian mumbled in response, but he thought he heard the words, "We'll see about that." Fortunately for Adrian, and perhaps even Archibald, the conversation was brought to a halt by the sound of the lunch gong, and they went into the dining room. The table was overburdened with food and Kit found he could hardly restrain himself from cutting into the rib of beef before grace had been said.

With a little effort and persistence, Kit moved the conversation from Jane Facey to Vienna.

"I've always thought of Vienna as a splendid city," said Archibald, finishing off his third glass of wine.

"You've been?" asked Kit.

"Not yet," said Archibald, "but there is St Mark's Square and a dozen churches on every canal."

Kit looked at him. "I think you are confusing Vienna with Venice," he said.

Archibald took another sip of wine. "Possibly – possibly – but I'm sure Vienna is a wonderful city, even without the canals. Anyway, my sources tell me," said Archibald, tapping at the side of his nose, "that you were quite a success as an artist."

"I'm not sure about a success," answered Kit, "but I was fortunate enough to be introduced to Koloman Moser while I was there, and he sponsored me."

"He's being modest," interrupted Adrian. "Kit exhibited with Gustav Klimt."

"I exhibited a few pieces in an exhibition that featured work from the Vienna Secession. However, it was only the once and I think they thought it too modern. I came back wanting to bring Cubism to England."

"And are you succeeding?" asked Archibald.

"Unfortunately, I haven't found a single cube yet."

Archibald laughed. Adrian rolled his eyes. He had heard this attempt at wit by Kit at least three times before.

"But I have received a commission for a few pieces – landscapes in mixed media."

"Congratulations," said Adrian, "you didn't say."

"It's only a few pictures of Munstead Wood. Otherwise, I am afraid to say that I have been having the quietest of times."

Chapter 34

There is nothing like a war to bring an old soldier out of retirement and for the first time in a decade, Admiral Charles Penrose Fitzgerald was positively enjoying himself. Admiral Fitzgerald was sixty-seven years of age and was waiting to be lowered into the ground when Gavrilo Princip fired his pistol in Sarajevo. Two months later he found that once again he had a purpose. After the initial rush to join up, the numbers of men who were prepared to enlist fell and the armed forces found that they needed to recruit. The government, frightened that conscription might prove politically unpopular, left it to the army and navy to play on pride and persuasion. "Your Country Needs You," Lord Kitchener pointed out. Charles Penrose Fitzgerald created a much more effective way of convincing men to enlist; he established the Order of the White Feather.

The Order of the White Feather had only one strategy – shame. The application of that strategy was uncomplicated – have a young lady, preferably pretty, place a white feather, the mark of a coward, into a young man's hand. It was simple, cheap and effective; all the things a retired Admiral of the Navy approved of in any line of attack. When the Order was created, Charles Penrose Fitzgerald looked around for prominent women to support him. One of the women who enthusiastically took up the baton was Emily Lutyens, and she in turn persuaded her daughter and her daughter's friends to join.

Celia chewed at a lock of her hair as her mother talked about the plan of campaign. It was, in Emily Lutyens' words, "the perfect time to find shirkers." Christmas Eve and the shops in the West End would be packed with young men looking for that last-minute present for their lady friends. Each man would be acutely aware that what a woman says she wants and what she actually wants are often poles apart. There would be that moment of realisation that the small trinkets they had already purchased would be inadequate to get them

173

to the next stage of their relationship. With less than twenty-four hours until Christmas morning, many men would realise that there was only one thing left to do – throw money at the problem.

"So," continued Emily Lutyens, "Margaret, Jenny and Celia shall go to Liberty's and the others will divide up between Harvey Nichols and Harrods."

Admiral Fitzgerald made a short address. He spoke of a way of life that had survived for a thousand years and that could only continue with effort from those at home and determination from those at the front. "The Hun," he said, his finger indicting a faraway enemy, "are raping and will continue to rape the women of those countries we have pledged to defend. Decency, honesty, courage, optimism and devotion to God are the qualities for which we stand."

Celia had heard a dozen similar speeches over the last few weeks. She reluctantly picked up her packet of feathers and put them into her coat pocket and left with her two friends, who were keen to do 'their bit' for their country. Her mother smiled at her as she left, and she tried to smile back.

As they walked from Bedford Square towards the West End, Celia said to Jenny, "Did you know we now have two Belgian refugees living in two of our rooms on the top floor of the house?"

"What are they like?" asked Jenny.

"They're very nice. They're called Monsieur and Madame Delville. It was Mother's idea to have them stay but now I think she regrets it. Mother likes having her own space and I think they feel she is being rude when she ignores them from one week to the next, and they think Father's mad because he is always making his little jokes that they don't always understand."

"It must be difficult for them and for you having them in the house," said Jenny.

"Oh, it's not so bad for me," said Celia. "In fact, it's been quite nice having them stay. As you know, Mother's trying to do everything and anything to help with the war effort. She tried saving fuel but all the walls in the house became damp and now we have mushrooms coming through the plaster."

"I didn't like to say anything," said Jenny, "but your house did smell a bit."

"You two," said Margaret Ellis, who had so far ignored the conversation, "stop chatting and keep your eyes open for any young men not in uniform."

"I do wonder," said Celia to Margaret as they got closer to Liberty's, "whether it should really be up to us to tell someone that he has no decency, honesty, courage or devotion to God."

"Don't start that again, Celia," said Margaret. "There's a war on and we are going to have to play our part."

Celia ignored her and continued, "I know and I'm not talking about the rights or wrongs of the war but about this – handing out white feathers. What gives us the right to point a finger at someone and call him a coward?"

"Cowards or traitors," said Margaret, "it makes no difference to me why they won't support our country. If men simply refused to fight for what this country stands for then we shall lose this war. Do you really want to be ruled by Germans? You heard what they're doing to the women in Belgium. If we don't fight now, then it will be too late when the Germans are marching down the Mall! We're fighting for what we stand for and if we don't, then the empire will crumble and so will our democracy and everything decent that comes from being English. If our men aren't prepared to protect us now when they're needed, they should pack up their bags and get out."

"Margaret's right," said Jenny, who rarely contradicted anything her friend said, though often did not agree with her wholeheartedly.

"I am just saying," said Celia, oblivious to Margaret who had pulled up sharply and was looking directly at her.

"Listen, Celia," Margaret said, "decide whether you're coming or not but stop whining about it."

Liberty's was now in front of them. The wind blew cold and bitter on a grey December day. Although it was not even lunchtime, it was still quite dark. There was a hint of snow in the air. Flurries of snow had fallen over the last few days on London and the Somme. Wrapped up in a thick fur coat and wool gloves, Celia did not envy those who had only a soldier's coat and very little else to protect them against the cold. No wonder her Aunt Gertrude had organised the women in her village to start knitting socks for soldiers.

It was Christmas Eve and it seemed to Celia to be wrong to hand out white feathers on the day before Christ's birthday. However, she was in a minority and decided it was best to just follow the herd. She knew why the suffragettes had agreed to support the Order of the White Feather; there had been hints from the government that it would be the *quid pro quo* for getting the vote after the war. That was one of the reasons why her mother had taken up the cause, that and the fact that Krishnamurti had gone to France to work in a hospital. There was little for Emily to do in England, now her precious Krishnamurti had left, and she couldn't sit still for five minutes without another cause to pursue.

For a few weeks it seemed to Celia that her household had returned to normal. Her mother was home, and her father was back from India, although only temporarily. She enjoyed the sense that she was again part of a normal family, and then her mother had taken up with the Order of the White Feather. In a moment of impetuousness, she had also joined, hoping that she could build a bond with her mother. It would be something that they could do together.

However, she hated each time she went out with the Order. She would tap someone on the shoulder or say excuse me; they would turn, and she would thrust a feather into their hands. They would look down, uncertain of what was happening, and then they would look at her. It was that last look that

175

stayed with her; a haunted, pitiful look. One boy had started crying and she took back the white feather.

Celia had admired those three hundred thousand men who had joined up on the first day of the war. She remembered the excitement as the crowds went out onto the street and congregated at Buckingham Palace and cheered the King when he came out on the balcony. She remembered how she waved a flag when the Expeditionary Force marched out from London and off to the front and how everyone said, "It will all be over by Christmas." But Christmas was here, and the war had only just begun.

It was now that she was beginning to see the arrogance of how the English approached the war. Only four divisions of regular soldiers had been sent to Belgium and the presumption that four divisions would be enough to see off an army of foreigners had been shown up for what it was. France had sixty-two divisions on the Western Front but mostly made up of conscripts. Russia had one hundred and fourteen divisions of infantry on the Eastern Front, many of them just peasants, unarmed and often without a uniform or even shoes. Germany brought to the field a total of eighty-seven well-equipped and well-trained divisions of infantry – nearly four million men. The four English divisions had fought courageously, but by Christmas had been repeatedly beaten, driven back and had been wiped out. The army was now in desperate need of recruits, but she hated having any part in it.

Liberty's was bustling with shoppers. The three young women passed through the ladies' department into an area that sold household gifts and silverware.

"There's a man over there," said Margaret Ellis, "who's not in uniform."

"Where?" said Jenny.

"Over there," said Margaret, pointing across the shop. Margaret stared at him to see what he was doing. Her black hair had been cut short and just touched the collar of her dark jacket. Her plucked eyebrows were pencilled in and arched as she spoke, giving her a hawkish expression. "Come on, Celia."

"What is it?" said Celia who was a step or two behind them.

"There's a coward over there," repeated Margaret.

Celia caught up and looked to where Margaret was pointing again.

"I can only see his back," said Celia.

"He's standing there trying to decide what he should buy," said Jenny Stanton.

"Are you sure he's old enough? He might be just a boy," said Celia.

"Nonsense!" said Margaret. "He's eighteen or nineteen if he's a day."

"I'm not sure," said Celia.

"We're in it together," said Margaret. "We agreed."

"Come on, Celia," said Jenny, "we did agree."

"That's right," said Margaret, who with Jenny walked over towards the young man who stood at an open display cabinet looking at an assortment of hip flasks. Celia followed a few paces behind. It was only as they got closer that they saw that he was with a shop assistant and another man who was standing behind a pillar.

"There are two of them," said Margaret to Jenny and then she looked for Celia. "Come on, Celia, for God's sake. There are two of them."

The young man had finally decided on a hip flask made of sterling silver. The female shop assistant took it away to wrap it and the other man walked to a nearby counter to look at cigarette cases. Celia took a step forward, still unsure what she was going to do. However, Margaret Ellis pounced, tapping the young man on the shoulder. He turned and looked at Margaret.

"This is for you," Margaret said, forcing a white feather into the young man's hand. He looked down to see what he had been given.

"Excuse me?" he said.

"Why aren't you in uniform, shirker?" said Jenny.

"I'm only just sixteen," said the young man. The other man came back quickly. He looked around, perplexed. The young man looked past Margaret and Jenny directly at Celia.

"Celia," he shouted. Celia's eyes dropped quickly, and she stood motionless, feeling a spot of colour rising in her cheeks and then flushing out as if she had been caught stealing. However, resolving that she must do something, Celia went forward towards Basil Drewe. She mouthed an apology and turned towards her two friends.

"Leave him alone!" she said.

Suddenly she found that Kit Drewe was standing next to her. She felt his hand on her shoulder and he stood between Margaret and Jenny and Basil. Celia felt that the odds had changed as there were now three against two.

"Do you call this patriotism?" said Kit. "Giving a white feather to a boy just turned sixteen, who can't walk without a stick?"

Celia could see the uncertainty in Jenny Stanton's face, but Margaret Ellis sneered at Kit with a sense of palpable distaste.

"Are you congenitally stupid?" said Kit, directly to Margaret Ellis. "Can't you see he's only a boy?"

"Sorry," said Jenny, who took a small but distinct step backwards, "we thought he was older."

"And what about you?" Kit demanded of Margaret. Margaret's face remained unchanged.

"You take it," she said. "What's your excuse?"

"It's not my war."

"Then take it, coward," said Margaret. Kit took the feather from Basil's hand and threw it back at Margaret. It fluttered, harmless, down through the air.

"Come on, Basil, let's go."

"Coward," she said coldly.

"I haven't got Adrian's present yet," said Basil.

"We'll get it later, Basil, when this lingering smell has left."

"Coward!" shouted Margaret.

"Basil, let's go."

"Coward!"

Basil and Kit started to walk away. Celia saw Basil turn towards her as they went.

"Thank you," he said and then he and Kit were lost in the crowd that had gathered to witness the scene. Celia didn't go with them. She had nailed her colours to the mast and needed to know where she stood with her friends. It was not only that she had not participated in handing out the feather, but had actively stood against them. Jenny might forgive her, but Margaret Ellis was quite a different matter.

Chapter 35

No one who knew her, except perhaps her nanny from her childhood, would have thought Margaret Ellis could bawl like a Billingsgate fishwife. It surprised both Celia and Jenny Stanton. The range of colourful language and the expressive way she described what she considered to be betrayal, was worthy of the coarsest parts of the East End. When she had finished her face was flushed and her dark eyes twinkled with menace. She perhaps never looked as animated or as attractive again, having stepped over the bounds of public decency without the slightest feeling of embarrassment.

She did not wait for an answer but turned on her heel and left. Jenny Stanton wondered whether to follow but decided in favour of discretion and so waited to see what Celia would do. Celia stood with her mouth open for a few moments until she gathered her wits, looked around her and decided she no longer wanted to be the object of attention. She began to push her way through the crowd that had congregated to watch.

"Pardon me," she said as tried to get past a red-faced old man with whiskers. He did not move. She slipped as she attempted to get round him. The large pin, which held her hair in place, fell to the floor and her long hair dropped across her white face. A young woman pushed forward and helped her up. Celia again looked for the door. She suddenly realised she was crying, and the crowd was again looking at her. She pushed on and then she was free of the people. She saw the door ahead of her and ran for it.

When she had got quite free of the crowd Celia stopped and looked behind her. Jenny Stanton, red-faced and equally out of breath, was following her.

"Well?" Jenny asked.

Well, indeed, Celia thought and she considered what she ought to do next. "I suppose I'd better tell Mother what just happened," Celia said.

"How is she likely to take it?"

"Badly," replied Celia. "Those two men were second cousins; Basil and Christian Drewe."

"Gosh," said Jenny.

"There will be all hell to pay. You don't give Basil Drewe a white feather and call Christian Drewe a coward and just walk away."

"So, what will your mother do?"

"I don't know," said Celia and she really hadn't any idea how her mother would take the news. Celia decided that it was best to get home as quickly as possible and try and repair any damage done. Except for the commission to design parts of New Delhi, Castle Drogo was still the largest project that her father currently had. She knew that Sir Julius was quite capable of sacking her father if he thought she had anything to do with handing out the white feather. It would make a massive dent in the family income, which seemed to Celia to be in bad shape as matters currently stood. She decided that Jenny would have to make her own way home and she hailed a cab.

"Thirty-one Bedford Square," she said to the cab driver. Despite the cold, she felt flushed and unbuttoned her fur coat. She sat back in the taxi counting the minutes as it slowly honked and crawled its way back along Oxford Street.

"What's the matter, dear?" said Emily, looking at Celia's face as she flew into the living room. "Is there anything wrong?"

Now she was standing in front of her mother, Celia was unsure where to begin.

"You're not going to be pleased," she began. She realised immediately that this was perhaps not the best way to begin giving bad news. Emily's face took on a suitably concerned expression.

"You're not hurt, are you?" Celia shook her head. "But you have been crying."

It wasn't a question and Celia wondered what she looked like. She pulled a lace handkerchief from her small underarm bag.

"That's going to do no good, Celia," said Emily, looking at the small lace handkerchief. "You look absolutely frightful. Now you may appreciate why a lady carries around a bag that can hold more than a handkerchief and lipstick."

Celia looked at her bag. It had been a present from her Aunt Gertrude for her seventeenth birthday and was considered very fashionable by all her friends, particularly Margaret Ellis. However, even she had to admit that it couldn't hold much more than loose change and she had nothing within it to repair the damage of a deluge of tears.

"Come with me," said Emily, leading Celia to the bathroom. "Now sort yourself out and tell me what happened." Emily turned on the tap and filled the sink. "I assume that one of those shirkers was rude to you?"

"No, Mother," said Celia. She looked at herself in the mirror. Her eyeliner had run. She tried dabbing away the black streaks with cotton wool, but it proved unsuccessful. She suddenly thought that she must have looked a state running through Liberty's like that.

However, what she felt would be nothing to how Kit and Basil Drewe would be feeling. "Thank you," Basil had said to her; but why on earth had he thanked her? She was no better than Jenny or Margaret. They had all gone there with the express intent of handing out white feathers.

"We went to Liberty's as arranged and Margaret Ellis saw a boy and decided to hand him a white feather."

Emily sniffed and looked at Celia as she was speaking.

"Anyway, I wasn't sure he was old enough and told her I didn't want anything to do with it – but you know Margaret. Nothing I said would stop her and she went straight up to the boy and pushed a white feather into his hand. I hadn't seen the boy's face, Mother – honest – otherwise I would have stopped her." Celia paused and looked at Emily. She regretted not continuing and had to take a deep breath before ending the sentence. "And when he turned round, I saw that it was Basil Drewe."

"You stupid girl!" exploded Emily. "Didn't you think to look before you decided to give him a white feather?"

"I didn't want to do it, Mother, really I didn't! I told them but... well... they just went off and I followed."

"What happened next?" said Emily. "I want every detail – everything!"

Celia narrated almost every word said and everything that happened. She explained how Kit had come back and what Margaret had said to him. She decided, however, to leave out some of the coarser language that Margaret used afterwards.

"And after that I just ran."

Emily's face remained pensive.

"What are you going to do?" said Celia.

"Nothing," said Emily.

"Nothing! You can't do nothing."

"To use a favourite phrase of Sir Julius, there are times, Celia, when you simply have to let sleeping dogs lie. I shall of course telegram your father straight away and tell him what happened. He has to know, just in case Sir Julius contacts him. However, don't breathe a word of this to anyone, not to your friends and especially not to your sisters or your brother. I will speak to Jenny and Margaret. If Basil Drewe thinks that you had nothing to do with the whole affair and came to his rescue, then let's not dispel that impression."

* * *

Rose's wedding to Peter had taken place on a Saturday afternoon a week before Christmas, 1914. A few days later she had gone up to Liberty's in the West End to buy curtains in her lunchtime break. The rooms that Peter had rented needed to be painted and she was excited to make them her own. As a married nurse, she no longer had to share rooms at the hospital with the other nurses. Peter had also opened a joint bank account and when she moved into her new home, there was already a chequebook in her married name. She looked at the torn blankets over the windows and decided that one of the first things she would buy would be curtains. She decided that she would go looking for some modern fabrics at Liberty's and then wait until the sales; after all, even the wife of a lieutenant was not made of money.

She had not expected Liberty's to be so busy on Christmas Eve, but it seemed that everyone was doing their last-minute shopping. She had gone up to the third floor and had been disappointed with the materials that they had in stock – and the ones that she liked were priced extortionately, and even in the sales would be far too much. Buying curtains would have to wait to the New Year when she could visit a haberdasher that she knew in Blackheath. She would then get something that would be just as nice, but at half the price.

As she walked down the stairs, she realised she had not yet got anything for Peter for Christmas. In the commotion surrounding her wedding, she had completely forgotten about it. She desperately thought about what to buy him – she decided on a lighter, a Ronson, as Peter had started smoking. It was then that she had seen Kit Drewe.

Kit was in a crowd, but she would not have mistaken him anywhere. He was wearing a grey suit and a long black coat with an astrakhan collar. Basil was next to him, and he was now nearly as tall as Kit. She hadn't seen either of them since the previous August. She had forgotten how elegant Kit was. He was smiling and talking to Basil, who was laughing in return. Kit seemed to glide as he walked – the same way that he danced. Rose smiled to herself. She had never enjoyed dancing so much with anyone. Basil still had a cane, but the limp was now less pronounced. She decided to say hello and find out how Basil was, and so hurried down the stairs. In the crowds she quickly lost her sense of direction.

"Excuse me," Rose said as she bumped into a tall young lady with auburn hair pinned up high on her head.

"It was my fault," replied the woman in response. Two other women in front turned and Rose realised that they were all together.

"Come on, Celia," said one of the other women.

"What is it?" answered Celia to her friend.

"There's a coward over there."

Rose moved on. She looked up to help get her bearings but had no idea where Kit or Basil might be, and decided she should go back to the stairs and see if she could spot them. As she turned, she thought she could hear Kit's voice shouting above the crowd and pushed her way in the direction of the sound. A few moments later, she saw Kit standing in front of her no more than ten feet away. He was standing next to his brother with the girl with the auburn hair beside him. In front of them were the two other women. One of them, with short black hair and black eyeliner, was shouting "Coward, coward, coward" – the words were spat out with such venom that they sounded like curses. Kit's face was red; he raised his hand. For a moment Rose thought he might hit the woman, but instead he threw a white feather at her, and the woman turned and stormed away. Rose continued to stare as Kit and Basil made their way through the crowd.

The young lady with auburn hair stood motionless for a moment and Rose noticed there were tears running down her cheeks. Celia turned her head left and right. She looked straight at Rose who dropped her gaze, and then Celia started to push her way through the crowd. She had only taken a step or two when she lost her footing and fell. Rose ran forward and helped her up.

"Are you all right?" Rose asked, but she did not get an answer as the girl scampered off.

Rose then looked down by her feet and saw a hairpin. The end glinted and she bent down to pick it up. It was silver and topped with a pearl. Rose looked at it for a moment; it was probably worth a month's pay and for a moment she thought about putting it into her pocket. She hoped she could catch up with Kit and Basil but when she got to the exit they were nowhere to be seen. She continued to look around and then decided that she ought to hand the hairpin to someone at the shop as she was certain that the girl would come back to see if it had been handed in. It was then that she saw the other girl.

"Excuse me?" said Rose, walking up to the young woman.

"Yes?" said Jenny Stanton.

"Are you a friend of that woman with auburn hair?"

"Yes," said Jenny a little hesitantly.

"She dropped something. I wanted to make sure it got back to her."

Jenny Stanton asked what it was, and Rose held out the silver and pearl hairpin. Jenny Stanton insisted on taking Rose's address in case Celia wanted to send her a note thanking her. Rose returned to the store and bought a lighter, which was far more expensive than the Ronson she had initially thought about, a Dupont. She decided to pay for it from her own savings; after all, she did not want Peter to know how much she had spent on his present.

It was five hours later when Rose returned to her apartment in Balham. She sneezed as she walked through the door. The rooms were still dusty; however, it was just too cold to air the place out and the small coal fire in the living room hardly gave out any heat.

"Bless you," Peter said as he sat reading the paper. She looked down at the wedding ring on her finger – she was still not used to it. She shivered in the cold December evening air and then slammed the door behind her.

"Someone trod on your grave?" asked Peter.

She shook her head while looking at Peter. He still seemed exhausted, and his face was haggard and grey. She wanted to talk about their future, but with him stationed on the front line in Ypres it seemed as if she was tempting fate.

"I'd never been to Balham until we moved," Rose began.

"I know it's not much," replied Peter, who continued to read his paper.

"I wasn't complaining," said Rose. "I know I'll grow to love it here once it's decorated. I went looking for curtains today."

Peter looked up. "You didn't buy any?" he asked. "When the war's over I hope that we'll be able to get something much better than just an apartment in Balham; so don't waste my money on things that aren't really necessary."

"It's just some curtains I was looking for to make the place more cheerful. I'll get some cheap material from a haberdasher in Blackheath and get my mother to make them."

"So where did you go? Did you go over to Blackheath?"

"No," said Rose. "I went up to the West End and had a look at the shops."

"And did you see anything?" asked Peter.

"Well, not exactly," answered Rose.

"Not exactly is not an answer."

"Well, I saw Basil Drewe and his brother."

Peter folded the paper and placed it on the table.

"And which brother would that be?" he asked, his voice quiet and slightly trembling.

"Kit. Kit Drewe," she answered equally as quietly.

"And what did you say to him?"

"I didn't speak to him," said Rose. "I promise."

Peter stood up and looked at Rose. "That's not like you," he said. "If you saw an old friend, you'd make a point of speaking to them."

"But I didn't," said Rose. "I promised you. I promised you when I agreed to marry you that I would never see him again and I haven't."

Peter smiled. "But you have seen him."

"No," said Rose, her face going red. "It was just an accident and all I was going to say was hello to them."

"So you were going to speak to him?"

"Just to say hello," insisted Rose. "Just to say hello, I wasn't going to say anything else."

"And why should I believe you?" said Peter. "You promised never to see him again and as soon as you cast your eyes on him, you go running over to throw your arms around him."

"It wasn't like that at all."

"And what were you planning to do? Give him a kiss for old times' sake?"

"No," said Rose. She started crying. "No, it was nothing like that."

"Don't you think it's strange that almost every time I've seen you in the last six months, Kit Drewe has been with you? What am I supposed to think?"

It was then that he slapped her face.

Chapter 36

Emily Lutyens sat at her writing desk and pulled a shawl around her shoulders to ward off the cold. The fire in her room had burnt down to a few grey embers, the heat of which could not be felt more than a few inches away. The dying coals occasionally hissed and spat as they slowly burnt to nothing. She resisted the urge to pick up the poker and stab at the fire. Emily thought about ringing for the maid and asking for the fire to be relit but decided against it; after all she had chosen to do what she could to help the war effort.

It had not been a good morning. Madame Delville, her malcontent refugee whom she had taken in from Belgium, had been up to see her twice that morning. First, she had come alone but on the second occasion was accompanied by her husband, a feeble excuse for a man who had stood by the door looking apologetic and saying nothing. Madame Delville had started by complaining about the cold and damp in her whining Walloon accent.

Out of the goodness of her heart, thought Emily, she had given those two a roof over their heads – but did they thank her? Not a bit of it! Madame Delville regularly intruded into her life of meditation, often complaining about something and nothing. Today she had said that she had more chance of dying of tuberculosis in this cold and damp English house in which she had been forced to live than being shot by the Germans in her own home.

Emily had let out a deep breath and rather wished that the Germans had got to her first.

When the Delvilles had gone back to their own rooms they were clearly unsatisfied, and Emily was left annoyed and frustrated. She wondered why they couldn't just leave her alone. Was it too much to ask for a little peace and quiet? She had her correspondence to do and almost nothing had been done that morning because of one irritating interruption after another. She had yet to read her letters. There was one from her husband, one from Krishnamurti and a final letter from Frances Drewe.

Emily had worried on Christmas Day and Boxing Day about Celia's previous meeting with Kit and Basil Drewe. She had immediately telegrammed her husband, who was still in India, about the incident and he had sent a message back by return saying that she should do nothing but bide her time. However, biding her time was not one of Emily's strengths. She had been on tenterhooks all over the Christmas holiday and on more than one occasion was about to telephone Frances Drewe. However, she did not have to wait too long for a response from Frances Drewe and that morning, the day after Boxing Day, she had received a letter. She had taken it up to her room with her other correspondence when she was interrupted by Madame Delville. She opened the letter with more than a bit of trepidation.

"My dearest Emily," the letter began. She read the letter quickly and then let out a deep breath. Her eyes went back to the paragraph she had just looked at to ensure that she had not misread it.

"Once again," Lady Drewe wrote, "your daughter has stepped in when others might have walked by. Both Basil and Christian spoke about her courage in pushing forward and protecting Basil." Emily continued to read. The letter finished, "We are holding a New Year's Eve ball and would be delighted if you, Edwin, Celia and the rest of the family could attend. Hopefully this is not too short notice. Yours most sincerely, Frances – RSVP."

Next to Emily was a small sheaf of writing paper. She picked up a sheet and placed it in front of her. The watermark was barely visible through the cream paper. She picked up her pen which was still in the inkwell and wrote at the corner of the paper. "31 Bedford Square, Holborn, London". Below she wrote in full the date: "27th December 1914" and began:

"My dearest Frances,

Thank you for your kind words about Celia.

We should be delighted to attend the New Year's Eve Ball at Wadhurst Hall, apart from Edwin who is currently in India designing the new capital city, New Delhi, which now takes up most of his time (except, of course, that he is still devoted to completing the design of your marvellous castle on the moor).

I look forward to seeing you.

With kindest regards

Emily"

She placed the letter in an envelope and addressed it. She would send it down by hand.

The last letter that she read was from Krishnamurti. He wrote that he was coming back to England from France and wanted to see her. He said that, although he had wanted to work in the hospitals and look after people, it had not proved possible. Many of the invalids would not even let him touch them because he was an Indian. Nitya had decided to stay on as an orderly in the French town of Albert, but he had found the work too wearying. As a postscript he added that he missed her more than anyone else.

She looked at the fire which was almost out. She decided that she had had enough of sitting in the cold and rang for the maid to bring up more coal. She even decided to send another bucket of coal up to the odious Madame Delville.

Chapter 37

Kit Drewe could not remember having ever eaten so much over such a short period. On Christmas Day he had seconds of everything, even the Christmas pudding. On Boxing Day he made short work of the remainder of the turkey. For the rest of the week, he spent his time lolling around Wadhurst Hall with regular visits to the kitchen. On the thirtieth of December, his mother had looked up from the breakfast table and asked whether he was still likely to fit into his dinner suit. Adrian and Basil had burst out laughing and Kit had replied somewhat sniffily that 'Of course he could. He never put on weight.'

That 'of course' turned out not to be entirely correct. In the preceding four months since the purchase of his dinner suit, Kit found that he had put on a few inches around the waist. He regretfully concluded that perhaps most of it may have been added over the last week.

"They're only tight in one or two places," he said emphatically to Adrian, who watched him struggle into his dinner suit trousers. "See," he continued, "just a little snug."

"Trousers that snug," replied Adrian, "are only ever worn by Dilly boys."

"Well, what am I going to do?" asked Kit. "I can't get them to a tailor and back in time by tomorrow."

Adrian gleefully concluded that there were only two options: to let one of the maids have a go at letting out his Jermyn Street tailored trousers, or start a regime of dieting and exercise. Regretfully, Kit found himself agreeing to eat only a 'sparrow's portion' and undertaking some modest exercise.

"I suppose," said Adrian, "that if we start straight away, we can stroll down to Ticehurst station and meet the two-fifteen train from London." When Kit had discussed 'exercise' he had not thought that a four-mile walk from Wadhurst Hall to Ticehurst station would be on the cards. However, ten minutes later

189

he was wearing a warm jacket with a good pair of boots and on the driveway of Wadhurst Hall.

"But why do we have to walk?" he asked. "Poley's taking the motor to the station, so why don't we just go with him?"

"Because," said Adrian, without giving any further attempt at an answer. Kit realised that complaining further was unlikely to have any effect, except that Adrian might set off at a good pace and he did not fancy jogging to try and keep up.

As he walked along the path, Kit noticed how little Wadhurst Hall had changed since he was a child. The rows of cedars that edged the driveway were still tall and bushy with dark greyish-green needles. They seemed unaffected by time, barely changing over the years since Kit had played beneath them. He had once known how many trees were on each side, having counted them on the numerous occasions he had ridden his bicycle up and down that path. He had now forgotten the number but recalled that on one side there was one more trunk than on the other, the result of a tree having been struck by lightning.

He looked up at the sky as he walked. The clouds were low, dark and pillowy. He hoped they would not break and that he and Adrian would avoid being caught in the kind of winter downpour that had been all too common over the last few days.

"So, are you going to tell me what's bothering you?" asked Adrian as they turned into the road towards Ticehurst.

"There's nothing wrong," said Kit. "Whatever gave you that idea?"

"Well, you've been moping around the house for the last week with a face like a wet weekend and all the burdens of Sisyphus."

"I have not," said Kit.

"Everyone's commented," said Adrian. "Basil said that he thought it might have something to do with what happened at Liberty's."

It was the first time anyone had mentioned the white feather since he had taken Basil home. It was a conversation that had been left hanging like the sword of Damocles and Kit had been happy to leave it there. Anyway, he thought, it would be unfair to burden Adrian with his small problems when he was being sent off to the front just after the New Year. He just wanted to forget it. When he thought about it, he felt himself getting annoyed. What did it matter what some stupid girl with a white feather thought of him, or a crowd of shoppers he would never see again! He knew he was not a coward, and he did not care what anyone thought – anyone except for Basil. He hated to think that his younger brother might actually think him a coward. Basil had gone through so much pain because of him and borne it without complaint or criticism. Whatever respect Basil had for him, he did not want to lose.

"It really hasn't been bothering me," said Kit.

"And you shouldn't let it," added Adrian.

"I won't." Kit hesitated for a moment. "I don't know if you will understand this, but I don't hate the Austrians and the Germans. When I count up everyone I know, I happen to have more friends in the Austrian army than in the British army. As I've said a hundred times before, this isn't my war."

"I suppose I can understand that," said Adrian. "Although it's your friends that will be firing at me."

The brothers let the conversation end without any inclination to judge. They carried on walking, alone except for the crows in the trees above the ploughed fields, who screeched out warnings. Adrian smoked. Kit hit at stones with his walking stick, knocking them swiftly along the road. They had walked just under two miles when Kit asked:

"So how are things with Father?"

"What do you mean?"

"When we last spoke, you said that he might have financial worries."

"You know Father," said Adrian, "he keeps his cards close to his chest but from what I can gather, he is rather banking on getting this supply contract."

"So, it's just cash flow?" said Kit.

"Not exactly. It seems your friends in the Austrian navy are good at spotting any ship which Father has an interest in. He's lost a fortune so far and if things carry on, he'll need to start borrowing. He said that without the government contract, things might soon start getting a little tricky."

Kit took out a packet of cigarettes from his pocket and lit one. "And what about you?"

"There's nothing to tell," replied Adrian.

"Well, we're going to Ticehurst station to meet Miss Jane Facey. How do you feel about that?"

"You do know there's nothing in that silly story Archibald Drew was telling. Mother has just got this idea into her head that it would be a good idea if I married into a titled family. It seems that Mother and Edith Facey have seen each other on a few occasions since Father started doing business with Facey. Fortunately, Father seems dead against it; he doesn't like Lord Facey at all."

"So why are we walking over to the station to meet her?" asked Kit.

"Father asked if I would. He thought Lord Facey might appreciate it if I turned up to welcome his daughter and make her feel at home."

"A Freudian slip?" said Kit.

"Pardon?"

"A Freudian slip," Kit repeated. "If you don't want to marry her, then better not make her feel too much at home."

"Look," said Adrian, "I've no idea what she's like. As I said, I have only ever seen her on one or two occasions and that's an end to the matter."

When Kit and Adrian arrived at the station Poley was already there, sitting in the front of the Isotta Fraschini fast asleep. They decided not to wake him and went onto the platform, their coats wrapped round them to ward off the chill of the December afternoon. The train was surprisingly on time. It slowed as it came into the station, steam hissing from its brakes and pulled up with a shudder. Adrian and Kit looked up the platform and saw the slender figure of a young woman getting out of the first class carriage. A guard lifted a trunk from her carriage and placed it on the platform.

"She's coming well prepared," said Kit, guessing that with Poley asleep at the wheel he would be the one to carry the trunk to the car.

Jane Facey watched them as they approached along the platform and waved to Adrian. Adrian greeted her like an old friend and Kit introduced himself. Kit thought to himself that they seemed to be a little more than just casual acquaintances. She was not particularly tall and looked older than twenty-three. Her mousy hair was tied up and she wore heavy-rimmed brown tortoise-shell glasses. She had a plain but charming face, a slight tilt of the nose, a full mouth and cornflower-blue eyes. She was not unattractive, thought Kit, but by no means beautiful. Adrian bent down and picked up her trunk with an ever-so-slight but audible groan.

"Can I help?" asked Kit. "You look like you're struggling."

"Not at all," said Adrian, through clenched teeth.

"If you're certain?"

"Quite," said Adrian who had started sweating with the effort.

Kit turned to Jane.

"How was your trip down?" he asked.

"It seemed to last forever. There were soldiers everywhere – coming and going in different directions."

"They're sending out fresh troops over the next two weeks, but then you probably knew that," said Kit. Jane smiled back at him. He continued, "And Adrian's regiment is also moving out in three days' time but that's all he's told us. He won't even say where he's going."

"They're going to Neuve Chapelle," said Jane.

Adrian looked over. "It's supposed to be a secret."

"Not from the daughter of a member of the cabinet," replied Jane.

Adrian placed the trunk beside the motor and Poley, who had woken when the train arrived, lifted it into the boot.

"There's only room for two in the back," said Adrian to Kit. "You'll have to sit up with Poley."

"I'm sure we can all squeeze in," said Jane.

"Or you could always finish your walk back to Wadhurst Hall," Adrian casually suggested.

"Sitting with Poley is fine with me," said Kit. "I think I've done enough exercise to last me the rest of my life."

Chapter 38

The Wadhurst Hall Ball was indeed a splendid event. In a county where New Year's Eve balls were two-a-penny, it always delighted Lady Frances Drewe that absolutely no one ever refused her invitation. She stood side by side with her husband, Sir Julius, looking on as her guests arrived, ensuring that each received a glass of champagne and *hors d'oeuvres* of smoked salmon, steak tartare or caviar. Sir Julius stood quietly in his dinner suit, hands in his pockets, with a look of complete indifference to the whole affair.

Tall candelabras were placed beside the main doors to ward off the chill of the last crisp December evening of 1914. The footmen in their scarlet livery opened doors to cars and carriages and ushered guests into the main receiving hall where the butlers, dressed in their black morning clothes, first took their capes and coats and then escorted them to Sir Julius and Lady Frances. Each guest was made to feel special, as if the ball had been arranged for them alone. They were then moved effortlessly to the ballroom where a sixteen-piece orchestra sat squashed in a corner playing a medley of waltzes, foxtrots and even occasionally a tango in deference to younger tastes.

Celia Lutyens' younger sisters gasped when they entered the ballroom. On one side of the room were mirrors and on the other, large windows that went up to the ceiling and which in daytime gave undisturbed views across the gardens. There were six chandeliers which sprinkled light down on the dancers. At the far end of the ballroom was an arch that led to the large wood-panelled drawing room where tables had been covered with white linen and flowers, cutlery and crockery for the evening dinner. Everyone was saying that this was the event of the season – the elder ladies as they watched the dancing; the young women as they, with apparent effortlessness, coordinated their steps on the maple-stripped dance floor; and the young men who desperately tried to be more confident and assured than their years permitted.

Celia Lutyens walked with her mother, her brother and her two younger sisters towards a group of empty chairs on the far side of the ballroom. Mary and Elisabeth Lutyens looked up at their elder sister, both fizzing with excitement. In the bright, glittering room of glass and mirrors, the two young girls walked with heads turning and mouths open. Each wore identical yellow silk dresses with matching ribbons in their hair like a pair of lemon sherbets. Robert, who initially had expressed his keenness to attend the ball, was beginning to change his attitude as he suddenly realised that he would soon have to get up the courage to ask someone to dance with him. He began to adopt a pose of indifference to the idea of dancing, one that was fashionable with each generation of boys who have turned sixteen.

Celia walked nonchalantly and seemed to care not one iota for the music or the dancing. She had been to numerous balls as a debutante that year and knew that she needed to create just the right impression. She should not appear too excited, as that would give the sense of being unsophisticated; however, it was just as bad to appear too severe because then one risked frightening away anyone who might wish to dance with you. She had once been told that when entering a ballroom, one should always chat casually. She therefore turned to her younger sisters and asked who was wearing the most fabulous dress. They looked around and together pointed to a young woman with mousy hair, wearing an ivory ballgown.

Celia looked over to where the girls had pointed and the young woman, sensing she was being watched, looked back. Celia smiled and slightly nodded her head. The woman smiled back.

"So what do you think of your first ball?" asked Celia.

"Oh, it's lovely," said Mary, wide-eyed from looking at the dancers. The youngest sister, Elisabeth, continued walking open-mouthed.

"You'll catch a fly," said Emily Lutyens sharply at her daughter, but Elisabeth continued to stare around her as if in a trance. She was captivated by the music that made her want to spin around and around until she was dizzy. Elisabeth twirled her skirts around her ankles as she followed her mother to some empty seats at the far end of the room.

They had not sat for more than a few minutes when a young man in a dinner suit came over and asked Celia in a country accent whether she would like to dance. Celia looked at her card and agreed to a foxtrot later in the evening. The young man left and two soldiers one after the other came up and asked her to dance. Emily Lutyens leant over to Robert and whispered something in his ear. He waited for a moment and then got up and went looking for someone with whom he could dance.

"What did you say to him?" asked Celia.

"I said that if he didn't put his skates on and ask one or two girls to dance, he would end up having to talk to me all evening."

After five minutes of sitting, Mary and Elisabeth decided that they needed to go off and explore. They were given strict instructions by Celia not to break anything, get underfoot or otherwise cause a nuisance. They left chastened by the orders but as soon as they were out of Celia's sight, everything that she had said to them was forgotten.

The orchestra started to play another waltz and Celia looked at her card. The young woman with the ivory dress was dancing with a soldier with glistening dark hair and a short moustache. He was taller than her by a few inches and Celia noticed that he danced better than she did. As they spun around, she noticed it was Adrian Drewe. She had been looking for him as she had wandered in. She had not seen him for three years and the fact that he danced beautifully and better than his partner amused her.

"Do you know that young lady over there," said Celia to her mother, "the one with the ivory dress dancing with Adrian Drewe?"

Emily Lutyens looked across the dance floor. "Her name is Jane Facey," she said. "Her father is something in government. I've only met them once or twice with your father. They are not really my type."

Celia watched as she danced. She didn't dance badly but every step was so predictable and placed. It was if she had learnt to dance from a textbook and memorised each step to perfection. However, she did not seem to have any sense of the rhythm of the music, as if it were an irrelevant part of dancing. Adrian Drewe however carried her around the dance floor. He seemed to ebb and flow with the music, guiding her effortlessly. His feet lightly moved backwards two steps and sideways two steps and then backwards again.

"Robert's coming back with someone," said Emily to Celia.

Celia looked to see her brother, Robert, heading towards them with another young man who walked with a pronounced limp. They were chatting like old friends. Celia immediately recognised Basil Drewe and had a feeling of slight trepidation. In comparison to her brother, Basil Drewe was tall; taller by at least two inches. He even looked older than her brother – it was something about the set of the jaw and the eyes. Looking at them together, Celia realised why Margaret Ellis had thought that he might be eighteen.

"Good evening, Lady Emily," said Basil, "Celia."

Celia let her mother talk and for once did not care what she said or even whether she talked about theosophy. In fact, she hoped her mother would start telling Basil about Krishnamurti because then, she knew, she would never stop talking. Celia feared that she might be asked about why she was in Liberty's and then would be forced either to lie or to admit that she was also there to hand out white feathers. However, her mother did not mention Krishnamurti and nor did Basil ask her about that day. Instead, Robert came to her aid and interrupted the conversation by saying that Basil had a cricket bat signed by

Jack Hobbs and that he had promised to show it to him.

She took a deep breath when they had gone and settled back in her chair. She looked at her dance card and saw she was taken for the next three dances. Two women in their mid-fifties had sat down beside her and while looking at the dancing she listened to them speaking. One had an American accent and the other was distinctly English.

"It seems to me," said the woman with the clipped English accent, "that this is the most opulent ball the Drewes have ever held. She must have decided to do this because her eldest son is going to the front soon."

"I thank God that she did," replied the American. "I can't remember ever having such a dull Christmas. It doesn't seem to matter how much money one has, there's nothing here to spend it on in England at the moment." She took a sip of champagne. "So where are these Drewe boys?"

"I saw the eldest boy, Adrian, dancing when we came in. I'll point him out if I see him again. The youngest was standing here when we came in; he was the taller boy. The middle one, Christian, is standing over by the arch, smoking." The American looked over towards the reception room and Celia also instinctively looked.

"He's quite striking," said the American woman. "In fact, I bet he turns a few heads."

Celia stared at Kit and had to agree. It was a mixture of the green eyes and dark hair and the way he stood. He had a nonchalance about him that on someone less attractive might give the appearance of being louche. He scanned the people on the dance floor, occasionally looking at someone longer if he found them interesting or attractive. Celia recalled that when she had first met him, he had that disconcerting and annoying habit of looking elsewhere when talking to her; but watching him now as he surveyed the ballroom, she agreed that he was 'quite striking'.

Celia could no longer hear the conversation as the orchestra raised the volume for the last few phrases of the waltz and then the sound faded. Celia clapped her lilac-gloved hands. As the applause died down the band struck up the next foxtrot. Celia strained her ears to hear more but could not pick up another morsel of the conversation and then noticed that someone was standing just before her. She looked up to see the young man with the country accent and got up to dance with him.

Mary and Elisabeth ran back to their mother when they saw Celia dancing.

"Look how wonderfully Celia dances," Elisabeth said to Emily.

Celia followed the lead of her partner, conscientiously keeping her eyes lowered. It was evident to Celia after just a few steps that her dance partner was more used to wading in mud on a farm than moving his feet on a dance floor. She hoped that by looking down she could at least avoid a trampled toe. After the foxtrot had finished, she breathed a sigh of relief and when her partner asked whether she was free to dance later, she made the excuse that her card was full.

The next two turns were much more satisfactory and one of the soldiers danced quite well. She sat back down afterwards with her mother and her two younger sisters. She had not sat for long before Adrian came over, said that it was a shame that she was not dancing and asked whether she would like to accompany him.

He escorted Celia onto the ballroom floor, turned, and put his left hand on her waist. He smiled as the music started and he moved backwards quickly taking her with him. Celia smiled back at him. She breathed deeply as they moved round, the hem of her dress whipping around her ankles. She could tell each step he was about to make by the posture of his body and how his weight shifted from one foot to the other. It was not until she had been dancing for a minute that she looked at him and noticed that he was once again smiling.

"You dance extraordinarily well," he said. "You must dance all the time."

"Only when I'm not out riding."

"I don't ride half as often as I would like."

Adrian did not take his eyes off Celia as they continued to dance around the room. Celia looked in the mirrors as their waltz went on but could only for the briefest moments distinguish her reflection with Adrian. She thought how well they danced together. The noise of the music and the fall of footsteps on the hard wooden floor seemed to deafen Celia. Adrian said something to her, but she did not hear.

"I'm sorry," she said, "I didn't catch that."

"It was nothing," he said. "I only said how perfect you looked."

*   *   *

Those privileged to see the whole of the Drewe family together on its last social occasion before the devastation of the war, could not help but notice the opulence of the occasion. They represented a cross-section of a certain class of English society, which had come to the fore. They owned more than the landed classes and were to the middle classes as important, if not more important, than the aristocracy. They were what the middle classes aspired to become. These families had, for a hundred years, worked to be the pinnacle of society and were now fully in their prime. However, like any tree that reaches full maturity, there is nothing but decay and sickness and, ultimately, death to follow.

On New Year's Eve of 1914, the wealth of the Drewes could be seen at its height. Fine wine, champagne, a buffet of smoked salmon, prawns, lobster and cold roast sirloin made the spirit of even the most parsimonious person melt. If meanness thrives on an empty stomach, then not one of the guests at the Drewes' ball could have complained that there was nothing to excite a censorious palate. Sir Julius and Lady Drewe sat at a table in the middle of the drawing room with Lord Cecil and Edith Facey and other distinguished guests. Adrian sat at an adjacent table with Jane Facey and a few officers and their partners from Adrian's regiment. Kit avoided eating, as he felt that the trousers of his dinner suit were still nipping at his waist. Basil Drewe and Robert Lutyens found a quiet corner and turned the pages of Wisden's almanack and discussed the finer points of batting averages.

On the walls in the great wooden drawing room there were portraits of long-dead aristocracy, who had been distantly related to Lady Frances Drewe. The paintings had been hung soon after the Drewes bought Wadhurst Hall. They looked down year after year as one ball followed the next. They had seen the slight but perceptible changes which had occurred that year. There were more candles and glitter and the champagnes were only of the finest vintage, sirloin now replaced rib of beef and lobster was served as a staple. If Sir Julius had money problems, then no one would have guessed it that evening. They did, however, notice that Sir Julius was more detached from the festivities and his family than he had ever been.

Emily Lutyens and her family were seated at a table at the back of the drawing room some distance from the Drewes. Emily automatically objected to this positioning. She made the point to the gentleman sitting next to her, a magistrate, recently widowed, that she was a relative of Lady Frances Drewe and ought to have sat adjacent to her hosts. The magistrate nodded in sympathy, but Celia was certain that he thought them the most inconsiderate snobs.

"And where's Robert?" said Emily plaintively. "You would have thought that with the money I have spent on his education he would have better manners than to leave four women sitting on their own."

"I'll get him," said Celia, relieved to find an excuse to leave the table. "I saw him in the next room with Basil Drewe." She walked slowly towards the ballroom where she had last seen her bother. Kit Drewe was standing by the open door to the ballroom, and she stopped for a moment to talk to him.

"It's a fabulous party," she said.

"I'm pleased you're here," Kit replied. "I hardly know anyone apart from my family and, of course, the servants."

Celia turned to look at the people who were about to commence their dinner.

"Would you like a cigarette?" asked Kit.

Celia looked over to where her mother was sitting. She knew Emily would disapprove. She leant over and took one from Kit's cigarette case. She knew even fewer people than Kit but did not mention it. Around the corner she could hear her brother, Robert, talking to Basil Drewe. They had been talking about cricket when she had arrived, but the subject had changed to the Royal Flying Corps. She heard Basil saying that the aeroplane would revolutionise warfare and Robert responded that, at best, it could only ever be used for reconnaissance. They did agree, however, that it would be desperately good fun to go flying.

A small painting in a frame was resting against the wall by Kit's feet.

"What's that?" asked Celia.

"There will be an auction later," said Kit. "There are a few things that are donated from galleries or wealthy friends but at the end of the evening, all the family will donate something which is precious to them. I thought I would auction one of my paintings."

Kit stopped talking, again tuning in to Basil's conversation.

"And," said Basil, "there would be no reason why I couldn't fly. My leg wouldn't prevent me from getting my wings."

"The only downside is the uniform," replied Robert, "it's a bit bland. Not like your brother's."

"The Royal Garrison Artillery has probably the best uniform, but I wouldn't like to join them. My brother Adrian says that they hardly see any action and that he's as safe as a church mouse."

"And what about your other brother?" said Robert. "What regiment has he joined?"

There was a silence for a moment. Basil said, as nonchalantly as he could, that his brother Kit hadn't joined up yet.

"He doesn't think it's his war," Basil tried to explain.

There are times when youth has its disadvantages and sometimes one speaks before weighing the consequences. There was no malice, but Robert could not stop himself from remarking: "How can anyone think that? If I were older, I'd join up in a shot."

"I know, and if I could, so would I," replied Basil.

"He's not a coward, is he?" asked Robert.

"No! It's nothing like that. Nothing like that at all. Kit is no coward," said Basil. However, as Basil spoke his voice was hesitant, almost apologetic.

"I didn't mean that," said Robert.

"It's just that he doesn't care what you or I or anyone else thinks. He'll show everyone he's no coward."

Celia looked at Kit, who was looking down at the painting. His face was flushed but he didn't say anything; he continued to smoke. Celia decided it was time to break up the boys' conversation and went into the ballroom. She told Robert that he was wanted. As she returned to her table, she walked past Kit who was handing the painting to one of the staff.

"Take it back to my room," he said. "I've thought of something better for the auction."

Chapter 39

Adrian Drewe sat next to Jane Facey, trying to explain how to arrange artillery against a superior force. His black hair was rich and thick; his moustache clipped fashionably short and, as he discussed the positioning of cannon, his emerald eyes shone. He held in one hand a glass of champagne. He had set down bread rolls on the table, representing the artillery of the Germans, and cruets of salt and pepper were the British guns. He posited a theory as to why the German strategy was misconceived. In order better to understand the strategy, Jane Facey had moved her chair so close to his that when he leant forward across the table to remove or reposition the bread rolls or cruets their arms would brush. Once he had finished his exposition on the doomed strategy of the German High Command, he leant back and offered Jane a cigarette from his cigarette case. She refused the cigarette but commented on the exquisite silver case. 'To Adrian – Christmas 1914' was engraved on the front. A present from Kit, Adrian explained.

"So, what's life like in training?" asked Jane.

One of the other officers at the table described the camp in Aldershot and how all the wooden huts where they lived were spread out like spider legs around a set of communal washrooms. None of them have any heating, he said, even now in winter, except for some old pot-bellied stoves in the middle of the hut with a pipe going out the roof.

"So much of it is so ridiculous," Adrian added.

"Why?" asked Jane.

"Because," said Adrian, "we are made to do things that when rationally considered are just mad. I have to polish my own boots. Every day I have to spend twenty minutes with a soft cloth and a tin of parade gloss buffing up my boots and belt until they shine like glass. Then I go out on parade and am made to drill on a muddy courtyard until the boots are caked with mud. The next day it starts all over again. We all know how to polish boots, but we are still made to do it day in and day out. The point is that I have spent probably up to a week just polishing boots when I could have been learning something useful."

"And what is the worst thing about the army?" asked Jane.

"The food," said the other officer without hesitation. "Porridge and reconstituted egg for breakfast. For lunch – burnt sausages that are blackened on the outside and raw on the inside. Awful! The food's almost as bad as that served up at Eton."

Jane laughed.

"It's baffling," continued Adrian. "Although we are training to be officers the sergeants treat us like some underprivileged regulars. You just have to keep your head down and, most of all, don't stand out."

"It all sounds perfectly beastly," said Jane. "You must be looking forward to going off to the front."

"We are," said the other officer.

"And are you going to have an auction again this year?" said Jane to Adrian.

"Yes," Adrian replied. "There are some donations from companies and art houses which are auctioned off first and then there are little mementoes that are provided by the family."

"Have you given something for the auction?" she asked.

"I'm afraid I can't tell you what it is," he said. "It's supposed to be a complete surprise."

"Whisper it to me," Jane insisted. She placed her hand around his waist and leant closer to him.

"It really is supposed to be a secret," answered Adrian.

"Suit yourself," she replied and removed her arm. Adrian looked at her. She really was quite difficult, he thought, but his father had made it clear that he should try to make her feel at home.

"I'm auctioning an old silver hip flask," said Adrian urbanely. "I received a new one from Basil this Christmas."

"And what is Kit auctioning?" she asked.

"Kit will be auctioning a painting. Whenever he is here, he always auctions a painting," whispered Adrian. "And now," he continued, "we really should go back to the ballroom."

"I would love to," she said, "but you're not going to leave me alone again and go off dancing with that young girl with the auburn hair."

"Not at all," said Adrian, "she's just a distant cousin whom I haven't seen for an age. I'm surprised you don't know her – her name's Celia Lutyens."

"I know her by name," replied Jane. "We have a mutual acquaintance, Margaret Ellis, and I'll introduce myself to her later. Anyway, please don't leave me alone for too long – distant cousins, especially when they are attractive, do have a habit of being a distraction."

Chapter 40

A butler in a black morning suit tapped at a crystal glass and then paused for a moment. When he was certain that the majority of people had stopped speaking, he said firmly in his rich baritone voice, "My Lords, Ladies and gentlemen, the auction for the wounded veterans of Bexley Cottage Hospital will take place in the great hall in fifteen minutes."

"Come along," said Celia to her two youngest sisters. "If you want to see the auction we'll need to get to the front of the crowd." She found Robert and they all made their way through the ballroom to the receiving hall.

"Why are they having an auction?" asked Elisabeth. "I wanted there to be more dancing."

"It's for the wounded soldiers," explained Celia.

"Exactly right."

Celia turned to see who had spoken and found that she was standing next to Adrian Drewe.

"Hello," she said, "have you met my brother and my two sisters? This is Robert and the two girls are Mary and Elisabeth."

Elisabeth curtsied to Adrian and then added, "This is the first ball I've been to because I'm only eleven. It's very splendid."

"Thank you," answered Adrian.

"Mary's three years older than me," added Elisabeth.

"We saw you dancing earlier with the lady in the ivory dress," said Mary.

"I also danced with your sister," replied Adrian.

"Who danced better?" asked Elisabeth.

Celia tried to shush her; however, Adrian leant forward and whispered, "Celia."

"Have you been to the front?" asked Celia.

"I go in a week or so," said Adrian. "Since Marne the Germans have attacked again and pushed us back to the Belgian border with France. We have dug in, but God only knows what will happen next. We need more men if we are to stand a chance of winning this war."

"You know you shouldn't take the Lord's name in vain," said Mary.

"Sorry," said Adrian, who looked at Celia and smiled.

Elisabeth, who found any discussion on the war boring, looked at Adrian and asked, "What do we do at an auction?"

"Well," said Adrian, "there are lots of things which will be sold and if you want anything you can bid for it."

Elisabeth's face lit up.

"Really! Can I bid for anything?"

"Don't be silly!" replied Celia. "You don't have any money."

"Are you going to bid for anything?" asked Mary.

"I don't know," said Celia.

"Do you have any money? I remember Mother and Father gave you twenty pounds on your last birthday," said Elisabeth.

"It's none of your business," remarked Celia.

The butler with the baritone voice walked to the top of the stairs and hit a dinner gong. The sound of the brass reverberated in the receiving hall, which was now full of people and noise.

"You'll have to excuse me," said Adrian. "It's a tradition that Basil, Kit and I give something to be auctioned."

"What are you going to auction?"

"It's a secret," answered Adrian, "or supposed to be."

The dinner gong sounded again.

"The auction will be starting in a minute or two and I am supposed to be with the rest of my family." Adrian walked towards the stairs.

"Good evening, Miss Lutyens," a woman's voice said from behind Celia, who turned. "We haven't been introduced," said Jane Facey, who then proceeded to make an introduction. "Will you be bidding for anything?"

Celia said she doubted that there was anything she wanted. Jane replied that she might want to bid for a silver flask which was being auctioned by Adrian.

"Isn't that a secret?" asked Elisabeth.

"It's supposed to be," said Jane, "but Mr Drewe and I are close friends." Jane then turned to Celia. "Talking of friends, did you know we have a mutual acquaintance in Margaret Ellis? I was sorry to hear about your argument with her; it's so tragic when old friends fall out."

Jane walked away into the crowd and Celia glared after her.

When the dinner gong was beaten for a third time, Celia looked up to see Sir Julius standing next to his wife with Adrian, Kit and Basil. There was still that similarity between Sir Julius and Adrian, but Sir Julius had aged in the last few years. The grey could be seen on his temples and in his moustache. There were also slight rings around the eyes. Adrian was about three inches taller than his mother and, as far as she could guess, a little taller than both Kit and Basil. She noticed how Sir Julius looked disinterested in what was happening. He smoked a cigar, occasionally saying something to Basil and Adrian.

Lady Drewe was thin and elegant. She exuded health, spending hours out and around her estate. She knew by name each of the farmhands and their families. Her light brown hair was tied up high above her head and held in place with a large clasp made of lapis lazuli. She resembled Kit with her high cheek bones and thin nose, although he was taller with darker hair and green eyes; a concession to the fact that he had genes from two parents.

"Ladies and gentlemen," began Sir Julius. "Thank you for attending this evening and your kind support at this annual auction as part of our New Year's Eve celebration. This year Lady Drewe has chosen the charity that is close to both our hearts. All money raised will benefit the invalids at the Bexley Cottage Hospital for wounded soldiers." There was a round of applause and Sir Julius waited for it to die down before continuing. "Lady Drewe would now like to say a few words about the cause we are supporting this evening."

"It was not difficult to choose a cause to support this year," she began, her voice resonant with emotion. "Our eldest son Adrian will soon be leaving for the front. As a mother I have my deepest reservations – of course – but as an Englishwoman I am so proud of him." There was another round of applause. Celia looked at Kit, whose face had a determined expression.

"Now," continued Lady Drewe firmly, "the auction will begin. Please bid generously." She turned to her three children and beamed with pride when she looked at Adrian.

The butler in his black morning suit banged the gong again. He waited a minute to let the applause for Frances Drewe subside and then explained to the crowd that there were catalogues describing the items to be auctioned. He said that those who wanted to bid should take a numbered card and hold it up over their heads to signify that they were bidding.

Celia felt a tug at her arm and Elisabeth said in a whisper: "When does the dancing start again?"

"Soon," replied Celia. "This shouldn't last more than thirty minutes. Robert has gone to get a catalogue for us and a card."

"I'm very tired," said Elisabeth.

"There's no one in the drawing room right now," said Celia. "Why don't you find yourself a quiet corner and close your eyes? If you like, I shall get you when the dancing starts again?"

"Would you?" said Elisabeth. "But do please remember. I don't want to miss any of the dancing." Elisabeth left and Mary also decided it might be best to keep her company.

The butler had stopped speaking and another man in the Drewe family livery was holding a small limestone sculpture. Celia had missed the introduction to this piece and looked down at the one-page catalogue which Robert handed to her. As she looked up again, the auctioneer was already taking a bid for fifty-five pounds. The bidding continued between a tall man with wispy hair and a rather portly lady until it was sold to the lady for eighty-one pounds. There followed three more pieces of art – two paintings and another sculpture. One oil painting of two dogs by a fireside by a British artist called James Hardy was bought by Lord Cecil Facey. After the artworks, a number of pieces of jewellery and perfumes from Paris were sold.

"Finally," said the butler who was conducting the auction, his voice now a little hoarse, "we come to the most interesting part of the evening." Celia looked down at her catalogue: 'Personal gifts of Sir Julius, Lady Drewe and their family.'

"Each year," the butler continued, "we auction gifts donated by each member of the Drewe family."

Sir Julius and Lady Frances donated a two-week stay at their villa near Bath, together with their chef and servants. It fetched a respectable bid of thirty-five pounds. The bidding for Adrian's sterling silver hip flask started at two pounds and went up slowly by two shillings at a time. Celia then heard Jane Facey's voice behind her call out five pounds. Jane held a card over her head. Celia had a sudden desire to outbid her.

"Are there any other bids?" shouted the butler. "No? Then going once, going twice..."

Celia thought about raising her hand but decided she had no use for a man's hip flask.

"Sold," shouted the butler.

The next item to be auctioned was Basil's cricket bat signed by Jack Hobbs. Robert Lutyens managed to acquire it for three pounds, which he assured Celia was quite a bargain.

"The final item to be auctioned..." the butler paused, "is from Mr Christian Drewe, who has asked that he conduct the auction for this item."

Kit went over to where the butler was standing by the dinner gong.

"What I am auctioning," said Kit, "is myself. The person who is prepared to bid the highest amount can name the regiment that I should enlist in."

There was a stunned silence.

"I'll bid ten pounds if you'll join the Royal Garrison Artillery," said Adrian. A round of applause followed, but the butler stepped forward and said that Adrian was ineligible to bid as it had been agreed that one member of the

Drewe family could not bid for something offered by another member of the family. Kit looked over to Adrian apologetically.

"Who will start the bidding then?" said Kit.

"Eleven pounds," said the American lady whom Celia had sat next to earlier, "if you join the Guards."

Celia looked at Robert. "What did Basil say about the Royal Garrison Artillery?" she asked.

"Nothing much," replied Robert.

"No," said Celia, "he said something like he would be as safe as a church mouse."

"If there are no further bids," said Kit in a loud voice, "then going once..."

"Yes," answered Robert, "he said something like that."

"Twelve pounds," shouted Celia, "for the Royal Garrison Artillery."

"Thirteen," replied the American lady.

The bidding went up quickly. "Eighteen," said Celia.

"Nineteen," answered the American lady.

"Nineteen pounds and ten shillings," responded Celia.

"Twenty pounds," bid the American lady.

Celia paused. She had no more money.

"If there are no further bids," said Kit looking at Celia, "then at twenty pounds I'm going once, going twice."

"Twenty pounds," Celia said.

"I'm afraid," began Kit, "that the bid already stands at twenty pounds. You have to make a higher bid."

Celia turned to Robert and asked how much he had got on him.

"Nothing," Robert said, "I spent every penny I had bidding for the cricket bat."

"I'm sorry," said Celia, blushing furiously, "twenty pounds is all I have. I'm afraid I haven't a penny more." Kit looked at her and grinned, just fractionally.

"Twenty pounds and a kiss would be a perfectly proper bid."

There were a few whistles and a few of the younger men cheered.

"Then I bid twenty pounds and a kiss," said Celia, to scattered applause.

Kit suddenly noticed that the American lady had raised her card above her head indicating that she intended to make another bid.

"He's half your age and if you carry on, you'll look desperate," whispered the Englishwoman with the clipped accent to her American friend. The American woman looked at Kit, inwardly sighed, and dropped her arm.

"No other bids?" said Kit. "So, the highest bid is with Miss Celia Lutyens for twenty pounds and one kiss – going once, going twice..." Kit paused.

"Twenty-five pounds," a woman shouted. Celia turned and saw Jane Facey holding her card above her head. "And I would like to nominate Ticehurst's local regiment – the Royal West Kents." Several resident Ticehurst dignitaries cheered when they heard their local regiment's name.

"Are there any other bids?" said Kit. He looked at Celia but she lowered her head. "Then sold to Miss Jane Facey."

The music had started again and the throng of people who had been at the auction moved into the ballroom.

"Excuse me," said Adrian to Celia as she walked from the reception hall into the ballroom. "It was very decent of you to try and bid so much."

"I wanted to," said Celia. "I thought it was a very brave thing he was doing."

"Anyway... I just wanted to say thank you."

Celia started to walk away.

"Perhaps we can have a dance later if your card is not full," said Adrian.

"I would love to," she said, trying not to sound too eager; "but I hope you will excuse me, I promised to find my sister when the dancing started." Celia began walking through the ballroom towards the drawing room. Elisabeth had already missed one dance and Celia was sure that she would complain when she was woken up. She was halfway across the ballroom when someone touched her on the shoulder, and she turned. Kit stood in front of her.

"I'm sorry that I can't collect that kiss," he said.

Celia looked at him amused. "But someone outbid me," she said.

"If I had my way, I would have taken your bid."

"Now you're flirting with me," said Celia.

She then saw Elisabeth standing in front of her, tears down her face, accusing Celia of not waking her up and ruining her evening.

*   *   *

The journey back from Wadhurst Hall to London was slow. Elisabeth and Mary had fallen asleep in the back of the car underneath a blanket. It was just as well, thought Celia. Elisabeth had been in a foul mood since she had woken up. Robert turned over the cricket bat in his hand, occasionally running his fingers over the signature of Jack Hobbs, as if he hoped to obtain some of the great batsman's prowess. Lady Emily said nothing. Celia assumed that her mother simply did not want to wake the two young girls. When they arrived back at 31 Bedford Square, Mary and Elisabeth were whisked upstairs and Robert retired. Celia and Lady Emily went into the drawing room.

"Did you enjoy the evening?" said Celia.

"Enjoy it?" said Emily. "How could I enjoy it when I was left alone for hours on end with nothing to do and no one to speak to and then I hear that my eldest daughter is acting like some common street girl, flirting with one brother and offering kisses to the other."

Chapter 41

The daffodils on Wandsworth Common had wilted and the stems waved in the spring breeze, nodding forwards and backwards like a crowd at a tennis match following the flight of the ball. Windows were opened to let in the air. Women stood and talked over garden fences as their washing blew dry in May 1915. The war remained the main topic of conversation and they spoke quietly about the horrors of the Dardanelles. Everyone was asking what would the new coalition government do? And then there were the Irish troubles; but there had always been Irish troubles of one variety or another for as long as Rose could remember.

Rose's journey from Balham to St Thomas' Hospital proved remarkably easy. On a good day she could get from door to door in less than forty minutes. In these first few months since her wedding, she got a letter from Peter every week. The correspondence was often heavily censored as Peter liked to detail the facts about where he was and what he was doing. She remembered getting one letter from him which had been blacked out from almost top to bottom. His life did not change. She knew he was still in Ypres and that he was spending most of his time in the mines. What is there to write when you have no friends and you spend most of your time underground, he once wrote. By the eighth letter he was repeating what he had written before.

Rose felt, by then, that all the conversation had been sucked out of their relationship. Five months into a marriage and they had nothing new to say to each other. She even knew now how he would end each letter: 'your obedient servant.' He could almost be writing to her father. There was no emotion but the recitation of fact and cliché.

Spring would have passed almost unnoticed in a small town like Ypres in the northwest of Belgium, except that the Germans were using a new weapon – poisonous chlorine gas. The allied casualties stood at sixty thousand in just five weeks of fighting. Almost immediately the effects were felt in the hospitals of London as train after train of wounded soldiers were brought home. The soldiers' uniforms were still bloodstained, dirty and soiled; their bodies would be riddled with lice. They would have their uniforms stripped from them by red-faced nurses and their clothes would be collected and burnt. The soldiers became known as the PBI – the Poor Bloody Infantry.

Each day as Rose went into work, she imagined that Peter would be there wounded. She had no idea what she would say if she saw him or how she would look after him. She felt a surge of relief when, day after day, his name did not appear on the roster of newly admitted soldiers; it was relief for all the wrong reasons. She also hated the crowds that now gathered in front of the hospitals, the ports and the train stations. Waving at the mutilated soldiers had become a national pastime. In another age these same people would have come to watch a hanging. Rose hated all of them and then someone would run forward and hand a soldier a bar of chocolate or cigarettes, and, for a moment, they would be forgiven.

It was on a day very much like any other that she arrived at the hospital. New casualties were being moved back to England and Rose even hoped that things would soon quieten down. The second battle of Ypres had ended and the last of the most seriously injured were being brought home. As Peter was stationed in Ypres, she asked many of the injured whether they knew him. None of them had met Peter but then, as the infantry said, you didn't really get to know those who worked in the mines – they kept themselves to themselves. Even though every building in the town had been damaged and the great Cloth Hall, built in the thirteenth century, had been flattened, none of this affected the miners. Their existence consisted of little air and the fear of suffocation. They were so far underground that they hardly knew that a war was going on above them. It was on this day a young second lieutenant was admitted into the hospital.

Edward Stanton had short black hair and a moustache, and he spoke in the short, crisp tones of one who had been to public school. He had not been shot, gassed or even burnt. What made him different from the other wounded men and officers was that he had not slept in thirteen days. The other officers didn't speak to him and thought him a malingerer. Rose had, however, come across a similar case once before and the soldier had committed suicide by the third week of not sleeping. When she first saw Edward Stanton, she was shocked by how insane he looked. He sat upright in bed, black-eyed and shaking. The shaking, like a fit, affected him every minute or two and was so severe that he could not hold anything. He did not speak much, except at night when everyone was asleep.

"You remind me of my sister," he said to Rose one evening.

"Do I look like her?"

"It wasn't how you look," replied Edward, his voice shaking as another seizure took hold of him. "You're far prettier – though please don't repeat that to her. It's just that when you think no one is watching, you look like you're carrying the burdens of the world on your shoulders."

"Oh," said Rose and put her hand to her chest where her St Christopher hung. "Does your sister know you're here?" she asked.

Edward nodded his head and wrapped his blanket around him, hoping that this might stop the uncontrollable tremors. "She's coming tomorrow to see me and bringing her best friend. I had hoped, well... that's a long story..." He paused and waited for the shaking to die down. "Is there anything the doctors can give me to stop this damned shaking? I really don't want to let them see me like this."

"We can give you something to sleep," said Rose.

"No!" said Edward. "I can't sleep anymore. Whenever I sleep I see them – all the young men that I sent forward in the last push. They were all killed on the Ypres salient. They tried to run back but the gas swallowed them up and when it blew away, they were choking to death."

Rose sat on the bed next to him.

"When I close my eyes, I can't breathe and then I start choking. All I want to do now is get back to my company," Edward said. "I just feel so damned useless, worse than a coward. I would have preferred to have had my legs blown off than this." He started to cry. Rose wanted to put her arm around him, but she knew never to get close to a patient.

Ten minutes after she left him, Dr Harold Gillies found Rose sitting alone in the nurses' room. She asked him what could be done for Stanton. Dr Gillies said he would look at the case and said that the usual treatment was opiates, but that he knew of someone who had been distilling an extract from St John's wort which had had some success with sleep disorders.

"I shouldn't become involved," said Rose, "but I just can't help it."

"Most injured soldiers die because the treatment they get on the frontline is hopelessly inadequate. You could do a lot more if you were stationed at the front. You know I'm going out to France in a couple of weeks, and I could do with any help I can get."

"I'll think about it," said Rose.

"Well think about it quickly," replied Gillies. He turned and walked out of the nurses' station and back towards his office.

Rose stood up and saw her reflection in a mirror on the wall. She looked tired. She was tired – every nurse was. However, she also looked sad. She knew that Peter would be getting leave in a few months' time and dreaded the thought of his return.

She knew that she needed to get away.

Chapter 42

Edward Stanton's father, P.D. Stanton KC, was a small, rather thin gentleman with unkempt grey hair and pince-nez glasses. He walked through the men's ward at St Thomas' Hospital with an air of disdain, taking little note of what he saw. His daughter and her friend had to hurry to keep pace behind him. He walked directly to the nurses' station and asked where he could find his son.

The conversation between Edward Stanton and his father did not last long. It was carried out in the manner of the best cross examinations, where P.D. Stanton asked the questions in such a manner that only a 'yes' or 'no' answer could be given. He left the ward within ten minutes of arriving. Jenny Stanton and Celia Lutyens stayed and sat down beside the bed.

"Edward," said Jenny, "you look frightful."

"Jenny!" said Celia.

"It's quite all right, Celia," replied Edward, "I know I look frightful." He started shaking again.

"I'll get the nurse," said Jenny.

It seemed like an age to Celia before Jenny returned with the nurse. Celia sat, not knowing what to say to Edward. The last time she had seen him was nearly nine months ago when they had gone out to see a new play in the West End. He was, at that time, a junior officer in the army, having chosen the armed forces as a profession. Edward's father had hoped that he might follow him into the law but an average intellect and a dislike for public speaking had put an end to that.

"Do you remember when we last met?" asked Celia.

"Your father threw me out of the house." A further fit of shaking seized Edward. He caught his breath and continued, "I didn't even have a chance to get my jacket and had to walk back to Bayswater."

Jenny returned and sat next to Celia and the nurse began reading the chart hanging on the end of Edward's bed.

"Celia," Jenny whispered in her ear. "This was the nurse who picked up your hairpin at Liberty's. You remember the hairpin with the pearl at the end?"

Celia looked at the nurse. She did not recognise her at all; she could not remember even seeing a nurse on that day.

Rose returned a brief look before continuing to read the chart.

Celia quickly lowered her eyes. She knew she should have written to Rose to thank her for handing in the hairpin, but she had wanted to forget that day. She still felt ashamed of herself, and those feelings worsened when she had found out that her mother, and the other women from the Order of the White Feather, were only supporting the war because the government had promised that in return for their support, they would get the vote. It seemed such a betrayal. And now, when they brought those soldiers home wounded, she did not know how to look at them, nor what to say.

"Celia," said Edward, "are you all right?"

"I was miles away," said Celia. Jenny continued to chat away to her brother. Celia stood up and walked over to where Rose stood.

"Can the doctors stop these fits he's having?" she asked. Rose looked at Celia.

"They'll stop when he starts sleeping again."

"Doesn't he sleep at all?" Celia asked.

"He sleeps," answered Rose. "No one can keep themselves awake for this long, but he sleeps for only a few moments at a time before he wakes himself up."

"So what can be done to help him?" asked Celia.

"He needs to forget and then to rest. He needs to talk to friends and family. His sister will probably do more good than a hundred nurses."

"Would it help if I came to see him?"

"Yes, miss," said Rose. "You can tell that he enjoys your company."

"Thank you," said Celia. "I would like to help more."

"A lot of young ladies are now volunteering as auxiliary nurses," explained Rose. "There's a shortage of nurses in our hospital as many trained nurses are going out to France to work in the field hospitals."

"I'm not sure I would make a good nurse," said Celia. She paused for a moment and then added quietly, "I also wanted to thank you for handing in my hairpin. It was a present."

"Oh, that," answered Rose. "I had almost forgotten. Can I ask you a question, miss?"

"Of course."

"That afternoon in Liberty's, did you know those gentlemen – Basil Drewe and his brother?"

"They're distant cousins of mine," said Celia, "but how do you know them?"

"I looked after Basil when he had the metal plates replaced in his leg and his brother Christian visited him every day. I was hoping, miss, that you might be able to tell me how Basil and Mr Christian are?"

"I think Basil is in his last year of school at Winchester. I believe that he wants to study jurisprudence at Oxford. As for Christian, he's an officer in the army – the Royal West Kents. They're fighting out on the Somme right now."

"Mr Christian enlisted? When he talked to me, he said he would never join up. Do you know what made him change his mind?"

Celia lied. She said she didn't know but she could guess.

"And he's not been injured, miss?" asked Rose.

"No," said Celia.

"Could I ask a favour, miss? If you hear anything about Mr Christian, then could you please write to me and," she paused a moment, "if you see either him or Basil, please tell them that Rose, Nurse Hall, sends her best wishes, though I doubt either of them will remember me."

"I will," said Celia, though she thought the request quite strange. "And I'll also come back to see Lieutenant Stanton as often as I can," she added.

*　　*　　*

Every day for the next three weeks, Celia came and talked to Edward Stanton until he was sent to convalesce at a hospital in Kent. Despite the fact that she did not do anything more than talk to Edward, she felt that her visits helped him. After a week he began to sleep for short periods at a time and she would sit and hold his hand. By the second week his convulsions became less frequent.

Celia wrote to him when he went to the convalescence home and managed to visit every few weeks. During this time, Edward Stanton gradually returned to full health and in the late summer of 1915 he returned to active duty in the front lines. Celia during this time had obtained a place at Girton College, Cambridge to read English. However, having spent weeks with Edward Stanton and having seen the other soldiers at St Thomas' Hospital, Celia found the academic lifestyle in the cloistered college stifling.

Rose Hall also left St Thomas' Hospital in June 1915 to work in the hospital at Albert on the Somme. She wrote a letter to Peter explaining her decision, but it was nothing more than a shadow of the truth. The hospital in Albert was run by an old soldier from the Boer War – Colonel Hill. He was a tall man with a full head of grey hair and a moustache. His uniform was pressed and his long brown boots immaculately polished. Rose always felt her own eyes dropping down towards her own stained uniform whenever she saw him. He did not disguise the fact that he thought that nurses at the front lines were inappropriate – he considered that it detracted from the task in hand.

Rose spent the next year apologising for being in Albert, but she did not once regret her decision.

PART VI

Chapter 43

Christian Drewe opened his journal and wrote:

"1st July 1916

In the last month all reason has fled. The Germans started a heavy bombardment of our positions three weeks ago. The shells fell and fell; it was incessant, it rarely stopped. Day and night the bombs fell until finally our dugout began to crumble. At the beginning of the third day, of bombing the roof came down on us and we had to dig ourselves out. Some of my regiment were suffocated or crushed to death. We tried to make our way down to the deeper bunkers. Of course, they were full and the only way we could get in was to crawl on top of those already there. The injured had little strength to complain and those most grievously injured drowned in pools of their own blood as they slept. Many of the men down there were already hysterical, it was the never-ending noise, the relentless pounding of the great artillery guns. Every so often a soldier would not be able to stand it any longer and would want to run out and we had to hold him down to keep him there in comparative safety. The noise even drove the rats mad. They would scurry wildly about and hide with us in our shelters, seeking refuge from the terrific artillery fire.

During that time we had nothing to eat or drink while shell after shell burst above us. It brought back all my worst nightmares.

One thing in the trenches is certain – after a prolonged bout of shelling, an attack will come, it always does. After the firing stopped, I dragged myself from the bunker. For a minute I was unable to see anything in the sunlight, but my eyes soon adjusted and there were groups of German soldiers advancing quickly over no man's land. I shouted for the men to load the machine guns and we began to fire and they fell like scythed blades of corn and then they were stopped by the endless rolls of barbed wire. Only a few of them made it across. In the late afternoon we cleared our lines. I went around one corner of our trench and there was a young German soldier getting out and trying to run back to his own lines. I shouted at him to surrender and he looked back at me and raised his gun. I think we were both scared to death, but I recovered my wits quicker than he did and I was able to push his rifle away and run my bayonet through his stomach. He fell clutching his wound. I thrust again, again and again and then blood poured out of his mouth and he died.

When I looked down at him, he was no older than Basil. I wanted to cry but couldn't.

What more can I write? No one has yet crafted words for this horror and all that's left is madness and vanity!"

Once he had finished writing, he placed the journal with his other things that he would leave behind. His personal belongings would be sent back to his parents if he died. Perhaps his journal would survive, but he guessed that the censors would destroy it. However, he felt he had to place the words neatly on paper as a permanent testimony to the lunacy surrounding him. It was also a cathartic experience; a bloodletting in case he survived.

He stood in the entrance of his dugout feeling the cool wind, waiting for the sun to rise on that first morning of July. His soldiers were sitting half-asleep in the half-blown-down trenches. They had had a long night of praying and listening in the blackness. Even a quarter moon and a heavenful of stars failed to pierce the dark. Christian could sense the fear as the soldiers waited with their knees pulled up to their stomachs, with nowhere to move. They sat shoulder to shoulder breathing in short, determined breaths, passing cigarettes among themselves. They had been told that at precisely six-thirty the artillery would start firing and an hour later they would attack. Christian knew that line after line of soldiers were, like him, waiting for the morning. He looked up at the night sky no longer fearing the dark. Morning was coming far too quickly.

"Kit's afraid of the dark." No! He was no longer Kit and he would never be afraid of the night again. He was Lieutenant Christian Drewe who had killed a boy not much older than his younger brother.

An hour passed and the blackness gave way to grey and soon the sky turned a light blue that seemed to herald in the most perfect July morning. Another hour later the artillery started to fire again – Christian looked at his watch, right on cue. He wondered where Adrian was – perhaps somewhere behind him firing the heavy artillery shells across no man's land.

No one in the trenches spoke as the shells were falling. There were only brief moments of respite – and then he heard the shrieks from the German lines. His men would only then start speaking as if to try to cover the sound, but Christian could tell that the words were being forced out, uttered through ground-together teeth. His men waited, fearing the silence and the screams across the fields and the explosions somewhere in front of them. They waited, hidden in soiled trenches on a little piece of earth in a field in France, for the moment Christian would place the whistle to his lips and blow for them to attack.

Christian had been at the Somme for nearly three months in a world entirely made up of men. A world of trenches that went on forever and that had been built up and knocked down and built up again. Across the battlefields and across the sea and then across the green gardens of Kent was a woman's world. For those who had been there for a long time, the distance seemed even greater. Once you had been there you could not talk to anyone who hadn't experienced the Somme.

The Somme changed the language of life and because those soldiers would not be understood they became annoyed and upset by everyone's inability to appreciate the world they lived in. Many men who had gone home on leave had spent it in silence. For most soldiers the sympathetic strangers of elder generations were the worst. It was always strange that, after two weeks, the soldiers wanted to return to that man's world where their lives in the trenches were the most real thing they could imagine. It was the same with the wounded soldiers who desperately wanted to get back to their friends. It was a jealous war that kept on calling the soldiers back to it.

Christian Drewe looked at his watch again. There was not much longer to go and he crouched with his men, his back wedged into the wall of the trench, his head down and his neck aching. The company sergeant sat on his left and a private on his right, a new recruit who had recently come up to the front. In the last few days scores of men had been brought up; each one seemed younger than the last. He had realised that most of them had not received the proper training, but they were there nonetheless because numbers were needed. They all looked the same – fresh-faced and scared. Christian had no intention of getting to know any of them. There seemed little point.

His men had taken up their places during the night and were ready to attack. Each man had been given ammunition, a hot breakfast and a measure of rum to dispel the fear. All he had to do was to blow his whistle and his men would then stand, pick up the duckboards on which they stood and follow him. There would be two waves. The first men out of the trenches would put the duckboards over the barbed wire and then they would cross.

Christian had left his men alone during that night. They would only be embarrassed by his presence and struggle for something to say. He therefore only joined them when the sun was coming up and the artillery fire was about to commence. Many of the old regulars had been able to catch snatches of sleep during the night, but the new boys had stayed awake shivering and petrified. Christian knew that if he looked over the top of the trench, he would be able to see the German lines across the Mash Valley. It was the name the Intelligence Corps had given to this valley that was once full of cornfields, beside the hamlet of La Boisselle. Someone, somewhere, had thought that a common soldier would not be able to remember a French name. On the other side of the Mash Valley was the Sausage Valley. Bangers and Mash, Christian thought to himself. Someone had a sense of humour in HQ.

At headquarters, fifty miles away in a chateau in Montreuil-Sur-Mer, General Haig had taken the view that seven days of the heaviest bombardment the world had ever seen would be enough to break down the German fortifications. However, Haig hadn't seen these fortifications. They had been built with German efficiency and thoroughness and Christian was certain that even if they bombed them for seventy days it wouldn't make a blind bit of difference. Germans didn't build inadequate fortifications or neglect them. Christian had lived in Austria for long enough to know that both the Austrians and Germans would take pride in their construction. The Germans had come and they meant to stay.

Christian thought about the strategy once more. The men were to walk forward in an orderly line until the German lines were taken. Officers should restrain their men from running or crawling and an officer must at all times be with his men. Unsupervised soldiers, Christian was told, would not know what to do when they got to the German trenches. Christian looked at his pocket watch again. Ten minutes past seven. Only another twenty minutes to go.

"Sergeant Frasier," Christian said to the company sergeant, "I assume that the rum is being handed out?"

"Aye, sir. It's coming down the line now."

"Then, sergeant," continued Christian, "would you have a message passed down the line to Major Rees? Wish him a good morning and tell him that we are in position and ask him whether there are any last orders."

"Beggin' your pardon, sir," said a young recruit sitting on Christian's other side. Christian turned and saw that the young soldier was shaking. "Will we meet much resistance?"

"We're hoping to get across no man's land before they can get back to their positions."

"And what about the barbed wire, sir?"

"Our shelling should have destroyed most of it." Christian noticed that his sergeant was listening to what he said and added: "Keep close to me and Sergeant Frasier."

"Yes, sir," replied the private.

"Sergeant Frasier," said Christian, "if for some reason I'm not here, ensure that this soldier has a double ration of rum."

"A double ration, sir?"

"That's what I said."

Christian looked at his watch; fifteen minutes to go. He wondered if there would be a message from Major Rees. His mouth was dry. There was still a chance, he thought, that HQ may have changed its mind and that General Haig had finally listened to sense. He looked down the line, half hoping for someone to come running round the corner of the trench and tell him that there was a change in orders. He carried on staring – no one came.

"Are you waiting for someone, sir?" said the sergeant.

"No, Sergeant Frasier," replied Christian.

He lowered his head and pulled down his steel helmet. He noticed that the sides of his brown calf-length boots were smeared with mud. He had a desire to rub them clean with a cloth but stopped himself. He looked at his watch again.

"Sir, there's someone coming," said the private next to him. Christian looked and saw a man scampering along the trench as if his life depended on it. Thank God, thought Christian, it's a message from Rees. The soldiers moved their legs to allow the runner to get through. Each soldier's eyes followed him as he passed. When he got to Christian he was out of breath.

"Major Rees sends his respects, sir," said the runner. He took a few deep breaths.

"Yes," said Christian impatiently, "what is it?"

"Major Rees asked me to say, 'Nothing from HQ. No change in orders.' He also said, 'Good luck, sir.' Any message in return?"

Christian looked at him blankly. "No... no, thank you."

The runner returned down the line.

Christian watched him until the trench cut back and he lost sight of him. Rum was soon brought up and ladled out and the private who had been sitting next to Christian was given a double ration, which he swallowed in one long gulp from his bivvy tin.

"What's your name, private?" asked Christian.

"Poley, sir."

"A west Kent name isn't it?" said Christian. "My father has a chauffeur called Poley."

"He's my father, sir."

Christian looked at the young soldier. He hadn't recognised him, although he had spent the last forty-five minutes no more than two feet away from him.

"George Poley?"

Even looking again, Christian didn't recognise him. All the new recruits looked the same; young faces, shaved heads and smelling of fear. Perhaps even if his own brother had been sitting next to him, he would not be able to recognise him.

The shelling started to intensify, as the gunners made one last effort to fire everything they had, and the air vibrated with the concussions. Christian looked at his watch once again – twenty past seven. The roar of the heavy artillery became deafening.

"Sergeant," shouted Christian, "when this stops, I want the smoke canisters fired immediately! I don't want the men walking exposed into the fire of machine guns." Christian looked towards Poley. "This is important," Christian said directly to him. "Don't try to carry on if you're hit. A wounded man is worse than useless fighting in the trenches. If you do get hit, go down and stay down. Wait till night and then crawl back. Cover yourself as well. The Germans will rake the ground with bullets if they hear a sound." Christian looked at his watch again. The minutes seemed to be going too quickly.

Suddenly, the earth felt as if it had moved back a yard and then forward. Sergeant Frasier stood up immediately and peered out above the trench in an attempt to see the damage that the mine had caused under the hamlet of La Boisselle. However, a second wave of vibrations stronger than the first hit them and knocked Frasier off his feet.

Christian stood up and looked out across no man's land to where the remains of La Boisselle had stood. The earth was gradually rising into the air. He clung to the front of the trench as the vibrations continued; time seemed to hang so that the ground came up incredibly slowly and unnaturally. The explosion extended for nearly fifty yards. The earth heaved upwards and brought with it the remains of houses, trees and barns. Christian could hardly believe it when the ground continued to rise into the air, perhaps two hundred feet and then, as if freed from any constraint of nature, it all blew apart. The great elm trees of Picardy, some taken up with the explosion, turned over, exposing their roots to the blue sky before shattering into splinters.

"Get down!" shouted Christian, as masonry and wood suddenly started falling on the trench.

A minute passed before Christian regained his focus. The barrage of the heavy artillery continued coming relentlessly but he couldn't hear it. The explosion of the La Boisselle mine had momentarily deafened him to the noises around him. He looked for his sergeant and saw him standing on the top of the trench, his rifle held in his right hand high above his head.

Christian could barely hear anything as the sound of the explosion was still pounding in his ears. He looked down the line, wondering whether it would be possible to lead his men. Most of them were pressed hard against the wall of the trench. One soldier was screaming – a shard of elm tree was sticking out of his leg. Christian could just hear the screams, or at least he thought he could. And then it went quiet as if all the noise had been sucked out of the world. Even the screaming soldier ceased shouting and Frasier got back into the trench.

"Fire the canisters, sergeant!" shouted Christian. "Fire the bloody canisters!" A wave of tiredness suddenly swept over him – exuberance and exhaustion all mixed together. He had been waiting for this moment all night, but now it had come he did not know whether he had the strength left to get out of the trench and march across no man's land. He knew, however, what was expected of him. Christian looked at his watch. Seven twenty-nine.

"Hold your positions, men," he shouted.

Lieutenant Christian Drewe held his pocket watch in one hand and then placed his whistle into his mouth. Thirty more seconds. The smoke continued to billow out of the canisters towards the German lines. Sergeant Frasier looked at him. Suddenly Christian felt sick and began to shake. Twenty more seconds. He carried on staring at his watch. The second hand seemed to drag itself around the face of the dial. His mouth was still dry and then he began to blow.

The 6th battalion of the Royal West Kents climbed out of their trenches where they had been for the last nine months and walked slowly into a bank of grey smoke. They got out of the trenches lice-ridden and exhausted, but Christian knew they would fight.

As Christian clambered over the top of the trench, the noise increased and seemed to surround him. The soldiers threw the duckboards on the barbed wire and they crossed easily enough. They now walked forward into the smoke. Suddenly Christian had no idea where anyone was – no idea where Frasier was or Poley – no idea whether his men were in front of him or behind him. He carried on walking, blinded to what was going on around him. He could smell cordite and hear the unrelenting sound of guns firing.

"Keep a steady line!" he heard Sergeant Frasier bark. "Keep a steady line!"

Christian walked slowly forward across the potholed cornfield where the crops had been blown into inexistence. As he walked, he began to hear a hissing noise that grew louder and became unrelenting. It sounded like a train passing through a tunnel. The smoke blew on ahead and then started dispersing. He looked to his side and behind him; he had come no more than fifty yards. Poley was a few steps to his right, but he could not see Frasier.

"Keep the line," he shouted. It was then that he noticed that some of his soldiers were falling; knocked off their feet by something he could not see. The hissing continued. Christian suddenly stumbled. A form lay in front of him. For a second Christian did not recognise his company commander, Major Rees. He did not stop to check him – after three months at the front he knew what a dead man looked like.

In front of him Christian could see the Germans' barbed wire. The smoke had nearly lifted completely. He turned to look how many men were with him and was amazed for a moment at how few British soldiers he could see. Grenades started to explode. Suddenly, Christian could not stop himself; he started running forward. He was no more than fifty yards from the hedges of barbed wire when an explosion knocked him off his feet. Winded but not hurt, he got up. Poley ran across to help him.

"Are you all right, sir?" Poley yelled.

"Fine I think," said Christian. He looked down at his stomach, his arms and his legs.

There was no blood, no tears in his uniform. He steadied himself and once again started running forward. He had taken about two dozen paces, reached the rows of barbed wire, when a wall of flame engulfed him and he staggered backwards, falling into a shell hole. He screamed, rolling in the damp mud to put out the flames and clutching at his face. He continued screaming. For a second, he heard Poley shouting and then he passed out and remembered nothing more about the attack on the Somme.

*   *   *

George Poley threw himself down the side of the large crater where Christian Drewe had fallen. Christian was screaming when he got there, and he could see the collar of Christian's jacket was still smouldering. He pulled out his water can and poured the contents on Christian's face and collar. It hissed and steamed; he could suddenly smell burnt meat. Christian screamed once more before he passed out. The side of his face was blistered and jelly was seeping from one empty eye socket.

Poley stared at the body, horrified; he thought that no one that badly burnt could live for long. He did not want to touch Christian again, but what was he to do? His father would have known what to do. He tried to imagine his father sitting opposite him. He would take stock of the situation. He would check to see what was in the kitbags; find out if there was a knife or bandages or even some morphine. He would then inspect Christian's injuries. Christian shook violently as Poley removed the kitbag from around his shoulder. Once again George Poley stared at Christian, wondering whether he was conscious; his eyelids were open and he seemed to stare up at the sun with one good eye and the other empty socket like a hollow moon.

Warm gusts of air swept up through the Mash Valley in hot surges that carried with it the smell of explosives. The firing continued and Poley could hear shouting from near the shell hole. He blanked out the sounds around him and focussed on treating Christian. He had found some bandages in Christian's kitbag and knew he needed to bandage Christian's face to stop it becoming infected. There was no morphine, gauze or antiseptic. He was worried that without gauze, the bandages might stick to Christian's face but he thought the risk of infection the most serious problem. He hoped that Christian would not start screaming again. He took Christian's water bottle and wetted a bandage. He placed it on Christian's face and the screaming began again – it was a whole life's experience in a single inexpressible day.

"Bloody hell, sir," he shouted, "shut up! Shut the fuck up!"

George Poley put his hands over his ears and closed his eyes. "Shut up, shut the fuck up, fuck, fuck, fuck... fuck!"

Poley breathed quickly and heavily. Try to think rationally, he thought. Finish off what you're doing. He could imagine the look of disappointment on his father's face as he sat in a mud crater, his hands over his ears, his eyes closed, almost in tears. He drew in another lungful of air. He couldn't stand the noise. He opened his eyes. He saw the bandages and the water bottle. He snatched up the canteen and poured water on another strip of bandage and tied it around Christian's blistered face. His body convulsed upwards and his arm swung up, catching Poley in the ribs. Christian stopped moving and Poley looked at him, unsure whether he was still alive. He moved closer and could hear Christian's shallow breathing through his mouth.

Do it now, he thought to himself. Put the bandages on now. He picked up the water canteen to wet another bandage but only a few drops were left.

"Shit!"

He raised his head above the crater's edge and saw a dozen soldiers lying near him. He heaved himself over the lip of the crater and crawled towards the nearest soldier and then, taking his bayonet, he cut the strap of the water canteen and pulled it away from the soldier, and rolled back towards the crater.

When he was safely back, he took a drink from the canteen and then poured a trickle into Christian's mouth. Christian seemed to swallow it and then choked, bringing the water back up. He moved Christian to the side of the trench so that his head was upwards and again he poured a few drops into Christian's mouth. This time Christian swallowed. Poley decided not to try and force any more water down him – not for the time being. He finished putting the bandages on Christian's face.

There was nothing to do but lie in the crater and hope that Christian Drewe would not die. He remembered what had been said to him: "wait until nightfall and be as quiet as possible; the Germans will rake the ground with bullets if they hear a sound." He looked up at the sky, it appeared to be just after midday.

Those in command, somewhere safe from the threat of bullet and explosion, were just sitting down for lunch. General Rawlinson, commander of the British Fourth Army, sat at a large table trying to decipher what had gone on with the hope of determining how the day should progress. At about two-thirty he took the decision to renew the offensive. Too far away to feel the pulse of the battle or to receive intelligence quickly, the general took the view that they really ought to attempt to mitigate the failures of the morning and if there was to be a failure then it had to be a glorious failure. He decided over his lunch and a small crystal glass of Hock that the second and third lines of reserves should now go forward and somewhere in his stomach he sensed that the afternoon's event would be even more ineffective than those of the morning.

George Poley waited as the afternoon attack took place and stayed quiet. A few wounded soldiers tried to make their way back as the offensive took place. Few survived. Poley had no idea whether it was a British or German attack. He almost hoped that it might be German so that he could surrender; however, as the attack was taking place the noise of the whistles seemed to disturb Christian. Poley crawled over next to him.

"It's me, sir, it's George Poley. Don't worry, I'll get you back," he whispered in Christian's ear. "I'll get us both back, sir – don't you worry about that."

There was no answer; albeit in response Christian ceased shaking as if calmed by the familiar voice and his weak, ragged breathing resumed.

Suddenly, George Poley could take the suspense no longer. He slowly raised his head above the lip of the crater to see what was going on. Everywhere there was a stench of burnt meat. He wanted to cry. Suddenly he heard whistling around him and quickly brought his head down.

"They're withdrawing, sir," said Poley, "withdrawing before they even got going," but again there was no answer – just the slow, weak, ragged breathing. The guns of the Somme ceased firing. Poley picked up a handful of dust. It had probably been good farmland once, he thought, and he wondered how quickly all signs of the war would be wiped away and the fields of corn return.

Nothing much happened for the rest of the afternoon, or so Poley thought. He heard only the single shots of a rifle, the screams of the injured and the mad cries of magpies out of Authuille Wood. Poley rolled over and lay on his back, looking up at the late afternoon sky and the cotton wool clouds that restlessly tumbled around. He had begun to get used to the sounds of Christian's ragged breathing and the screams or the recoil of a rifle. He had heard them for the last ten hours and he knew it was another five hours before it would become dark. He still feared that Christian would not survive being dragged back.

He sat up – he desperately wanted to be at home – away from the noise and the smell and the disease; from the rats and the lice and the never-ending feeling that this might be one's last breath. There was none of the glory that he had been told there would be. At eighteen years of age, George Poley could think of nothing better to do while crouching in a crater in Mash Valley, in the department of the Somme, but to cry.

"What are ye doin' down there, laddie?"

Poley stared upwards for a moment, unable to connect the voice or to make sense of what was being said. Out of the red lulling swell of the early evening Poley recognised Sergeant Frasier's stocky figure. He continued to stare mesmerised at the outline of Frasier who stood on the edge of the crater apparently unconcerned or perhaps even unaware of the bullets buzzing around about him. Frasier continued to look at Poley. None of it made sense. He rubbed his eyes with the back of his hand.

"It's Lieutenant Drewe," said Poley, "I need to get him back."

Frasier looked down at Christian's body with its face bandaged.

"He's as good as dead," answered Frasier.

"I'm not going without Lieutenant Drewe." Poley was emphatic and picked up his rifle. He began breathing hard. He looked at Frasier and gritted his teeth together. He could at least make a show of being determined.

"Well, what are ye goin' do with that, laddie?" Frasier asked. He raised his own rifle and looked down the barrel at Poley. "Ye better think what yer goin' tae do next 'cause I'll nae have a problem with blowin' yer fuckin' brains out."

Poley put his gun down.

"I need your help to get Lieutenant Drewe back." Poley's voice trembled.

Frasier jumped down into the crater. He walked over towards Christian.

"Don't touch him," Poley shouted and again picked up his rifle.

Frasier stared at Poley and with one swift movement knocked the rifle to one side. "Ye don't go aimin' a fuckin' rifle at me, laddie."

"What are you going to do?"

Frasier looked at Christian.

"They made a fuckin' mess of him."

Frasier once again turned to look at Poley. He could see that he was nothing more than a boy, scared and wet behind the ears. Frasier had that morning seen more than a thousand boys no older than George Poley die. He hadn't the stomach to see one more killed.

"Yer fuckin' lucky I'm nae gonna kill ye," said Frasier, standing nose to nose in front of Poley. Slowly his head moved back. "But no one points a rifle at me." Rapidly Frasier's head went forward, smashing into the bridge of Poley's nose and he buckled to his knees before passing out.

Chapter 44

"Are ye awake, laddie?"

George Poley lifted his right hand to his nose and winced.

"Yer name, soldier?" Sergeant Fraiser asked.

"George Poley, Private 46235."

"So ye reckon yer gonna try and drag Lieutenant Drewe back tae our lines?"

Poley watched as Frasier took a sip of water out of the canteen. He thought about reaching over and taking back his water bottle but decided against it. Frasier looked at him staring at the canteen and handed it over. Poley took a sip and wondered whether he ought to try to give a little water to Christian. He suddenly realised that Christian wasn't making any noise; he couldn't even hear the ragged breathing. He moved towards Christian, but Frasier leant over and grabbed him.

"Leave him, laddie; ye won't wake him."

"He's not dead?" asked Poley, shaking Frasier's arm away.

"No. I gave him some morphine to keep him unconscious."

"Morphine?"

"I had some. Do ye always ask so many bleedin' questions?"

"When do we try and get him back?" continued Poley, ignoring Frasier.

"When it's as black as hell, and not a minute sooner."

It was nearly dusk, but it would be at least another four hours before it was as black as hell, thought Poley.

"What now, sergeant?" Poley whispered.

"Well, ye seem well in with the lieutenant," whispered Frasier in reply. "We have a couple of hours t' kill, so tell me somethin' about Lieutenant Drewe."

Poley looked over at Christian. He had no idea where to start. He had known the Drewe family all his life. Talking about them seemed a betrayal; however,

231

he had spent most of the day sitting in silence or listening to screaming and he wanted to pass the time.

"Lieutenant Drewe's father is Sir Julius Drewe. Perhaps you've heard of him – he owns the Home and Colonial Stores. My father works on his estate; he's worked for the Drewe family for nearly twenty years." He looked over to where Christian was lying. "I last saw Lieutenant Drewe eighteen months ago – it was on the day he joined up."

Poley remembered the New Year's Eve ball at Wadhurst Hall as if it was yesterday. He had helped the kitchen staff clear plates from the dining hall and had to wear a stiff collar and a black jacket like the butlers. He remembered itching at the starched collar all that evening, feeling it was worse than a Sunday. He remembered watching as the auction took place.

"It happened at their New Year's Eve ball. They were talking about it for weeks afterwards."

He recounted the story of the auction to a rapt Frasier.

"Nobody really knows why he signed up, but my father reckoned when you are just one voice against hundreds, you soon get exhausted, like swimming against the tide. My father reckoned that Lieutenant Drewe just wanted to shout back at the world that he weren't no coward."

* * *

And with a silence of held-in breaths, night came. For over an hour, neither Poley nor Frasier whispered a word but around them they could sense a throb of activity. From what had been said to him, Poley knew that now was the time when soldiers would try to limp or crawl their way back to their own lines, feeling their way as they went. Occasionally, flares would go up and hang in the sky, their accusatory light identifying the crawling, undead soldiers. The soldiers would then cease moving. Occasionally Poley would hear the snap of a rifle or the burst of a machine gun – sometimes a groan.

The crater in which Poley and Frasier huddled was a hundred and fifty yards from the German line, three quarters of the way across no man's land. In front of them they heard German voices. They were starting to round up prisoners. Poley could just about make out Frasier's shape in the blackness – he was looking back at the German line, holding his rifle and bayonet ready. Poley also picked up his rifle and aimed into the blackness in the general direction of the German lines. He waited quietly; his breathing became more pronounced. He tried to quieten it and breathe more regularly but his heart was beating too quickly. He heard a German shouting and then shots and afterwards the concussion of stick grenades. The German voices did not come so close to them again.

From pitch-darkness to sunrise was five hours. Frasier had said that to try to get back as soon as night had fallen would be a mistake – that would be the time when the Germans would be vigilant. Wait, he had said, wait for at least two hours. Frasier reckoned that it would take them an hour to get back to their own lines as they would have to crawl.

"Ye cannae walk or ye'll be trippin' over holes and corpses," he had said.

It was ten past two when Frasier gave Christian a second injection of morphine.

"If he makes a sound," Frasier whispered to Poley, "we leave him – yer agreed on that."

Poley nodded his head but knew that he had yet to reach a decision on what he would do if that happened. He could hear Christian's breathing – shallow and weak – and hoped that he would stay unconscious. They waited a few moments to be sure that the morphine had taken full effect and then from the ridge of the crater they started pulling Christian. He did not utter a sound, but the full weight of his unconscious body immediately made Poley's arms ache. Frasier, small, squat and built like an outhouse, appeared not to be bothered by the weight. The only light that Poley could see was the stars above them. He felt insignificant beneath these tiny specks of light, so far off that some had burned out before their light had arrived in the night sky.

Frasier was able to move quicker than Poley, and within a few minutes he was sweating. He crawled forward and suddenly his hand touched a corpse. He moved his hand away quickly. He could feel Frasier's eyes staring at him. Poley shifted his body round and pushed the corpse away and then continued to pull Christian after him as he also crawled forward. Inch by inch they moved back towards their own lines. After ten minutes Poley's arms became leaden and tired. He struggled to pull the weight; he started breathing harder as he pulled Christian towards him a few inches at a time. He also began to hear Frasier breathing and then again he found himself against the cold skin of a corpse. He pushed it away and then took a deep breath before pulling at Christian's arm. The ground in front of him seemed to fall away.

"It's a crater," he whispered to Frasier.

"Pull him into it," Frasier whispered back.

They clambered down the side and found themselves on top of a pile of corpses at the bottom. A flare went up and Poley could see that the crater was about thirty feet across.

"Get yer breath, laddie," Frasier whispered. "He's heavier than he looks."

Poley nodded.

"We can carry him across the crater. It'll be easier than draggin' him and no one will see us."

Poley again nodded. The flare went out and Poley peered into the darkness. They agreed to wait until the next flare went up and they could see where they were walking. He had seen the twisted pile of limbs each indistinguishable from the others before the flare died away, as well as its reflection on the metal of the barrels of the rifles, the steel helmets and the brass buckles.

The next flare went up high above them and they picked up Christian underneath his arms. He moaned. Frasier looked at him but said nothing. They began climbing over the bodies. "Let's get Lieutenant Drewe to the far end of the crater," said Frasier. They waited there for the flare to fall softly to the ground and the light fade. Once again in the blackness they moved, dragging Christian. It took them another forty minutes to get back to their own lines. They clambered over a duckboard and then had to convince a sentry that they weren't Germans counter-attacking.

Poley, who had his arms around the waist of Christian to hold him up, felt he was about to collapse.

"For Christ's sake," he gasped, "help me get Lieutenant Drewe on a stretcher."

"You won't find a stretcher bearer here," said the sentry. However, he helped Poley bring the body of Christian into the safety of a trench. Poley looked up and down the line – he could see some half-shaded light coming from a dugout down the line. A mass of bodies was piled up beside the trench.

"They're all dead," said the sentry. "There are thousands of them – everywhere. If I were you, I'd leave your officer here. With a bit of luck they'll get to him early tomorrow as he is an officer."

"Where's the nearest hospital?" asked Poley.

"Albert," said the sentry.

"And where's that?" demanded Poley.

"It's about two miles straight behind you but there's thousands of wounded everywhere. Even if you get him there, no one will be able to look at him. You're wasting your time. Just leave him here with the others – get yourselves something to eat and a drink."

"Don't waste yer breath," said Frasier to the sentry. He turned and looked at Poley. "I suppose yer'll want me to help ye carry him there?"

Chapter 45

Even in the early hours of the morning, just before daybreak, the French town of Albert was alive with activity. A basilica stood in the main square and had been turned by the English army into a hospital. The gaslights around the square gave out a dim glow. Groups of soldiers stood in shadows, many smoking and some drinking. Before the steps of the basilica, row after row of soldiers were laid out on the cobbles. Orderlies in white coats moved from one body to the next, like ghostly apparitions, inspecting injuries. They covered the dead, who were quickly removed and piled one on top of another. Those still living were moved a step closer to the door of the church – a little nearer to sanctuary.

Inside the church was pandemonium. Blood lay in pools on the floor. The smell of decay, faeces and carbolic soap was everywhere. Supplies of morphine were now almost non-existent and what was left was reserved for the officers. The soldiers screamed as their wounds were washed in a weak antiseptic solution, biting hard down onto tough leather belts. Rows of makeshift operating tables were at the far end of the basilica, underneath a stained-glass window of Christ on the cross, his side pierced by a spear. It was into this chaos that Poley walked. No one paid him the slightest attention.

Poley had decided to look for a nurse as he assumed that the doctors would ignore him and order him out. He walked slowly down through the nave and climbed on the bema, where the altar had once stood. Everyone seemed busy. He saw another four tables in the semi-circular area of the apse where surgeons were amputating limbs. There were nurses there and a few male orderlies holding down the screaming soldiers, but he decided they would resent being interrupted. He turned around and saw a nurse walking towards a side door, carrying a set of surgical instruments. He chased after her.

"There's an officer with me, miss," Poley shouted at her.

She stopped and turned towards him. A lock of her jet-black hair had escaped from under her nurse's hat. She looked at him with her large eyes. She seemed exhausted; she seemed so tired, as if she were carrying the sins of the world.

"I've got an injured officer with me, miss," Poley repeated.

"Bring him to the front," said the nurse, "and an orderly will take his details."

"You don't understand, miss," said Poley. "He's nearly dead and I've been tryin' to get him here since morning."

"You'll have to take him around to the front."

"Please, miss, can't you look at him?"

"I'm not a doctor," said the nurse quietly. "He needs to see a doctor."

"Please, miss. I don't think Lieutenant Drewe will live much longer if he ain't seen."

The nurse went white and dropped the tray she was carrying.

"Are you all right, miss?" asked Poley.

"What did you say his name was?" she demanded.

"Lieutenant Drewe."

"His full name."

"Lieutenant Christian Drewe, miss."

"He's injured?" She grabbed hold of Poley's arm. "Where did you say he was? Take me to him now."

"He's with our sergeant, behind the church, where they're layin' out the corpses," answered Poley, leading her towards the side door.

"Hurry!" Rose shouted at him.

*　*　*

An old nurse with callused hands brought Poley and Frasier a mug of tea. She said nothing but then she never said much. She was a Baptist minister's daughter who had grown up frequenting the chapels of the Yorkshire dales. Her father had had a taciturn way about him which she inherited.

The sun began to rise and the clouds appeared red, a warning to faraway shepherds. Poley and Frasier sipped at their tea, sitting on cold stone steps at the side of the basilica. Frasier closed his eyes. Poley shook slightly with tiredness. The bodies of the dead, piled up at the back of the church, no longer attracted their attention. The white-coated orderlies had given up trying to hide the corpses under white sheets. Perhaps, thought Poley, it was because there were too many bodies or perhaps they had run out of sheets. Around him he could hear a buzzing sound; it was similar to the sound of bullets whizzing past, and then he realised that as the dawn sun was rising, the flies had come to feast.

In the distance the guns started their heavy pounding once again. Poley looked at Frasier and considered if he should ask whether they ought to make their way back to their regiment but decided against it. He had done his part – no one could ask him to do more – or call him a coward. Frasier sat with his eyes closed, cupping the mug of tea in his broad hands. Better not disturb him, thought Poley.

They had hardly touched their tea when the side door to the basilica opened and Rose came out. She turned towards the front line when she heard the guns pounding.

*   *   *

The heavy artillery forewarned a new intake of wounded and Rose Hall wondered where in hell they would put the new casualties. There were still rows of wounded at the front of the basilica; they kept on coming in a relentless wave. Many of the injuries were identical – flesh torn from the body and shattered bone. There were also some bayonet gashes where soldiers had made it across to the German trenches and fought hand to hand. A few soldiers had burns; they had been caught by the flamethrowers – the *Flammenwerfer*. Not many survived being burnt and therefore statistically Christian Drewe could consider himself lucky, but Rose knew how serious the injuries caused by the flamethrowers were and did not think him fortunate at all. The flamethrowers spewed out an oil that stuck to the flesh, causing a permanent disfigurement and, having seen the extent of the burns, she knew that Christian, even if he did survive, would need skin grafts.

She remembered him from that first day when they met at Fenchurch Street Station. She remembered him as Kit Drewe. There had been a fog – a real pea-souper – and he had wandered into the concourse café. He had nowhere to sit and had asked if he could sit down at her table. She remembered looking up at him as he read his paper and then he had suddenly stopped reading and frowned. He had dark brown hair, a slight cleft in his chin and beautiful green eyes. She remembered the green eyes and how well dressed he was. When he frowned, she found herself asking whether he was well. When she thought about it now, it was a ridiculous question – he looked perfectly well. In fact, he looked perfect.

As she had got to know Kit, she found that he was so different to Peter in almost every way. He was rarely serious. He danced divinely. He laughed at her jokes. He was all the things that Peter was not – and he was unattainable. Kit could have chosen a dozen prettier nurses – he was one of the most eligible bachelors in England – rich, talented, handsome. There was no reason why he would give her a second thought. And then he had kissed her one night and for a moment she had hope, before Peter had taken that hope away from her.

She looked down at her black shoes. She had wanted to tell Poley and Frasier how the operation on Kit's face was going; she also wanted to get back to Kit but as soon as she had stepped outside, the emotions had welled up in her so that she could not speak. She hadn't slept for twenty-four hours, and standing in the rays of the morning sun made her feel like she wanted to cry. She had no idea when she would sleep again; she felt too tired for sleep. None of the nurses had gone back to their quarters and although some now napped through exhaustion on chairs in the basilica, not one of them had thought about leaving.

Her blue nurse's uniform hung shapelessly around her. She had taken off her white headdress and pinafore and had given them to an orderly to be bleached in boiling water.

Poley looked up at her and waited for her to speak. When she didn't, he could not help himself saying, "Miss?"

Rose looked at him for a few moments more before gathering herself together and replying.

"He's being operated on at the moment. The doctors are cutting away the skin around his eyes and mouth. They are hoping to save his left eye but," she paused, "there's nothing to save on the right side. That nurse who brought you tea is assisting the doctors. She suggested I come and see how you are."

She now looked at Poley who was looking up at her. She hadn't realised how young he was, probably not much older than eighteen, she thought. Another young boy with a lifetime of experience in his eyes.

"We're fine," Poley lied. "I couldn't leave without finding out how Lieutenant Drewe was. I knew him, you see, before the war. I grew up on his father's estate."

"I also knew him," said Rose, "and his brother Basil. Anyway, I wanted to thank you both for saving him. If you hadn't got him here when you did, I doubt whether he would be alive now."

"And he's out of danger now, is he?" asked Poley.

"No," said Rose; "but if he survives the operation then we can at least hope."

"And when will the operation be over?"

"In an hour or so. If you want, you can wait at the back of the nurses' quarters; there's an outhouse there and a washroom where you can get cleaned up or there's a bar across the square where you might be able to get something to eat later. I doubt if it's open at this time."

Poley looked at Frasier who had opened his eyes.

"There nowhere where we can get somethin' to eat now, miss?" asked Frasier.

"There's ham and bread at the nurses' quarters. I'll take you there and get you something."

Poley and Frasier stood up and followed Rose as she walked down the passageway at the side of the basilica. She looked out across the square at the hundreds of bodies still lying there. The stench of excrement was growing worse every hour. She wondered how they could ever deal with the bodies lying there, let alone another intake. She turned and walked away slowly, ignoring the cries and screams that haunted the square. At the edge of the town square, a group of Indian orderlies stood sharing a cigarette. They were huddled in a small circle in their long white coats with red crosses on their pockets; conscientious objectors who had come to help because their conscience dictated that they must do something. One of the orderlies, a tall man with long black hair and dark skin, smiled at Rose as she went past. She knew him as Nitya but was too emotionally drained even to smile back.

Poley kept pace with her and Frasier stayed a step behind, as if he were an unwanted guest at a party to which he had not been invited.

"We won't know for a while whether he'll be able to see again," said Rose. "We have our best surgeon treating him and he can do marvellous things reconstructing the face. I'm sure he'll live." The last few words were more as a comfort for herself and she tried to smile, although she did not really feel it was anything to smile about. It was better to smile than to cry. "It's incredible what Dr Gillies can do." The tears began to fall down the side of Rose's face.

"Don't take on, miss," said Poley.

She wiped her eyes with her uniform sleeve. "I'm just a little tired."

An accordion played from the bedroom window of a house that they passed. Poley looked up, finding his attention caught by a sound so quintessentially French.

"He practises every morning and then plays for centimes in the market square in the evening," said Rose, who had noticed that Poley was looking to see where the sound was coming from. "He's also blind," she added. She carried on walking and Poley continued to look up at the window as he followed behind her. As they passed away from the house and the noise of the accordion died away, Poley turned to see where Frasier was. He was already thirty yards behind and was only now turning into the street. His feet shuffled along like those of a tired tramp. He seemed to have shrunk in size, not nearly as stocky and ferocious as when he was charging out across no man's land. Poley called out to Rose to wait up, but she had already stopped and was now opening the door to a large, detached house, a few metres back from the pavement. She stood beside the heavy wooden door with a red cross painted on the front, until Poley walked over with Frasier behind him.

"Go round to the back and I'll get you something to eat."

Rose left them ten minutes later to return to the basilica. In that time, they had eaten the bread and ham. They agreed to wait until they heard news whether the operation was a success. Frasier had said that he'd kill for a bath and didn't care one iota whether there was hot water or not. As soon as Rose had left, he pulled off his lice-infested clothes and sunk himself into the water and fell asleep immediately as he rested his head on the back of the tin bath.

Rose lit a cigarette as she walked back to the basilica. The tobacco smoke whirled in the air as she walked – restless and soon to fade. Alone, her thoughts turned back to Kit Drewe. It had been eighteen months since she had last seen him and now he lay on a table in the hospital, unrecognisable. She would not have known him, his face being so badly burnt. She would have walked straight past him but for the fact that young George Poley had told her who he was. She didn't want to have feelings for him. What good would they do? He was different; she was married and everything had moved on. She tried to convince herself that she would not care whether he lived or died. She threw her cigarette on the ground as she got closer to the basilica and stepped on it. She said to herself once again that she would not care whatever happened to him, but found herself crying as she climbed up the seven steps to the church.

Lieutenant Christian Drewe was still unconscious when she arrived back at the field hospital but during every break, she sat next to him and talked. She didn't know whether he understood or not. At the end of the day she was told that they would be moving him by ambulance to the hospital at Amiens. The surgeons said there was nothing more they could do for him in a field hospital except give him morphine. Rose held his hand and told him that when they both got back to England, she would find him and they would go dancing once again in the Lyons' Corner House. She told him that when the war was over they could go to Vienna and drink champagne in the bars and listen to the opera singers. She told him that if he wanted then she would look after him for as long as he needed her. He made some sounds, but she was not sure whether he was trying to speak or trying to breathe. She took off her St Christopher, kissed it and fastened it around his neck.

* * *

Rose looked at Kit as he slept in the field bed. She had rubbed in an antiseptic, placed gauze on the wounds and bandaged Kit's face after the operation. Dr Gillies told her that he had lost his right eye and that his left eye had been damaged. He doubted whether he would see again and he needed to be transferred to Amiens as soon as possible and then back home. Rose closed her eyes. She had hardly slept for the last few days, catching snatches of sleep when she could. Dr Gillies left her and she kept her eyes closed as she sat beside Kit and held his hand.

She dreamt that she was back in London, back with Peter. She had not seen Peter since the previous Easter. Peter had given up the apartment in Balham; he said it was a waste of money and they had stayed at a hotel. Rose hated that they had to stay in a hotel, as if it was an indecent liaison. Peter had hardly spoken whilst he was with her. He sat reading his paper, occasionally scratching himself. She tried to tell him about her decision to go and work in a field hospital, but he didn't seem to care. She said that she wanted to do more to help; she added as an afterthought that if Peter were injured, she hoped that she might be there. He didn't answer. He stared at her when she got undressed to go to bed and she felt uncomfortable. When he slept, he tossed and turned and kept her awake. Sometimes he woke up in the night and shouted at her.

She had played out the part of a dutiful wife and had lain in bed listening to his slow and irregular breathing as he slept. She imagined that he was riddled with lice and she wanted to scratch herself. She couldn't continue her life like that. She hardly slept at all during the first night they were together and got up early the next morning, as quietly as possible, not wanting to wake him. It was cold and she looked for her dressing gown. It was hanging on the door and she walked across the room.

"What time is it?" Peter had said, his eyes still shut.

"I don't know," she replied.

"Do you love me?"

She lied.

*   *   *

Six hours later she was awakened when a hand was placed on her shoulder. Dr Gillies stood beside her.

"It's time for him to go," he said.

The orderlies carried Christian to a lorry with a red cross painted on the side. He was carried by the young Indian orderly, Nitya, and laid out on the floor of the truck with a dozen other injured soldiers.

"Was he a close friend?" Nitya asked.

"I hardly know him," said Rose.

"Then he's very lucky," replied Nitya, "to have someone who cares for him so much."

Rose watched the ambulance as it took Christian Drewe to Amiens.

241

She didn't cry when the ambulance left but instead made a decision that when she got back to England, she would find him. If she still felt the same when her leave was due, she would write to Peter and tell him of her decision. She needed to explain things to him. He would never understand, he would feel betrayed, and he would hate her. She felt a moment's indecision – fear at what Peter might do. But what could he do? Slap her again? It would be nothing compared to what Kit was enduring.

It was a marriage that had lasted seventeen months – hardly a marriage at all.

PART VII

Chapter 46

The Endsleigh Hospital for the Rehabilitation of Wounded Soldiers had once been the Endsleigh Palace Hotel. It was a vast, squat, rectangular, grey stone building with large windows in heavy iron frames. It had been built at the start of the industrial revolution as a *grande* hotel for the comfort of northern millowners coming to London. It had, in the hundred years from its construction, become run down and all that was left was a sense of faded grandeur – worn burgundy carpets and unfashionable drapes. Water had got into the building and the plaster on the walls of the top floor had de-bonded. The owner of the hotel decided it was not worth the cost of renovating the building and therefore, as Edwin Lutyens remarked, it was sold for a song.

In the latter part of 1915, Dr Haden-Guest, a surgeon who had practised on the front line, came up with the idea of turning the old Endsleigh Palace Hotel into a hospital. His circle of friends were wealthy and he was full of motivation and therefore the project was up and running within a few months. He asked for money from Gertrude Jekyll, who gave generously, and from Emily Lutyens, who gave her support. He also asked the help of a young Indian man, Jiddu Krishnamurti, whom he had met the previous year while in France.

When Celia decided to help at the hospital in September 1916, she wrote to her tutors in Cambridge saying that she was planning to delay her second year – possibly indefinitely. She was not upset. In the preceding twelve months, all the life had been sucked out of Cambridge and those who had not enlisted walked around with their heads down. The city felt cold, and she was pleased not to be going back. She wrote the letter without telling either of her parents about her plans. She spent that weekend trying to find the right time to tell them. Her mother had Krishnamurti in tow once again and her father was in a foul mood. He blamed it on problems with the design of New Delhi, but she suspected that the reason was closer to home. Celia could not find the right moment, so she blurted the news out over dinner on the Sunday evening. She said she had written to her tutors and that she had also spoken to Dr Haden-Guest, who had agreed she could start working at the Endsleigh Hospital on the following day. She was surprised by her mother's reaction; Emily Lutyens, who so rarely smiled, beamed.

"You'll be working with Krishnamurti," Emily said.

Her father said nothing.

*   *   *

Working at the Endsleigh Hospital was not what Celia had anticipated. Years at school doing lessons with the St John's Ambulance Association had not prepared her for this. She had expected to be changing dressings and comforting the injured. The truth was that most of her first day involved collecting and sluicing out bedpans, and by the time she went home her arms and legs ached, and she worried that she would never escape the smell of faeces. The second day was no better, nor the third. The ward sister shouted at everyone irrespective of rank and ability, and the matron was so ferocious that Celia considered that she might be a direct descendant of the gorgon.

In contrast, Krishnamurti, who spent the weekdays studying for his entrance exams for university, would come in on a weekend in striped trousers, a cream shirt and black Lobb shoes. He would casually talk to the nurses and doctors. She never saw him cleaning bedpans and didn't seem to do any of the manual work that was assigned to her. Whenever Celia saw Krishnamurti she would fume. He was popular with the doctors and other nurses – more popular than she was. The doctors would not spend a moment speaking to her and the other nurses seemed to think that she wasn't pulling her weight, as she sometimes complained about how tired she was, whereas Kirshnamurti appeared not to have a care in the world.

The top two floors of the building were still being refurbished when the hospital opened. The works were being undertaken by a group of volunteers and some tradesmen who were supervising them. They were working from the bottom up so that rooms could be converted into wards and become operational in stages. After a few weeks at the hospital, Celia was told that a new ward had been completed and therefore a further influx of injured soldiers would be turning up. The ward sister asked Celia to inspect the rooms in order to help determine what would be needed in terms of bedding, bedpans and linen. Celia was pleased to be away from her usual mundane routine and was inquisitive to see what was being done on these floors, which were barred to everyone except those who were helping with the refurbishment.

One large ward had been made operational on the second floor. The walls of the first dozen rooms had been removed to create a ward for thirty-six soldiers. At the far end of the ward many of the rooms had been turned into storerooms or bathrooms. The beds had been placed in the ward, but they were covered with dust. The sister explained to Celia that the room would have to be cleaned from top to bottom. Celia found herself volunteering to help, hoping to get on the good side of the ward sister, and was left to start the cleaning of the ward and prepare a list of what bedding and other linen would be required. She was told to use some of the volunteers who were preparing the final ward on the top floor to assist her in cleaning the ward and went looking for some help.

Celia could not help smiling when she saw Krishnamurti in a pair of dirty overalls with a large scrubbing brush in one hand and the pail of bleach and water in the other, scrubbing at a wall. His jacket, tie and waistcoat were hanging on the back of a chair.

"I don't think I've ever seen you in overalls," said Celia.

Krishnamurti looked round at Celia and his face broke into a smile and his brown eyes lit up.

"Come to help?" he asked.

"I was hoping that I could get you and some of the others to help clean the ward below," said Celia. "It's covered in dust and until we get it spotless, we can't move any soldiers in."

"I am afraid I am the last one here," said Krishnamurti. "We usually start around seven in the morning and finish about four." Celia looked at her watch; it was five-fifteen.

"You're still here? It's all a bit menial for the new messiah isn't it?"

Krishnamurti looked at Celia again. His smile faded.

"I got in a bit late this morning," he answered. "I had to get some trousers for a soldier who had lost a leg."

"Sorry," Celia said. "I only meant..."

"I know what you meant," said Krishnamurti interrupting her. "Anyway, do you want some help or not?"

"If it's only us two then we're likely to be here all night," answered Celia.

"Then let's stop talking and get started. I'll see if I can round up a few nurses or a doctor or two."

Krishnamurti recruited three nurses and two doctors to the cause and together they finished cleaning the ward just after eleven p.m. Celia did not feel nearly as tired as she often felt, even though she had worked twice as long. People spoke to her and for the first time in nearly a month, she felt welcome.

Given the hour, Celia suggested that Krishnamurti stay at her home and, also because of the long journey back to Wimbledon where he currently lived, he willingly agreed.

"You know it's not how I think of myself," he said, as they walked the half mile from the hospital to Bedford Square. "I don't think of myself as anything special."

"But you *are* special," said Celia. "You're worshipped by hundreds of people, including my mother..."

"By some people," Krishnamurti answered. "But most people I meet have no idea who I am, and it's pleasant sometimes to feel that you're just like anyone else. It can be the most frustrating thing that each of your actions is examined to see if it is something miraculous."

"I thought you would love the adulation – I would."

Krishnamurti shook his head. "You can't say you're without your admirers," he added.

"What do you mean by that?"

"Emily told me that there was a young man who has been keen on you for the last few years, the brother of one of your friends."

"Edward Stanton."

"Yes," said Krishnamurti.

"But I'm not interested in him," said Celia.

"Is there anyone who interests you?" asked Krishnamurti

"Adrian Drewe," Celia replied. She was surprised that she had told him. She hadn't told anyone except Margaret Ellis. It had been a secret between Celia and her once best friend, but she found Krishnamurti also had a key to enter into the secret rooms of her mind. Perhaps, thought Celia, that was what made Jiddu Krishnamurti special – one instinctively trusted him.

It was the first of a string of conversations they had each weekend. They drank a cup of Earl Grey before starting work. By the end of the first conversation, Celia had warmed to Krishnamurti. By the third conversation, she was sharing confidences with him. She found he listened and was more interested in her than himself. She told him about the first time she had met Adrian Drewe at Castle Drogo and how he seemed so much older than she was. She recounted Basil's accident and how Adrian had carried back his younger brother, and how a young engineer, who was supposed to be looking after the two boys, had been dismissed by Sir Julius. As Celia told the story to Krishnamurti she tried to remember the name of the engineer, but after five years the name had fled from her memory.

On another occasion she spoke to Krishnamurti about the day she had gone to Liberty's to hand out white feathers. How unexpectedly she had found herself against her friends and stood shoulder to shoulder with Kit and Basil Drewe. She said she felt worse than a fraud when Lady Drewe asked her to the New Year's Eve ball and how she had danced with Adrian Drewe. It was a dialogue that all went one way. Krishnamurti would stand with his hands wrapped around a mug of tea, leaning against a wall, saying nothing, simply listening attentively. She sometimes spoke in an animated way and then the next day her mood might be reflective. He would look at her without staring, empathise with her in his gestures and stance. He could make his tea last ten minutes or half an hour, allowing her to speak without her ever feeling that she needed to hurry. After five weeks, Celia felt that he was her closest friend.

"This is going to be my last day here," said Krishnamurti one morning as they drank their cup of Earl Grey.

"Why?" said Celia. "I didn't know you were going. What will you do?"

"I failed my entrance examinations and the now the last ward is complete there is nothing left for me to do."

"Can't you work as an orderly or something?"

Krishnamurti handed over his empty mug of tea to Celia. "I'm going to America. I think it will do me good to get away from the stuffiness of London."

"I'll miss our chats every weekend," said Celia.

"I'll miss them as well, but I shall see you this evening. Emily has asked me to dinner tonight, so it's not goodbye just right now."

"I might not get the chance later and while we're alone – well, there's something I've wanted to ask you. We are friends, aren't we?"

"Of course," said Krishnamurti.

"And you won't be cross?"

"No."

"It's this." Celia took in a short breath and then stared downwards. "Do you believe that you'll one day become the messiah?"

"Ah," said Krishnamurti. He moved his head slightly closer to hers and she smelt a slight scent of aniseed on his breath. "I have no idea what the future holds and no one can read the words that are not yet written."

*   *   *

Krishnamurti pushed back his chair and stretched out his legs.

"An excellent dinner, Emily," he said.

Celia looked up from the almost untouched dish of three-bean stew in front of her. She looked at Krishnamurti's empty, bread-wiped bowl and realised that he must simply have no sense of taste. From the corner of her eye, she saw her father – the same look of disbelief was on his face – and she knew instinctively that he was having the same thought.

"What are you two smirking at?" asked Emily.

"Nothing," answered Celia and her father together. Celia lifted another spoonful of the stew to her mouth and managed to swallow it without pulling a face and then placed her spoon and fork on the plate beneath the bowl to signal she had finished.

"No wonder girls today are all skin and bone," said Emily, "you've hardly eaten anything."

"Just leaving room for dessert, Mother. Is it Peach Melba?"

Emily shook her head slightly. "Cook couldn't find any peaches or anything fresh at a decent price. I'm afraid that it's tinned fruit in jelly."

"Tinned fruit in jelly!" spluttered Lutyens; however, he managed to stop himself from saying anything further.

"Everyone's making little compromises, Father," added Celia.

Lutyens took his pipe out of his pocket, chewed at it for a moment and then placed it back in the pocket. Emily had recently banned the smoking of what she termed as 'the offensive instrument' within the house. If Lutyens wanted to smoke, he knew he would have to go outside. Cook came in, cleared the plates away and returned with a terrine of jelly stuffed with tinned fruits. Celia ate it, noting how each piece of fruit had been regularly cut into faultless rectangles and each was perfectly tasteless.

Emily brought the conversation back to what Krishnamurti would be doing next, where he would be staying and when he would come back to visit her again. Krishnamurti in turn tried to avoid talking about himself and instead asked Celia how her day had been.

"We filled up the new ward," she answered, "with officers who had fought on the Somme. I saw on the admission list the name of Lieutenant Christian Drewe."

"Julius' boy!" said Emily. "I didn't know he'd been wounded."

"All I could find out was that his face had been burnt," said Celia. "A nurse who works on that ward told me that he will need skin grafts."

"But he was so handsome," continued Emily.

"And there's concern about his sight. I'll see him tomorrow."

Krishnamurti took his pocket watch from the breast pocket of his suit and opened the cover.

"I hope you won't think me rude if I leave shortly."

"Do you have time for coffee?" asked Emily.

Krishnamurti nodded his head. "Shall we take it in the garden?" he suggested. "It's such a pleasant evening for early November and Edwin can have his pipe."

The scent of camomile rose from the lawn as Lutyens and Krishnamurti sat under the gazebo at the far end of the garden. Krishnamurti was commenting on how mild the weather had been for November and was sure that a cold snap was coming. Lutyens filled his pipe and lit it. He took a few puffs before placing the bowl of the pipe to rest in an ashtray.

"Tell me," said Lutyens, interrupting Krishnamurti's monologue about the weather. "Your brother, Nitya, is he still at the Somme?"

"For the moment," answered Krishnamurti. "He's helping as an orderly at the hospital in Albert. He'll be finished there soon, and I hope he'll join me in America."

"Ah," replied Lutyens. "Have you spoken to him recently? Is it as bad as everyone is saying?"

"He says it's worse. After the attack in July the Germans built up their resources and counter-attacked."

Krishnamurti waited for Lutyens to ask his next question but instead Lutyens picked up his pipe, inhaled and then blew a cloud of sweet-scented bluish smoke into the air and stared quite silently at the garden. Krishnamurti decided to explain his last remark, hoping that it would fill the silence.

"Albert is a small town. There's not much there at all but a square, a few restaurants, a hotel and a basilica that has been turned into the hospital. It's called Notre-Dame de Brebières. Nitya said that after the attack in July there were bodies piled three deep outside the hospital. There weren't enough doctors, nurses or even medicine. They just tried to patch the soldiers up and as soon as they could they moved them on to the main hospital at Amiens. It was quiet for a few months afterward and then when the Germans counter-attacked they shelled the town. The square was hit, the hospital hit – they even flattened the nurses' quarters."

"I heard about that," said Lutyens, "although it wasn't reported. The authorities thought it would be bad for morale. I was told that it had a big red cross painted on the roof, but the Germans still fired on it."

"Nitya said that the building was put next to an ammunition dump. He thought it was nothing more than a stray shell. You know that none of the nurses survived except those working at the hospital."

"Yes, I had heard," said Lutyens. "I toured that part of France with Emily twenty or so years ago. We went to Albert and saw the basilica. It's a modern building – red brick and white stone, I think. There's a large golden statue of the Virgin and Christ Child on the top."

"Nitya said that the basilica is now badly damaged and the statue now leans almost at nearly ninety degrees and that a French engineer had gone to the top of the church and tied it so that it doesn't fall into the square below."

Lutyens picked up his pipe, but it had gone out.

Chapter 47

Lieutenant Christian Drewe could hear voices in the blackness. He had been moved from one hospital to the next until he had lost track of time and precisely where he was. They operated on him, injected him full of morphine and operated again. The doctors told him that they were trying to save his left eye but at best, if he ever regained his sight, he would have partial vision only. They told him that he had been badly burnt and they would need to graft flesh from his buttocks onto his face. At least the morphine dulled the pain. He didn't want to be there – had never wanted to be there. He often thought about falling asleep and never waking up again.

The Endsleigh Hospital was the last in a long line of hospitals. He had started at Albert and had been moved shortly afterwards to Amiens. He had stayed there for a few weeks or more and then he had returned to England. They had admitted him to Barts where they had operated twice and now to the Endsleigh.

In a well of blackness all the hospitals appeared the same, except for that first hospital at Albert. He had passed in and out of consciousness and he could hardly recollect anything but the pain and that she had been there. He had known her immediately. He had heard her voice when he woke with the taste of anaesthetic in his mouth. '*You maaade me looove you... I didn't wanna do it, I didn't wanna do it.*' He had tried to sing the words as he had done once before but consciousness seemed too far away. People had called her Nurse Hall. He did not understand why they didn't call her by her proper name, Rose Braithwaite. It confused him for a while. He didn't even have time to speak to her before they moved him to another hospital. He was there for weeks and then he had the boat journey back to England. He moved his hand to his neck where a St Christopher hung. He made a wish and, if wishes had wings, Lieutenant Christian Drewe would have been back in Albert with her.

Chapter 48

Celia took Krishnamurti's hand as they walked from her home in Bedford Square towards Waterloo Station.

"I'm pleased that we became friends," she said.

Krishnamurti looked up at the sky. It was not yet dark enough to see the stars.

"A penny for them," said Celia.

"I was just thinking about home and my family."

"It's strange," said Celia, who also looked up at the night sky. "Mother talks constantly about you; she has done for years but I really don't know much about you before you came to England."

"There's not much to tell. I was born in a small hill town called Madanapalle, which is about a hundred and fifty miles west of Madras. I was the eighth child and in accordance with Hindu custom, my parents called me Krishnamurti, because Sri Krishna had also been the eighth child. My family are Brahmins..."

"What are Brahmins?" asked Celia.

"According to Hindu faith, at the moment of creation the Brahmin caste came forth from the mouth of the god Brahma. We're thought of as a sacred caste and chief caste of all created beings. In Sanskrit the word Brahmin means possessor of secret knowledge and we alone may interpret the sacred text – the Vedas."

"So, you're like priests?"

"Something like that," continued Krishnamurti. "Just before my birth my mother had a premonition that I would be a remarkable child, and the day after I was born an astrologer cast my horoscope and gave a prediction that I would be a person with a very wonderful destiny."

"Is that why Mrs Besant and the Reverend Leadbeater chose you, because of the prediction?"

"No. As far as I'm aware neither of them knew anything about that."

"What made them choose you?" asked Celia.

"My father was a member of the Theosophical Society in India and, after my mother died, he wrote to the society asking for a position at their headquarters in Adyar. We moved there in January 1909 and one day, soon afterwards, I was summoned to the office of the Reverend Leadbeater who said that I had an aura around me."

"Mother told me about this years ago," interrupted Celia. "Everyone has an aura, but it becomes stronger the more highly evolved you are."

"That's precisely it," continued Krishnamurti, "and Leadbeater thought that my aura was the brightest he had ever seen."

Celia and Krishnamurti started to climb up the steps at the front of Waterloo Station. It had taken them thirty-five minutes to walk from Bedford Square to the station and in that time Celia had done little more than listen to Krishnamurti as they walked. Dozens of people were milling around the station, mostly men. Some wore suits – all but the very eldest had armbands to show that they were in reserved professions. Many of them were soldiers, going to or from the war. The thumping of the steam engines made it almost impossible for any conversation to be carried on. Only the shriek of whistles being blown by guards made any impression in the din.

"I'll leave you here," shouted Celia.

She watched as Krishnamurti walked to the platform where the train for Wimbledon had just arrived. Passengers were pouring off the train, many in uniform, and for a moment she could have sworn she saw Adrian Drewe.

PART VIII

Chapter 49

"You really don't have to come to the hospital," said Celia.

"Of course I do," said Emily Lutyens. "I wouldn't be able to look Frances Drewe in the eye knowing that her son was there, and I hadn't visited."

Celia opened the front door of their house in Bedford Square and walked out beside her mother. Overnight the weather had changed. It was colder and the sky was the colour of flint. Winter was on its way. Celia pulled her coat collar up.

"Are you wrapped up well?" said Emily as they walked. "When the weather is like this you're much more likely to catch a cold, and you see so many silly girls today running around wearing hardly anything."

"Yes, Mother," Celia groaned. Emily had hardly been around to look after her for the last few years and now that she was twenty, she was getting lectures about what to wear. Anyway, there was nothing wrong with what she was wearing; it was the fashion to wear a skirt that was above the ankle. They crossed the road into Montague Place and the distant sound of traffic could be heard as buses rumbled along and cab drivers impatiently blew on their car horns trying to get somewhere quickly for someone else's benefit.

"Is this the quickest way to the hospital?" asked Emily, as they walked through Montague Place and into Malet Street.

"Yes, Mother," said Celia.

"If you say so," said Emily. "You do seem to be out of sorts this morning, dear."

"I was just thinking about Christian Drewe. You know it's the strangest thing, but I thought I saw his brother Adrian last night when I was walking to the station with Krishnamurti."

"And talking of Christian," said Emily, "I forgot to mention that I bought him a little something to keep his spirits up."

"What have you brought him, exactly?" asked Celia.

"Krishnamurti's book, *At the Feet of the Master.* I thought it might cheer him up."

"Mother, he's lost his sight – you might as well have brought him the *Telegraph* crossword for all the good it will do."

"Celia, you should learn to stop looking at everything in such a negative manner. It's not an attractive attribute for a young lady – and decent society notices that kind of thing. If Christian can't read the book, I shall read it to him."

Celia had read the book and doubted whether a reading from her mother would keep anyone's spirits up. She had her own copy, a present from her mother. It had been neatly filed away and was hidden on her bookshelf somewhere between Keats and Locke.

As they turned into the bottom of Gordon Street, a chill wind blew. The buildings, dreary and dirty from the London smog, seemed to be nothing more than shadows in the grey morning. The only colour came from the blue and buff coats that Celia and Emily wore. It was an almost colourless day and the traffic noise blended into a long, constant, oppressive moan. Celia lowered her voice.

"Mother, please understand that Christian is badly burnt. He may not want to see anyone. He may not want to see you." Celia placed a particular emphasis on the last word. "It's a miracle he's alive. The surgeons have been grafting skin on his face for the last two months. Are you really sure this is a good idea?"

"Celia," said Emily, "the best thing for Christian is for everyone to treat him normally. If you treat him differently, he'll feel different. I would come and do the same thing whether he had lost a leg or had influenza."

Celia pushed open the heavy wooden doors to the hospital. A rush of warm air came out.

With a shrug of the shoulders Celia said, "He can only say 'No'."

*   *   *

Emily paused for a moment.

"These are the opening words from Krishnamurti's book," she explained. "He says that it is not enough to say that the words are true and beautiful; a man who wishes to walk along the Path must do exactly what is said."

Christian Drewe gave no indication that he had heard her, and with his face wrapped in bandages Emily could not tell whether he was even awake. She continued reading for a few more minutes before she stopped again and waited a moment to see if there was any reaction. She looked at the St Christopher

259

that hung around his neck and, despite not knowing whether he was conscious or not, she continued.

"Theosophy offers a chance to find the Path to enlightenment whereas yours is a vengeful god, Christian. He allows wars in his name and pestilence across the world. He even permits his saints, like St Christopher, to be martyred in his name."

Emily had not taken off her buff coat despite the fact that the ward was warm. She found it difficult to look directly at Christian.

"It's not mine." The words spoken by Christian were barely audible. He seemed to lisp and under the heavy bandaging the lisp was accentuated. He put his hand to the cold metal of the St Christopher around his neck.

"Why do you wear it?" asked Emily.

"A gift," he replied. "It doesn't work." Christian tried to laugh but instead he started choking. He raised his head; the St Christopher turned over as he continued to cough, and Emily saw that one word was inscribed on the back: 'Rose'.

"Do you want me to get you a nurse?" Emily asked.

Christian continued to cough. He attempted to get himself higher up in bed and Emily leant over to help him. Christian pushed her hand away.

"I can manage." The coughing stopped. "A glass of water, please."

"Pardon?" said Emily, who was having trouble understanding what he was trying to say. Christian repeated himself. Beside the bed was a small table on which stood a glass jug covered by a doily. The doily was beautifully and intricately crocheted and the design, creation and provision of fifty of them had been the combined war effort of two maiden sisters from East Dulwich. Emily picked up the jug and poured a glass of water. The doily fell silently behind the table, unnoticed by Emily. She placed the glass in Christian's hand.

Christian moved the glass slowly towards his lips. He took a small sip and then another. He held out the glass and Emily took it and placed it back on the table. Once again, she sat uncomfortably looking at Christian's face which, except for an area around the mouth, was wrapped in bandages. She noticed that where the bandages were wrapped around his left cheek, they were now damp. She watched the dampness spreading out. She doubted that she would have the strength to sit through this if it were her own son Robert who was lying there. She didn't want to cry but she could not stop her eyes filling up with tears.

"It's not so bad," said Christian.

"Sorry?" said Emily, who had again not heard what he had said.

"It's not so bad," Christian repeated again.

"No," said Emily, "you'll be as right as rain in no time." But neither of them believed it.

She breathed a deep sigh of relief when she saw Celia coming towards her and did not object to being dismissed when Celia said she needed to change Christian's bandages.

Celia pulled a screen around the bed and undid a safety pin that held the bandages together.

"Are you ready?" she asked and began undoing the dressing, not waiting nor expecting a reply. Christian did not move as she began to unwind the bandage from around the top of his head. Celia spoke continually as layer after layer came away. She felt it was like unravelling a mummy and when the bandages had been removed, the left-hand side of his face appeared in some places raw and in others petrified. She did not remove the two round dressings over his eyes. Celia wondered what he remembered about that morning on the Somme; whether he recalled the smell of explosives or the screaming or the men who had dragged him back to his own lines? Did he remember the pain? She wanted to ask him what it was like. She also wanted to know what it was like to live in a world without light or colour. However, she asked no questions but continued to tell him about the weather outside and what was in the newspapers. He winced as she cleaned his face and started to bring his hand up.

"I've got to clean the wounds," she said and moved his hand to his side.

She spoke about nothing in particular. In the previous months she had learnt the art of banal chatter, skipping lightly from one subject to the next. It was as much for her benefit as for his. She had been told not to get too close to her patients and that she would function effectively only if she did not let her reserve down. However, her emotions had flooded in as soon as the bandages were stripped away. She had only ever met Christian four times before, but she felt responsible. She wanted to grab hold of Margaret Ellis and drag her to the hospital by her hair and shout at her that "she had done this," that "they had done this." However, she had not seen Margaret Ellis since that morning at Liberty's. Jenny Stanton told her that Margaret felt she had been betrayed by Celia and did not want to see her again. She knew that Margaret and Jane Facey were acquaintances, but they could have each other, Celia thought. She continued to clean the wounds, giving no impression to Christian about how she was feeling until he suddenly took a deep breath and bit on the side of his cheek.

"Sorry," she said. He didn't reply. "I'm so sorry about everything."

"Why?" he asked. "You have nothing to be sorry about."

Celia took a deep breath, took out a clean bandage and began to re-dress the wounds. She needed to clear her head and talk again about the inconsequential.

"I assume Mother didn't convert you to theosophy?" Celia asked, trying to lighten the conversation.

"You assume I don't believe already," said Christian. She watched as his jaw tried to make the words and how saliva escaped through the rip in his cheek as he spoke. She wrapped the bandage over the bridge of his nose.

"Do you believe then?"

"No. How can anyone have any faith," he answered, "when we still do this to each other?"

"Did you know that, up until a few days ago, Krishnamurti was working here?" She remembered that Christian had been at that talk given by Krishnamurti, her mother and Annie Besant at the Drury Lane theatre.

"Krishnamurti is nothing," he shouted. "If he was the messiah, he'd stop this."

"Sorry."

"You've seen me! I'll never see again. They should have buried me. No one can live like this." Two of the stitches on the side of his face tore away as he shouted, and the wounds started bleeding.

Celia backed away. The noise alerted the matron who came over to where Christian was sitting up in bed. He continued to shout.

"Now, Lieutenant Drewe," the matron said sternly, "quieten yourself. This is no way for an officer of the British army to act."

"Sorry," Celia repeated again and again.

*　　*　　*

Adrian Drewe had stood in a corridor of the Endsleigh Hospital for over an hour. He had first been shown to the visitors' waiting room where a half-dozen other relatives sat saying nothing. He had soon found the silence stifling and went out into the corridor where he could at least smoke without a sour-faced woman staring at him. After ten minutes a doctor introduced himself and said that he may have to wait for some time as his brother had become distressed that morning. When he had asked how long 'some time' would be, the doctor shrugged and said that it would be when his brother was less anxious. Adrian had answered that he had no intention of going before seeing Christian and asked the doctor to keep him advised about the condition of his brother.

Adrian looked out of the window onto Gordon Street watching the rain clouds gather. He exhaled a thin bluish stream of tobacco smoke and then saw someone in his peripheral vision. He turned and looked at a tall, thin nurse. She had the same emerald eyes that both he and Christian had and he couldn't help staring for a moment. She looked concerned.

"Major Drewe," she began.

He recognised her voice and interrupted her. "I had no idea that you worked here, Celia."

He took the cigarette from his mouth and stepped on it, extinguishing it with the ball of his foot. "How is my brother?"

Celia sensed she was being scrutinised and felt uncomfortable in her formless uniform. She raised her hand to a loose wisp of hair that had escaped the restraint of her nurse's cap and replaced it back into the position where it belonged.

"He..." she hesitated, "Christian is seriously injured. Have you spoken to a doctor yet?"

"There was one earlier, but he didn't say much."

"As you know, he has been having skin grafts. The right-hand side of his face was badly burnt."

"And what about his sight?" asked Adrian.

Celia hesitated. She had already said more than she was supposed to. She added quietly: "We're hopeful, but you will have to ask the doctors. I'm afraid I don't know much more. Sorry."

"And when can I see him?"

Again, Celia hesitated. "He said he wanted to be left alone – that is, he said... I don't think he'll see you."

Adrian took a step closer to Celia. Celia dropped her gaze. He was close enough for her to smell his cologne, the scent of sandalwood.

"Ask him. No, tell him that I won't go without seeing him. Tell him he has my word that I don't intend to leave without seeing him even if I have to camp here for the three days of my furlough."

"But he was adamant."

"Just tell him," said Adrian. She raised her eyes and found that he was staring at her. She lowered her gaze again. "Please," he added.

Celia turned and went back into the ward. She swore under her breath. 'Damn it, why had he asked her to do this? Why couldn't he have asked anyone else?' She thought that the last person that Christian would want to speak to was her. They had to inject him with an opiate to quieten him after the outburst earlier that morning.

She stood at the door of the ward for a full two minutes before summoning the courage to go in and speak to Christian.

"I know," she began, "that I'm probably the last person whom you want to talk to right now but Adrian's here." Christian said nothing. "Will you see him?" she asked.

"No," he muttered though his bandages.

She repeated what he had said word for word. Celia waited for a moment but there was no reply. "Please see him?" she begged.

"Why?"

"Because he needs to see you."

Celia waited a moment. Christian said nothing but there was a barely perceptible nod of the head. Celia turned and had to check herself from running back through the ward.

*　*　*

Later that morning Celia felt a tap on her shoulder, which made her jump.

"Sorry," said Adrian. He looked shaken and his eyes were full of tears.

"How can I help?" she asked, but her voice was a little too high-pitched. She took a breath and tried to sound confident. "What can I do for you, Adrian?"

"I want to know how he'll be. I've spoken to the doctors," his voice trembled just a little, "but they have a habit of telling you nothing."

All her emotions welled up. She wanted to say that everything would be all right. She wanted to hold him, but they had drummed into her not to become involved.

"I don't know any more than what I told you this morning."

"But you could find out?"

Celia felt a lump rise in her throat. She couldn't speak to him in the hospital. If the matron saw them talking, she would be skinned alive.

"I could speak with the consultant who is dealing with him, and I can tell you what he says at lunchtime," she said. "I have a half-hour break, but I really shouldn't be telling you. You should speak to his doctor."

"I know an Italian restaurant not too far away. We could have some spaghetti there. They know me and they're quick."

Behind her, Celia heard the door squeak and she turned to see the matron looking at her. God, thought Celia, if I'm gone for more than thirty minutes, she'll kill me.

"I'll meet you outside the front door in an hour," she said quietly and moved away from Adrian. Adrian walked slowly back down through the ward. He didn't look at the matron and the matron appeared oblivious to him. She walked over to where Celia was standing.

"Get back to work, Nurse Lutyens," said the matron. "There's no one here to flirt with now."

*　*　*

La Trattoria was a small Italian restaurant near Gray's Inn. It was run by a balding Italian man and his portly wife, who, to balance the deficit of her husband's loss of hair, had grown more than the faintest hint of a moustache. Cristina, their daughter, waitressed and washed up and when the restaurant was closed was a friend to soldiers on leave.

"*Buongiorno*, Major Drewe," Signor Archenti boomed out in his deep baritone voice and then wiped his hands on the tea towel that was tucked into the apron. "How are you?"

"*Bene, grazie*," Adrian replied, shaking the pudgy outstretched hand. "A table for two, please. We're in a hurry, I'm afraid."

They were taken to a table near the window.

"Signora Archenti cooks probably the best pasta in London," Adrian said as the restaurateur sat them down and passed them the menus.

"*Si*, there's no doubt about that," said Signor Archenti, looking down at his bulging stomach. Cristina Archenti was there a few moments later with a basket of bread and a jug of water.

"*Buongiorno*, Major Drewe," she said. "We haven't seen you for months." She swept her black hair away from her face. Celia picked up her menu and pretended to study it while listening to the conversation.

"I'm just here for the day."

"And how is your brother...?"

"Christian?"

"Yes, Kit."

"He's been injured, I've just been to see him."

"I'm so very sorry," said Cristina. "Please, I hope he gets better soon."

"Thank you," replied Adrian.

"And what would you like?" she asked Adrian. Adrian looked across the table toward Celia: "What will you have?" he asked.

"*Risotto ai funghi*, please," Celia said.

"I shall have the mushroom risotto as well."

"The salmon tagliatelle in cream sauce is very good," Cristina suggested.

Celia looked at the woman's waistline and decided to stay with the risotto.

"Perhaps another day," said Adrian.

Cristina walked away with the order.

"Have you ever been to Italy?" Adrian asked.

"Once. I stayed for a few months in a town near Rome. We rented an old palace called the Villa Grazioli which used to belong to Cardinal Antonio Carafa. Father had been asked to design the Royal Pavilion in Rome and we decided to turn it into a holiday."

"And did you learn to speak Italian while you were there?" asked Adrian.

"Not exactly," replied Celia. "When I knew we were going I took lessons

265

for a few months beforehand. I just thought the whole city was breathtaking, especially the Vatican. I became giddy staring up at the frescoed ceilings."

The food came and they ate and talked about Christian. Celia told Adrian what the doctor had said to her. The surgeons were hopeful that in time they could operate and restore Christian's sight but in the meantime, they wanted to focus on repairing the burnt skin around his face. She said that he would be likely to stay at the Endsleigh for the next few months before being sent to convalesce, and then she hoped he would return home.

Adrian paid the bill and they walked out to the sound of church bells in a square nearby striking half past one. Celia got in the front of the car next to Adrian, who started the engine.

"So, he should be out of hospital in three or four months," said Adrian.

"That depends on him," answered Celia. "Some patients want to leave hospital and get back to their lives. Others just linger. We've found that there are some patients who never want to leave and can't cope with living in the world outside. They need almost constant care and Christian may also need to learn to cope with blindness if he doesn't get his sight back."

"He didn't talk much when I saw him, but he made it clear he didn't want to go back to Wadhurst Hall. I suggested that when he's better he comes and stays at my house in Drewsteignton, it's just standing empty."

"I know it's not much of a comfort, but you should know I'll watch over him while you're away." Celia reached over and squeezed Adrian's arm.

"Thank you..." Adrian briefly took his eyes off the road and looked at Celia. "And it is a comfort." Celia now looked at him for a few seconds. She knew she was blushing. The car pulled up outside the Endsleigh Hospital. Adrian leant over and kissed her lightly on the cheek. He held his cheek next to hers for a few moments. When he moved away from her, Celia felt that she was short of breath and her hand moved up instinctively to touch the side of her face.

"I'll see you tomorrow," said Adrian.

"I'm working," replied Celia.

"I meant when I come to see Christian."

"Of course – yes – of course – I realised that."

Celia blushed again.

Chapter 50

Every afternoon a group of officers in Christian's ward would play cards. Whist, rummy, brag, pontoon – groups of four sat playing their games. It had become such an entrenched part of their routine that they would not know what to do if the card games were for some reason cancelled. These were the soldiers who were so badly maimed that they could not or would not leave the ward. Celia called these patients the 'would-nots' and the 'could-nots'. Disabled either physically or emotionally or both. They rarely had visitors and did not want to see anyone. They were going to be in hospital for years – their wounds would be treated at the Endsleigh Hospital and then they would move on to convalescence homes where many would be forgotten. These were the injured soldiers that people gawped at in the street. For many, one institution or another would become their homes for the rest of their lives with children and bitter wives coming to visit on birthdays and Bank Holidays.

Another group of soldiers sat at the opposite end of the ward talking and looking out of the windows. They did not want to be in the Endsleigh Hospital. They wanted to be at home with their families and did not care about their disabilities, what people thought of them or how they looked. They were the ones who would shout back at the gawping strangers. They still had pride in their uniform. Celia called these patients the 'can-dos.' She admired them for their resilience and determination but found she had little in common with them. It was easier to talk to the would-nots and could-nots who were grateful for any kindness from a nurse.

Celia had noticed that, since joining the ward, Christian had not joined either group. He had still not made up his mind in which camp he belonged.

The would-nots and could-nots noticed even the smallest change in what went on around them. They knew that something was in the air. They had seen that Celia had been late returning from lunch the previous day and had received a dressing down from Matron for being ten minutes late. At half past five in the evening Adrian had not yet visited and Celia was feeling concerned. The empty cups of tea still had not yet been cleared away and sat on the bedside tables. The could-nots talked between themselves as to when she would return to clear away the tea things. They said that if Matron saw the mess, Celia would be in for another scolding. When, however, she finally got round to clearing away the cups and saucers she realised that Christian was not in his bed.

"Where's Lieutenant Drewe?" she asked the patient in the next bed.

"Ggggone," he stammered. "Sssssomeonnne cccame." The patient pointed towards the visitors' room at the end of the ward. Celia left the clearing up of the tea things and with an effort stopped herself dashing through the ward. She opened the door to the visitors' room. It smelt of disinfectant. It always smelt of disinfectant as it was so rarely used, because so few people came to see these patients. Christian was sitting at a table facing the door. Celia could only see the back of the person talking to him but she knew instinctively from the broadness of his shoulders, his posture and the cut of his hair that it was Adrian. From the table a thin wisp of bluish smoke curled up into the air from an ashtray.

"Can I get you something?" asked Celia.

"Tea," lisped Christian from underneath his bandaged face.

"And for you, Adrian?" she asked.

Adrian turned to look at her.

"Nothing – thank you," he said.

"How long have you been here? I didn't see you arrive," said Celia.

"About five minutes ago. I need to speak to Christian. There are some things I need to tell him, and I won't be able to visit tomorrow."

"I'll get Christian his tea and leave you." She turned and walked back through the ward.

Adrian picked up his cigarette, drew hard on it and blew a smoke ring.

"What is it?" asked Christian.

"I've been sent up to Ypres. We need to defend the city and it's a hell of a place."

Adrian put out his cigarette and then lit another. He sat silently for a few seconds before continuing. "Stupid, I know, but I sometimes think I won't get back from there. When I first saw what was left of the town it froze me to the bone. It's being shelled badly and to protect our position they moved my siege battery forward. We're losing a lot of men."

"Don't," said Christian.

Adrian looked down at the table. "If I don't make it, I want you to have the house in Drewsteignton. I think I was happiest when I lived there. I can even reinstate the housekeeper and cook full-time if you want to have it."

"Stop," said Christian. "Please."

"It needs to be said. I've sent a letter to Father's solicitor just in case." The cigarette was slowly burning down to a long, thin piece of grey ash.

"There's another thing that I need to tell you," continued Adrian. "When I arrived at Ypres I started working with some engineers. Strange chaps – either obsessed with building things or blowing them up. I got to know their commanding officer Rory Campbell. He told me that when we were ready to make a push on the German lines I might need to work with one of his best engineers, a Major Peter Hall, but that he was away on compassionate leave."

Christian said nothing but moved his hand to the silver St Christopher around his neck.

"He's been away for over a month now – actually since the 8th of October. You may not know but that girl you were keen on, Rose I think her name was, well, they married. I wanted to talk to you about her yesterday – but lost my nerve…"

"What about her?" asked Christian.

"It happened when the Germans bombed Albert."

"Just tell me, damn it!"

"She was killed." Adrian paused for a moment expecting a response, but none came. "They were married last Christmas, Hall and Rose. As far as I know, it wasn't much of a marriage. She came out to the Somme soon afterwards and they didn't see each other again."

"And what else?" asked Christian.

"It happened in the first week of October. The Germans had been bringing more and more reserves up and they started attacking the British position near Albert on the 5th of October." Adrian paused again. "It started about six p.m. The first bombs hit the square. They started ringing the bells in the basilica. It was getting dark and the blasts lit up the sky. After a few minutes the shelling stopped but only for a short time and then it moved to the west side of town. You could hear the rumbling as the shells exploded. There was then a huge detonation as the ammunition dump was hit. However, at that time most people were running around trying to help those that had been hit in the first round of shelling."

Adrian leant over to the ashtray. His cigarette had now burnt away. He crumpled the ash of the cigarette and lit another.

"Did you know that they had put the ammunition dump next to the nurses' quarters? They thought that if they painted a big red cross on the nurses' quarters then the Germans wouldn't attack the ammunition dump." Adrian took a puff of his cigarette. "Once the shelling had stopped," he continued, "they realised that the nurses' quarters had been hit. The doctors were still treating the wounded, but a group of Indian orderlies ran over to give what help they could. The nurses' quarters had been flattened – no one was sure whether it had been shelled or whether the explosion from the ammunition dump had destroyed it. The orderlies tried to move some of the debris. I suppose they hoped that if any of the nurses had got to the basement, they might have survived the blast but the heat and the smoke made it impossible. A few of them seemed not to care for their own safety, pulling away the burning rafters of the house and shouting out – asking whether anyone was still alive. However, after a time they had to give up."

"No one survived then?" asked Christian.

"No one," said Adrian. "The fire burnt for most of the next day. When they could remove some of the debris, they found that the floor above the basement had caved in. They pulled out the bodies of five nurses. Some bodies they couldn't find, I suppose they had been incinerated in the blast."

"Did they find Rose?"

"Christian," said Adrian slowly, "they couldn't identify anyone; the bodies were so badly burnt."

Adrian put down his cigarette.

"Three days later, Hall arrived at Albert. He must have pulled a few strings. They said that he was half mad when he arrived. He wouldn't, or couldn't, believe that Rose had been killed and started pulling the debris away stone by stone. After an hour his fingers were bleeding. Some of the orderlies tried to stop him but he took out his revolver and threatened to shoot them. When they came back later in the evening, they found him unconscious and exhausted. He was sent home to recover."

Christian's hand dropped from the St Christopher around his neck to the table and he rubbed the tips of his fingers along the tabletop. A splinter of wood stood proud, and he slipped his nail under it. He suddenly ripped up the splinter which tore into the soft tissue under his nail.

Behind the bandages and behind the dressings he could picture Rose that very first day they met, sitting in the tearooms on the concourse of Fenchurch Street Station. She had been reading a book and was concentrating. Her large dark eyes went backwards and forwards following the words across the page. He remembered that her nose was small and straight and her mouth was slightly too wide, especially when she smiled. He thought her smile enchanting but he rarely ever saw her smiling. When he had first heard her voice in the hospital at Albert he immediately had the same picture in his head. She spoke to him for what seemed like days as he floated in and out of dreams.

Adrian waited for a few minutes, just watching his brother.

"Is there any chance?" asked Christian.

"None."

Christian stood up. He reached out his hand to feel the wall. He had misjudged the direction and began to topple. Adrian jumped up and prevented him from falling.

"Can I help?" asked Adrian

"No!" Christian answered.

In his head Christian could hear the words of that song again and again. '*You maaade me looove you... I didn't wanna do it, I didn't wanna do it.*' He imagined her face again and remembered her smiling as he had danced around a lamp post. He had become giddy as he danced and then he had kissed her; it all went black.

Chapter 51

The following day Celia walked a different way to work, along by the British Museum. It was a bleak November day and the sky was as grey as the old building. There was a hubbub around a newspaper vendor. She heard someone shouting that the battle of the Somme was over and that the Germans had retreated back to the Hindenburg Line. She wanted to join in the celebration, but she had been in more than enough trouble recently with the matron and so hurried on to work. She had even been blamed for the incident yesterday with Christian when he had passed out. She had come back with a cup of tea to find Adrian shouting for help. Together they had managed to get Christian into bed and he was then sedated because he was so agitated.

She had spent half an hour with Adrian before he left. He didn't want to leave the hospital until he was sure that Christian was fine, but the matron had insisted. He was almost as agitated as Christian and paced around the visitors' room. He had to go back to Belgium the following day and said that he could not come back until he was next on leave after Christmas. He had told Celia briefly about the death of Rose. The name seemed familiar to Celia, but she could not recall why. Adrian said that he would arrange for Basil to come up and see Christian. He said he would come back and thank her when he was next in town.

When she turned into Gordon Street, her pace quickened. A horse-drawn van was motionless beside the pavement, its driver stood with his hand to the horse's nose. The old grey horse stamped its foot excitedly. Three cars had pulled up behind the van and were waiting for it to move on, each driver intermittently sounding his horn. The noise made the horse more excited. Only a girl on a bicycle could get past. She wore a tartan beret and long red scarf and Celia noticed the explosion of colour on the colourless day. She would have to get a tartan beret and a red scarf.

She wondered whether Christian would still be in the hospital after Christmas. The consultant had told her that he would need to have further skin grafts. The process was slow because each graft had to heal before the next operation. It was only when all the operations had been completed that Christian would be able to speak properly again. Then they could start to think about operating on his remaining eye. However, the consultant was not hopeful that even partial sight could be restored.

Celia arrived at the hospital, pulled off her coat and her gloves and made her way to the nurses' room. Everyone was talking about the retreat of the Germans from the Somme. A new nurse was saying that this was the beginning of Germany's defeat. Celia changed into her uniform; a blue shirt, white pinafore skirt and white headdress with a blue cross on it. The matron handed her a rota and yesterday evening's notes with instructions that she was to deal with changing dressings in the enlisted men's ward. She looked down and saw that one of the newly admitted soldiers had died during the night. He had been there only a week and had been prescribed opiates to dull the pain. Celia had been with him every day since his admittance.

The young nurse continued talking, saying how it was likely that there would be fewer and fewer injuries.

"Shut up, Joan," Celia said.

"Pardon!" replied the young nurse.

"I said 'shut up'. If the Germans are retreating, then they're likely to fight harder than ever."

"Well, I was just saying..." began the nurse, but Celia had turned and was leaving without listening to the answer.

When Celia finally took a break at lunchtime, she found Basil sitting next to Christian's bed. He seemed much older than she remembered. He also seemed much sadder than a boy of his age should be, but given how badly Christian had been injured, that was to be expected. He had his cane next to him as he sat. She decided not to interrupt them and to come back after she had eaten lunch. When she returned twenty minutes later, Basil had gone and she sat down next to Christian. She was asking him how he was when a voice behind her said, "Hello." She turned around.

"How are you, Basil?" she asked.

"Fine. Adrian telephoned me and asked whether I could visit, and he persuaded the school to let me have a day off."

"Yes, he told me," said Celia. "When did Adrian leave?"

"He's going this afternoon," said Basil. "My parents and he are visiting Lord and Lady Facey before he catches the train from Charing Cross."

"So, he's going to be in town?"

"Yes."

"Is he coming to visit Christian?" she asked.

"No. He said he would be pushed for time."

Chapter 52

Adrian Drewe was not in a good mood and thoughts were tumbling around his head. He tried not to think about his future but as the car took him further away from the Facey's estate and into the suburban sprawl of Romford, he once again considered a life back in Belgium. It was only three in the afternoon but already the day was on the wane. The last rays of a setting sun occasionally streaked through the window of the car. He lit another cigarette. His regiment had recently been repositioned to the small hamlet of Vlamertinge just outside Ypres. There was little there except for a desolate landscape and the bitter cold. It was a wind that cut to the bone.

Adrian wanted to talk to someone but the only person with him was the chauffeur, Arthur Poley, and it was quite impossible to openly talk with the staff. Not only would it be embarrassing for Poley, but it would also be demeaning for Adrian. He had joined with two friends from his university days – Lionel Peters and Archibald Don. Peters had died on the Somme and he had not heard from Don in months. He had an urge to tell Poley to drive up to the Endsleigh Hospital but there wasn't time, and anyway what would Christian say? Christian had been the only one who had ever stood up to his father. Sir Julius had told him that he would be ruined if he didn't renew the government contract. Adrian didn't see what he could do but Sir Julius continued that Jane Facey had taken more than a liking to him. It appeared that Cecil Facey would renew the supply contract if he were given more stock in the Home and Colonial and his daughter's future could be assured. Bankruptcy or a marriage to Jane Facey; these seemed to be the options that his father had put forward to Adrian, and he did not know how to say 'no'.

Christian would have done what he wanted and lived with the consequences, but he had responsibilities. As the eldest son he had a duty to his family. It made the decision easier; and, anyway, his father did not permit dissent. Once

Sir Julius had made up his mind there was no moving him, whether he was proven right or wrong, and his father had already mapped out Adrian's future.

"Shall we make the train on time, Poley?" asked Adrian.

"Yes, sir," replied Poley, "and with a few minutes to spare."

"Do you have any message for George?" asked Adrian.

"I have a letter for him, sir. If you wouldn't mind passing it on to him," replied Poley.

"The family is very grateful to George; even if we don't say it as often as we should. You should be very proud of your son."

"I am, sir, and I'm also indebted to Sir Julius arranging for George to be transferred to your regiment."

"Well, don't worry, Poley, I'll keep an eye on him."

"Thank you, sir. It'll put Mrs Poley's heart at rest to know that you're looking out for him. I don't think that she could bear to lose a second son."

"We were all terribly sad to hear about Luke."

"It's kind of you to say so, sir."

Adrian closed his eyes. He wondered how his own father would feel if he were killed. He assumed that Sir Julius would go through that mandatory period of mourning, but he could not imagine him wasting away in some grief-stricken torment. He guessed that his father would be back at work within two weeks, trying to keep his businesses afloat.

The conversation with Sir Julius the night before came back into his head. Sir Julius had explained that all his money was tied up in his shipping contracts, that he had mortgaged most of the Home and Colonial Stores but unless he won the new government contract, he would have to stop work on Castle Drogo and sell Wadhurst Hall. The last few months had seen ship after ship that he owned being sunk by German U-boats and Lord Facey was now hinting that there was pressure on the government to split the supply contracts. People were worried that Sir Julius didn't have the financial reserves to weather the losses he was incurring. Sir Julius now needed Facey more than he had ever done before and Facey knew it.

Adrian had not been down to see the castle for months but understood that things were again going slowly as they only had two stonemasons working at that time. His father was again talking about reducing its size, making it smaller and less costly. His father did not see why each granite stone had to be hand-cut and said that the work would progress faster if modern building techniques were employed. Lutyens complained that if the changes that Sir Julius wanted were made it would spoil the castle's symmetry. There seemed to be a stand-off between the two men.

Lunch with the Faceys had been arranged weeks before when Adrian had told his mother he was coming home for a week's leave. It galled Adrian to think that his father could read him so well. Was he so easy to predict? How had his father been so sure that he would say yes to an engagement with Jane Facey? However, he had agreed without much hesitation. The thought of making his mother homeless made him sick and so he had sat next to Jane over lunch a few hours earlier with both of their parents. His father and mother had decided to stay with the Faceys for the day. Sir Julius and Lord Facey had business to sort out and his mother said she wanted to get to know Jane better. They had drunk champagne with lunch and even his father had a glass. Jane was in her element, playing at being demure when she spoke to Adrian and confidently telling his mother where they would live. Of course, she said, they would keep the house in Drewsteignton, so that they would have somewhere to stay when they visited, but they would have to start looking for a small house off Regent's Park. Adrian should stand for Parliament, she said. Adrian had so much talent and all he needed was a woman's direction.

Adrian felt that his whole life was being taken apart brick by brick. The only saving grace was that they had decided not to publish their engagement. Jane agreed it was better to keep things quiet and that they should have a small intimate wedding; after all, everyone was scrimping and saving and large society weddings were frowned upon at the moment. The truth, as Adrian saw it, was that Facey could hardly award a new contract to Sir Julius and then, on the same day, announce the engagement of his daughter to Adrian.

Just then, his thoughts turned to Celia Lutyens. She had been infatuated with him when she was fifteen. She had followed him around doe-eyed, chewing at a loose lock of her hair. However, he had hardly seen her in the five years since. He thought that she must wince every time she thought about that weekend at Drewsteignton. But she was no longer fifteen; no longer boyishly thin with unruly auburn hair. He had to admit that she had become a beautiful young woman. He would like to see her when he was next on leave, to thank her for looking out for Christian.

"We've arrived at Fenchurch Street Station, sir."

The car had come to a halt and Adrian looked out of the window at the hundreds of soldiers milling about. They were all heading back to the front. He was certain that most of them would not return. He took a deep breath and told himself to stop feeling morose. He had survived in the Royal Garrison Artillery for over two years and the war could not go on forever.

"Do you have that letter for George?" Adrian asked.

"It's here, sir... and, sir... you will keep an eye out for George?

"You have my word."

Chapter 53

"The Corps of Royal Engineers," said Colonel Campbell, giving the Christmas toast, "has existed in one form or another for nearly eight hundred years. William the Conqueror had engineers when he invaded England and over a hundred years ago, we received a Royal Warrant."

Peter Hall sat on the colonel's right-hand side. He had hardly heard a word that was being said but he knew what would be next. Colonel Campbell always gave the same speech at the mess table on Christmas Day.

"And our motto '*Quo Fas et Gloria Ducunt*'..." continued the colonel.

"Where right and glory lead," said Peter under his breath. He had not realised that he had spoken out loud.

"Exactly," continued the colonel. "Where right and glory lead, serves to inspire us to greater achievements." The colonel looked at Peter to make sure he wasn't going to be interrupted again and then raised his glass. "The Royal Engineers." The officers stood, raised their glasses and drank.

The meal ended and Peter wandered to a corner of the mess room. No one followed him or came to talk to him. Everyone in the officers' mess knew he was probably the best engineer in the regiment, but he had not been to the right school and therefore could never be trusted – not fully. He had gained his commission on the back of a recommendation and but for that he would never have been made an officer.

Peter sipped at his glass of port. He had only returned to the regiment that morning after three weeks away on compassionate leave. He had received his orders that morning to go back to the mines at Vimy Ridge. He had spent longer there than any other officer. He should have resented the posting, but he accepted it with a sense of fatalism. At least he would be away from the other officers who did not even pretend to like him. At least he would be buried underground like his wife. There was now so much death that life no longer made sense to him.

He slept fitfully that night and in the early morning took a lorry south out of Ypres towards Vimy Ridge. He looked back at what was left of the town. There was not one building that stood unscathed. The town had been built up over the centuries and destroyed in a few months. It seemed so much easier to knock things down then build them up. The town passed from sight and the mutilated landscape with its broken trees and craters, trenches and fortifications continued to taunt him. When he left, he had thought that working once again in the mines would be more than he could bear, but by the time Peter Hall came to his journey's end, it was the only place on earth where he wanted to be.

He arrived at the mines just before midday. He made his way to his quarters which he had left two and a half months earlier and called for his batman.

"Pritchard!" shouted Hall. "What the bloody hell has been happening since I've been away?"

"We lost Sub-Lieutenant Jenkins," said Pritchard. "He came in looking for a periscope one day last week but couldn't find it. I'm not sure what happened next, but I was told he just stuck his head over the top. Bad luck really – no more than a chance in a thousand. Must have been a sniper waiting 'cause in that split second he took a bullet. Just bad luck really."

"Bad luck?" Hall's voice trailed off. "I suppose it was just that, bad luck. Anything else, Pritchard?"

"Just some post, sir. It came soon after you left. I would have sent it on normally, but I wasn't sure where you'd be and they told me you were coming back soon so I thought I oughta hold on to it." Pritchard moved to the back of the dugout where a shelf had been nailed to the wall. On it stood a bible, a shaving mirror and a photograph of Rose. Hall watched as his batman opened the cover of the bible and removed a letter.

Peter reached out his hand and took the letter. He looked at the handwriting and knew immediately who had written it. He stood in the doorway of his dugout, tore open the envelope and began reading.

2 October 1916

Dear Peter,

I decided not to reply to your last letters when I got them knowing that if I responded I would just be telling one more lie on top of all the other lies.

I have never been unfaithful to you, nor have I done anything that would place a blemish on your name. However, I cannot continue to be your wife. It was unfair for me to marry you as I did. It was done for all the wrong reasons. I knew you loved me and hoped in time that I could grow to love you, but this has not happened. Indeed, the opposite has occurred and I feel we have grown further and further apart. I am ashamed of myself as I know that when you read this it can only cause you hurt.

I think it also fair to tell you that I saw Christian Drewe recently. He was seriously injured on the Somme and has been sent back to England to recuperate. I know that he's from a different class and we live in different worlds, but when I saw him my heart broke. As I have said I have never been unfaithful, but I cannot go on feeling this way.

I am happy for you to divorce me. I deserve nothing better.

Please know that this is sent with my heart full of sorrow.

Yours very truly,

Rose

Peter Hall looked northwards at the grey clouds hanging over Ypres, folded the letter neatly and put it in his jacket pocket. "Better get going!" he shouted to Pritchard and walked along the trenches towards the deep mines.

He could not believe it. He would have given her anything she had wanted. He had rented an apartment for her; made sure she didn't want for money and given her a position. He didn't even complain when she had decided to come out to the front. She had said that she would be there if he was injured. He no longer knew whether to believe anything she had said! He clenched his fists as he walked. He wanted to shout at her and then tell her that he would forgive her anything, but what he could not live with was the thought that she had gone. If she were somehow alive, then perhaps he could have made everything fine again.

Chapter 54

Celia had seen it coming. It had started at the beginning of the Christmas vacation when her brother Robert came back from his first term at university. He arrived with his bag and went upstairs, his shirt hanging out slightly from the back of his trousers. No longer a boy, thought Celia, but still her little brother. For the next few days he sat around brooding without even a word for the dog. When he looked at the newspaper he turned first to the list of the war dead and his eyes would slowly go down the page. Celia put it down to a concern for his friends, so many of those who had enlisted had lied about their age, been sent to the front and had been killed. Each evening when she got home from the Endsleigh Hospital, he would be sitting in the bay window at the front of the house, staring out towards the street lamp and the darkness beyond. The fire in that room was always replenished at lunchtime and would now be nothing but a few embers. She always shivered when she entered that room. When she asked him what was bothering him he answered that there was nothing wrong. She didn't believe him.

A week before Christmas, Celia heard that Jenny Stanton's youngest brother, Frederic, had been killed in a skirmish just south of Trieste. He had been a year younger than Celia and a year older than Robert. Robert had known him since prep school. On the day after New Year's Day 1917, news came that Edward Stanton had been killed in Flanders. No one in the house spoke about it. She wrote to Jenny but she did not get an answer. However, the news seemed to weigh on Robert's mind. He now seemed even more distracted. Celia also noticed that he was particularly short with his mother. He almost grunted when she spoke to him. Fortunately, thought Celia, her father was due back from India the following day and Celia hoped that having him there would give Robert the chance to talk to someone.

On the 3rd of January 1917 a flurry of afternoon snow covered the grass at 31 Bedford Square. Edwin Lutyens slowly climbed up the three stone steps to his house and rapped hard on the door. The temperature had dropped sufficiently so that the snow was beginning to settle on the roads and roofs and, with a driving wind, Lutyens had to stuff his hands back in his pockets. The collar of his coat was pulled tight around his neck and his fedora hat was fixed firmly. He shivered, waiting for the maid to open the door. Behind him a taxi driver huffed and puffed as he pulled down Lutyens' luggage from the top of the cab. Lutyens turned to watch him, a man only a few years older than himself in his early fifties. One of his trunks clattered to the ground. No tip for him, thought Lutyens to himself.

Celia opened the door and smiled.

"Sorry, lost my keys. I think I must have packed them. Stupid thing – my memory's not what it once was." Lutyens walked into the hall. Celia kissed him on his cheek as he took off his hat and coat.

"We expected you at lunchtime. If you're hungry, we could make up an omelette?" Celia kept the door open as the taxi driver carried the three trunks up the steps and placed them in the hall. She gave him thruppence and he left with a thank you and a better impression of those who lived in Bedford Square than he had when he started work earlier that morning.

Emily had also heard the door and came down the stairs from her bedroom.

"How are the children?" he asked.

"Fine," said Emily. "Mary, Elisabeth and Robert are all upstairs."

"And how are you?" said Lutyens turning to Celia.

"Well."

"I didn't think I'd see you."

"I'm working nights this month. I shall be going to the hospital after dinner."

Emily picked up her husband's coat which he had placed on the banister and put it in a heavy oak cabinet. She examined the brown fedora that Lutyens had placed on the letter table.

"Is this new?" she asked.

"I bought it in Rome on my journey back."

Celia looked at it. "Very artistic," she added, "you probably look like Oscar Wilde with it on."

"Your father looks nothing like Oscar Wilde!" said Emily.

Emily put the hat away and opened the door to the front room where Celia had arranged for extra coal to be placed on the fire.

"I met him once," Emily said to Celia as they walked into the room. "Oscar Wilde, I mean. I met him when I was very young, about fourteen, I think. My father had been posted to Paris as the ambassador and he turned up at the embassy. He was amusing and not nearly as odious as we had all expected, though he was fearfully conceited. He told me that the key to telling an epigram that people remembered was to add 'Oscar Wilde said' at the end. Now run along, dear. I have to speak with your father."

*   *   *

Edwin Lutyens came back from India with a wealth of stories and his children sat quietly at the dinner table listening. He did not desist from telling one anecdote after another as the courses rolled from one to the next until finally coffee and cheese arrived. In the moments when he paused to think or play with his pipe, one of the younger children would butt in with a question. He mainly talked about India. He told them about the claustrophobic heat and the smell of spices and rancid cooking oil from the vendors who thronged the train stations. Celia smiled as he talked. She knew she had been to India when she was a baby and Robert had been born there, but she had no recollection of the place.

"It's a place that we shall soon lose," said Lutyens. "All the energy and drive has been sucked out of the country. There is none of the restlessness that I saw in South Africa when I was there. I think it is because we have lost the will to govern, and once the Indians shake the tiredness out of their own eyes we shall be gone. They are a strange people – an old people full of their own sense of history, culture and religion and at the moment they are sleeping; but it is not a deep sleep. There is a movement towards independence with new young leaders who are trying to understand their own country because it has so many different cultures and religions."

"As I've said before, Edwin," said Emily, "why don't we hand it back now? We don't have any right to stay. You know my views on Home Rule."

"That reminds me," he said, beginning a new story. "I forgot to tell you that I had some trouble on the way back home. As the ship sailed out of the port of Marseille, we spotted two German U-boats." He waved the stick of celery at Robert as he spoke. "The guns on our ship started firing – boom, boom, boom – and we were given inflatable Gieves waistcoats to wear and we all marched up on deck just in case we were hit. The U-boats didn't fire and submerged once we had spotted them. However, we kept firing for about an hour. When we got round the rock of Gibraltar we knew we were pretty safe. I kept the Gieves waistcoat and inscribed a message on it for your mother."

"What does it say?" asked Robert.

"I wrote 'If anything should happen to me you have only to take out the cork and listen to your husband's last breath.'"

"I wish I had been there," said Robert.

"That's not a wish I share," said Emily.

"But then you don't want me enlisting, do you?"

"We can talk about it later."

"No!" shouted Robert. "Let's talk about it now." Robert's face was flushed and if Celia had not seen that he had refused wine with his dinner she would have thought him drunk. "When this war started there were a lot of people who went around handing out white feathers and you encouraged them, Mother." He did not look at Celia. "And now that I am old enough to join up you want me to avoid doing my duty."

"You're still a child," said Emily. "I won't sit in a hospital crying for you. I won't let you get killed or burnt or maimed. You only just turned eighteen last week and I'll do all I can to stop you."

"I want to do my duty! I don't want to be thought a coward. When I see Jenny Stanton next, what will she think when she sees me? Which of her two brothers would she wish back and me dead in his place?"

Robert took another deep breath.

"I can't live like that."

Celia found herself crying as she sat at the table. She did not know when the tears had started. Her father had taken off his glasses and was rubbing his eyes. Celia looked at her mother. Emily was watching Robert. There was no hint of emotion in her face, and Celia realised that her mother had known that this was coming.

Edwin Lutyens put on his glasses and turned his chair round so he could talk directly to his son.

"Not only do I understand your position," Lutyens began, "but I sympathise with your position."

"Edwin!" shouted Emily. "Don't. You promised."

"But," said Lutyens, "your mother has raised you and I have agreed to defer to her wishes. I have agreed not to encourage you."

"You can't stop me," said Robert.

"But we don't have to help you," said Emily.

"I just need my birth certificate and then I can enlist as an officer."

Lady Emily took her napkin from her lap and placed it on the table.

"You don't have one," she said to Robert.

"What do you mean I don't have one? I found Celia's; where's mine?"

"Robert, you weren't born in England. We were in India at the time when you were born. There was no way to register your birth and I didn't really think about it too much when we got back to England. You don't have one."

Emily held out her hand.

"Don't lie to me!" he answered.

She brought her hand back and looked at him coldly. She suddenly thought that she could prevent him enlisting if she could stop him getting a birth certificate.

"How do I get one?"

"One of your parents has to register you and if we don't, then there's nothing you can do."

"There is one thing," answered Robert. "I need a birth certificate in order to become an officer. I don't need a birth certificate to enlist in the ranks. If you don't register my birth, I will join up as a private in the first regiment that'll have me. They're not really that fussy nowadays." Robert looked at his father for support.

"Emily," said Lutyens, "try and see Robert's position."

"I won't do it," said Emily firmly.

"See sense," said Lutyens. "It's better for him to be trained as an officer than to be shipped to France in the ranks. Please, Emily."

"I'll get him his birth certificate," she said finally, "but don't think I'll ever forgive you, Edwin. You promised to support me, not stab me in the back."

The next morning, Emily Marion Lutyens made a solemn declaration at Mansion House in the City of London in accordance with the Statutory Declarations Act, that her eldest son Robert Cedric Lutyens had been born on the 27th of December 1898 at Lucknow in the dominion of India and that as there was no place to register his birth and therefore he was without a birth certificate. In the twenty-ninth month of the war against Germany and for the price of a shilling stamp, Robert Cedric Lutyens, just turned eighteen, was certified by his mother and the Lord Mayor of London as having been born.

After leaving Mansion House, Emily Lutyens walked back to Holborn and in that hour and a half made up her mind to go to America at Easter for the remainder of the war. She would need a few months to arrange things. Later that day, and without telling her husband, she booked passage on a ship to America with her two youngest children.

At least, she thought, she could spend the rest of the war with Krishnamurti.

Chapter 55

The ebb and flow of death and life became the norm for Celia and although her moods sometimes swung from depression to elation she remained, most often, on an even keel. She worried about her brother and hated her mother who was arranging her trip to America. Work was still hard but there were now newer nurses whom Matron preyed on. The cold snap of January had passed and February, although still chilly, was warmer. Christian Drewe was recovering well in a convalescent home in Wiltshire. In fact, that morning she had received a letter from him saying that he hoped to be leaving for Drewsteignton within the month. He had made good progress in the two months at the Endsleigh Hospital and from his letter Celia was pleased to see that he was learning to cope with his blindness.

Her hours and the days passed more quickly now that she was not routinely sluicing bedpans. Eleven turned into twelve and twelve turned into one and then lunchtime was gone. She worked quickly and efficiently. She seemed to have more time to talk to the injured soldiers and although she felt part of the hospital, she had made the decision to leave to look after Christian Drewe. They had got on better in the two months after he was admitted. He had quietened and become more determined; finally, he had joined the 'could-dos' on one side of the ward.

At five o'clock she looked out of the window. Underneath the streetlamp in Gordon Street a man was smoking, one hand in his pocket. Celia recognised him immediately. He threw his cigarette to the ground, stood on it with the ball of his foot, took out a silver cigarette case and lit another. The smoke seemed to dissipate into the grey evening. He looked at his pocket watch – and Celia in turn checked hers. She thought about going out to see him, but she remembered the previous dressing down from Matron and something in the back of her mind told her that he would wait and that it would do no harm to make him stand there in the cold evening for half an hour longer. The minutes seemed to stretch out forever. Matron was again doing her rounds and Celia busied herself with making sure her ward was spotless.

"I believe Lieutenant Drewe's brother is waiting outside for you," said the matron when she had finished her inspection.

"Is he?" answered Celia.

"He is... and Nurse Lutyens... no one would particularly miss you if you went a few minutes earlier this evening."

Celia managed to get changed, powder her face and apply lipstick all in less than five minutes. She took a deep breath before opening the main door of the hospital.

"You're here," she said, trying to sound surprised.

"I thought you might want a lift home," replied Adrian.

"I don't live far."

"I just wanted..." Adrian threw his cigarette to the ground. Celia looked at him. His green eyes with his black eyelashes looked back at her for a second and then he dropped his gaze. "...to thank you." He was smiling; she hadn't seen him smile the last time he was at the hospital. "So would you like that lift?" Celia nodded. Adrian lifted his hand and waved at a parked car about twenty yards away. The car lights turned on and it began to move slowly forward. Celia looked at him.

"I borrowed my father's Packard; it's a little more comfortable than my old Ford."

"Are you staying at Wadhurst Hall?"

"Yes."

The car slowed and stopped in front of them. He pulled open the door and she stepped into the motor. A wrap of silver fox fur lay on the back seat.

"Bedford Square, Poley," Adrian said to the chauffeur.

Adrian closed the door and sat beside Celia. He offered her a cigarette.

"I don't think I shall have time to finish this before we arrive."

Adrian pulled down a tube, blew through it and shouted: "Poley, drive a little slower."

"Now I feel as if I've been kidnapped," said Celia.

"At this speed you could jump from the motor and hardly scuff your shoes," replied Adrian, "and as I said before, I wanted to thank you. My mother told me that you agreed to move to Drewsteignton to look after Christian. He'll need as much help as he can get and I appreciate what you're doing."

As Adrian was speaking, Celia placed her cigarette in a black ebony holder and lit it. She took the cigarette holder from between her lips. The black ebony was smeared with her red lipstick.

"You don't have to thank me," she answered. "Your father sorted things out with the hospital. When Christian is discharged from the convalescent home, I will stay with him for a month or so to make sure he can cope and then I will come back for a few days each month to make sure things are progressing smoothly."

"I was also told that you spent a lot of your own time with Christian, helping him to speak again after his skin grafts."

"I promised I would help him," said Celia. "And what about you? When do you go back to the front?"

"In a few days' time."

"And will I see you again?"

"When I'm next back in England. I promise I will come down and see you in Drewsteignton if you're there."

"I'll hold you to that."

The car pulled up to a halt. Arthur Poley opened the door and Celia got out followed by Adrian. She stood at the bottom of the stone steps to her house. She thought about inviting him in but there was no one there except for her mother and the servants. The house would be cold and damp and Adrian wouldn't even be allowed to smoke if he wanted to. She shuffled for an uncomfortable moment wondering what to say to him. Goodbye was all she managed and she started climbing the steps to the front door.

"Goodbye," Adrian replied.

She put her key in the latch and then turned, thinking that Adrian would be climbing back into the car. He hadn't; he stood watching her.

To hell with it, she thought and dashed down the stairs and across to where he stood, kissed him and then ran into the house.

PART IX

Chapter 56

By slow and uncertain degrees the train made its way towards Exeter. Celia sat with her head resting against the window, looking out at the fields and embankments with their scattering of buttercups and dandelions. Her father sat opposite, absorbed in his drawings and on occasion she would look at him. She had tried near Farnham to talk to him, but he was wrapped up in his work. For the last hour she had done nothing more than daydream. She looked at her watch. The train was already two hours late. Why on earth, she thought, couldn't the trains run on time? On the Continent the trains ran on time. Sheep on the track, the guard had said! How could it take thirty-five minutes to move a few sheep? And then there was a signal failure at Honiton. The train whistle blew and suddenly the carriage was thrown into darkness as it went through another tunnel.

"How is one supposed to work," Lutyens said, exasperated by the darkness, "when every five minutes you are disturbed by one thing or another?"

In the blackness Celia smiled to herself. "Sorry, Father, what did you say?"

"Nothing – nothing of any importance." As quickly as the darkness had come, it lifted. Celia expected her father to go back to his drawings but to her surprise he started to fold them up one after another and place them in his old leather Gladstone bag.

Celia tried once more at conversation. "I wonder how Mother is?"

"Emily? Oh, Emily's fine. I got a letter from her this morning."

"You didn't tell me."

"Didn't I? Are you sure – well perhaps not, my memory's not what it once was."

"What did she write? How are Mary and Elisabeth?"

Lutyens scratched his head and thought for a moment. "She first asked about Robert and you. Then she wrote that Mary and Elisabeth were enjoying

America although they had both been terribly seasick on the journey across and that they are staying in New York for a month or so before going to see Krishnamurti. Oh yes, and she also sent something called peanut butter, which is all the rage in America."

"So, Mother's *still* intending to stay with him?"

Lutyens did not answer but took out his pipe from the breast pocket of his suit, filled it with tobacco and lit it.

"And what about you, Father? Now everyone has gone perhaps we can talk more. I would like to know about what you're doing."

Lutyens inhaled deeply of the rich tobacco.

"There's plenty for me to do. There's India, there's Drogo and then there's my war work. When I was recently in France, I saw the battlefields with all the obliteration of human endeavour and achievement. There were fields of poppies and wildflowers everywhere. I realised then why your Aunt Gertrude loves flowers. They don't discriminate against an unexploded shell or the leg of a garden seat in Surrey. I was then shown the graveyards – hundreds of them – spread out, haphazard and in need of time and care."

"But what have you been asked to do, Father?"

"There are so many dead now that they can never bring all the bodies home. The War Office has requested that Baker and I design the cemeteries where the bodies will be buried. There has to be a theme to them, and I want to design something non-denominational – not just a cross." His pipe had gone out while he had been speaking. He did not relight it but continued to chew on the stem.

"Have you had any thoughts about the design?"

"Just something simple," said Lutyens. "Perhaps a stone. A stone of remembrance. Something that is not linked to any creed or religion. A symbol that can be used by those of all faiths and none."

"Of all faiths and none," said Celia.

"Exactly," said Lutyens, "And what about you, Celia?" he asked.

And what about me? thought Celia to herself.

"My work keeps me busy I suppose," she replied. However, it wasn't what she wanted to say. She had started to think about what she could do after the war. She had been thinking about going back to university and completing her degree. But then what? She didn't want to work with injured soldiers once the war had finished, she wanted a fresh start. Finish her degree in literature and then, perhaps, teach?

She had taken a large collection of books with her when she first went to Drewsteignton two months ago. They were mainly novels and some books that she had from her time at Girton. After a few days, when Christian and Celia had worn out all conversation about their mutual interests, she began reading to him from one book after another. *The Mystery of Dr Fu-Manchu* was his favourite. "The greatest genius which the powers of evil have put on the earth for centuries." He repeated the words after Celia had read them.

When they were not reading, they would go through each room in the house one after another. Celia would initially tell him where everything was placed and then he would navigate the room, avoiding chairs and tables. With the housekeeper, they removed everything that could be knocked over and every sharp edge. He learnt the layout of the rooms quickly. He could picture them like a photograph in his mind.

While she was there, she had got to know every nook and cranny of Adrian's house. She had looked out of every window as he must have done; she had stood in the library and wondered what his favourite books were. She remembered that first day when she saw the house; she had had a moment's trepidation that she might dislike everything in it. What if Adrian had no taste and the house was stuffed with Victorian clutter? She didn't want to be disappointed and had tentatively knocked on the door. However, she had found nearly everything to be perfect. The walls had been painted white and were bare except for a few modern paintings in the hallway and living room. She had liked the paintings; some abstract and some in the style of Klimt. The rooms also were uncluttered with simple furniture of plain lines. It was the type of furniture she would have chosen. The only thing which she did not care for was an ornate silver frame with a photograph of Adrian and his parents and the Faceys. He was standing next to Jane Facey. It was not the photograph that she objected to and, she thought to herself, that the girl couldn't help being plain. However, she took objection to the frame. Whoever had bought it, she concluded, did not know Adrian, because Adrian would have chosen something much simpler.

As the train got closer to Exeter, Celia wondered once again whether Adrian would be there. Christian had dictated a letter saying that he hoped his brother might be back on leave. She read and reread the letter. She played over in her mind what she would say to Adrian when she saw him. She had kissed him. However, he had never done anything to suggest that he had the same feelings. She blushed. She hoped he would not make fun of her. She could bear anything but being teased by him. She looked at her father, smoking and deep in his own thoughts. He had grown old and comfy, like a good slipper. His hair had turned completely grey and the top of his head had gone bald.

"Do you mind if I ask you something?" she said. Lutyens nodded his head. "Do you still love Mother?"

Celia had expected her father to look shocked by the question, but he wasn't. He chewed on the stem of his pipe and concentrated for a moment before answering.

"I've never loved anyone else but your mother," he said and took out a match and lit his pipe.

Celia looked down at her shoes. She thought about his answer for a moment before looking back at him.

"Did you know that you were in love the first time that you saw her?"

"Yes." Lutyens crossed his arms in front of him.

"And you miss her?"

"Of course." Lutyens shuffled in his seat. His eyes moved around the carriage.

"Why didn't you try and stop her from going to America?"

"You can't stop your mother doing anything. If I had tried it would have made matters worse."

"But it's made you unhappy," said Celia.

"It would have made me even sadder to know that I had made my Emily unhappy. Now," said Lutyens opening up his bag and taking out one of the drawings he had just folded and put away, "I just want to check one more thing before we meet Sir Julius and go up to the castle."

Celia's eyes wandered back to the windowpane. They were now slowly going through the outskirts of Exeter. Her father's feelings for her mother seemed so unselfish. It was so different to what she was feeling. She resented that she would be going back to London in three days' time and that she did not know whether Adrian would be there or not. She resented the fact that the war had taken Adrian away from her and might not bring him back.

The train pulled up at Exeter station in short, sharp jolts. Celia and Lutyens got off the train and for a moment Celia thought that Adrian might me there. She hadn't checked what she looked like in the mirror in her vanity case. After four and a half hours on the train she was certain that she looked a fright. How could she be so stupid, she thought to herself.

*   *   *

"You're late," said Sir Julius as Celia and her father got into the car.

"Sheep on the track," replied Lutyens by way of explanation, "just outside Farnham."

"It *still* doesn't disguise the fact that you're late," said Sir Julius sharply. "We'll go straight to the castle as I've now wasted the whole morning."

A slow cloud of despair rose within Celia. She would have to sit with her father and Sir Julius for the next few hours as they sniped against each other over what the castle would look like and how much it would cost.

A gang of boys was standing beside the car, some looking into the chauffeur's compartment and others were attempting to peer into the back of the vehicle. Julius pulled down the window and shouted at them to clear off. One of the boys stood his ground defiantly, looked at Julius and seemed in two minds whether to say something in return but as his friends were already running down the road, he decided to follow suit without exchanging words.

"It's going to the dogs," said Sir Julius.

"What is?" asked Celia.

"This country," said Sir Julius shaking his head. "It's all going to the dogs. No respect. No respect for anyone or anything nowadays."

Celia could see the boys as they ran away laughing and then looked at Sir Julius and deep down, she was pleased that the country was going to the dogs. It was all just a bit too stuffy. Stuffy old men wearing stuffy suits and dressed in starched collars making money from a war run by stuffy generals and stuffier politicians. She lowered her head and tried not to smile and then wondered whether Adrian would one day turn out to be like his father. She suddenly did not feel like smiling.

They began the thirty-two-mile journey to Castle Drogo. It took them a little time to get out of the city centre and then past the Victorian tenements. Once they had reached the outskirts of Exeter, they picked up speed.

"A top speed of fifty miles per hour," shouted Sir Julius to Lutyens above the engine noise. "Mind you, she's damned hard to handle when she's going flat out."

Sir Julius sat back on the tan leather seat of the motor and crossed his legs. He wore a charcoal grey suit, a cream silk shirt and Homburg hat. Celia thought that he appeared more at ease than when she had seen him at the Wadhurst Hall New Year's Eve ball. He looked less tired. When she had been staying down in Drewsteignton with Christian, he had told her that Sir Julius had lost almost everything because of the war. He said that Sir Julius had convinced the government that despite the losses to his ships he would still guarantee the amount of tonnage they wanted, even if he had to sell the shirt on his back. Sir Julius could have lost everything on the turn of a card, but he said that fortunately, with the help of Lord Facey, things had swung back in his favour. His contract with the government had been renewed and his ships were now getting through from America.

The car slowed and turned off the main road and entered the undulating countryside of Dartmoor. The road changed from dark, smooth asphalt to a cinder track. Celia noticed the change. No longer did they have to shout over the sound of the engine but as the car moved slowly forward along the cinder track, a quieter and different sound could be heard, like the cracking of a thousand eggshells.

Celia could smell something quite woody and musky. She looked out of the side window across the moor with its mixture of grass and heather. The heath land rolled away in waves of purple, green and gold. The air was rich with the taste of the heathers. If Celia had been alone, she would have stopped the car, run into the fields and turned circles with her head back and her arms outstretched.

"You used to have a Rolls-Royce, didn't you?" Celia heard her father say. Talk of cars bored her. She looked out of the window at the sapphire sky and barely heard the conversation.

"I've had a few automobiles – a Clément and an Isotta Fraschini," said Sir Julius. "I liked both, but they were always breaking down. The French and Italians can't make motors, they're just not practical, although I will give them their due, they produce the best chefs. Leave it to the Germans to build something reliable. If I had my way I would have a German automobile, a French sommelier and an Italian chef but given the state of things with Germany, I thought it unpatriotic to buy anything German. Therefore, I settled on a Packard – it's American, built better than a Cadillac and better value for money."

"It's a nice automobile," Lutyens added.

"What are you driving now?" asked Sir Julius.

"We decided to economise for the war effort," replied Lutyens.

Celia began listening more acutely to the conversation. She hated being thought of as poor. All her friends seemed to be wealthier than her. None of them did without maids or didn't have a motor. She could see little point in her father being considered a great architect if it meant that they had to scrimp and save.

"Quite right," said Sir Julius, "we've been tightening our belts at Wadhurst Hall. Everyone's been prepared to do their bit. I wasn't able to let go of the Italian chef, though," Julius added with a slight grin. "Some things a gentleman just can't do without. Life would hardly be worth living would it, eh?" Celia looked over to Sir Julius and concluded that if push came to shove, he could tighten his belt considerably more.

Fortunately Adrian's nothing like his father, thought Celia, they're like chalk and cheese; but she knew the analogy wasn't correct. There were strong similarities between father and son. They had similar looks. Both could be determined when they wanted to be. But, she thought, there were as many differences as similarities. Adrian had charm and passion and a sense of duty. Adrian made one feel special when he spoke to you. Adrian had thrown caution to the wind and enlisted the day that war was declared. Celia could not imagine Sir Julius would ever have done the same, even as a young man.

The sounds inside the car once again changed. The cinder track had finished, and they were now travelling again on tarmac. Celia looked out of the window as they went through the village of Drewsteignton. Sir Julius was not even going to stop for Christian. They would be arriving at the castle within a few minutes. She remembered when she had first come to the castle, there had not been a road at all but a single muddy cart track. The wet sheen of the surface of laid tarmac had begun to dull and the road was starting to show signs of its age as nature tried to claw back what Sir Julius had taken. Suddenly the hedges disappeared and on the right-hand side of the road there was a driveway with two white pillars of stone. The car turned into the driveway.

"Now pull up fifty yards on your right just where the driveway splits," said Lutyens. "Pull up there," he continued, pointing his finger forward to another vehicle, "beside that motor." Celia looked at the vehicle, an old Ford, and recognised it immediately as Adrian's. Why hadn't her father told her that Adrian was here? She looked at her dress; it would have to do, she thought. She could hardly unpack her things and get changed into something less plain on a building site.

"Why didn't you tell me Adrian would be here?" she said to her father.

"I didn't think to," said Lutyens, surprised by her tone of voice.

Men, she thought to herself. Hopeless.

"Adrian came up with Christian earlier," said Sir Julius. Celia tried to peer away into the distance, but the road curved up and then dipped so that she could see little further than a stone's throw away. Where was he? What would she say to him?

"Now," said Julius to Lutyens. "What do you want to show me? I've done what you asked and haven't visited the castle for the last two months."

Lutyens started to explain why he had asked Sir Julius to come to the site. "I wanted you to see what the castle could one day look like when it's complete."

"I know what it will look like," interrupted Sir Julius. "I've seen your drawings."

"But I want you to experience the castle."

Celia interrupted them.

"I'm not sure I understand. How can you experience something that's not there? I walked up here only a few months ago and there was almost nothing but the foundations and some half-built bits of the walls."

"We employed a new foreman about eight weeks ago," said Lutyens. "He's a Scot, called Frasier, who helped carry Christian when he was injured on the Somme. He was injured but not too badly. We took him on to speed up the work on the castle."

"But nothing much can be done in eight weeks," said Celia.

"You'll see," said Lutyens. "Where's Adrian?"

The chauffeur sounded the car horn three times. Celia saw Adrian first. He was as she remembered him; tall, athletic with jet-black hair and a short thin moustache. He appeared in his uniform and swung his swagger stick in his left hand, clipping the heads off any dandelions that had been brave enough to grow on the path. He did not hurry – he appeared more interested in beheading the dandelions than anything else. Celia felt a pang of self-doubt as she watched him. She wondered why he was not hurrying. She wondered if he knew that she was there. He seemed so self-absorbed in what he was doing. As he approached, he took out his watch and looked at it.

"Good afternoon, sir," he said to his father.

"Adrian."

Adrian held out his hand to Lutyens.

"Good afternoon, sir. I telephoned the station about an hour ago and was told that your train would be delayed."

"Sheep on the track," said Lutyens.

"I take it then that you haven't eaten?" Adrian glanced down at the waistlines of his father and Edwin Lutyens.

"Not a bite," said Lutyens.

"I missed luncheon as well," added Sir Julius.

"I doubt if it will be fatal," replied Adrian with a smile and he turned to Celia. "I did, however, take the liberty of preparing a small picnic for us while they see the castle – I hope you don't think it impertinent."

"Not at all," said Celia.

Lutyens, however, not only thought it impertinent but distinctly cruel, and as the four of them walked in the direction of the castle his stomach rumbled in protest.

Chapter 57

The path led them over a small hillock. Celia followed her father who led the way towards the castle with Sir Julius next to him. She walked beside Adrian and asked him what it was like in Belgium. Celia let him talk about himself and expressed her concerns when he mentioned anything that seemed remotely dangerous. She knew that even the most reserved man cannot resist talking about himself if a woman was prepared to listen. He only spoke about the war in general terms and said that what he had missed most was his family and home cooking.

"And I have George Poley in my regiment," he said, "the chauffeur's son."

Celia nodded. She had heard about Arthur Poley's son who had dragged Christian back across the whole of no man's land and received the Military Medal for his bravery.

"He was always volunteering for one thing after another and as I had promised his father to look after him, I had to make him my orderly in order to stop him getting himself killed."

"I'm sure he's very safe with you."

"You know," said Adrian, "you have a habit of putting me at ease? I remember that day I met you at the hospital. When I saw you, I knew immediately who you were."

"You did?"

"Of course. How could I forget you?"

"Can I ask you a question?" said Celia. "Do you know why my father is being so mysterious about the castle? I gather he asked Sir Julius not to visit here for the last two months."

"Didn't he tell you?" said Adrian with a note of surprise. "I assumed you knew."

"He hasn't said a word."

"Christian said he didn't think your father would tell you, but I thought he would."

"Tell me what?" She looked around.

"It's around the next bend," said Adrian.

"What is?"

"The castle."

"But why all the mystery? There are only the foundations and a few walls to see."

"You really don't know?" Adrian said. "Come on then, we shall have to catch up with the other two. I wanted to see my father's face when he rounds the next bend anyway. Do you mind running?" Celia nodded her head and Adrian started to trot to catch up with his father and Lutyens. Oh God, thought Celia to herself, what on earth had possessed her to nod her head? Nowhere in her picture of that afternoon had running featured. She hoped that she would not go bright red in the face or perspire inordinately. She had a horrible image of her standing before Adrian like an overcooked beetroot. However, in for a penny, in for a pound and Celia sprinted after him as fast as she could.

Celia reached her father first – but only just. She overtook Adrian with a few yards to go but she suspected that he let her. As they turned the next corner the sight in front of her took Celia's breath away. Rising from the edge of the escarpment and stretching towards her for a hundred yards appeared the completed castle with an octagonal tower and battlements. Celia stood in disbelief before she noticed the look on Sir Julius' face.

"I thought it would take another ten years to build," she said to no one in particular.

Adrian leant towards her and whispered, "It's not real."

Celia turned and looked at him blankly.

"What do you mean it's not real? It's standing in front of me."

"Christ!" exclaimed Sir Julius as he caught his breath. He stood motionless for a moment before taking a few steps forward into the open space. His eyes ranged left and right. "How is it possible?" Once again Sir Julius' eyes wandered down the length of the castle and the octagonal tower with its granite-looking stone where, above the main wooden door, was carved a lion rampant. Julius looked at it – he could just read the inscription below it from where he stood. It was the Drewe heraldic emblem, the lion with its one paw outstretched and the mouth gaping. *Drewe Nomen et Virtus Arma Dedit* – Drewe is the name and valour gave it arms.

"How is it possible?" Sir Julius said again.

"Come on," said Adrian quietly to Celia, "he'll realise in a minute that it's nothing more than a theatre set."

Celia looked at him slightly bemused. "What do you mean?"

"Your father came up with the idea and has had men working on it for the last six weeks. When you get closer you'll see."

Celia walked forward closer to the castle. Suddenly she saw that there was no depth to the rampart walls and that there were cracks between the various wooden panels. Sir Julius, however, stood motionless behind her, enthralled with an image of what he would one day possess.

*   *   *

Near the castle, beside the escarpment, where Basil Drewe had fallen six years previously, Christian Drewe listened. He heard his father's voice, a little quicker than normal, thrilled by what he was seeing. There were also those faint traces of a Lancashire accent that emerged whenever Sir Julius became animated. Lutyens' voice in contrast was assured. The shabby, old, balding man who liked so much to tell anecdotes and stories, was relishing his moment. High above their deep voices he heard Celia, her voice skipping along at the speed of a gazelle. Christian could always tell when she was excited. Try as she might, she could not hide it in her voice. Her tone went up and her words tumbled out. Finally, there was Adrian. He spoke in a measured tone that seemed to exude confidence. However, Christian could hear a slight hesitancy in Adrian's voice, as if he were hiding something.

Christian pictured each one of them in his head. He imagined Celia wearing a long dress, probably white, he thought, with small flowers embroidered on it. He recalled the day he met her at Munstead Wood when he had been asked to paint some pictures of Gertrude Jekyll's gardens. He remembered her from that precise moment; he did not think of her wearing a ballgown or in a nurse's uniform but in a long, white, cotton dress. Lutyens would be wearing that terrible brown three-piece suit he always wore, which smelt of pipe tobacco. He smiled with the thought that he would smell Lutyens approaching before anyone else. His father would be wearing his charcoal grey suit and cream silk shirt and his favourite Homburg hat. Adrian would, of course, be in his uniform. He pictured Adrian dancing with Celia. He remembered that evening of the New Year's Eve ball well. He remembered that everyone had praised Adrian for his bravery in joining up and that Basil had seemed so unsure what to say when it was suggested that he was a coward.

He sat facing the gorge. He liked the feeling of the air blowing against his face. He looked as if he were staring out intently across the rolling moorland at the violets and yellows of gorse and heather. However, he could see nothing and so he listened. He heard the conversations and the sound of the river Teign far below in the gorge. He heard the birds and other animals, and the wind as it twirled and swirled out of the gorge and made the tree branches creak.

Adrian and Celia were getting closer to him. Their voices were becoming louder. He turned in their direction. Christian listened to Celia as she laughed at one of Adrian's bad jokes and knew that there was nothing he could do or say to stop the inevitable.

He suddenly felt tired. He would ask Adrian to fetch Poley so that he could be taken home. There were too many people, and he didn't want to have to sit with them and answer the inevitable questions of how he felt. Once again, he began withdrawing into himself as he had done over the last few months. He still found being in company hard, especially with more than one person. He wrapped his scarf around his face and pulled his wide-brimmed hat down. Even though he was blind, he knew that people who saw him were instinctively repelled by the way he looked. Often during the long nights, he would slowly run his hands over his face, feeling the lumpy, pock-marked parts and the empty socket where his right eye had once been. On these occasions he sometimes felt that it was a blessing that he had lost his sight. He was blind to the world and could ignore what the world thought of him.

He had spoken for a long time to Adrian that morning as they had walked on the moor.

"Is it still hell out there?" Christian had asked. "What is Ypres like?"

"I'm not sure I can tell you," replied Adrian. "I don't think there are words in any language sufficient to describe that place. It's so physically and emotionally exhausting that it wears you down. How can you explain that? Words are insufficient; they belittle what we've done and betray those who've experienced it."

More and more Christian thought about what had taken them into war. He concluded that the establishment would prefer to be annihilated than lose face. Arrogance and vanity; it was inherent in the upper-class British character. It was inherent in his father and in Adrian and in himself. Adrian called it duty.

They had walked slowly for about two hours that morning. Adrian had kept them to the paths and tracks and Christian had linked his arm around Adrian's so as not to fall. It was a little later than nine when they returned to the house; Christian had heard the church bells of Drewsteignton strike the hour. Adrian suggested that the following morning Christian should try sitting on a horse. He had laughed at the suggestion – the thought of blindly sitting on top of a horse scared him witless. He was certain to fall and between the stirrup and the ground there was only just enough time to repent. When they had returned to the house and were having breakfast, Adrian told Christian about his engagement to Jane Facey. He admitted that he had been pressurised by his father and that Lord Facey's price for resolving his father's financial problems was a marriage to Jane.

"Everyone does their duty," he told Christian. "Even if we don't want to. It's what makes us English."

Christian sniffed and said nothing.

Chapter 58

The scent of honeydew melon hung between them. A sun as yellow as the fruit they had just eaten was high above them. The view across the moor seemed endless and Celia sat quietly taking in the panorama. The purple heather, dashes of yellow gorse, bracken and the candy pink of bird's-eye primrose seemed everywhere. Little on the moorland had changed for a thousand years. Before the Romans came there had been thriving communities living on the moors, but they had been ground into extinction by the hardness of the land and time. The only reminders of their once ferocious existence were small tors, stone circles and the pathways that crossed the moor and linked one village to another. Over time everything was consumed by the moor and now high on the Teign gorge stood an imaginary castle.

Adrian took out his cigarette case and lit himself a cigarette. He lay back on the tartan rug looking up into the clear blue sky. Celia watched him out the corner of her eye.

"What are you thinking about?" asked Celia.

"I was just thinking how almost perfect this is."

"You've been staring up into the sky for so long I thought you had forgotten I was here," said Celia.

Adrian rolled over onto his side and looked at her. "How could I forget you were here? I was just watching a bird circle in the sky."

Celia looked up trying to see what Adrian had been staring at.

"I can't see anything."

Adrian moved over to where Celia was sitting. "Lie on your back." He took her hand, stretching it upwards. "There," he said, directing her finger to a small grey speck in the sky. "Can you see it?"

"Yes," said Celia. "What type of bird is it?"

"It's a shrike. If you carry on watching, it will find its prey in a minute or two and swoop down and grab it."

Adrian could feel her hand trembling as he held on to her. He turned his head to look at her.

"Do you want to kiss me?" he breathed into her ear.

"You're very presumptuous."

"So that's a 'no'."

"Yes."

"It's a 'yes' then."

"Not only presumptuous but impertinent," said Celia. "I'm not going to kiss you when my father is standing no more than one hundred yards away." She brought her hand down and lightly stroked the side of his face. "So, behave yourself."

Adrian got up slowly. When he was upright, he tucked his green army shirt into his trousers.

"What will you do when you leave the army?"

"Come home to Drewsteignton and never do anything serious again."

Celia also got up and they began to walk back towards the castle until they saw Sir Julius and Lutyens coming in their direction.

"Do you think your father liked the castle?" asked Celia.

"Liked? I don't know. He was impressed by it."

"Do ask him," said Celia. "I want to know."

Sir Julius and Lutyens had been looking at the castle for the best part of an hour. In that time Sir Julius had been told about the windows overlaid with stone mullions, the telephone exchange, the inner courtyards, and atrium. He had even been told about the budget and had not baulked. They walked towards Adrian and Celia.

"There is still some food left," Celia shouted out to her father. Lutyens did not need to be encouraged and picked up his pace. He took off his Panama when he arrived at the picnic and wiped his forehead on his shirt cuff. Lutyens' stomach was beginning to believe that his throat had been cut and so was relieved to find that the 'leftovers' consisted of more food than both Sir Julius and he could devour. The cold pheasant had not been touched, nor the paté, salmon, cheeses or the pickled walnuts. Lutyens ignored a plate of canapés and went straight for a pheasant leg. In between mouthfuls he asked Celia what she had thought of the castle.

"It's not how I imagined it would look," Celia said. "I always pictured it being more classical. One can imagine that it will survive as long as the empire."

"I hope it will last a little longer than that," said Lutyens, picking up a piece of pie. He looked back at the castle. "Yes. It looks as if it could always have been here – as if it had existed for a thousand years." Lutyens looked around. "Sir

Julius told me that Christian was here."

"He had to go," said Celia, "he said he wasn't feeling well."

"I'm sorry to hear that; but I am pleased to see that Adrian didn't stint on the picnic. You two must have the appetites of midges," said Lutyens, helping himself to a glass of champagne and a sliver of foie gras on Melba toast.

"I had enough," said Celia. "But I think Adrian wanted a little more." She looked over to Adrian who was now talking with his father ten yards away. Sir Julius was again staring at the castle.

"Do you like it?" Adrian asked his father.

"Yes," said Sir Julius emphatically. "I was worried that it would be vulgar – American – but the one thing you can say about it is that it's not a pastiche of anything. It's an original."

"What did Lutyens say about the castle?" she heard Adrian ask Sir Julius.

"He just said, '*mi casa, su casa*'," replied Sir Julius.

Adrian laughed and his father snuffed in exasperation. "Artist types; you never get a straight answer from them," said Sir Julius quietly.

Celia continued to look over her father's shoulder towards Adrian and smiled at him. He smiled back and came over to where she was.

"What are your plans for the next few days, sir?" said Adrian to Lutyens.

"Dinner with you and Sir Julius tonight and then I am here tomorrow to discuss the building works with the stonemasons and the engineers. I shall tell you a wonderful story about Death after dinner. I heard it when I was coming back from India. I bumped into a young writer called Devon or Somerset or something or other, and he told me this Mesopotamian fable about Death meeting someone in Samarra. The gist of it is that it is impossible to avoid your destiny."

"And when will you be round to see Christian?" Adrian asked Celia.

"Just after ten tomorrow," replied Celia.

Once again Adrian turned towards Lutyens. "I am trying to get Christian out of the house, sir. I said I would take him riding early in the morning before anyone is up. Would you like to join us?"

Lutyens shook his head. "Thank you, Adrian, but I don't ride nowadays."

"What about you, Celia?"

"I would love to."

Lutyens studied Adrian. Of course he didn't ride. Anyone could see from the size of his waist that he didn't ride – that he hadn't done anything more exerting than a bit of sightseeing in twenty years. The boy was sharp, Lutyens thought to himself.

"And how is Christian?" asked Sir Julius.

"He's very angry. Angry with everything and everyone," replied Adrian. "I thought that getting him out might do him some good. We walked up to Watchet

Hill this morning, very slowly, his arm in mine. I saw a huntsman there with a small pack of hounds chasing across the moor. I find it so strange that some people here just don't know there's a war on."

Chapter 59

It was the possessive instinct that Celia inherited from her mother. A score of Lyttons that had come before her mother all had that instinct. Celia's father had a different character. He designed buildings which were owned by others and he moved from one job to the next. However, for Celia, the desire to possess was part of her character. She had been offered a kiss and had yet to collect it. It was hers to have when she wanted and, like anyone with a possessive instinct, she had no intention of giving up something which was rightfully hers. She woke that morning meaning to call in the debt.

The dawn sunlight first appeared in stripes through the shutters of Celia's room and slowly crept down the wall towards her bed. It had been too warm during the night to sleep under the eiderdown and she had pushed it away with her feet to the bottom of the bed so that it had rolled up like a bolster. Celia looked up at the ceiling, worrying that if she closed her eyes she might fall asleep again. She was not used to being up at this time of the morning; 'not an early riser' her nanny had more than once remarked when, as a child, she appeared for breakfast still in her night clothes. She placed her feet on the floor and walked to the window, opened the shutters and let the brightness stream in. She was surprised by how brilliant it was. Her room overlooked the church with its overgrown graveyard and beyond that the countryside fell away into a valley.

She had heard rumours about Adrian and Jane Facey over the last few months. Someone even suggested that they might soon get engaged. She had asked Christian about it but he said he didn't know anything. However, if she was going to do something about getting Adrian, then she would have to act sooner rather than later. Her mother wasn't there to help and so she would have to manage things herself. She imagined them living one day in the castle and every day they would go riding. The more she thought about it, the more she decided that the castle should belong to her; after all, when she had been fourteen she had spent days with a young engineer designing it. She tried for all her worth to remember the engineer's name but could not.

Stepping back from the window Celia undid the buttons of her cotton nightdress and let it drop to the floor. She looked at herself in the mirror. She knew she was beautiful; she knew that men turned and looked at her. She knew she had something that Jane Facey, with all her airs and graces, could never possess. She poured out a basin of water, washed and dressed in her riding clothes and then dabbed a small amount of perfume behind her ears. She left her room, walked along the hallway of the Globe Inn and downstairs. Each floorboard appeared to attempt to betray her presence. Adrian said he would knock on the back door of the inn. There were still a few minutes to wait. Adrian was not late. He knocked on the back door precisely as the church clock struck six. He stood with his hands behind his back for a few moments before Celia opened the door.

"Shhh," she whispered, "no one's up yet."

"Are you ready?" Adrian asked. Celia nodded her head.

"Where are the horses?"

"They're tied to the gate at the churchyard."

"Is Christian with them?"

"He declined to come."

Celia felt momentarily uncertain.

"We can't be too long then," she added.

Celia and Adrian walked round to the front of the inn and untied the horses. They led them slowly along the road. Edwin Lutyens, from his bedroom next to Celia's, heard the clopping of the hooves and watched them through the half-open shutters until they rounded a bend in the road and disappeared from sight. Lutyens stood for a moment looking out at a slight mist that would dissipate once the sun gained some height. He stepped away from the blinds, took off his round, steel-rimmed glasses and placed them on the bedside table. He went back to bed but he could not sleep another wink.

Adrian and Celia both mounted their horses. There was not a cloud in the heavens as they rode out on an almost forgotten pathway. The horses pulled eagerly at the reins and set off at a good pace. The mist in the valley moistened Celia's arms. The horses slowed as they started going up the far side of the valley and Adrian turned to look at Celia. They felt no awkwardness not speaking to each other as they rode. As they crested the hill Adrian pulled his horse up sharply. He waited for Celia to catch up and took out his cigarette case from inside his jacket pocket and offered a cigarette to Celia. She shook her head.

"You ride well," he said. "I thought we could canter for a mile or so until we get to the woods near Fingle Bridge."

"Where's Fingle Bridge?"

"Over there," said Adrian pointing to the northeast. Celia followed the direction of his arm toward an area of forest in the distance. It was made up predominantly of larch and birch that had died and had regrown at least half a dozen times since the days of Drogo de Teigne. "It's a small bridge that crosses the Teign at its narrowest part. It's where the grounds of the castle finish."

Adrian kicked his horse into motion again. He wore a pair of riding jodhpurs, a tweed jacket and knee-length brown boots. Celia followed just behind, watching Adrian as he rose in his saddle as the horse trotted downwards into another valley. Celia breathed deeply as she brought her crop sharply down on the gelding's flank, encouraging her horse to keep pace with Adrian's. The wind and the world whistled passed her as she rode across the moor. She continued to urge the horse forward. The moor was starting to wake and breathed out a smell of peat. She thought she could hear the morning song of the larks. Her cheeks began to colour as she again encouraged her horse with a quick swipe of the crop. They crested the next ridge and the horses began to gallop down towards the vast wood that appeared in front of them. Adrian pulled up as his horse came to the outskirts of the wood.

"Now where?" shouted Celia.

"It's not too far from here," said Adrian, as he dismounted. "There's a path over there. We'll leave the horses here and walk. Do you need a hand to dismount?"

Celia's first instinct was to say 'no'. She knew she could dismount from a side saddle with little difficulty but it looked inelegant and so she gratefully accepted his offer. He tied his horse and came over to her. Adrian's hands stretched up and took hold of her waist and lifted her down. Once her feet were on the ground, she looked up at him. His hands remained on the sides of her waist.

"Well, kiss me then," Celia said.

Adrian leant forward and his lips pressed on hers and she closed her eyes. That possessive instinct welled up in her again. She intuitively felt that he would come back from the war. He would be safe. She recalled that Basil had said that everyone in the Royal Garrison Artillery was as safe as a church mouse. She decided as they kissed that when he came back from the war that he would belong to her.

"I'm not sure kissing is going to be enough for us." Celia did not know whether she actually said the words or just thought them. She moved her head away and opened her eyes. Adrian was looking at her and then his eyes dropped and he looked at her mouth. Celia took a step back.

"Come on," she said, "you promised to show me Fingle Bridge." Adrian took off the saddlebag from his horse and made his way along the path in the woods. He held out his hand and she placed hers in his. They walked for what seemed an eternity to Celia but was no longer than ten minutes. Adrian spoke as they walked. She admired his self-possession. Her heart was thumping and she could scarcely take in what he was saying. He was talking about what he would do when he came back. She imagined herself with him for the rest of their lives.

Fingle Bridge was at the bottom of the escarpment and crossed the river Teign. It was an old stone structure that had been built at the time of Drogo de Teigne, over seven hundred years earlier. It had become worn and weathered by the passage of time but was still as sturdy as the day it had been built and would survive for a few centuries more. On one side of the bridge lay the woods, on the other was a pathway that a few miles on began to wind its way to the top of the escarpment.

"I sometimes come bathing here," said Adrian. "In the mornings when there's no one around."

They walked over to the crystal waters and Celia put her hand in the flow. It was icy cold.

"There's a story that when Drogo de Teigne fled from Henry II's hounds he ran along the river in order to put the dogs off his scent and got out here at Fingle Bridge. If he had carried on running in the water he might have escaped. The hounds picked up his scent and chased him up to the stone circle at Watchet Hill."

As Adrian spoke, he undid his saddlebag and pulled out a tartan rug that they had used the previous day.

"I brought breakfast," he said, taking out a loaf of bread, cheese and ham. "Unfortunately, the Clarence Hotel wouldn't deliver breakfast at this time in the morning, and this is all I could find in the larder."

"Breakfast?"

"And orange juice," he added. He spread out the tartan rug for them to sit on. "Now tell me something about you. I've been talking non-stop for the last ten minutes."

Celia sat down on the rug, curled her knees up and turned her face toward him. She looked up at him, affecting a slight pose, her chin almost on her shoulder. Her green eyes tried to look past him. She had one hand on the ground; the other she placed on her lap.

"There's not much to tell," she began. "I don't do anything more than anyone else. I just do what I can to help out in the hospital." She wanted to affect a false sense of modesty – but not too much. "I suppose when the war is over I will stop being a nurse and go back and finish my degree."

"What were you reading?" asked Adrian.

"Literature."

"I read Classics," said Adrian.

"I know."

"And after that?"

"Perhaps a teacher, I don't know."

"You would make an excellent teacher. Would you like something to eat?"

"No, not yet. Sit down next to me," Celia said. She smiled as he sat down next to her. She could smell sandalwood. She leant slightly forward so that her mouth was just a few inches away from his, sufficiently indicating that he could kiss her again. He put one hand to her neck and slid his fingers down the white skin. He inclined his head and moved forward, kissing her tenderly on the mouth.

Thinking about it afterwards, Celia knew her feelings went beyond love. She was still as infatuated as she had been that first day she had seen him in the garden of the Reverend Archibald Drew's garden. They had eaten outside until the dark clouds and the rain came. He had got soaked. She let him kiss her more passionately and slowly lay down on her back. She moved one arm around his shoulder. If he felt just half of what she felt for him, she could imagine him betraying both King and country for her. Afterwards, she thought, he would want to stay forever with her, hidden together out on the moor.

His hand moved to the buttons of her blouse. She now had to decide. She moved her lips away from his and took a breath. She knew that the next thing she said would probably be the most important words she had ever spoken. She looked at his bright eyes – the same colour as hers and she could see, reflected in the dark retina, herself looking at him. She knew that if she did not stop now then neither she nor he would be able to stop themselves afterwards.

"Yes," she said and kissed his neck. She moved her lips to his ear and slightly bit at it as he tore at the buttons of her blouse. Her hands went to his jacket; one by one the buttons came undone. She pulled his shirt out of his trousers and felt his smooth skin. She tried to put her hand into his trousers but the belt he was wearing prevented her. He stopped kissing her.

"There's something I have to tell you," he said.

"Shhh," she whispered.

Adrian undid his belt and then began kissing her again. Celia brought her arms up and clasped her fingers around the back of his neck. She could smell the scent of heather and horse and sandalwood.

Some distance away the church bells at Chagford struck the half hour.

Back in the hotel at Drewsteignton her father would be having breakfast. She knew that she would be late and she knew that she would have to tell him only a piece of the truth.

*　　*　　*

On the ride back they heard the church bells from Drewsteignton strike eight. They rode side by side. Occasionally she would stretch out her fingers and brush his hand, but they said almost nothing. As they reached the outskirts of Drewsteignton she suddenly needed reassurance.

"I will see you later?" she said.

"Of course."

"And when do you have to go back?"

Adrian looked at her.

"Lunchtime."

"Can't you delay it? Please! I didn't know you were going back so soon. Can't we just have a few more days?"

"If I could change my plans I would but they're set in stone. I'm meeting my father just after lunch and travelling back to town with him and then I go back to the front soon afterwards."

"It seems so unfair."

"It is unfair," said Adrian. "I would change things if I could."

*　　*　　*

Edwin Lutyens looked down at his newspaper. He had looked at it for the last half hour without reading a word. The carriage clock, which sat upon the mantelpiece of the cast-iron fire, chimed the half hour. He had now sat in the breakfast room for an hour waiting for his daughter to arrive and his appetite had long since fled. The waitress had tried to tempt him with a plate of kidneys, sausage, bacon and egg, but he only managed to nibble at some toast. He looked over towards the carriage clock. The hands of the clock confirmed the time – half past eight – he groaned audibly and the waitress, who was in earshot, came quickly to the table and asked whether he was feeling all right. He grunted something about being a little under the weather. The waitress, a girl around twenty years old, suggested liver salts but Lutyens shook his head.

"Perhaps I can get you something else. What about mint tea?"

"Mint tea," said Lutyens, "that's what my wife would have suggested."

"My gran'ma swears by it," replied the waitress. "She says that it'll cure just about any ailment and she isn't often wrong."

Lutyens looked up at the girl. She was maybe a year younger than Celia with black hair and dark eyes and a deep West Country accent.

"Do you come from Drewsteignton?" Lutyens asked.

The waitress nodded her head. "Born and bred here," she said. "Me and my husband have known each other since we were at school."

"Is your husband away at the front?" asked Lutyens.

"Yes," answered the waitress. "He used to work on the castle before the works stopped. When he comes back he hopes to carry on building the castle."

"And have you seen how it will look when it's completed?"

"Everyone in the village has, sir. We've all been there over the last two weeks."

"And what did you think?" said Lutyens, trying to keep the curiosity from his voice.

"To be honest, sir, it don't look very much like a castle to me." The young waitress brought her head a little closer and whispered. "Do you know it's being built for the Drewe family? My gran'ma says there's a curse on them."

"Why would she say that?"

"Something to do with Drogo; it's just superstition, sir."

Lutyens smiled at her. "I think I will have that mint tea." The waitress turned and walked towards the kitchen and as she went, he saw Celia walking into the breakfast room. He looked at his pocket watch to once again confirm the time. He stood up as his daughter arrived and waited for her to sit.

"Good morning, Father," she said. "Have you eaten?"

Lutyens shook his head. He grumbled under his breath that he had lost his appetite and then looked at Celia.

"Well, I'm famished," said Celia as she tried to attract the attention of the waitress. "I could eat a horse."

"And talking about horses, how was your ride?" asked Lutyens. He looked at her, but she pretended not to notice. She had changed into her best dress since getting back and Lutyens guessed that she had hurried. Her face was slightly flushed and there were a few beads of perspiration on her forehead. The waitress came over and Celia asked for some hot toast and tea. Lutyens waited for the waitress to go before repeating his question.

"Oh, I don't know," Celia said, "it was fine, I suppose. We rode out to Fingle Bridge and back."

"Fingle Bridge," repeated Lutyens. "That's a round trip of about three or four miles isn't it? I wouldn't have thought that it would take more than an hour."

"That's right, dear," Celia said looking directly at her father. "Unfortunately, Adrian's horse threw a shoe on the way back and we had to walk the last mile or so." She continued to stare at him. "How was the cooked breakfast?" She was speaking a little louder than normal.

"I didn't have an appetite this morning. I just told you I hadn't had breakfast."

"That's unlike you," said Celia. "Are you feeling under the weather?"

"Indigestion," he said. "And how were Adrian and Christian?"

"Oh, they were fine," said Celia.

"So, Christian went out riding with you also?"

"No, actually he didn't feel up to it."

"But you just said he was fine."

Celia took a deep breath.

"Why all these questions? I'm sorry I was late for breakfast and I'm sorry that you're not feeling well but as I said, Adrian's horse threw a shoe and I couldn't get back any earlier and that's rather it."

Lutyens made another indiscriminate sound and the rest of their breakfast passed without either of them saying a further word to each other.

Chapter 60

Adrian looked at Christian over the breakfast table and wondered what, if anything, he should say. Christian had seemed out of sorts from the moment he came back from his ride. There was a time when they would have talked but he was no longer the same brother. It wasn't the blindness or the burns to his face; it was the way he had withdrawn from the world. He now seemed angry at everything and everyone. The self-confidence that he once had was being slowly drained from him.

Through a mouthful of soft-boiled egg Adrian asked, "Will you change your mind about tomorrow?"

Through a mouthful of toast and marmalade Christian answered: "No."

"I'll miss you if you're not there."

"You'll have no time for me. I'll stand in a corner being stared at."

"It won't be like that," said Adrian.

"Of course it will be like that. Even Mother can't look at me without crying."

"So you're determined not to come to my wedding?"

Christian took another bite of toast and chewed on it slowly.

"About that," said Christian. "Are you sure that you're making the right decision?"

"No," said Adrian. "And today I'm even less sure than I was yesterday."

"What do you mean by that?"

"Nothing."

They finished breakfast without any further exchange. Adrian picked up the newspaper and noisily turned the pages. Christian went back to his Braille book. After ten minutes Christian took his fingers away from the page.

"So nothing happened on your ride this morning?" asked Christian.

"Nothing, except what I told you previously; the horse threw a shoe."

"And how is Celia?"

"You're full of questions today," said Adrian.

"And you're not telling the whole truth," remarked Christian.

"Why on earth do you say that?" said Adrian, throwing his newspaper on the breakfast table.

"Because the horse didn't throw a shoe. I heard you when you rode past here into the village."

Adrian got up. "I don't appreciate being called a liar." He slammed the door as he walked out.

"And you smelt of her perfume," Christian added after he left.

Celia called soon after Christian had finished his breakfast, which is to say sometime just after ten. He was still in the breakfast room when he heard the bell ring. In that room he heard more than people guessed. He heard snatches of conversations as the villagers walked past. He heard the people who stopped at the front gate and talked about him. He heard about how he scared the women and the children of the village.

Christian heard Celia walk through the hallway towards the kitchen. She would say hello to the housekeeper and the cook before she came and saw him. It was typical of her, thought Christian. She looked after the people not as well off as she was, tipped cabbies just a little too much and always found out what the servants wanted for Christmas. She was so different in so many ways to him – and Adrian. Christian stood with his back to the fireplace when Celia entered. He felt her look at him and heard her breathe out a little too quickly. Even Celia could not hide her feelings.

"Good morning, Christian, how are you?" she said suppressing all emotion from her voice.

"How do I look?"

She took a step closer to him. He could feel her standing an inch or two away from him. He could smell her perfume; lavender water – she always wore lavender water. He felt her look him up and down. He could picture her; tall, lithe with long, auburn hair and wearing a hint of lipstick – looking intently at the burns on the side of his face.

"You'll do," she said. It was the kind of answer that he had come to expect from her. She didn't lie to him but he had got used to the fact that she often did not answer the question asked.

"Adrian said..." there was a lengthy pause which Celia did not interrupt, "that his horse threw a shoe this morning." He could feel the sense of relief. "You know he's going back to the front soon?"

"I know," she said.

He turned in her direction and could sense the tenseness in her. "You might as well be star-crossed lovers."

If Christian could have seen her, he would have known that her eyes had closed. The few tears when they came fell down the bridge of her nose, soundlessly as the coming of autumn dew. She pretended that they did not exist.

"Why are you saying that?" she asked. There was anguish in her voice as if she was scared to hear the answer.

"Because it's true." He still lisped slightly from the operations on the side of his face. A bead of perspiration appeared on his temple. "Don't blame him – we all have to do our duty."

"I know he has to go back to the front. Is there something else?" she said.

"You'll have to ask Adrian."

She composed herself and said that she would need to look more closely at the scarring. She reached up and touched the side of his face. He winced as if she had slapped him, although he felt almost nothing.

"Did that hurt?" she asked.

"No, I don't know why I jumped."

Her hand went back to the side of his face, and she applied a little more pressure to one of the scars. He felt she was being a little rougher than usual, as if she was trying to hurt him. She breathed deeply, her face coming close to his. He could again smell lavender and this time there was the faintest hint of sandalwood. The two scents did not blend.

"How does that feel?" she asked, pressing one of the scars.

"Fine," he answered.

"It shouldn't feel fine," she said. "It should hurt."

"You get used to that kind of pain."

"What kind of pain don't you get used to?"

"The type that makes you feel as if you're a circus attraction."

"So, you're still not going out?"

"I've been out once or twice. When I got settled I received a few invitations from people in Exeter. You know the types – young women with too much time and money who spend their days chattering about other people. They just wanted to gawp at me. One girl even screamed. I decided not to go again."

Celia took out a kidney-shaped metal dish, some swabs and antiseptic lotion from the brown bag she had brought. She walked over to the curtains and pulled them shut.

"We talked about this, Christian, when I was down here last. There are always going to be people who will do things for the wrong reasons. I'm sure that they don't mean to be cruel. However, it's often embarrassment. When they see you, they don't know how to act and therefore they just stand with their mouths open, gawping."

"If it was just the stupid people I wouldn't care." Christian felt his way to a chair and sat down, "but it's everyone. I was in the garden the other day when some relic from the Boer War walked up the driveway and told me I ought to be inside. He said I should be ashamed letting myself be seen where decent folk might pass."

As soon as Christian had started to talk, he found himself unable to stop. Without the bandages, which Christian now refused to wear, he could talk more clearly. He looked as if wax had been melted onto the side of his face. The graft still felt sore, but he no longer cared. He had been told to keep the bandages on but like every other man alive, never listened to his doctor's order. The housekeeper came into the breakfast room with a bowl of steaming water. She left saying she would be back in an hour to clear up and shut the door.

Christian was made to sit on a chair under the chandelier. He noticed how Celia seemed to stop every time there was a creak of the floorboards upstairs. He noticed how she never mentioned Adrian. She chatted less than usual as if afraid to say what was on her mind. He decided not to say any more about Adrian. After all, he concluded, it had nothing to do with him.

The carriage clock chimed eleven as Celia finished her examination. She was expressing her satisfaction with the way the grafts were healing when there was a knock on the door. Celia opened it thinking it was the housekeeper to take away the bowl and stood looking up at Adrian.

"I thought you were the housekeeper." She blushed.

"Not disappointed I hope," Adrian replied. He didn't blush.

"I was just going to take the bowls out to the kitchen."

"Would you like a hand?"

"I can manage," she replied, "thank you."

Christian listened to the exchange behind a wry smile, although no one would have been able to tell. He doubted whether Celia really understood Adrian. Adrian was bound to follow a path that he had been expected to follow since he was a child. His parents had mapped his life out and Celia played no part in their schemes. She seemed not to see what was so clear to him.

Celia took out the basin of water to the kitchen and Christian turned towards Adrian.

"You would probably like to be alone with Celia."

Adrian looked down the hallway. Celia was still in the kitchen.

"Yes," he said.

"She's pretty and intelligent... too good for you anyway."

"I don't know what I shall say to her," Adrian added.

"Tell her the truth."

"The truth will hurt her."

"A lie will hurt her more."

Adrian walked over to the curtains and opened them. The sun streamed through, lighting up the breakfast room. Around him dust particles swirled. He moved over to the breakfast table with the dust following in his wake and poured himself a cup of coffee before sitting down. He half wondered what he would say when Celia returned. It might be easiest to pretend that the morning had not happened. From his chair he was able to see Celia down the hallway in the kitchen still washing her hands in the sink, under a steady stream of steaming water. He watched her as she moved around in a cotton dress with its print of flowers, fuchsias, he thought, on a background of white. She had her hair tied up and he could see her white neck. The truth was not a pleasant option and it meant burning his bridges, and this one was especially well made.

When Celia returned from the kitchen, she perched on the arm of the chair. She trembled slightly. Christian got up and excused himself. Adrian let his fingers play on the small of Celia's back.

"I know you have to go in the next half hour, so promise that we shall see each other again," she said.

Adrian's hand went around her waist and she turned to look at him.

"I can't," he said. He looked at her deep green eyes. "How can I give you promises when I'm going back to the war?"

"Swear it," she insisted.

"I can't."

Celia moved her head forward and kissed him, pushing her fingers through his black hair.

"If you promise me, I know you will," she said.

"Are you crying?" asked Adrian.

Celia put the back of her hand to her cheek and wiped away the tears. "I'm just being silly."

Suddenly she turned, having seen something through the corner of her eye. On the window sill sat a black cat watching them enigmatically.

"Did you tell Christian about us?"

"No," said Adrian, "of course not. I didn't say a word to him. I just told him what we had agreed, that my horse threw a shoe."

"He was just a bit beastly earlier on but now I have you for half an hour," said Celia, "and I don't want you to say one more word that makes me sad."

She leant down and kissed him again.

Chapter 61

Outside the window of the train, the steam billowed up and the noise of the embarking troops made it almost impossible to hear. Adrian sat in the corner of a carriage drumming his fingers on his silver cigarette case. Other officers who had squeezed into the carriage were chatting amongst themselves, but Adrian sat deep in thought. The repetitive tapping of his fingers could not be heard above the noise. It felt an eternity since he had been at Drewsteignton; however, it had only been three days. He had picked up his father from the Clarence Hotel in Exeter and then taken the train from Exeter to Waterloo. They were at the Faceys' estate at Havering-atte-Bower later that evening.

The journey up from Exeter with his father had been tense.

"It's just wedding nerves," his father had said, the Lancashire accent becoming pronounced.

"But I don't love her, sir," Adrian had replied.

"It's your decision, Adrian," Sir Julius had answered, "but if you make the wrong one, we'll be ruined."

Sir Julius once again explained that the only reason why the government was not looking at other suppliers was Lord Facey's unconditional support.

"And that support, Adrian, comes at a price. Both Facey and I each have forty percent of the shares in the company and tomorrow you get twenty."

"And what would happen if I don't go through with the marriage?"

"Your interest in the company passes to Jane. Needless to say, I shall no longer be required to manage the company and your allowance will cease."

"But we'll be able to manage?"

"Don't be stupid, Adrian. You couldn't manage on a major's salary. Your imported Turkish cigarettes cost more than you earn and then there's your car, your mortgage, the staff, and last but not least, your tailor."

"I'm not concerned about myself."

"But will you tell your mother that she has to leave her home because you decided you didn't want to marry Jane Facey? Make no bones about it, Adrian, Wadhurst Hall would have to go under the hammer. I'm mortgaged to the hilt because of this war and that damned castle doesn't help. This contract with the government is keeping us afloat and now the Americans are sending ships to escort our convoys, I might even start making some money again. So will you tell your mother that her home has to go?"

Adrian didn't have an answer.

"Now sit down, Adrian," Sir Julius continued, "and give me one of your expensive cigarettes." Adrian took out his silver cigarette case and offered his father a smoke. "If you had doubts you should have said months ago. However, we're men of the world. I agree Jane is no Lillian Gish, and everyone will turn a blind eye if you choose to seek your pleasures elsewhere."

Sir Julius went on to comment that the Lutyens girl appeared quite amiable. There was something a little crude in the rest of the conversation that turned Adrian's stomach. He admired his father's determination but sometimes the lack of breeding showed. He hoped he was better than that.

The marriage ceremony the next day was small and not as crass as he feared. Only Jane's inner circle of friends were invited, a few of the closer relatives and one or two cabinet ministers. Her maid of honour was Margaret Ellis, who still had short, raven-coloured hair and dark eyes. When Adrian saw her, he realised that Jane had made a mistake in choosing her, as most of the men watched her rather than the bride. The service took place at the local church near the oak tree where it was said that Edward the Confessor had once given a ring to a beggar who had asked for alms.

The secrecy of the engagement and the wedding also meant that no one from the press intruded except a chosen correspondent and photographer from *The Times*. Although he thought it a nightmare, Adrian realised it could have been a lot worse.

They had spent the night in the lodge of the Faceys' estate, a gift from Lord Facey to his daughter and new son-in-law. It was a six-bedroom gatehouse on the estate. It had been decorated by Jane in the most awful fabrics and heavy flock wallpaper. Adrian's heart sank when he saw it. It was nothing like his house in Drewsteignton and he wondered how long it would take before Jane managed to ruin that. They talked for a little before she went up to get ready for bed. In that time, he sat in the drawing room regretting his decisions and drinking two large whiskies. He came up and undressed in their room. It was pitch-black and he wondered where his pyjamas had been put; he decided not to ask and got into bed naked. He took the lead and she lay there with her eyes closed. He thought of Celia and how different it had been. There was no passion or emotion with Jane. It was just a physical act of release that he was expected to perform. Afterwards it felt awkward; he had nothing to say to Jane. He did not sleep well.

The following morning, he agreed that they should go on a proper honeymoon when he was next on leave. They breakfasted on the lawn of the lodge and then walked to the main house to see their parents before Adrian went back to Belgium. He left with Jane at eleven a.m. for Fenchurch Street Station.

The train whistle blew. Adrian's fingers still drummed on the cigarette case. He looked out of the carriage window. The platform was clear except for the guard who was waving a flag at the driver. The train lurched forward a few feet. At the end of the platform a crowd of people waved and cheered. He could hear nothing above the noise of the train and then he spotted Jane, waving her hand. He put his hand out of the window and waved back. A few seconds later he lost sight of her.

"A sweetheart?" asked the officer sitting next to Adrian.

"Not exactly."

Chapter 62

Celia threw a cut crystal vase at the wall of her bedroom and then broke into tears.

She breathed fiercely and irregularly, she looked for the next thing to hurl. Her eyes rested on a bowl of face powder on the dressing table and it soon felt her wrath, breaking into a dozen pieces and spraying the whitish powder onto the wall in a semi-circle like a half moon. The tears did not stop her anger and downstairs Edwin Lutyens buried his head in a copy of *The Times*, dreading to interfere. The servants looked at him and on occasion he would look back with a plaintive expression which seemed to say, "What can I do? I'm only her father."

A sheet of ivory paper lay on the bed, half screwed up with a press cutting. Margaret Ellis had signed the letter and there was only one line: "*She just wanted him more!*" A cutting from *The Times* dated the 2nd of July 1917 reported the marriage of Major Adrian Drewe and Jane Facey. It stung at her pride to think that she had given herself so cheaply and that the next day he had married Jane Facey. She almost screamed when she thought that he hadn't said a word before they had made love. He had let her play at being the doe-eyed, love-sick schoolgirl and he must have been laughing at her all the while. Damn him! thought Celia. Let him have plain Jane with her awful taste in furnishings and insincere and backbiting friends. She decided that she wouldn't let it bother her. She would go downstairs and breakfast with her father as if nothing had happened. She washed her face. Her breathing became more regular, and she walked towards her bedroom door but, seeing a small bottle of *Le Muguet* perfume on a bedside table, she picked it up and threw it towards the wall for good measure.

Edwin Lutyens started to reread the main story about Henry Puyi, the last emperor of China, when he heard Celia coming down the stairs. He had found, in his twenty-two years of marriage, that it was often better not to enquire why a woman was in a foul mood. Too often their irritation could turn quickly on the nearest person to hand. If Celia wanted to talk about matters, he would be there to listen; although no doubt, he concluded, it would have been better if Emily was there or any woman. He thought about cabling Gertrude Jekyll to come up but Gertrude with her Victorian view of life would probably be of little assistance. She hardly understood young girls today, but then who did?

Even Lutyens noticed that Celia's face was blotchy. He decided it was best not to stare and pretended to continue to read his paper. Celia poured herself a cup of coffee and took a plate of scrambled eggs, two pieces of toast and some peanut butter. He looked at the mixture on Celia's plate and his nose automatically wrinkled. Both Celia and Lutyens had agreed to maintain the vegetarian diet that Emily had imposed, despite the fact that both had grumbled unceasingly about it throughout the last six years. Somehow the continuation of having vegetarian meals was a joint act of denial that they had been abandoned by both a wife and a mother. It was as if both refused to admit that Emily had gone, even if it was only intended to be semi-permanent. Lutyens also insisted that the bed linen in Emily's room be changed every week and that the maid thoroughly dust her room. They both lived in a world of denial and so Lutyens watched Celia sit down to breakfast and both proceeded with an unhealthy English disposition which ignored the obvious fact that both had broken hearts.

Celia spread the peanut butter on the toast and covered it with the scrambled egg. She picked it up with her fingers and took a bite.

"Do you really like that stuff?" Lutyens asked.

"What, the peanut butter?" said Celia through a mouthful.

"Yes, that stuff."

Celia swallowed and sniffed as well. "Actually, I do. I've got a real taste for it at the moment. I'm pleased that Mother sent it to us from America."

"I had a letter from Emily this morning."

"What did she have to say? May I read it?"

"She said that Krishnamurti had moved to a small town called Ojai, which is an American Indian word meaning 'nest'. She says that it is miles away from Washington and that there is very little there, but Krishnamurti wants to go there to meditate. She says that the house is in a long, narrow valley of apricot orchards and orange groves and that it is as hot there as it is in India. She would like to move from Washington to Ojai in the next month or two if she can find a school for the girls, otherwise she will have to get them tutors. She sends her love to you. She asks us to pass her best wishes to Robert when he next comes home." Lutyens handed the letter to Celia, who ran her eyes down the letter and continued to bite into her toast.

"She didn't say when she was coming home," said Celia, handing the letter back to her father.

"I'm sure she'll be back as soon as the war is over."

"May I have the paper after you've finished with it?" asked Celia.

"Of course," said Lutyens, "what do you want to look at?"

"I want to see if anyone I know has been killed in the war."

"That's not like you," said Lutyens. "Is there anyone in particular?"

"Major Drewe."

"I'm sure he'll be fine," answered Lutyens.

"More's the pity," replied Celia under her breath.

Lutyens stopped speaking. His gaze dropped to the table and he picked up his knife and fork. Not knowing what he should say, he took a mouthful of food and slowly chewed it. There was something in Celia's tone of voice that made it clear that he had started to tread on thin ice. There was something quite cruel in not only what was said but the tenor of it, and he thought it better not to ask. He did not know what had happened between Adrian and Celia that previous week at Drewsteignton and did not want to guess. He believed that time had a way of curing these things – forget and forgive. And for the second time that morning he buried something with a stoical English temperament.

As he finished the last mouthful of his toast he glanced up at Celia. The colour had not returned to her face. There was something pinched in her expression, which surprisingly reminded him of his wife. He did not know what she was thinking but that expression of bitterness did not auger well. He didn't want to leave her and go to work but he did not want to stay either. He always found these moments difficult. Perhaps five years ago, when Celia was a child, they could have spoken but their worlds were now so very far apart. She was her own person. She did what she wanted and to hell with the consequences, he thought. Emily had instilled in all her children a feeling of independence but where was she when her eldest child had taken a knock?

"Is there anything you need?" Lutyens mumbled.

Celia did not respond immediately. She thought for a few seconds and then answered, "Tell me a story. I haven't heard one of your stories for an absolute age and I think I was happiest when you used to come home from your trips abroad with a suitcase full of stories and tell them to me and Robert, Elisabeth and Mary before we went to bed."

"Is that all?"

"Yes; but it has to start with once upon a time."

Lutyens paused for a moment.

"Once upon a time there was an island where the waves washed upon the shores of nothingness and licked the edges of the night. On this island all the feelings of the world lived: Happiness, Sadness, Envy, Spite, Knowledge and many others including Love. When the Lord God Brahma created the universe, he told the feelings that they would have to leave the island as it would be consumed by creation, so all built boats and left except for Love. Love was the only one who stayed and waited until the last possible moment and when the waves began to consume the island, Love looked out to sea and cried for help.

"Arrogance was passing in a small boat and Love said: 'Arrogance, can you take me with you?' Arrogance answered, 'No. If you were so foolish not to build yourself a boat, why should I help you?' Love then called out to Vanity who was also passing in a handsome vessel. 'Vanity, please help me!'

"But when Vanity heard her name, she turned and saw her reflection in a mirror that hung in her boat and she forgot about everything else but the face that looked back at her. Sadness was also close by so Love now pleaded with Sadness, 'Sadness,' she said, 'please let me go with you.'

"'Oh... Love, I am so sad that I need to be alone with my grief!'

"Suddenly, there was a voice, 'Come, Love, I will take you.' It was an elder. So overjoyed was Love that she forgot to ask the elder where they were going and when they arrived at dry land the elder went his own way. Love, realising that she had not thanked the elder or even asked his name, went in search of Knowledge, another elder.

"'Who helped me?' asked Love.

"'It was Time,' Knowledge answered.

"'Time?' asked Love. 'Why would Time help me?'

"Knowledge smiled with deep wisdom and answered, 'Because only Time is capable of understanding how valuable Love is.'"

Celia didn't finish her scrambled eggs.

"I think I shall go back to my room," she said, "I have a letter to write."

PART X

Chapter 63

Rubble lay where once the Cloth Hall had stood. The remnants of the east wall rose up from the ground and grey slate tiles lay scattered like playing cards thrown by a petulant child. It was a place without shade or shadow where soldiers hurried, fearing the next round of shelling. Adrian also quickened his step as he walked out onto the levelled square. They hadn't yet got round to burying the dead. He lowered his head and pulled his steel helmet tightly down. Adrian's memories of Ypres were of a city of ochre and burnt sienna, a bustling place of medieval buildings. There was little left of the once great city.

Adrian did not feel the need for unnecessary talk. He let George Poley walk in front of him as they went towards a hole in the city wall where once the Menin Gate had stood. Weariness made his head swim and brought unwanted recollections. Spectres and dreams merged. He thought about his new wife and his new lover. He was newlywed, and already unfaithful, if not in deed then in thought, and he was troubled by these feelings of guilt.

"Is it far to go, sir?" asked Poley.

"Not far," replied Adrian, "just keep walking."

Poley went on a few more paces and then turned to look at a group of Germans sitting huddled in a corner by the old city ramparts. A corporal and two privates with rifles stood close by, keeping guard and smoking. The Germans talked to each other, flagrantly ignoring the English soldiers' calls for them to shut up. Adrian cast a quick glance at them. They were mostly boys – not much older than seventeen, he guessed – who had given themselves up voluntarily after the last week of shelling, and looking at them sitting, smoking and talking he guessed that there was little need to guard them. They looked almost pleased to be out of the war.

"Tell the last man in the line to close the Menin Gate," Poley shouted at the German prisoners as he went past. However, there was no longer any gate to close or even an arch. Nothing remained except some debris and the gap in the ramparts which Poley and Adrian now walked through.

"Shut up, Poley," Adrian said. He was not in the mood for humour. He looked ahead of him along a road that led up towards Pilckem Ridge. None of this matters, he thought. After so many deaths, who would care if there were another hundred thousand or even a million more deaths? How can you grieve when what has happened is beyond comprehension?

They walked past soldiers lying dead in the gutters beside the road. Occasionally they would see civilians who had panicked and fled their homes. Most of the bodies were mutilated, arms or legs missing. Sometimes there were only parts of people. They were already being devoured by flies and maggots. Adrian tried to ignore the dead. He needed to focus his mind, to collect his thoughts and look and listen. It was the only way to survive.

Adrian and Poley walked on to where the road forked. Adrian looked up the road. The engineers had done a decent job of keeping the road open – filling the potholes and repairing the shoulders as they crumbled into the morass of waterlogged fields. Adrian pulled out his cigarette case and took a cigarette. The inscription was being slowly worn away – *Christmas 1914, From Kit*, it had once clearly read. Poley was looking at the cigarette case and he offered him one.

"Are we really going up to Pilckem Ridge, sir?" asked Poley, taking a light from Adrian's cigarette. Adrian was, however, lost in his own thoughts and did not answer. He continued to stare along the road, looking at a lorry that was coming slowly towards them. "It bloody well stinks up there, sir, beggin' yer pardon. The first time I went up there I noticed that smell and didn't realise that it was just the decaying bodies in the mud and then I smelt the chlorine gas, like boiled pear drops it was. I only notice it now when a shell goes off in the mud and then you can really smell it."

Adrian answered without looking. "Yes, we're going to Pilckem Ridge." He felt tired and his head ached. He had not slept well since getting back to the front.

The lorry came ever closer. Adrian started thinking about the orders that had been given to him that morning. He would be going to help relieve the attack on Pilckem Ridge. It was vital to hold the position if there was going to be a push at the end of the month. The attack would be in the last week of July. Adrian listened attentively to the briefing. For now they needed to hold the lines and Adrian was placed in charge of five light batteries which were to be moved up to the front line over the next few weeks. Moreover, the colonel had said, these batteries could be used to push forward a mile and a half when the attack came. Headquarters thought they would be carried forward with the men. Adrian asked how they were going to move pieces of artillery which weighed a ton through a quagmire. He was told that he would have to liaise with a major from the Royal Engineers who was designing some special duckboards for the task. Adrian had stopped himself asking any more questions. He would wait and see but suspected that the idea was doomed to failure.

The lorry pulled up and a thin, sinewy officer got out. He was untidy and unkempt but Adrian recognised him immediately. For the first time in six years Adrian found himself face to face with Major Peter Hall.

*   *   *

Necessity's sharp pinch forced Adrian to listen to the briefing. His headache had gone but his head was still groggy. To make matters worse he had been billeted with Peter Hall and Hall had made no bones about the fact that he was unwelcome. They had spent the whole of the previous evening studiously ignoring each other. Adrian had therefore woken up in a bad mood and he tried not to let his mind wander. Hall's briefing was less than clear as to why he and his men had been moved up to the front line. Hall, like many other engineers Adrian had met, was obtuse when it came to explaining things. Hall talked about engineering principles and his audience was neither able to understand nor interested. Adrian saw his men flagging as they listened. Hall ended his briefing by saying that therefore the ground was not impassable, and an attack could succeed. The infantry could advance and the sappers would ensure that the artillery was brought forward across no man's land until they took Westroosbecke and Passchendaele Ridges.

"And what if it rains?" asked Adrian. "How do you plan to move my artillery over waterlogged ground?"

Hall looked at Adrian, astonished that he had been interrupted.

"Do you know how much a six-inch howitzer weighs?" continued Adrian. Hall gave no hint as to whether he knew the answer or not. "Well, let me remind you," persisted Adrian. "It weighs over one point three tons. We usually use three-ton lorries with four-wheel drive to move these guns. On this terrain we are going to have to use pack horses. It will take six men to help the pack horses and then I doubt they could get more than a hundred yards or two. We then have to move the shell casings..."

"We have been working on that, Major Drewe," Hall answered. "As I've said, we need the field artillery to protect the new front line. This has been our main problem over the last two years. We push forward beyond the range of the artillery and are open to counter-attack."

Adrian let out a sigh. He had no wish to die on a forlorn hope.

"But how are you going to move my artillery?"

As Hall talked, the sound of rain could be heard on the corrugated iron of the dugout in which they were meeting.

"We're designing some new duckboards which will allow the cannon to roll on them over the ground."

"It can't be done," said Adrian. "We tried that on the Somme."

"You'll be disassembling the artillery, Major Drewe, and then rebuilding it."

The soldiers from Adrian's regiment started talking loudly.

"Quiet," said Adrian to his men. "As I remarked, Major Hall, the total weight is over a ton. Even broken down there is no way to carry these guns."

"I didn't say it was going to be easy, Major Drewe."

After the meeting broke up, Adrian sat wondering how precisely they would move the artillery across the waterlogged land. It seemed to him that he and his men would be exposed, without cover, as the pack horses slowly dragged the equipment over the ground. It was reclaimed land, originally under the sea level and the shelling that had taken place in the last two years had broken every land drain for twenty miles. He wondered whether he would order his men on a fool's mission – it was his duty and he had always thought that duty was enough. He reflected on the path he had chosen. Duty, it was such a curious word in the abstract; duty to what or to whom? A man could owe a duty to his country, to God, or to his family. He could owe a duty to all these things and to many other things. The problem, as Adrian saw it, was that when one owed so many duties there would be a time when they conflicted. Everything he once believed in seemed now to be in conflict with his feelings. He had always been so certain of everything in his life and now he was beginning to question it all. Why should he fight an enemy he did not hate or pray to a God he did not believe in? However, he realised that perhaps the biggest sin was to have married a woman whom he did not love. The answer of 'duty' no longer seemed adequate.

He remembered his last meeting with Christian when he had left Drewsteignton and gone to meet his father. Christian had touched a nerve that he had not realised was even exposed. He tried to remember what Christian had said. "You do this only for yourself and no one else; you do it because you're vain." Adrian had ignored him and left with a sour taste, but the cold fingers of uncertainty wrapped themselves around his conscience and in the last eight days he had begun to reflect on whether there was any truth in what had been said. Why was it that he wanted to be the top of the class, the best oarsman, the first over the top? Did he revel in the praise? However much he did not want to admit to it he did enjoy that feeling that comes from being seen as the best.

The forced silence that had begun between Hall and Adrian continued, except when they had to talk out of necessity. Adrian found Hall perversely fascinating. He noticed the changes that had occurred in the last six years. The years working in the mines had made Hall gaunt and his thin moustache, like his hair, was tinged with grey. Hall rarely stood upright and squinted when he went outside in the light. He was almost stoat-like in his bearing and appearance. Hall was fastidious about many things but gave almost no consideration to his appearance. If Adrian had passed him in the street, he would have thought him nearly fifty. He looked two decades older than his real age, but Adrian was aware that everyone who had worked in the mines looked older. It was probably the hardest job in the army and Adrian knew that he probably wouldn't have survived more than a month working underground.

They carried out practice run after practice run of moving the six-inch howitzers by pack horse. Under the weight of the guns the duckboards twisted in the mud, throwing the groups of soldiers and the animals off balance. After spending the day caked in mud Adrian was tired and irritable.

"Will you believe me now – it's bloody well impossible," he said to Hall that evening. "And worse than that," Adrian argued, "the men who are carrying the weaponry are exposed to the enemy's fire. They are sitting ducks! It's certain death." Hall responded with just one word – orders.

As the evening darkened, Adrian sat silently in the dugout watching Hall write in his journal. It was something Hall did every evening. If he admired one quality about Hall it was the taciturn way in which he just got on with things. It appeared that he did not care about what went on around him. He would be the last person that Adrian would want to have sitting next to him at a dinner party. Hall just lacked the ability to engage in small talk, but then the front line was not suited to small talk. For some inexplicable reason he recalled his grandmother. She was a ferocious widow of eighty with white hair who started each conversation with a roll call of her contemporaries who had recently passed away. She'd have a lot to talk about here, thought Adrian, and suddenly he burst out laughing. Hall looked up from his journal.

"Sorry," said Adrian, "something tickled me."

Hall's eyes went back to his writing; however, for a moment he had lost his train of thought and licked the lead of his pencil before starting again.

"Do you ever worry you're going to die?" asked Adrian.

"No," answered Hall.

"Me neither," said Adrian; "well, not until I got posted here. For the first time since the war started, I feel the cards are stacked against me."

"I suppose we can't cheat death if it's in God's plan."

"I'm not sure I really believe in God," said Adrian, "but I do believe in destiny."

Hall continued writing in his journal. Adrian pulled out a letter from his wife which he had received a little earlier that evening. It said exactly the same as the last letter he had received from her and when he had finished reading it, he folded it up and placed it back in the envelope. There was one other letter he had received, and he did not know the writing on the envelope. He opened it. It was a short note.

"I read of your marriage. There are some things which even time cannot forgive. *Celia.*"

Adrian sat up and swung his legs off the bed. He walked over to a table where a ewer of water was placed. He poured a small amount into a small clay china bowl and washed his face. A wave of nausea took hold of him, and he ran outside to vomit.

Chapter 64

Adrian looked out into the darkening indigo sky. In the distance, far to the south, he could see the sheets of light from artillery fire. It was impossible to tell who was shelling who. To the north were storm clouds. He hoped that they would blow quickly past.

"Oh Christ!" he said. He still held Celia's letter in his hand, and he thought about what she had written. He wanted to talk to someone, but he knew no one there, except Poley. He did not know anyone to confess to and seek forgiveness. He could find the army chaplain, but what good would it do? He did not believe that absolution came from a few Hail Marys. His contrition was genuine, but the penance he would be given would not be enough. He looked up at the sky – who else was there? The sound of the artillery once again reverberated in his head and, lost in thought, he failed to notice the blanket that covered the entrance to his dugout being pulled back or the head of Peter Hall peering through.

"You look like shit," Hall said.

Adrian shrugged in response. He continued to look down the front line to where shells were still exploding in the distance. The beating in his head continued and he brought his hand up and rubbed his eyes. Hall continued to watch him silently and Adrian turned to him and said:

"I hurt someone whom I care about." Adrian waited for a response. Hall's eyes seemed red and dry in the light from the dugout. He looked so very tired. Adrian had sympathy for him. He hadn't slept well since he had come back to the front. Every time he closed his eyes and began to fall into a sleep he would wake with a start.

"Do you want to talk about it?" asked Hall. Adrian shrugged again and then started speaking.

"Did you know I enlisted as an officer on the day war was declared? My father called me an idiot." As soon as he had started talking Adrian found that he could not stop. He was telling Hall about things which he would not generally share with anyone. "However, my parents accepted it and I could tell they were proud of me doing my duty for King and country. I can't even come close to guessing how many men I've killed. The thought keeps me awake at night. And what about you?"

Hall had not come out wanting to start a long conversation but having been asked a direct question he found no way to retire without appearing rude. He stepped out from the dugout.

"I've been here too long," he said, "too long at the front, too long in the dirt and the death and the constant noise and stench. When I close my eyes, all I hear is screaming."

Adrian took out his cigarette case from the breast pocket of his jacket and offered a cigarette to Hall.

"I hate everything about this place," continued Hall, "and because I've been here for longer than any other officer, I'm expected to get through it better than anyone else. You know what will be coming next. As soon as the Germans think that we are ready to attack they will try a counter-attack. They will probably send over gas, and it doesn't matter how often you tell all the new recruits what will happen, when it does come they will be utterly unprepared."

"I've never experienced a gas attack," said Adrian. "The gas never gets back to the heavy artillery. We do the drills, of course."

Poley arrived a few minutes later carrying a bucket. Adrian looked at him and thought he had got so much older during the war. He remembered Poley as a boy, the same age as Basil. The soldier he saw walking towards him was not the same lad. He was hardly recognisable with his long face and large teeth and a high forehead which was accentuated by his shaven head. He was taller than most of the other men in the regiment with bluish eyes and hollow cheeks.

"I thought I would try and get some of the water out your dugout, sir," said Poley, holding up the bucket in Adrian's direction.

"Don't bother, corporal," replied Hall looking at Poley, "you'll be there for a month of Sundays before you make a difference."

Poley stopped and looked at Adrian, who nodded his head to signify that Poley need not try to clear out the water. Hall continued: "We've blown up every land drain and with the rain and the high water table it's a hopeless task."

"I suppose another damp night with the rats then," said Adrian, watching Poley as he went back the way he had come and disappear around a corner.

"Well, goodnight then," said Hall, who threw the end of his cigarette into the mud and turned back towards the dugout. However, having started talking Adrian did not want the conversation to end so abruptly and had yet to say what was really on his mind.

"I think that death makes the world a darker place," Adrian blurted out. Hall turned and again looked at him. "When someone is killed I think that the world becomes a little dimmer, as if a tiny light has been extinguished. Just a tiny light in a hundred million lights and most people won't notice it. It's not as if they have died of old age when that light has naturally faded away. It's when someone is cut down before their time, before God's chosen time, the world then gets a little dimmer. You read about people lying on the battlefield with expressions of contentment on their faces. I've never seen it. The only faces I've seen are those who are scared, or in pain or know the horror of it all. It's the same when people deliberately sin."

"What do you mean?" asked Hall.

"When a person does something that hurts another then the world just becomes a little greyer." Adrian looked at Hall whose red eyes stared back. He wondered whether he ought to continue with the conversation but felt compelled to go on.

"I got married two weeks ago and it was for all the wrong reasons."

"Why?" asked Hall.

"Because I thought it my duty to help my family."

Hall continued to stare at Adrian, waiting for him to go on. However, it took a few moments before Adrian spoke again. He looked down at the letter in his hand.

"But there was someone else and I should have told her that I was getting married, but I didn't. I should have done lots of things and I didn't."

Adrian looked at the letter in his hand. "It's from her," he added.

"Write to her," said Hall. "Tell her how you feel. I'll let you have some time alone if you want."

"Thank you," said Adrian. Hall walked up the line of the trench. Not a bad chap, thought Adrian, once one gets past the dourness.

The two kerosene lamps in the dugout flickered as Adrian pulled back the curtain and walked down the three steps and into the waterlogged room. As he moved towards his bed he saw a black object on Hall's bed scuttling for cover. Adrian went over to where the rat had been sitting to make sure it had not crawled into the bedding. On top of Hall's bed lay his journal, open at the page where he had been writing. He looked at the entry.

"11 July 1917

My dearest Rose,

I know you'll never read this but I refuse to believe that you're gone. I shall continue to write to you every day and one day when I see you again – here or in a different world – you will know how much I have missed you and how sorry I am. Today was no better than yesterday – it rained in torrents. There is going to be another push soon. I hope that it stops raining as this morning there was a deluge and I was out with a few gunners from the Royal Garrison Artillery until I was soaked and coated in mud. We need to haul their cannons up to the front lines as soon as possible and this mud is horrible and absolutely impassable. On the first attempt to move these guns we had the muzzle of one gun stuck deep in the mud, which defeated our most desperate efforts to move it for hours. The Hun seems to know we're here 'cause they strafed blue hell out of us unceasingly throughout the day. I had the idea of widening some duckboards and that might give them more stability. I shall see if we can get some made up later this week...

Adrian's eyes skimmed down the entry.

"Just before tea one of the dugouts got blown in. It must have taken a direct hit and Drewe and I ran to see what we could do. The place was horribly wrecked and I doubted that anyone could have survived the explosion but Drewe just waded in with a shovel and orders and got the men digging. He does not worry about his own safety but I cannot like him. I sometimes wonder how anyone keeps their head when everything that is normal comes to an end. Suddenly we heard some horrible groans from inside and we all renewed our efforts with the greatest difficulty, and at last we extracted a battered-looking figure and hurried him off on stretchers to the dressing station. We returned to our shelter and found it submerged. It's an awful life – Drewe seems to be feeling the pressure of it all today but what do I care."

Adrian turned back a page. Once again there was another entry dedicated to Rose. He kept on turning the pages backwards. Each entry started with Hall stating that he refused to believe that Rose was dead. He looked at the first entry. It was written six months earlier – just after Christmas.

"What are you looking at?" said a voice from behind him. Adrian turned to see Hall standing at the door of the dugout watching him.

"Nothing," replied Adrian. "There was a rat... I was just... I'm sorry."

Hall walked over to the bed and took the journal and closed it. Adrian felt he needed to say something, but he didn't know what.

Chapter 65

It was about a faraway place that Adrian dreamed, a world of undulating valleys and the scent of lavender. It felt like home; he could smell it and see the hedges full of meadowsweet. In his imagination he was there, and he wanted to remain there for the rest of his life. However, the skies became flintish and the dream dissolved, and he saw in his mind an image of his wife. She was planning his house in the city and his career in politics. The smell of lavender, however, stayed with him.

Celia! What could he say to her? Her face faded away and merged with his wife's and he awoke sweating in the darkness. He took deep breaths and finally when he could no longer remember his nightmares, he closed his eyes again. Once again, he dreamed of the moor and when he was last there with Christian. He dreamt of the huntsman and his hounds chasing insanely – endlessly – over Watchet Hill.

He awoke shaking. He knew he would not go back to sleep and so lay in the blackness of the dugout with his eyes open, hoping that his latest nightmare would fade away. But the images stayed and the thumping in his head returned. He lay quietly, trying not to breathe loudly, listening to the rats splash in the water on the floor. By degrees the room seemed to get lighter, and he could make out the still figure of Peter Hall in the other bed across the dugout.

The beginning of the British bombardment gave Adrian the excuse he needed to get up, wash and get out. He shaved in a metal bowl with a little water. His tired arms pulled the razor across his face as he peered with heavy eyes into a small fragment of a mirror. He didn't know how much longer he could stand being in the front line with the unceasing noise. He lit himself a cigarette and put the case on his bed as he brushed off caked mud from his jacket. He made a decision. He would go back to Ypres that morning and then arrange for the transport of the remainder of the field artillery to the front. He had planned to do it the following day, but he could think of no reason why he should not go now. It would at least give him a day or two away from the front line and from Hall. It was nearly five o'clock when he left the dugout. There was a transport leaving at five-thirty and he decided he would get Poley.

It had rained during the night and the dark storm clouds still loomed overhead. He had to steady himself on the slippery duckboards on more than one occasion. He felt claustrophobic as if the world was pressing down on him. His hand went to his jacket pocket, but he could not find his cigarette case. He swore; he rarely swore. He would have to go back and perhaps have another encounter with Hall.

The artillery barrage ended. He stopped walking and listened to the silence. It gave him time to think, time to gather his thoughts. He stood motionless and deliberated about what he should say to his wife and then he remembered having dreamt about her in the night. He knew he had to write to her and tell her the truth. It might lead to divorce, but the idea of a never-ending loveless marriage appalled him. He would provide grounds. She could claim cruelty or neglect; it didn't much matter to him. His father had a lawyer he could use. And then there was Celia – that was another matter. She would never forgive him. He expected nothing from her but rejection. He had lied to her by his silence and by his acts. He would accept his punishment and live alone, away from society. He thought again about what she had written.

He started walking again, a little faster towards where Poley was billeted. He found Poley still asleep and woke him.

"I want to be on a truck to Ypres in fifteen minutes," he said quietly, trying not to wake up the other soldiers. "Get dressed." Poley opened his brown eyes slowly. "Get yourself dressed," repeated Adrian, a little louder. The soldier in the next bunk grunted and rolled over. Poley got up. He scratched his shaven head and started to do up the buttons on his tunic. He put on his tin hat and picked up his rifle. His pack, which he had placed on the bedpost the night before, had gone.

"The bastards," Poley muttered under his breath.

"What is it?" asked Adrian.

"Someone's stolen my pack."

"Requisition new equipment when we get back," said Adrian. "I just want to get out of here."

Adrian turned away expecting Poley to follow. Poley hesitated. It was not in Poley's nature to abandon anything.

"But, sir," said Poley.

"Just get a bloody move on. There's a truck going in just over ten minutes, and I don't want to miss it."

Poley followed Adrian. He watched Adrian as he walked along the winding trench. A few birds warbled in the early morning. Poley speculated about where the birds lived; where they flew to when the firing started. He hadn't seen a scrap of living vegetation in nearly a week at the front. He listened to the chirping and wondered what the birds were saying to each other. Did they think the human race mad? Did they look down from the skies and ask why for three years these men had converged on a quiet salient and blown into inexistence every tree and bush?

They had travelled three quarters of the way back to Hall's dugout when the German barrage started. The ordnance flew over them to the second line of the British defences. Poor bastards, thought Adrian as he pulled down his tin helmet firmly on his head. Adrian could feel the pounding as the shells exploded sixty yards behind him. He expected the smell of cordite to swell over him any moment, but the wind had changed and the smoke was being blown away. Adrian quickened his pace and Poley, bending himself over to keep his head down, tried to keep up. The explosions continued and Adrian could hardly hear anything except the blasts, not even the screams. They seemed to be blown away by a forgiving wind. He pressed on towards Hall's dugout.

"Gas!" Adrian heard a soldier shout from along the trench. Adrian started to run and Poley tried to keep up with him, his lank and lean figure running down the line of the trench hell for leather. "Gas!" Other soldiers started to take up the call and then soldiers started rapping their bayonets on empty shell cases to ring out the warning.

Adrian scrambled back into Hall's dugout. No one was there. He pulled out his respirator and threw the spare to Poley.

"Gas, gas, gas," he heard soldiers shouting from the trenches above him.

"Put it on," Adrian shouted at Poley.

Poley placed the gasmask over his head and started to tuck it into his tunic. It was Adrian who saw the rip in the mask. It ran from the ear all the way down to the neck.

"Stay here," he shouted through his own mask. Poley tried to pull the material together. "If the gas gets in here try to hold your breath," screamed Adrian. "Whatever you do don't breathe in the gas, it will kill you! Just stay here!"

Adrian clambered out of the dugout. The green gas was being blown quickly towards him and was filling the trenches. Soldiers were tightening up their gasmasks and fixing their bayonets to their rifles. The gas crept along the floor of the trench with its sickly green phosphorescent glow. Adrian realised he did not have time to get to the stores and back before his dugout would be flooded with gas. He went back inside. Poley was already beginning to choke. The green gas was filling up the dugout and finding its way through the tear in the mask.

"Hold your breath, Poley," Adrian shouted through his mask. "Just hang on and don't breathe."

Suddenly Poley's body jerked back, and he started pulling at the mask around his face.

"Leave it, Poley," Adrian shouted once again. "Leave it!" But Poley was tearing at the mask. Adrian grabbed hold of Poley. "Don't breathe," he shouted. Poley stared back at him. His dark brown, watery eyes were wide.

Adrian took a step a back, releasing his grip on Poley's shoulders. He pulled out his revolver and aimed it towards Poley's head. He paused and remembered a promise he had made to Poley's father. He dropped the revolver and then raised his hands to his respirator and removed it.

"Put it on," Adrian shouted, handing over the gasmask. Poley pulled off his mask and put the tube of the respirator in his mouth and then exhaled. Poley breathed and began to cough but suddenly Adrian could hold his breath no longer.

*　　*　　*

Sir,

It is my painful duty to inform you that a report has this day been received from the War Office notifying the death of Major Adrian Drewe of the Royal Garrison Artillery which occurred at Ypres, Belgium on the 12th of July 1917, and I am to express to you the sympathy and regret of the Army Council at your loss. The cause of the death was killed in action.

If any articles of private property left by the deceased are found, they will be forwarded to this Office, but some time will probably elapse before their receipt, and when received they cannot be disposed of until authority is received from the War Office.

Application regarding the disposal of any such personal effects, or of any amount that may eventually be found to be due to the late soldier's estate, should be addressed to "The Secretary, War Office, London, S.W.," and marked outside "Effects".

I am, Sir, Your obedient Servant,

Rory Campbell (Colonel) Officer in Charge of Records.

The telegram fell out of Sir Julius' fingers and floated to the floor. He suddenly started sweating and caught hold of the corner of his desk. He breathed hard; the room spun around him. He could not think for a few moments. He had to sit down. He bent over and picked up the telegram and put it in his pocket. Calm yourself, he thought. Have a drink. He got up but was unsteady on his feet. He held onto the bureau in his office, took out the whisky bottle and poured himself a large glass. He knew that one wasn't going to be enough – he knew he needed another before he could face his wife. There was a cloying dryness in his throat and then he felt a heavy weight on his chest.

He moved to the window to get some air. It had been his intention that one day his businesses would go to Adrian. He began to cry and the tears ran down his cheeks. He turned away from the window in case the gardener came past and saw him. He looked around his study. It was austere with little indication that he shared his life with other people. There was a photograph in the silver frame that stood on the bookcase and he went over and took hold of it. A family portrait in a formal pose, it was the last time that all of his children had been together. He remembered the occasion when it had been taken. It was just before the last New Year's Eve ball which they had held. Adrian was standing in the centre of the picture, the centre of attention.

He was unable to stop the tears. He took out the telegram and looked at it again. Somehow he hoped the words would have changed, that the army had made a mistake, but he knew that they didn't make mistakes when advising of losses. *The cause of the death was killed in action*. What exactly did it mean? It said absolutely nothing in its own convoluted way. How had his son been killed? He would have to find out. He would speak to Adrian's regiment, make some enquiries. His left hand trembled again. 'Perhaps,' he thought 'it might be wiser not to ask.'

Somewhere out across the lawns, out of sight and down by the water meadows, would be his wife. She would be talking to one of the gardeners or the farmers who tended their small allotments. She would be back in the next hour. She always came back for tea at three and, as usual, he would join her in the arboretum. They would sit at a small, white wrought-iron table on two small, white wrought-iron chairs and drink tea from china cups. She insisted and he consented to this custom, although the chairs were quite uncomfortable. There was not much that she demanded and when he was at home at Wadhurst Hall he gave in to this whim. He would tell her there, but how to tell her? How do you say to a mother that her boy is dead?

Sir Julius read the telegram for the third time. He still wanted to believe that it was a mistake. He read through it word by word. Could there be another Adrian Drewe in the same battalion? He knew the answer. This time he screwed up the telegram in his fist and threw it at the wastepaper basket. It missed and bounced across the black and white marble floor. How to tell her? He didn't know. He hoped she would be back soon and instantly changed his mind and hoped that she would stay away for an eternity so he could avoid the moment. Perhaps he could just pass her the telegram. Let her read it and not say a word; but that was the coward's way out and he would not do that. He looked at his pocket watch – two-fifteen. She would be coming back soon.

He thought about Castle Drogo – the embodiment of his family's line. What would he do with it now? It was to have been his legacy to Adrian. He would never have started it but for Adrian. It was only Adrian who had ever shown any interest in the family name. It was too late to stop it now, but Sir Julius wondered if it were possible to reduce its size. By rights it should go to Christian, but Christian had no love for it. He made a mental note to call Lutyens.

Finally, there was Jane to consider. He wondered whether Adrian's wife would be reading a similar telegram right now or whether, because Adrian had only recently got married, they would have her address. He would call her after he told his wife the news. He would arrange everything that needed to be done. They would go to France and bring back their son. He might have to pull a few strings to do it, but he was certain it could be arranged. There had been others at his club who had done the same. His wife would tell Basil and Christian and he would telephone Jane. Then, where to bury Adrian? They could bring his boy home and bury him at Castle Drogo. It seemed fitting. There should also be a chapel. He remembered that Lutyens had once suggested that there be a chapel but he had dismissed the idea as a waste of good money. He would call Lutyens tomorrow – he must do that. He looked at his pocket watch. It was half past two.

His left hand was still shaking. He started to leave the study to make his way to the arboretum but stopped. He looked at himself in a mirror by the door. His face was ashen and his hair was out of place. He took out a comb to straighten his parting; one more small act of vanity. The castle, money, everything he had; he realised that it all meant nothing.

The weight in his chest became heavier and he was sweating profusely when he collapsed.

Chapter 66

After she received the news of Adrian's death, Celia had sleepless nights and tears. At times she hated him, at times she felt betrayed by him, but soon she realised that she still loved him. She did not eat much and seemed to live in the past; in her memories she possessed him absolutely. With him she had felt alive. In the present she was depressed and then she would become angry. When she failed to have her period that month, she thought nothing of it. When she missed her third cycle, the bulge in her stomach started to show.

Lutyens telegrammed Gertrude Jekyll who came up from Munstead Wood. He needed someone to take control of the situation and with Emily abroad there was no one better than Gertrude Jekyll in a difficult situation. However, he had not taken into account Gertrude's Victorian values or Celia's apathy to the world. They clashed immediately. Gertrude told Celia that she would have to go abroad until the baby was born and then have the child adopted. Celia would not hear of it. Faced with Celia's unflinching obstinacy, Gertrude quietly and determinedly set about a series of actions which she believed might at least limit the chance of a scandal. She sent a wire to Emily in America. It was followed by a telephone call and then a further wire. The exchanges were frank. By the end of the day, Celia no longer had a job or a home in England.

By the start of November 1917, the story that Emily Lutyens was suffering from severe influenza was being circulated by Gertrude Jekyll and Edwin Lutyens. Gertrude saw it as the perfect deception. It was an illness that was serious to the extent of being life-threatening but once overcome would leave no stigma. The story was circulated that Celia was needed to tend to her two younger sisters, who had to be kept away from their mother during her recuperation. Celia's disappearance on the next boat bound to New York could be explained by this simple lie. On the day that Celia was to travel to America,

Gertrude Jekyll looked back at the last month and concluded that this had been her most productive time for an age.

Emily received the news from Gertrude Jekyll with a feeling of despair. As she read the telegram from Gertrude, her mouth was pinched. She would have to leave Ojai where she lived in a house near to Krishnamurti and go back to New York. She counted it as another black mark against her husband. She had only been gone six months but in that time he had managed to bring her family to the precipice of ruin. She agreed that bringing Celia to America was the only option and then to hide her away somewhere. She agreed with Gertrude that they would need to work on Celia to convince her to have the little bastard adopted. Give it a year or two and then return to London, suggested Gertrude. Emily reflected on how inconvenient this would all be. How no one would say anything, but others might guess and those little looks of sympathy that she would receive would cut.

While all this went on around him, Edwin Lutyens continued as if nothing had happened. He did not know what he was supposed to do and so he let those who were prepared to act make decisions. He pretended that things had not changed and made no mention of the fact that his daughter was leaving in order to hide a rather unpleasant truth. On the day that Celia left to go to America she asked for one last story, but he couldn't remember any and chewed on his unlit pipe. She waved goodbye as she sat in the car with Gertrude Jekyll. He waved back and she could have sworn that he was crying. The car pulled away taking Gertrude back home to Munstead Wood and her on to Plymouth. Celia and Gertrude said little to each other on the journey. Gertrude had made no bones about the fact that what Celia had done was unforgiveable. Celia would not accept that she had made a mistake. She refused to believe that a child born of love could be wrong; only time would tell. The goodbyes, when Gertrude got out of the car, were cold.

"How much time have I got?" said Celia to the chauffeur, as the car headed southwest. She was told that she had plenty of time. She asked whether there was enough time to make a short diversion to Drewsteignton. The driver looked at his watch, said that even with the diversion she would have an hour or two to spare. She decided she would see Christian one last time.

Adrian's house appeared a little greyer to Celia than she remembered it. The stone was just a touch shabbier under a bleak sky and a cold, unpleasant November wind came off the moor and up through the valley. It chilled Celia to the bone. On the slate roof of the house a mischief of magpies, seven in number, screeched at each other. An overfed black cat feigned disinterest and licked its paw, meticulously cleaning around each of its claws. It hoped that one of the birds would be expelled from the group and in its haste fly down and come within reach. The black cat had sat in the same place almost every day for the last three years and although in that time it had not caught a magpie it remained hopeful, even if such hope was misplaced. It believed that anything was possible. On this day the cat did not intend to spend long outside. It was far too cold and as soon as lunchtime came it would walk, with dignity and purpose, to the back door of the house where Adrian once lived, to eat a meal prepared by the cook who continued to care for Christian Drewe.

Celia's possessive instinct pulled at her heart. She had so wanted to marry Adrian and that dream now lay buried near Ypres. At twenty-one she believed that her life lay in the past and the future held no attraction but a fatherless child and a censorious family. The overfed black cat watched her intently for a moment or two before going back to its grooming. The cat did not care about the past, which it considered an irrelevance. It did not matter that in the last three years none of the magpies had been caught; it might happen today. Living was about the present. It was something that cats instinctively knew.

Celia knocked on the door of Adrian's house and waited. It would be her last farewell. At one time she thought about writing to Christian, but she did not know what to say and then someone would have to read it to him. She could not explain how she felt in a letter. Even if they only spoke for the briefest of minutes, she wanted to say goodbye. They had both been hurt in different ways by the war and she knew that his scars ran deeper than hers and she still blamed herself.

She did not go and see the cook. She did not want to be seen by her or for anyone to guess. She was taken by the housekeeper into the reception room at the back of the house . Christian came in a few moments later. It always took her a moment or two to become accustomed to the way he looked. She had seen him a hundred times since he had been wounded, but there was always that immediate feeling of repulsion, as if he had become something less than human. She still marvelled how he had survived his injuries. He had been out on the battlefield, wounded, for the whole night, blinded and bleeding. How George Poley and that sergeant had dragged him back was a miracle. Celia did not take off her coat.

"I'm going to America," she said. "My mother is ill and before I left, I wanted to give you something."

She moved forward to where he stood and kissed him on the cheek.

Christian said nothing for a minute. A tear ran down the side of his face. He wiped it away and then said: "There's something I have for you as well." He moved away to the bureau by the window and ran his hand along the green leather before he found what he was looking for.

"I know you rarely smoke but..."

Celia looked at the dented case. The inscription was barely readable, and she tilted it in the light.

"It was sent back soon after Adrian's death. Apparently, it had been lost in his dugout and, well, it's a long story but finally it was sent to me."

Celia placed the cigarette case in her bag. "Thank you," she said. "I have a question as well. It's something that's been troubling me; do you know how Adrian died?"

"He gave his life to save George Poley," said Christian. "Poley's mask was ripped along the side and Adrian couldn't stop the gas getting in. When Poley started choking, Adrian gave him his own mask."

They said goodbye at the door.

"I think I know how you must feel," said Christian. "For what it's worth I know that he loved you."

They hugged.

"You need to move on with your life," she said to Christian. "We both do."

"I'll do my best," said Christian.

Celia got back in the car. It turned around and left the small village of Drewsteignton, gaining speed along the tarmacadamed road. Celia looked out of the window; she knew that for a few moments she would see the plot where the castle was being built. The road turned back on itself and she saw the few shards of granite wall rising up on top of the escarpment. The theatre set which had been built had blown down or had been taken away; she did not know which. She thought that she was looking at a ruin and wondered whether it would ever be built now that Adrian was dead and Sir Julius had suffered a heart attack. For the first time since she was a child Celia did not care.

She unbuttoned her coat and placed her hands on her stomach. She could feel the swelling under her cardigan. Despite what her mother thought or what Gertrude said, she would bring up the child. The world could go and hang! That child would be her most precious tie to Adrian and no one could take that away from her.

She also realised that she had to move forward – make decisions to stand upon her own two feet in an unforgiving world. She knew that she had to take her own advice and put away the past, and she felt within her a rage to live.